TERMINAL

ALSO BY ROBIN COOK

ROBIN COOK

TERMINAL

G. P. Putnam's Sons ▼ New York

G. P. Putnam's Sons
Publishers Since 1838
200 Madison Avenue
New York, NY 10016

Published simultaneously in Canada
Library of Congress Cataloging-in-Publication Data

Cook, Robin.
Terminal / Robin Cook.

p. cm.
ISBN 0-399-13771-8 (acid-free paper)
I. Title.
PS3553.05545T47 1993 92-30678 CIP
813'.54—dc20

Printed in the United States of America
1 2 3 4 5 6 7 8 9 10
This book is printed on acid-free paper.
∞

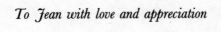

To Jean with love and appreciation

ACKNOWLEDGMENTS

I would like to thank Matthew Bankowski, Ph.D., for his patience and generosity in tolerating my questions about his arena of expertise, and for his willingness to read and comment upon the original manuscript of *Terminal.*

I would also like to thank Phyllis Grann, my friend and editor, for her valuable input. I would also like to apologize for any deleterious effects the lateness of the manuscript of *Terminal* may have had on her longevity.

Finally I would like to thank the basic science departments of the College of Physicians and Surgeons at Columbia University for providing me with the background that makes it possible for me to understand and appreciate the fast-paced developments in molecular biology.

Science without conscience is but
the ruin of the soul.

—*François Rabelais*

PROLOGUE

January 4
Monday, 7:05 A.M.

Helen Cabot gradually awoke as dawn emerged from the winter darkness blanketing Boston, Massachusetts. Fingers of pale, anemic light pierced the darkness of the third-floor bedroom in her parents' Louisburg Square home. At first she didn't open her eyes, luxuriating under the down comforter of her canopied bed. Totally content, she was mercifully unaware of the terrible molecular events occurring deep inside her brain.

The holiday season had not been one of Helen's most enjoyable. In order to avoid missing any classes at Princeton where she was enrolled as a junior, she'd scheduled an elective D&C between Christmas and New Year's. The doctors had promised that removing the abnormally heavy endometrial tissue lining the uterus would eliminate the violently painful cramps that left her incapacitated each time she got her period. They'd also promised it would be routine. But it hadn't been.

Turning her head, Helen gazed at the soft morning light

diffusing through the lace curtains. She had no sensation of impending doom. In fact, she felt better than she had in days. Although the operation had gone smoothly with only mild post-operative discomfort, the third day after surgery she had developed an unbearable headache, followed by fever, dizziness, and most disturbing of all, slurred speech. Thankfully, the symptoms had cleared as quickly as they had appeared, but her parents still insisted she keep her scheduled appointment with the neurologist at the Massachusetts General Hospital.

Drifting back to sleep Helen heard the barely perceptible click of her father's computer keyboard. His study was next to Helen's bedroom. Opening her eyes just long enough to see the clock, she realized it was just past seven. It was amazing how hard her father worked. As the founder and chairman of the board of one of the most powerful software companies in the world, he could afford to rest on his laurels. But he didn't. He was driven, and the family had become astoundingly wealthy and influential as a result.

Unfortunately the security that Helen enjoyed from her family circumstances did not take into account that nature does not respect temporal wealth and power. Nature works according to its own agenda. The events occurring in Helen's brain, unknown to her, were being dictated by the DNA molecules that comprised her genes. And on that day in early January, four genes in several of her brain's neurons were gearing up to produce certain encoded proteins. These neurons had not divided since Helen was an infant, which was normal. Yet now because of these four genes and their resultant proteins, the neurons would be forced to divide again, and to keep on dividing. A particularly malignant cancer was about to shatter Helen's life. At age twenty-one, Helen Cabot was potentially "terminal," and she had no idea.

January 4, 10:45 A.M.

Accompanied by a slight whirring noise, Howard Pace was slid out of the maw of the new MRI machine at the University Hospital in St. Louis. He'd never been more terrified in his life. He'd always been vaguely anxious about hospitals and doctors, but now that he was ill, his fears were full-fledged and overwhelming.

At age forty-seven Howard had been in perfect health until that fateful day in mid-October when he'd charged the net in the semifinals of the Belvedere Country Club's annual tennis tournament. There'd been a slight popping noise, and he'd sprawled ignominiously as the unreturned ball sailed over his head. Howard's anterior cruciate ligament had snapped inside his right knee.

That had been the beginning of it. Fixing the knee had been easy. Despite some mild problems his doctors ascribed to the aftereffects of general anesthesia, Howard had returned to work in just a few days. It had been important for him to get back quickly; running one of the nation's largest airplane manufacturing firms was not easy in an era of sharply curtailed defense budgets.

With his head still stabilized in the vise-like apparatus for the MRI, Howard was unaware of the technician's presence until the man spoke.

"You okay?" he asked as he began to release Howard's head.

"Okay," Howard managed to reply. He was lying. His heart was thumping in terror. He was afraid of what the test would reveal. Behind a glass divider he could discern a group of white-coated individuals studying a CRT screen. One of them was his doctor, Tom Folger. They were all pointing, gesturing, and, most disturbing of all, shaking their heads.

The trouble had begun the day before. Howard had awakened with a headache, a rare occurrence unless he'd "tied one on," which he hadn't. In fact, he'd not had anything to drink since New Year's Eve. After taking a dose of aspirin and eating a bit of breakfast, the pain had abated. But later that morning in the middle of a board meeting, with no warning whatsoever, he'd vomited. It had been so violent and so unexpected, with no preceding nausea, that he'd not even been able to lean aside. To his utter mortification, his undigested breakfast had spewed over the boardroom table.

With his head now freed, Howard tried to sit up, but the movement caused his headache to return in full force. He sank back to the MRI table and closed his eyes until his doctor gently touched his shoulder. Tom had been the family internist for over twenty years. He and Tom had become good friends over the years, and they knew each other well. Howard did not like what he saw in Tom's face.

"It's bad, isn't it?" Howard asked.

"I've always been straight with you, Howard . . ."

"So don't change now," Howard whispered. He didn't want to hear the rest, but he had to.

"It doesn't look good," Tom admitted. He kept his hand on Howard's shoulder. "There are multiple tumors. Three to be exact. At least that's how many we can see."

"Oh, God!" Howard moaned. "It's terminal, isn't it?"

"That's not the way we should talk at this point," Tom said.

"Christ it isn't," Howard snapped. "You just told me you've always been straight with me. I asked a simple question. I have a right to know."

"If you force me to answer, I'd have to say yes; it could be terminal. But we don't know for sure. For the present we've got a lot of work to do. First thing we have to do is find out where it's come from. Being multifocal suggests it's spread from someplace else."

"Then let's get on with it," Howard said. "If there's a chance, I want to beat this thing."

January 4, 1:25 P.M.

When Louis Martin first awoke in the recovery room, he felt as if his throat had been scorched with an acetylene torch. He'd had sore throats before, but nothing had even come close to the pain he'd felt as he tried to swallow after his surgery. To make matters worse, his mouth had been as dry as the central Sahara.

The nurse who had materialized at his bedside seemingly out of nowhere had explained that his discomfort was due to the endotracheal tube the anesthesiologist had inserted prior to his operation. She gave him a damp washcloth to suck on and the pain had abated.

By the time he was wheeled back to his room, a different pain had started, located somewhere between his legs and radiating into the small of his back. Louis knew the cause of that discomfort. It was the site of his surgery to reduce an enlarged prostate gland. The damn thing had been forcing him to get up to urinate four or five times each night. He'd scheduled the surgery for the day after New Year's. Traditionally that was a slow time for the computer giant he ran north of Boston.

Just as the pain was getting the best of him, another nurse gave him a bolus of Demerol through the IV which was still attached to his left hand. A bottle of fluid hung on a T-shaped pole protruding from the head of his bed.

The Demerol put him back into a drugged sleep. He wasn't sure how much time had passed when he became aware of a presence next to his head. It took all his strength to open his eyes; his eyelids felt like lead. At the head of his bed was a nurse fumbling with plastic tubing coming from the IV bottle. In her right hand was a syringe.

"What's that?" Louis mumbled. He sounded inebriated.

The nurse smiled at him.

"Sounds as if you'd had one too many," she said.

Louis blinked as he tried to focus on the woman's swarthy face. In his drugged state, the nurse was a blur. Yet she was correct about how he sounded.

"I don't need any more pain medicine," Louis managed to say. He struggled to a half-sitting position, leaning on an elbow.

"It's not pain medicine," the nurse said.

"Oh," Louis said. While the nurse completed the injection, Louis slowly realized he still didn't know what he was being given. "What kind of medicine is it?" Louis asked.

"A wonder drug," the nurse said, quickly capping the syringe.

Louis laughed in spite of himself. He was about to ask another question, but the nurse satisfied his curiosity.

"It's an antibiotic," she said. She gave Louis's shoulder a reassuring squeeze. "Now you close your eyes and rest."

Louis flopped back onto his bed. He chuckled. He liked people with a sense of humor. In his mind he repeated what the nurse had said: *a wonder drug.* Well, antibiotics were wonder drugs, there was no doubt. He recalled that Dr. Handlin had told him he might be put on antibiotics as a precaution after his operation. Louis vaguely wondered what it had been like to be in a hospital before antibiotics had been discovered. He felt thankful that he was living when he was.

Closing his eyes, Louis followed the nurse's suggestion and let his body relax. The pain was still present, but because of the narcotic, it didn't bother him. Narcotics were wonder drugs as well, and so were the anesthetic agents. Louis was the first to admit he was a coward when it came to pain. He could never have tolerated surgery back when none of the "wonder drugs" were available.

As Louis drifted off to sleep, he wondered what kind of drugs the future would bring. He decided he'd have to ask Dr. Handlin's opinion.

January 4, 2:53 P.M.

Norma Kaylor watched the drops fall into the millipore chamber hanging below her IV bottle. The IV ran through a large-bore catheter into her left arm. She had such mixed feelings about the medicine she was getting. She hoped the powerful chemotherapeutic agents would cure her breast cancer which, she'd been told, had spread into her liver and lungs. At the same time she knew the medicines were cellular poisons, capable of wreaking havoc on her body as well as on her tumor. Dr. Clarence had warned her about so many dreadful side effects that she'd made a conscious effort to screen out his voice. She'd heard enough. She'd signed the consent form with a feeling of numbed detachment.

Turning, Norma looked out the window at the intensely blue Miami sky, filled with massive bubbles of white cumulus clouds. Since her cancer had been diagnosed, she tried hard not to ask *why me?* When she'd first felt the lump she had hoped it would go away of its own accord, like so many lumps had done in the past. It wasn't until several months had passed, and the skin over the lump had suddenly dimpled that she'd forced herself to see a doctor, only to learn that her fears had been justified: the lump was malignant. So just before her thirty-third birthday she'd undergone a radical mastectomy. She hadn't fully recovered from the surgery before the doctors began the chemotherapy.

Determined to end her self-pity, she was reaching for a novel when the door to her private room opened. She didn't even look up. Staff at the Forbes Cancer Center was constantly in and out adjusting her IV, injecting her medicine. She had gotten so used to the constant comings and goings, they barely interrupted her reading anymore.

It was only after the door had closed again that she became aware she had been given some new drug. The effect was unique, causing the strength suddenly to drain from her body. Even the book she was holding fell from her hands. But what was more frightening was the effect on her breathing; it was as if she were being smothered. In agony she tried to get air, but she had progressive difficulty, and soon she was totally paralyzed except for her eyes. The image of her door being quietly opened was the last thing she knew.

1

February 26
Friday, 9:15 A.M.

"Oh, God, here she comes!" Sean Murphy said. Frantically he grabbed the charts stacked in front of him and ducked into the room behind the nurses' station on the seventh floor of the Weber Building of the Boston Memorial Hospital.

Confused at this sudden interruption, Peter Colbert, a fellow third-year Harvard medical student, surveyed the scene. Nothing was out of the ordinary. It appeared like any busy internal medicine hospital ward. The nurses' station was a beehive of activity with the floor clerk and four RN's busy at work. There were also several orderlies pushing patients on gurneys. Organ music from the soundtrack of a daytime soap could be heard drifting out of the floor lounge. The only person approaching the nurses' station who didn't belong was an attractive female nurse who Peter felt was an eight or nine out of a possible ten. Her name was Janet Reardon. Peter knew about her. She was the daughter of one of the old Boston Brahmin families, aloof and untouchable.

Peter pushed back from the counter where he had been

sitting next to the chart rack and shoved open the door to the back room. It was an all-purpose office with desk-high countertops, a computer terminal, and a small refrigerator. The nurses held their reports in there at the end of each shift, and those who brown-bagged it used it as a lunchroom. In the back was a lavatory.

"What the hell's going on?" Peter demanded. He was curious to say the least. Sean was against the wall with his charts pressed to his chest.

"Shut the door!" Sean commanded.

Peter stepped into the room. "You've been making it with Reardon?" It was part question, part stunned realization. It had been almost two months ago at the outset of Peter's and Sean's rotation on third-year medicine that Sean had spotted Janet and had asked Peter about her.

"Who the hell is that?" Sean had demanded. His mouth had gone slack. In front of him was one of the most beautiful women he'd ever seen. She was climbing down from the counter after retrieving something from the inaccessible top shelf of a wall cabinet. He could tell she had a figure that could have graced any magazine.

"She's not your type," Peter had said. "So close your mouth. Compared to you she's royalty. I know some guys who have tried to date her. It's impossible."

"Nothing is impossible," Sean had said, watching Janet with stunned appreciation.

"A townie like you could never get to first base," Peter had said. "Much less hit a home run."

"Want to bet?" Sean had challenged. "Five bucks says you are wrong. I'll have her thirsting for my body by the time we finish medicine."

At the time, Peter had just laughed. Now he appraised his partner with renewed respect. He thought he'd gotten to know Sean over the last two months of grueling work, and yet here he was on the last day of medicine surprising him.

"Open the door a crack and see if she's gone," Sean said.

"This is ridiculous," Peter said, but he opened the door several inches nonetheless. Janet was at the counter talking to Carla Valentine, the head nurse. Peter let the door shut.

"She's right outside," he said.

"Damn!" Sean exclaimed. "I don't want to talk to her right now. I've got too much to do, and I don't want a scene. She doesn't know I'm leaving for Miami for that elective at the Forbes Cancer Center. I don't want to tell her until Saturday night. I know she's going to be pissed."

"So you *have* been dating her?"

"Yeah, we've gotten pretty hot and heavy," Sean said. "Which reminds me: you owe me five bucks. And let me tell you, it wasn't easy. At first she'd barely talk to me. But eventually, utter charm and persistence paid off. My guess is that it was mostly the persistence."

"Did you bag her?" Peter asked.

"Don't be crude," Sean said.

Peter laughed. "Me crude? That's the best example of the pot calling the kettle black that I've ever heard."

"The problem is she's getting serious," Sean said. "She thinks because we slept together a couple of times, it's leading to something permanent."

"Am I hearing marriage here?" Peter asked.

"Not from me," Sean said. "But I think that's what she has in mind. It's insane, especially since her parents hate my guts. And hell, I'm only twenty-six."

Peter opened the door again. "She's still there talking with one of the other nurses. She must be on break or something."

"Great!" Sean said sarcastically. "I guess I can work in

here. I've got to get these off-service notes written before I get another admission."

"I'll keep you company," Peter said. He went out and returned with several of his own charts.

They worked in silence, using the three-by-five index cards they carried in their pockets bearing the latest laboratory work on each of their assigned patients. The idea was to summarize each case for the medical students rotating on service come March 1.

"This one has been my most interesting case," Sean said after about half an hour. He held the massive chart aloft. "If it hadn't been for her I wouldn't even have heard about the Forbes Cancer Center."

"You talking about Helen Cabot?" Peter asked.

"None other," Sean said.

"You got all the interesting cases, you dog. And Helen's a looker, too. Hell, on her case consults were pleading to be called."

"Yeah, but this looker turned out to have multiple brain tumors," Sean said. He opened the chart and glanced through some of its two hundred pages. "It's sad. She's only twenty-one and she's obviously terminal. Her only hope is that she gets accepted by the Forbes. They have been having phenomenal luck with the kind of tumor she has."

"Did her final pathology report come back?"

"Yesterday," Sean said. "She's got medulloblastoma. It's fairly rare; only about two percent of all brain tumors are this type. I did some reading on it so I could shine on rounds this afternoon. It's usually seen in young children."

"So she's an unfortunate exception," Peter commented.

"Not really an exception," Sean said. "Twenty percent of medulloblastomas are seen in patients over the age of twenty. What surprised everyone and why no one even came close to guessing the cell type was because she had multiple growths. Originally her attending thought she had metastatic cancer, probably from an ovary. But he was wrong. Now he's planning an article for the *New England Journal of Medicine.*"

"Someone said she was not only beautiful but wealthy," Peter said, lamenting anew he'd not gotten her as a patient.

"Her father is CEO of Software, Inc.," Sean said. "Obviously the Cabots aren't hurting. With all their money, they can certainly afford a place like the Forbes. I hope the people in Miami can do something for her. Besides being pretty, she's a nice kid. I've spent quite a bit of time with her."

"Remember, doctors are not supposed to fall in love with their patients," Peter said.

"Helen Cabot could tempt a saint."

JANET REARDON took the stairs back to pediatrics on the fifth floor. She'd used her fifteen-minute coffee break trying to find Sean. The nurses on seven said they'd just seen him, working on his off-service notes, but had no idea where he'd gone.

Janet was troubled. She hadn't been sleeping well for several weeks, waking at four or five in the morning, way before her alarm. The problem was Sean and their relationship. When she'd first met him, she'd been turned off by his coarse, cocky attitude, even though she had been attracted by his appealing Mediterranean features, black hair, and strikingly blue eyes. Before she'd met Sean she hadn't known what the term "Black Irish" meant.

When Sean had initially pursued her, Janet had resisted. She felt they had nothing in common, but he refused to take no for an answer. And his keen intelligence pricked her curiosity.

She finally went out with him thinking that one date

would end the attraction. But it hadn't. She soon discovered that his rebel's attitude was a powerful aphrodisiac. In a surprising about-face, Janet decided that all her previous boyfriends had been too predictable, too much the Myopia Hunt Club crowd. All at once she realized that her sense of self had been tied to an expectation of a marriage similar to her parents' with someone conventionally acceptable. It was then that Sean's Charlestown rough appeal had taken a firm hold on her heart, and Janet had fallen in love.

Reaching the nurses' station on the pediatric floor, Janet noticed she still had a few minutes left on her break. Pushing through the door to the back room, she headed for the communal coffee machine. She needed a jolt to get her through the rest of the day.

"You look like you just lost a patient," a voice called.

Janet turned to see Dorothy MacPherson, a floor nurse with whom she'd become close, sitting with her stockinged feet propped upon the countertop.

"Maybe just as bad," Janet said as she got her coffee. She only allowed herself half a cup. She went over and joined Dorothy. She sat heavily in one of the metal desk chairs. "Men!" she added with a sigh of frustration.

"A familiar lament," Dorothy said.

"My relationship with Sean Murphy is not going anywhere," Janet said at length. "It's really bothering me, and I have to do something about it. Besides," she added with a laugh, "the last thing I want to do is to be forced to admit to my mother that she'd been right about him all along."

Dorothy smiled. "I can relate to that."

"It's gotten to the point that I think he's avoiding me," Janet said.

"Have you two talked?" Dorothy asked.

"I've been trying," Janet said. "But talking about feelings is not one of his strong points."

"Regardless," Dorothy said. "Maybe you should take him out tonight and say what you've just said to me."

"Ha!" Janet laughed scornfully. "It's Friday night. We can't."

"Is he on call?" Dorothy asked.

"No," Janet said. "Every Friday night he and his Charlestown buddies get together at a local bar. Girlfriends and wives are not invited. It's the proverbial boys' night out. And in his case, it's some kind of Irish tradition, complete with brawls."

"Sounds disgusting," Dorothy said.

"After four years at Harvard, a year of molecular biology at MIT, and now three years of medical school, you'd think he'd have outgrown it. Instead, these Friday nights seem to be more important to him than ever."

"I wouldn't stand for it," Dorothy said. "I used to think my husband's golf fetish was bad, but it's nothing compared to what you're talking about. Are there women involved in these Friday night escapades?"

"Sometimes they go up to Revere. There's a strip joint there. But mostly it's just Sean and the boys, drinking beer, telling jokes, and watching sports on a big-screen TV. At least that's how he's described it. Obviously I've never been there."

"Maybe you should ask yourself why you're involved with this man," Dorothy said.

"I have," Janet said. "Particularly lately, and especially since we've had so little communication. It's hard even to find time to talk with him. Not only does he have all the work associated with med school, but he has his research too. He's in an M.D.-Ph.D. program at Harvard."

"He must be intelligent," Dorothy offered.

"It's his only saving grace," Janet said. "That and his body."

Dorothy laughed. "At least there's a couple of things to justify your anguish. But I wouldn't let my husband get away with that juvenile Friday night stuff. Hell, I'd march right in and embarrass the heck out of him. Men will be boys, but there have to be some limits."

"I don't know if I could do that," Janet said. But as she took a sip from her coffee, she gave the idea some thought. The problem was that she'd always been so passive in her life, letting things happen, then reacting after the fact. Maybe that's how she got herself into this kind of trouble. Maybe she needed to encourage herself to be more assertive.

"DAMN IT, Marcie!" Louis Martin shouted. "Where the hell are those projections? I told you I wanted them on my desk." To emphasize his displeasure, Louis slapped his hand on his leather-bound blotter, sending a flurry of papers wafting off into the air. He had been feeling irritable ever since he'd awakened at four-thirty that morning with a dull headache. While in the bathroom searching for aspirin, he'd vomited into the sink. The episode had shocked him. His retching had come with no warning and no accompanying nausea.

Marcie Delgado scurried into her boss's office. He'd been yelling at her and criticizing her all day. Meekly she reached across the desk and pushed a stack of papers bound with a metal clip directly in front of the man. In block letters on the front cover was: PROJECTIONS FOR BOARD MEETING FEBRUARY 26.

Without even an acknowledgment, much less an apology, Louis snatched up the documents and stormed out of the office. But he didn't get far. After half a dozen steps, he couldn't recall where he was going. When he finally remembered he was headed for the boardroom, he wasn't sure which door it was.

"Good afternoon, Louis," one of the directors said, coming up behind him and opening the door on the right.

Louis stepped into the room feeling disoriented. He hazarded a furtive glance at the people sitting around the long conference table. To his consternation, he was unable to recognize a single face. Lowering his eyes to stare at the packet of papers he'd carried in with him, he let them slip from his grasp. His hands were shaking.

Louis Martin stood for another moment while the babble of voices in the room quieted. All eyes were drawn to his face, which had turned ghostly pale. Then Louis's eyes rolled up inside his head, and his back arched. He fell backward, his head striking the carpeted floor with a dull thump. Simultaneous with the impact on the floor, Louis's body began to tremble before being overwhelmed by wild tonic and clonic muscular contractions.

None of Louis's board of directors had ever seen a grand mal seizure, and for a moment they were all stunned. Finally, one man overcame his shock and rushed to the side of his stricken chairman. Only then did others respond by racing off to nearby telephones to call for help.

By the time the ambulance crew arrived, the seizure had passed. Except for a residual headache and lethargy, Louis felt relatively normal. He was no longer disoriented. In fact, he was dismayed to be told he'd had a seizure. As far as he was concerned, he'd only fainted.

The first person to see Louis in the emergency room at the Boston Memorial Hospital was a medical resident who introduced himself as George Carver. George seemed harried but thorough. After conducting a preliminary examination he told Louis that he would have to be admitted even though Louis's private internist, Clarence Handlin, had not yet been consulted.

"Is a seizure serious?" Louis asked. After his prostate operation two months earlier, Louis was not happy about the prospect of being hospitalized.

"We'll get a neurology consult," George said.

"But what's *your* opinion?" Louis asked.

"Seizures with sudden onset in an adult suggests structural brain disease," George said.

"How about talking English," Louis said. He hated medical jargon.

The resident fidgeted. "Structural means exactly that," he said evasively. "Something abnormal with the brain itself, not just its function."

"You mean like a brain tumor?" Louis asked.

"It could be a tumor," George said reluctantly.

"Good Lord!" Louis said. He felt himself break out in a cold sweat.

After calming the patient the best he could, George went into the "pit," as the center of the emergency room was called by those that worked there. First he checked to see if Louis's private physician had called in yet. He hadn't. Then he paged a neurology resident stat. He also told the ER clerk to call the medical student who was up for the next admission.

"By the way," George said to the clerk as he was returning to the cubicle where Louis Martin was waiting. "What's the name of the medical student?"

"Sean Murphy," the clerk said.

"CRAP!" SEAN said as his beeper went off. He was certain that Janet had long since disappeared, but just to be sure, he opened the door carefully and scanned the area. He didn't see her, so he pushed through. He had to use the phone out in the nurses' station since Peter was hogging the one in the back room, trying to get last-minute lab reports.

Before Sean called anybody, he approached Carla Valentine, the head nurse. "You guys looking for me?" he asked expectantly. He was hoping they were because then the page would involve some easily performed scut work. What Sean feared was that the page was coming from either admitting or the ER.

"You're all clear for the moment," Carla said.

Sean then dialed the operator and got the bad news. It was the ER with an admission.

Knowing the sooner he got the history and physical done, the better off he'd be, Sean bid farewell to Peter, who was still on the phone, and went downstairs.

Under normal circumstances Sean liked the ER and its constant sense of excitement and urgency. But on the afternoon of his last day on his medicine rotation, he didn't want another case. The typical Harvard medical student's workup took hours and filled between four and ten pages of tightly written notes.

"It's an interesting case," George said when Sean arrived. George was on hold on the phone with radiology.

"That's what you always say," Sean said.

"Truly," George said. "Have you ever seen papilledema?"

Sean shook his head.

"Grab an ophthalmoscope and look at the guy's nerve heads in both eyes. They'll look like miniature mountains. It means the intracranial pressure is elevated." George slid the ER clipboard along the countertop toward Sean.

"What's he got?" Sean asked.

"My guess is a brain tumor," George said. "He had a seizure at work."

At that moment someone came on the phone line from radiology, and George's attention was directed at scheduling an emergency CAT scan.

Sean took the ophthalmoscope and went in to see Mr. Martin. Sean was far from adept at using the instrument, but after persistence on his part and patience on Louis's part, he was able to catch fleeting glimpses of the mounded nerve heads.

Doing a medical student history and physical was a laborious task under the best of circumstances, and doing it in the emergency room and then up in X-ray while waiting for a CAT scan made it ten times more difficult. Sean persisted, asking as many questions as he could think of, especially about the current illness. What Sean learned that no one else had was that Louis Martin had had some transient headache, fever, and nausea and vomiting about a week after his prostate surgery in early January. Sean had stumbled onto this information just before Louis began his enhanced CAT scan. The technician had to order Sean out of the CAT scanner room and into the control room moments before the study commenced.

Besides the technician running the CAT scanner, there were a number of other people in the control room including Dr. Clarence Handlin, Louis Martin's internist, George Carver, the medical resident, and Harry O'Brian, the on-call neurology resident. They were all grouped around the CRT screen, waiting for the first "cuts" to appear.

Sean pulled George aside and told him about the earlier headache, fever, and nausea.

"A good pickup," George said while he pulled pensively at the skin at the edge of his jaw. He was obviously trying to relate these earlier symptoms to the current problem. "The fever is the curious part," he said. "Did he say it was a high fever?"

"Moderate," Sean said. "102 to 103. He said it was like having a cold or mild flu. Whatever it was, it went away completely."

"It might be related," George said. "At any rate this guy is a 'sickie.' The preliminary CAT scan showed two tumors. Remember Helen Cabot upstairs?"

"How can I forget?" Sean said. "She's still my patient."

"This guy's tumors look very similar to hers," George said.

The group of doctors around the CRT screen began talking excitedly. The first cuts were coming out. Sean and George stepped behind them and peered over their shoulders.

"Here they are again," Harry said, pointing with the tip of his percussion hammer. "They're definitely tumors. No doubt at all. And here's another small one."

Sean strained to see.

"Most likely metastases," Harry said. "Multiple tumors like this have to come from someplace else. Was his prostate benign?"

"Completely," Dr. Handlin said. "He's been in good health all his life."

"Smoke?" Harry asked.

"No," Sean said. The people in front moved to give Sean a better view of the CRT screen.

"We'll have to do a full metastatic workup," Harry said.

Sean bent over close to the CRT screen. The areas of reduced uptake were apparent even to his inexperienced eye. But what really caught his attention was how much they resembled Helen Cabot's tumors, as George had said. And like hers, they were all in the cerebrum. That had been a point of particular interest with Helen Cabot, since medulloblastomas generally occurred in the cerebellum, not the cerebrum.

"I know statistically you have to think of a metastasis from lung, colon, or prostate," George said. "But what are the chances we're seeing a tumor similar to Helen Cabot's? In other words, multifocal primary brain cancer like medulloblastoma."

Harry shook his head. "Remember, when you hear hoofbeats you should think of horses, not zebras. Helen Cabot's case is unique even though there have been a couple of similar cases recently reported around the country. Nonetheless, I'll be willing to wager anyone that we're looking at metastatic tumors here."

"What service do you think he should be on?" George asked.

"Six of one, half dozen of another," Harry said. "If he's on neurology, we'll need an internal medicine consult for the metastatic workup. If he's on internal medicine, he'll need the neuro consult."

"Since we took Cabot," George suggested, "why don't you guys take him. You interact better with neurosurgery anyway."

"Fine by me," Harry said.

Sean groaned inwardly. All his work doing the history and physical was for naught. Since the patient would be admitted to neurology, the medical student on neurology would get credit for it. But at least that meant Sean was free.

Sean motioned to George that he'd see him later on rounds, then slipped out of the CAT scan room. Although he was behind on his off-service notes, Sean took the time for a visit. Having been thinking and talking about Helen

Cabot, he wanted to see her. Getting off the elevator on the seventh floor, he walked directly down to room 708 and knocked on the half-open door.

Despite her shaved head and a series of blue marker stains on her scalp, Helen Cabot still managed to look attractive. Her features were delicate, emphasizing her large, bright green eyes. Her skin had the translucent perfection of a model. Yet she was pale, and there was little doubt she was ill. Still, her face lit up when she saw Sean.

"My favorite doctor," she said.

"Doctor-to-be," Sean corrected her. He didn't enjoy the charade of playing doctor like many medical students. Ever since he graduated from high school he'd felt like an imposter, play-acting first at the role of a Harvard undergraduate, then an MIT fellow, and now a Harvard medical student.

"Have you heard the good news?" Helen asked. She sat up despite her weakness from the many seizures she'd been having.

"Tell me," Sean said.

"I've been accepted into the Forbes Cancer Center protocol," Helen said.

"Fantastic!" Sean said. "Now I can tell you I'm heading there myself. I've been afraid to mention it until I heard you were going too."

"What a marvelous coincidence!" Helen said. "Now I'll have a friend there. I suppose you know that with my particular type of tumor they've had a one hundred percent remission."

"I know," Sean said. "Their results are unbelievable. But it's no coincidence we'll be down there together. It was your case that made me aware of the Forbes. As I've mentioned to you, my research involves the molecular basis of cancer.

So discovering a clinic where they are having hundred-percent success treating a specific cancer is extraordinarily exciting for me. I'm amazed I hadn't read about it in the medical literature. Anyway, I want to go down there and find out exactly what they're doing."

"Their treatment is still experimental," Helen said. "My father emphasized that to me. We think the reason they've avoided publishing their results is that they first want to be absolutely sure of their claims. But whether they've published or not, I can't wait to get there and start treatment. It's the first ray of hope since this nightmare started."

"When are you going?" Sean asked.

"Sometime next week," Helen said. "And you?"

"I'll be on the road the crack of dawn on Sunday. I should be there early Tuesday morning. I'll be waiting for you." Sean reached out and gripped Helen's shoulder.

Helen smiled, placing her hand over Sean's.

AFTER COMPLETING report, Janet returned to the seventh floor to look for Sean. Once again the nurses said he'd been there only moments earlier but apparently had disappeared. They suggested paging him, but Janet wanted to catch him off guard. Since it was now after four she thought the best place to find him would be Dr. Clifford Walsh's lab. Dr. Walsh was Sean's Ph.D. advisor.

To get there, Janet had to leave the hospital, brace herself against the winter wind, walk partway down Longfellow Avenue, cross the medical school quadrangle, and climb to the third floor. Even before she opened the door to the lab, she knew she'd guessed correctly. She recognized Sean's figure through the frosted glass. It was mostly the way he moved that was so familiar. He had surprising grace for such a stocky, muscular frame. There was no wasted motion. He went about his tasks quickly and efficiently.

Entering the room, Janet closed the door behind her and hesitated. For a moment she enjoyed watching Sean. Besides Sean there were three other people busily working. A radio played classical music. There was no conversation.

It was a rather dated and cluttered lab with soapstone-topped benches. The newest equipment were the computers and a series of desk-sized analyzers. Sean had described the subject of his Ph.D. thesis on several occasions, but Janet still wasn't a hundred percent certain she understood it all. He was searching for specialized genes called oncogenes that had the capability of encouraging a cell to become cancerous. Sean had explained that the origins of oncogenes seemed to be from normal "cellular control" genes that certain types of viruses called retroviruses had a tendency to capture in order to stimulate viral production in future host cells.

Janet had nodded at appropriate times during these explanations but had always found herself more interested by Sean's enthusiasm than the subject matter. She also realized that she needed to do some more basic reading in the area of molecular genetics if she was to understand Sean's particular area of research. Sean had a tendency to assume that she had more knowledge than she had, in a field where advances came at a dizzying pace.

As Janet watched Sean from just inside the door, appreciating the V that his broad shoulders and narrow waist formed, she became curious about what he was currently doing. In sharp contrast to many other visits she'd made over the last two months, he wasn't preparing one of the analyzers to run. Instead he seemed to be putting objects away and cleaning up.

After watching for several minutes, expecting him to notice her, Janet stepped forward and stood right next to him. At five-six Janet was relatively tall, and since Sean was only five-nine, they could just about look each other in the eye, especially when Janet wore heels.

"What may I ask are you doing?" Janet said suddenly.

Sean jumped. His level of concentration had been so great he'd not sensed her presence.

"Just cleaning up," he said guiltily.

Janet leaned forward and looked into his startlingly blue eyes. He returned her stare for a moment, then looked away.

"Cleaning up?" Janet asked. Her eyes swept around the now pristine lab bench. "That's a surprise." Janet redirected her eyes at his face. "What's going on here? This is the most immaculate your work area has ever been. Is there something you haven't told me?"

"No," Sean said. Then he paused before adding, "Well, yes, there is. I'm taking a two-month research elective."

"Where?"

"Miami, Florida."

"You weren't going to tell me?"

"Of course I was. I planned on telling you tomorrow night."

"When are you leaving?"

"Sunday."

Janet's eyes angrily roamed the room. Absently, her fingers drummed on the countertop. She questioned to herself what she'd done to deserve this kind of treatment. Looking back at Sean, she said: "You were going to wait until the night before to tell me this?"

"It just came up this week. It wasn't certain until two days ago. I wanted to wait until the right moment."

"Considering our relationship, the right moment would have been when it came up. Miami? Why now?"

"Remember that patient I told you about? The woman with medulloblastoma."

"Helen Cabot? The attractive coed?"

"That's the one," Sean said. "When I read about her tumor, I discovered . . ." He paused.

"Discovered what?" Janet demanded.

"It wasn't from my reading," Sean corrected himself. "One of her attendings said that her father had heard about a treatment that is apparently achieving one hundred percent remission. The protocol is only administered at the Forbes Cancer Center in Miami."

"So you decided to go. Just like that."

"Not exactly," Sean said. "I spoke to Dr. Walsh, who happens to know the director, a man named Randolph Mason. A number of years ago they worked together at the NIH. Dr. Walsh told him about me, and got me invited."

"This is the wrong time for this," Janet said. "You know I've been disturbed about us."

Sean shrugged. "I'm sorry. But I have the time now, and this is potentially consequential. My research involves the molecular basis of cancer. If they are experiencing a hundred-percent remission rate for a specific tumor, it has to have implications for all cancers."

Janet felt weak. Her emotions were raw. Sean's leaving for two months at this time seemed the worst possible situation as far as her psyche was concerned. Yet his reasons were noble. He wasn't going to the Club Med or something. How could she get angry or try to deny him. She felt totally confused.

"There is the telephone," Sean said. "I'm not going to the moon. It's only a couple of months. And you understand that this could be very important."

"More important than our relationship?" Janet blurted out. "More important than the rest of our lives." Almost immediately Janet felt foolish. Such comments sounded so juvenile.

"Now let's not get into an argument comparing apples and oranges," Sean said.

Janet sighed deeply, fighting back tears. "Let's talk about it later," she managed. "This is hardly the place for an emotional confrontation."

"I can't tonight," Sean said. "It's Friday and . . ."

"And you have to go to that stupid bar," Janet snapped. She saw some of the other people in the room turn to stare at them.

"Janet, keep your voice down!" Sean said. "We'll get together Saturday night as planned. We can talk then."

"Knowing how upset this leaving would make me, I cannot understand why you can't give up drinking with your trashy buddies for one night."

"Careful, Janet," Sean warned. "My friends are important to me. They're my roots."

For a moment their eyes met with palpable hostility. Then Janet turned and strode from the lab.

Self-consciously, Sean glanced at his colleagues. Most avoided his gaze. Dr. Clifford Walsh did not. He was a big man with a full beard. He wore a long white coat with the sleeves rolled up to the elbows.

"Turmoil does not help creativity," he said. "I hope your leaving on this sour note does not influence your behavior down in Miami."

"Not a chance," Sean said.

"Remember, I've gone out on a limb for you," Dr. Walsh said. "I assured Dr. Mason you'd be an asset to his organization. He liked the idea that you've had a lot of experience with monoclonal antibodies."

"That's what you told him?" Sean questioned with dismay.

"I could tell from our conversation that he'd be interested in that," Dr. Walsh explained. "Don't get your dander up."

"But that was what I did three years ago at MIT," Sean said. "Protein chemistry and I have parted ways."

"I know you're interested in oncogenes now," Dr. Walsh said, "but you wanted the job and I did what I thought was best to get you invited. When you are there, you can explain you'd rather work in molecular genetics. Knowing you as I do, I'm not worried about you making your feelings known. Just try to be tactful."

"I've read some of the work of the chief investigator," Sean said. "It's perfect for me. Her background is in retroviruses and oncogenes."

"That's Dr. Deborah Levy," Dr. Walsh said. "Maybe you can get to work with her. But whether you do or not, just be grateful you've been invited at this late date."

"I just don't want to get all the way down there and get stuck with busywork."

"Promise me you won't cause trouble," Dr. Walsh said.

"Me?" Sean asked with eyebrows arched. "You know me better than that."

"I know you too well," Dr. Walsh said. "That's the problem. Your brashness can be disturbing, to put it mildly, but at least thank the Lord for your intelligence."

2

February 26
Friday, 4:45 P.M.

"Just a second, Corissa," Kathleen Sharenburg said as she stopped and leaned against one of the cosmetic counters of Neiman Marcus. They'd come to the mall just west of Houston to shop for dresses for a school dance. Now that they had made their purchases, Corissa was eager to get home.

Kathleen had had a sudden sensation of dizziness giving her the sickening sensation that the room was spinning. Luckily, as soon as she touched the countertop, the spinning stopped. She then shuddered through a wave of nausea. But it too passed.

"You all right?" Corissa asked. They were both juniors in high school.

"I don't know," Kathleen said. The headache she'd had off and on for the last few days was back. It had been awakening her from sleep, but she hadn't said anything to her parents, afraid that it might be related to the pot she'd smoked the weekend before.

"You look white as a ghost," Corissa said. "Maybe we shouldn't have eaten that fudge."

"Oh my God!" Kathleen whispered. "That man over there is listening to us. He's planning on kidnapping us in the parking garage."

Corissa spun about, half expecting some fearful man to be towering over them. But all she saw was a handful of peaceful, women shoppers, mostly at the cosmetic counters. She didn't see any man.

"What man are you talking about?" she asked.

Kathleen's eyes stared ahead, unblinking. "That man over there near the coats." She pointed with her left hand.

Corissa followed the direction of Kathleen's finger and finally saw a man almost fifty yards away. He was standing behind a woman who was shuffling through a rack of merchandise. He wasn't even facing toward them.

Confused, Corissa turned back to her best friend.

"He's saying we cannot leave the store," Kathleen said.

"What are you talking about?" Corissa questioned. "I mean, you're starting to scare me."

"We have to get out of here," Kathleen warned. Abruptly she turned and headed in the opposite direction. Corissa had to run to catch up with her. She grabbed Kathleen's arm and yanked her around.

"What is wrong with you?" Corissa demanded.

Kathleen's face was a mask of terror. "There are more men now," she said urgently. "They are coming down the escalator. They're talking about getting us as well."

Corissa turned. Several men were indeed coming down the escalator. But at such a distance Corissa couldn't even see their faces much less hear what they said.

Kathleen's scream jolted Corissa like an electric charge. Corissa spun around and saw Kathleen begin to collapse. Reaching out, Corissa tried to keep Kathleen from falling. But they were off balance, and they both fell to the floor in a tangle of arms and legs.

Before Corissa could extract herself, Kathleen began to convulse. Her body heaved wildly against the marble floor.

Helping hands got Corissa to her feet. Two women who'd been at a neighboring cosmetic counter attended to Kathleen. They restrained her from hitting her head on the floor and managed to get something between her teeth. A trickle of blood oozed from Kathleen's lips. She had bitten her tongue.

"Oh my God, oh my God!" Corissa kept repeating.

"What's her name?" one of the women attending Kathleen asked.

"Kathleen Sharenburg," Corissa said. "Her father is Ted Sharenburg, head of Shell Oil," she added, as if that fact would somehow help her friend now.

"Somebody better call an ambulance," the woman said. "This girl's seizure has to be stopped."

IT WAS already dark as Janet tried to see out the window of the Ritz Café. People were scurrying past in both directions on Newbury Street, their hands clasped to either coat lapels or hat.

"I don't know what you see in him anyway," Evelyn Reardon was saying. "I told you the day you brought him home he was inappropriate."

"He's earning both his Ph.D. and an M.D. from Harvard," Janet reminded her mother.

"That doesn't excuse his manners, or lack thereof," Evelyn said.

Janet eyed her mother. She was a tall, slender woman with straight, even features. Few people had trouble recognizing that Evelyn and Janet were mother and daughter.

"Sean is proud of his heritage," Janet said. "He likes the fact that he's from working stock."

"There's nothing wrong in that," Evelyn said. "The problem is being mired in it. The boy has no manners. And that long hair of his . . ."

"He feels convention is stifling," Janet said. As usual she found herself in the unenviable position of defending Sean. It was particularly galling at the moment since she was cross with him. What she'd hoped for from her mother was advice, not the same old criticism.

"How trite," Evelyn said. "If he was planning on practicing like a regular doctor, there might be hope. But this molecular biology, or whatever it is, I don't understand. What is he studying again?"

"Oncogenes," Janet said. She should have known better than to turn to her mother.

"Explain what they are once more," Evelyn said.

Janet poured herself more tea. Her mother could be trying, and attempting to describe Sean's research to her was like the blind leading the blind. But she tried nonetheless.

"Oncogenes are genes that are capable of changing normal cells into cancer cells," Janet said. "They come from normal cellular genes present in every living cell called proto-oncogenes. Sean feels that a true understanding of cancer will come only when all the proto-oncogenes and oncogenes are discovered and defined. And that's what he's doing: searching for oncogenes in specialized viruses."

"It may be very worthwhile," Evelyn said. "But it's all very arcane and hardly the type of career to support a family on."

"Don't be so sure," Janet said. "Sean and a couple of his fellow students at MIT started a company to make monoclonal antibodies while he was getting his master's degree.

They called it Immunotherapy, Inc. Over a year ago it was bought out by Genentech."

"That's encouraging," Evelyn said. "Did Sean make a good profit?"

"They all did," Janet said. "But they agreed to reinvest it in a new company. That's all I can say at the moment. He's sworn me to secrecy."

"A secret from your mother?" Evelyn questioned. "Sounds a bit melodramatic. But you know your father wouldn't approve. He's always said that people should avoid using their own capital in starting new enterprises."

Janet sighed in frustration. "All this is beside the point," she said. "What I wanted to hear is what you think about my going to Florida. Sean's going to be there for two months. All he'll be doing is research. Here in Boston he's doing research plus schoolwork. I thought maybe we'd have a better chance to talk and work things out."

"What about your job at Memorial?" Evelyn asked.

"I can take a leave," Janet said. "And I can certainly work down there. One of the benefits of being a nurse is that I can find employment just about anywhere."

"Well, I don't think it is a good idea," Evelyn said.

"Why?"

"It's not right to go running after this boy," Evelyn said. "Particularly since you know how your father and I feel about him. He's never going to fit into our family. And after what he said to Uncle Albert I wouldn't even know where to seat him at a dinner party."

"Uncle Albert was teasing him about his hair," Janet said. "He wouldn't stop."

"That's no excuse for saying what he did to one's elder."

"We all know that Uncle Albert wears a toupee," Janet said.

"We may know but we don't mention it," Evelyn said. "And calling it a rug in front of everyone was inexcusable."

Janet took a sip of her tea and stared out the window. It was true the whole family knew Uncle Albert wore a toupee. It was also true that no one ever commented on it. Janet had grown up in a family where there were many unspoken rules. Individual expression, especially in children, was not encouraged. Manners were considered of paramount importance.

"Why don't you date that lovely young man who brought you to the Myopia Hunt Club polo match last year," Evelyn suggested.

"He was a jerk," Janet said.

"Janet!" her mother warned.

They drank their tea in silence for a few moments. "If you want to talk to him so much," Evelyn finally said, "why not do it before he leaves? Go see him tonight?"

"I can't," Janet said. "Friday night is his night with the boys. They all hang out at some bar near where he went to high school."

"As your father would say, I rest my case," Evelyn said with uncamouflaged satisfaction.

A HOODED sweatshirt under a wool jacket insulated Sean from the freezing mist. The cinch for the hood had been drawn tight and tied beneath his chin. As he jogged along High Street toward Monument Square in Charlestown, he passed a basketball from one hand to the other. He'd just finished playing a pickup game at the Charlestown Boys Club with a group called "The Alumni." This was a motley assortment of friends and acquaintances from age eighteen to sixty. It had been a good workout, and he was still sweating.

Skirting Monument Square with its enormous phallic monument commemorating the Battle of Bunker Hill, Sean approached his boyhood home. As a plumber his father, Brian Murphy, Sr., had had a decent income, and back before it became fashionable to live in the city, he had purchased a large Victorian town house. At first the Murphys had lived in the ground-floor duplex, but after his father had died at age forty-six from liver cancer the rental from the duplex had been sorely needed. When Sean's older brother, Brian, Jr., had gone away to school, Sean, his younger brother Charles, and his mother Anne had moved into one of the single-floor apartments. Now she lived there alone.

As he reached the door, Sean noticed a familiar Mercedes parked just behind his Isuzu 4×4, indicating older brother Brian had made one of his surprise visits. Intuitively, Sean knew he was in for grief about his planned trip to Miami.

Taking the stairs two at a time, Sean unlocked his mother's door and stepped inside. Brian's black leather briefcase rested on a ladder-back chair. A rich smell of pot roast filled the air.

"Is that you, Sean?" Anne called from the kitchen. She appeared in the doorway just as Sean was hanging up his coat. Dressed in a simple housedress covered by a worn apron, Anne looked considerably older than her fifty-four years. After her long, repressing marriage to the hard-drinking Brian Murphy, her face had become permanently drawn, her eyes generally tired and forlorn. Her hair, which she wore in an old-fashioned bun, was naturally curly and although it had been an attractive dark brown, it was now streaked with gray.

"Brian's here," Anne said.

"I guessed as much."

Sean went into the kitchen to say hello to his brother. Brian was at the kitchen table, nursing a drink. He'd removed his jacket and draped it over a chair; paisley suspenders looped over his shoulders. Like Sean, he had darkly handsome features, black hair, and brilliant blue eyes. But the similarities ended there. Where Sean was brash and casual, Brian was circumspect and precise. Unlike Sean's shaggy locks, Brian's hair was neatly trimmed and precisely parted. He sported a carefully trimmed mustache. His clothing was decidedly lawyer-like and leaned toward dark blue pinstripes.

"Am I responsible for this honor?" Sean asked. Brian did not visit often even though he lived nearby in Back Bay.

"Mother called me," Brian admitted.

It didn't take Sean long to shower, shave, and dress in jeans and a rugby shirt. He was back in the kitchen before Brian finished carving the pot roast. Sean helped set the table. While he did so, he eyed his older brother. There had been a time when Sean resented him. For years his mother had introduced her boys as my wonderful Brian, my good Charles, and Sean. Charles was currently off in a seminary in New Jersey studying to become a priest.

Like Sean, Brian had always been an athlete, although not as successful. He'd been a studious child and usually at home. He'd gone to the University of Massachusetts, then on to law school at B.U. Everybody had always liked Brian. Everyone had always known that he would be successful and that he would surely escape the Irish curse of alcohol, guilt, depression, and tragedy. Sean, on the other hand, had always been the wild one, preferring the company of the neighborhood ne'er-do-wells and frequently in trouble with the authorities involving brawls, minor burglary, and stolen-car joy rides. If it hadn't been for Sean's extraordinary intelligence and his facility with a hockey stick, he might have ended up in Bridgewater Prison instead of Harvard. Within the ghettos of the city the dividing line between success and failure was a narrow band of chance that the kids teetered on all through their turbulent adolescent years.

There was little conversation during the final dinner preparations. But once they sat down, Brian cleared his throat after taking a sip of his milk. They'd always drunk milk with dinner throughout their boyhoods.

"Mother is upset about this Miami idea," Brian said.

Anne looked down at her plate. She'd always been self-effacing, especially when Brian Sr. was alive. He'd had a terrible temper made worse by alcohol, and alcohol had been a daily indulgence. Every afternoon after unplugging drains, fixing aged boilers, and installing toilets, Brian Sr. would stop at the Blue Tower bar beneath the Tobin Bridge. Nearly every night he'd come home drunk, sour, and vicious. Anne was the usual target, although Sean had come in for his share of blows when he tried to protect her. By morning Brian Sr. would be sober, and consumed by guilt; he'd swear he would change. But he never did. Even when he'd lost seventy-five pounds and was dying from liver cancer, his behavior was the same.

"I'm going down there to do research," Sean said. "It's no big deal."

"There's drugs in Miami," Anne said. She didn't look up.

Sean rolled his eyes. He reached over and grasped his mother's arm. "Mom, my problem with drugs was in high school. I'm in medical school now."

"What about that incident your first year of college?" Brian added.

"That was only a little coke at a party," Sean said. "It was just unlucky the police decided to raid the place."

"The lucky thing was my getting your juvenile record sealed. Otherwise you would have been in a hell of a fix."

"Miami is a violent city," Anne said. "I read about it in the newspapers all the time."

"Jesus Christ!" Sean exclaimed.

"Don't use the Lord's name in vain," Anne said.

"Mom, you've been watching too much television. Miami is like any city, with both good and bad elements. But it doesn't matter. I'll be doing research. I won't have time to get into trouble even if I wanted to."

"You'll meet the wrong kind of people," Anne said.

"Mom, I'm an adult," Sean said in frustration.

"You are still hanging out with the wrong people here in Charlestown," Brian said. "Mom's fears are not unreasonable. The whole neighborhood knows Jimmy O'Connor and Brady Flanagan are still breaking and entering."

"And sending the money to the IRA," Sean said.

"They are not political activists," Brian said. "They are hoodlums. And you choose to remain friends."

"I have a few beers with them on Friday nights," Sean said.

"Precisely," Brian said. "Like our father, the pub is your home away from home. And apart from Mom's concerns, this isn't a good time for you to be away. The Franklin Bank will be coming up with the rest of the financing for Oncogen. I've got the papers almost ready. Things could move quickly."

"In case you've forgotten, there are fax machines and overnight delivery," Sean said, scraping his chair back from the table. He stood up and carried his plate over to the sink. "I'm going to Miami no matter what anybody says. I believe the Forbes Cancer Center has hit on something extraordinarily important. And now if you two co-conspirators will allow me, I'm going out to drink with my delinquent friends."

Feeling irritable, Sean struggled into the old pea coat that his father had gotten back when the Charlestown Navy Yard was still functioning. Pulling a wool watch cap over his ears, he ran downstairs to the street and set out into the freezing rain. The wind had shifted to the east and he could smell the salt sea air. As he neared Old Scully's Bar on Bunker Hill Street, the warm incandescent glow from the misted windows emanated a familiar sense of comfort and security.

Pushing open the door he allowed himself to be enveloped by the dimly lit, noisy environment. It was not a classy place. The pine wood paneling was almost black with cigarette smoke. The furniture was scraped and scarred. The only bright spot was the brass footrail kept polished by innumerable shoes rubbing across its surface. In the far corner a TV was bolted to the ceiling and tuned to a Bruins hockey game.

The only woman in the crowded room was Molly, who shared bartending duties with Pete. Before Sean could even say anything a brimming mug of ale slid along the bar toward him. A hand grasped his shoulder as a cheer spread through the crowd. The Bruins had scored a goal.

Sean sighed contentedly. It was as if he were at home. He had the same comfortable feeling he'd get whenever he was particularly exhausted and settled into a soft bed.

As usual, Jimmy and Brady drifted over and began to brag about a little job they'd done in Marblehead the previous weekend. That led to humorous recollections of when Sean had been "one of the guys."

"We always knew you were smart the way you could figure out alarms," Brady said. "But we never guessed you'd go to Harvard. How could you stand all those jerks."

It was a statement, not a question, and Sean let it pass,

but the comment made him realize how much he'd changed. He still enjoyed Old Scully's Bar, but more as an observer. It was an uncomfortable acknowledgment because he didn't truly feel part of the Harvard medical world either. He felt rather like a social orphan.

A few hours later when Sean had had a few drafts, and he was feeling more mellow and less an outcast, he joined in the raucous decisionmaking involving a trip up to Revere to one of the strip joints near the waterfront. Just at the moment the debate was reaching a frenzied climax, the entire bar went dead silent. One by one heads turned toward the front door. Something extraordinary had happened, and everyone was shocked. A woman had breached their all-male bastion. And it wasn't an ordinary woman, like some overweight, gum-chewing girl in the laundromat. It was a slim, gorgeous woman who obviously wasn't from Charlestown.

Her long blond hair glistened with diamonds of moisture, and it contrasted dramatically with the rich deep mahagony of her mink jacket. Her eyes were almond shaped and pert as they audaciously scanned the room, leaping from one stunned face to another. Her mouth was set in determination. Her high cheekbones glowed with color. She appeared like a collective hallucination of some fantasy female.

A few of the guys shifted nervously, guessing that she was someone's girlfriend. She was too beautiful to be anyone's wife.

Sean was one of the last faces to turn. And when he did, his mouth dropped open. It was Janet!

Janet spotted him about the same time he saw her. She walked directly up to him and pushed in beside him at the bar. Brady moved away, making an exaggerated gesture of terror as if Janet were a fearful creature.

"I'd like a beer, please," she said.

Without answering, Molly filled a chilled mug and placed it in front of Janet.

The room remained silent except for the television.

Janet took a sip and turned to look at Sean. Since she was wearing pumps she was just about eye level. "I want to talk with you," she said.

Sean hadn't felt this embarrassed since he'd been caught with his pants off at age sixteen with Kelly Parnell in the back of her family's car.

Putting his beer down, Sean grasped Janet by her upper arm, just above the elbow, and marched her out the door. When they got out on the sidewalk Sean had recovered enough to be angry. He was also a little tipsy.

"What are you doing here?" he demanded.

Sean allowed his eyes to sweep around the neighborhood. "I don't believe this. You know you weren't supposed to come here."

"I knew nothing of the kind," Janet said. "I knew I wasn't invited, if that's what you mean. But I didn't think my coming constituted a capital offense. It's important I talk with you, and with you leaving on Sunday, I think it's more important than drinking with these so-called friends of yours."

"And who is making that value judgment?" Sean demanded. "I'm the one who decides what is important to me, not you, and I resent this intrusion."

"I need to talk to you about Miami," Janet said. "It's your fault you've waited until the last minute to tell me."

"There's nothing to talk about," Sean said. "I'm going and that's final. Not you, not my mother, and not my brother are going to stop me. Now if you'll excuse me, I have to go back in and see what I can salvage of my self-respect."

"But this can impact the rest of our lives," Janet said.

Tears began to mix with the rain running down her cheeks. She'd taken an emotional risk coming to Charlestown, and the idea of rejection was devastating.

"I'll talk with you tomorrow," Sean said. "Good night, Janet."

TED SHARENBURG was nervous, waiting for the doctors to tell him what was wrong with his daughter. His wife had gotten in touch with him in New Orleans where he'd been on business, and he had gotten the company Gulfstream jet to fly him directly back to Houston. As the CEO of an oil company that had made major contributions to the Houston hospitals, Ted Sharenburg was afforded special treatment. At that moment his daughter was inside the huge, multimillion-dollar MRI machine having an emergency brain scan.

"We don't know much yet," Dr. Judy Buckley said. "These initial images are very superficial cuts." Judy Buckley was the chief of neuroradiology and had been happy to come into the hospital at the director's request. Also in attendance were Dr. Vance Martinez, the Sharenburgs' internist, and Dr. Stanton Rainey, chief of neurology. It was a prominent group of experts to be assembled at any hour, much less at one o'clock in the morning.

Ted paced the tiny control room. He couldn't sit still. The story he'd been told about his daughter had been devastating.

"She experienced an acute paranoid psychosis," Dr. Martinez had explained. "Symptoms like that can occur, especially with some sort of involvement of the temporal lobe."

Ted reached the end of the room for the fiftieth time and turned. He looked through the glass at the giant MRI machine. He could just barely see his daughter. It was as if she were being swallowed by a technological whale. He hated being so helpless. All he could do was watch, and hope. He'd felt almost as vulnerable when she'd had her tonsils out a few months earlier.

"We've got something," Dr. Buckley said.

Ted hurried over to the CRT screen.

"There's a hyperintense circumscribed area in the right temporal lobe," she said.

"What does it mean?" Ted demanded.

The doctors exchanged glances. It was not customary for the relative of a patient to be in the room during such a study.

"It's probably a mass lesion," Dr. Buckley said.

"Can you put that in lay terms?" Ted asked, trying to keep his voice even.

"She means a brain tumor," Dr. Martinez said. "But we know very little at this point, and we should not jump to conclusions. The lesion might have been there for years."

Ted swayed. His worst fears were materializing. Why couldn't he be in that machine and not his daughter?

"Uh oh!" Dr. Buckley said, forgetting the effect such an exclamation would have on Ted. "Here's another lesion."

The doctors clustered around the screen, transfixed by the vertically unfolding images. For a few moments they forgot about Ted.

"You know it reminds me of the case I told you about in Boston," said Dr. Rainey. "A young woman in her twenties with multiple intracranial tumors and negative metastatic workup. She was proved to have medulloblastoma."

"I thought medulloblastoma occurs in the posterior fossa," Dr. Martinez said.

"It usually does," Dr. Rainey said. "It also usually occurs

in younger kids. But twenty percent or so of the incidents are in patients over twenty, and it's occasionally found in regions of the brain besides the cerebellum. Actually, it would be wonderful if it turns out to be medulloblastoma in this case."

"Why?" Dr. Buckley asked. She was aware of the high mortality of the cancer.

"Because a group down in Miami has had remarkable success in getting remissions with that particular tumor."

"What's their name?" Ted demanded, clutching onto the first hopeful news he'd heard.

"The Forbes Cancer Center," Dr. Rainey said. "They haven't published yet but word of that kind of a result gets around."

3

March 2
Tuesday, 6:15 A.M.

When Tom Widdicomb awoke at 6:15 to begin his workday, Sean Murphy had already been on the road for several hours, planning on reaching the Forbes Cancer Center by mid-morning. Tom did not know Sean, and had no idea he was expected. Had he known that their lives would soon intersect, his anxiety would have been even greater. Tom was always anxious when he decided to help a patient, and the night before he'd decided to help not one but two women. Sandra Blankenship on the second floor would be the first. She was in great pain and already receiving her chemotherapy by IV. The other patient, Gloria D'Amataglio, was on the fourth floor. That was a bit more worrisome since the last patient he'd helped, Norma Taylor, had also been on the fourth floor. Tom didn't want any pattern to emerge.

His biggest problem was that he constantly worried about someone suspecting what he was doing, and on a day that he was going to act, his anxiety could be overwhelming. Still, sensitive to gossip on the wards, he'd heard nothing that suggested that anyone was suspicious. After all, he was dealing with women who were terminally ill. They were expected to die. Tom was merely saving everyone from additional suffering, especially the patient.

Tom showered, shaved, and dressed in his green uniform, then went into his mother's kitchen. She always got up before he did, insistent every morning as far back as he could remember that he should eat a good breakfast since he wasn't as strong as other boys. Tom and his mother, Alice, had lived together in their close, secret world from the time Tom's dad died when Tom was four. That was when he and his mother had started sleeping together, and his mother had started calling him "her little man."

"I'm going to help another woman today, Mom," Tom said as he sat down to eat his eggs and bacon. He knew how proud his mother was of him. She had always praised him even when he'd been a lonely child with eye problems. His schoolmates had teased him mercilessly about his crossed eyes, chasing him home nearly every day.

"Don't worry, my little man," Alice would say when he'd arrive at the house in tears. "We'll always have each other. We don't need other people."

And that was how things worked out. Tom had never felt any desire to leave home. For a while, he worked at a local veterinarian's. Then at his mother's suggestion, since she'd always been interested in medicine, he'd taken a course to be an EMT. After his training, he got a job with an ambulance company but had trouble getting along with the other workers. He decided he would be better off as an orderly. That way he wouldn't have to relate to so many people. First he'd worked at Miami General Hospital but got into a fight with his shift supervisor. Then he worked at a funeral home before joining the Forbes housekeeping staff.

"The woman's name is Sandra," Tom told his mother as

he ran his dish under the faucet at the sink. "She's older than you. She's in a lot of pain. The 'problem' has spread to her spine."

When Tom spoke to his mother, he never used the word "cancer." Early in her illness, they'd decided not to say the word. They preferred less emotionally charged words like "problem" or "difficulty."

Tom had read about succinylcholine in a newspaper story about some doctor in New Jersey. His rudimentary medical training afforded an understanding of the physiologic principles. His freedom as a housekeeper allowed him contact with anesthesia carts. He'd never had any problem getting the drug. The problem had been where to hide it until it was needed. Then one day he found a convenient space above the wall cabinets in the housekeeping closet on the fourth floor. When he climbed up and looked into the area and saw the amount of accumulated dust, he knew his drug would never be disturbed.

"Don't worry about anything, Mom," Tom said as he prepared to leave. "I'll be home just as soon as I can. I'll miss you and I love you." Tom had been saying that ever since he had gone to school, and just because he'd had to put his mother to sleep three years ago, he didn't feel any need to change.

IT WAS almost ten-thirty in the morning when Sean pulled his 4×4 into the parking area of the Forbes Cancer Center. It was a bright, clear, summer-like day. The temperature was somewhere around seventy, and after the freezing Boston rain Sean felt he was in heaven. He'd enjoyed the two-day drive, too. He could have made it faster, but the clinic wasn't expecting him until late that day so there'd been no need. He spent his first night in a motel just off I95 in Rocky Mount, North Carolina.

The next day had taken him deep into Florida where the depth of spring seemed to increase with every passing mile. The second night had been spent in perfumed delight near Vero Beach, Florida. When he asked the motel clerk about the wonderful aroma in the air he was told it came from the nearby citrus groves.

The last lap of the journey turned out to be the most difficult. From West Palm Beach south, particularly near Fort Lauderdale and into Miami, he fought rush-hour traffic. To his surprise even eight-laned I95 coagulated into a stop-and-go mess.

Sean locked his car, stretched, and gazed up at the imposing twin bronzed, mirrored towers of the Forbes Cancer Center. A covered pedestrian bridge constructed of the same material connected the buildings. He noted from the signs that the research and administration center was on the left while the hospital was on the right.

As Sean started for the entrance, he thought about his first impressions of Miami. They were mixed. As he'd come south on I95 and neared his turnoff, he'd been able to see the gleaming new downtown skyscrapers. But the areas adjacent to the highway had been a melange of strip malls and low-income housing. The area around the Forbes Center, which was situated along the Miami River, was also rather seedy although a few modern buildings were interspersed among the flat-roofed cinder block structures.

As Sean pushed through the mirrored door, he thought wryly about the difficulty everyone had given him about this two-month elective. He wondered if his mother would ever get over the traumas he'd caused her as an adolescent. "You're too much like your father," she'd say, and it was meant as a reproach. Except for enjoying the pub, Sean felt little similarity with his father. But then he had been presented with far different choices and opportunities than his father ever had.

A black felt sign stood on an easel just inside the door. Spelled out in white plastic letters was his name and a message: Welcome. Sean thought it was a nice touch.

There was a small lounge directly behind the front door. Entrance into the building itself was blocked by a turnstile. Next to the turnstile was a Corian-covered desk. Behind the desk sat a swarthy, handsome Hispanic man dressed in a brown uniform complete with epaulets and peaked military-style hat. The outfit reminded Sean of a cross between those seen in Marine recruitment posters and those seen in Hollywood Gestapo movies. An elaborate emblem on the guard's left arm said "Security" and the name tag above his left pocket proclaimed that his name was Martinez.

"Can I help you?" Martinez asked in heavily accented English.

"I'm Sean Murphy," Sean said, pointing to the welcome sign.

The guard's expression did not change. He studied Sean for a beat then picked up one of several telephones. He spoke in rapid, staccato Spanish. After he hung up he pointed to a nearby leather couch. "A few moments, please."

Sean sat down. He picked up a copy of *Science* from a low coffee table and idly flipped the pages. But his attention was on Forbes' elaborate security system. Thick glass partitions separated the waiting area from the rest of the building. Apparently the guarded turnstile provided the only entrance.

Since security was all too frequently neglected in health care institutions, Sean was favorably impressed and said as much to the guard.

"There are some bad areas nearby," the guard replied but didn't elaborate.

Presently a second security officer appeared, dressed identically to the first. The turnstile opened to allow him into the lounge.

"My name is Ramirez," the second guard said. "Would you follow me, please."

Sean got to his feet. As he passed through the turnstile he didn't see Martinez press any button. He guessed the turnstile was controlled by a foot pedal.

Sean followed Ramirez for a short distance, turning into the first office on the left. "Security" was printed in block letters on the open door. Inside was a control room with banks of TV monitors covering one wall. In front of the monitors was a third guard with a clipboard. Even a cursory glance at the monitors told Sean that he was looking at a multitude of locations around the complex.

Sean continued to follow Ramirez into a small windowless office. Behind the desk sat a fourth guard who had two gold stars attached to his uniform and gold trim on the peak of his hat. His name tag said: Harris.

"That will be all, Ramirez," Harris said, giving Sean the feeling he was being inducted into the army.

Harris studied Sean who stared back. There was an almost immediate feeling of antipathy between the men.

With his tanned, meaty face, Harris looked like a lot of people Sean had known in Charlestown when he was young. They usually had jobs of minor authority that they practiced with great officiousness. They were also nasty drunks. Two beers and they'd want to fight about a call a referee had made on a televised sporting event if you suggested you disagreed with their perception. It was crazy. Sean had learned long ago to avoid such people. Now he was standing across the desk from one.

"We don't want any trouble here," Harris was saying. He had a faint southern accent.

Sean thought that was a strange way to begin a conversation. He wondered what this man thought he was getting from Harvard, a parolee? Harris was in obvious good physical shape, his bulging biceps straining the sleeves of his short-sleeved shirt, yet he didn't look all that healthy. Sean toyed with the idea of giving the man a short lecture on the benefits of proper nutrition, but thought better of the idea. He could still hear Dr. Walsh's admonitions.

"You're supposed to be a doctor," Harris said. "Why the hell are you wearing your hair so long? And I'd hazard to say that you didn't shave this morning."

"But I did put on a shirt and tie for the occasion," Sean said. "I thought I was looking quite natty."

"Don't mess with me, boy," Harris said. There was no sign of humor in his voice.

Sean shifted his weight wearily. He was already tired of the conversation and of Harris.

"Is there some particular reason you need me here?"

"You'll need a photo ID card," Harris said. He stood up and came around from behind the desk to open a door to a neighboring room. He was several inches taller than Sean and at least twenty pounds heavier. In hockey Sean used to like to block such guys low, coming up fast under their chins.

"I'd suggest you get a haircut," Harris said, as he motioned for Sean to pass into the next room. "And get your pants ironed. Maybe then you'll fit in better. This isn't college."

Stepping through the door Sean saw Ramirez look up from adjusting a Polaroid camera mounted on a tripod. Ramirez pointed toward a stool in front of a blue curtain, and Sean sat down.

HARRIS CLOSED the door to the camera room, went back to his desk, and sat down. Sean had been worse than he'd feared. The idea of some wiseass kid coming down from Harvard had not appealed to him in the first place, but he hadn't expected anyone looking like a hippie from the sixties.

Lighting a cigarette, Harris cursed the likes of Sean. He hated such liberal Ivy League types who thought they knew everything. Harris had gone through the Citadel, then into the army where he'd trained hard for the commandos. He'd done well, making captain after Desert Storm. But with the breakup of the Soviet Union, the peacetime army had begun cutting back. Harris had been one of its victims.

Harris stubbed out his cigarette. Intuition told him Sean would be trouble. He decided he'd have to keep his eye on him.

WITH A new photo ID clipped to his shirt pocket, Sean left security. The experience didn't mesh with the welcome sign, but one fact did impress him. When he'd asked the reticent Ramirez why security was so tight, Ramirez had told him that several researchers had disappeared the previous year.

"Disappeared?" Sean asked with amazement. He'd heard of equipment disappearing, but people!

"Were they found?" Sean had asked.

"I don't know," Ramirez had said. "I only came this year."

"Where are you from?"

"Medellín, Colombia," Ramirez had said.

Sean had not asked any more questions, but Ramirez's

reply added to Sean's unease. It seemed overkill to head security with a man who acted like a frustrated Green Beret and staff it with a group of guys who could have been from some Colombian drug lord's private army. As Sean followed Ramirez into the elevator to the seventh floor his initial positive impression of Forbes security faded.

"Come in, come in!" Dr. Randolph Mason repeated, holding open his office door. Almost immediately Sean's unease was replaced by a feeling of genuine welcome. "We're pleased to have you with us," Dr. Mason said. "I was so happy when Clifford called and suggested it. Would you like some coffee?"

Sean acquiesced and was soon balancing a cup while sitting on a couch across from the Forbes director. Dr. Mason looked like everyone's romantic image of a physician. He was tall with an aristocratic face, classically graying hair, and an expressive mouth. His eyes were sympathetic and his nose slightly aquiline. He seemed the type of man you could tell a problem to and know he'd not only care but he'd solve it.

"The first thing we must do," Dr. Mason said, "is have you meet our head of research, Dr. Levy." He picked up the phone and asked his secretary to have Deborah come up. "I'm certain you will be impressed by her. I wouldn't be surprised if she were soon in contention for the big Scandinavian prize."

"I've already been impressed with her earlier work on retroviruses," Sean said.

"Like everyone else," Dr. Mason said. "More coffee?"

Sean shook his head. "I have to be careful with this stuff," he said. "It makes me hyper. Too much and I don't come down for days."

"I'm the same way," Dr. Mason said. "Now about your accommodations. Has anyone discussed them with you?"

"Dr. Walsh just said that you would be able to provide housing."

"Indeed," Dr. Mason said. "I'm pleased to say that we had the foresight to purchase a sizable apartment complex several years ago. It's not in Coconut Grove, but it's not far either. We use it for visiting personnel and patients' families. We're delighted to offer you one of the apartments for your stay. I'm certain you will find it suitable, and you should enjoy the neighborhood as it's so close to the Grove."

"I'm pleased I didn't have to make my own arrangements," Sean said. "And as far as entertainment is concerned, I'm more interested in working than playing tourist."

"Everyone should have a balance in life," Dr. Mason said. "But rest assured, we have plenty of work for you to do. We want your experience here to be a good one. When you go into practice we hope you will be referring us patients."

"My plan is to remain in research," Sean said.

"I see," Dr. Mason said, his enthusiasm dimming slightly.

"In fact, the reason I wanted to come here . . ." Sean began, but before he could complete the statement, Dr. Deborah Levy walked into the room.

Deborah Levy was a strikingly attractive woman with dark olive skin, large almond-shaped eyes, and hair even blacker than Sean's. She was stylishly thin and wore a dark blue silk dress beneath her lab coat. She walked with the confidence and grace of the truly successful.

Sean struggled to get to his feet.

"Don't bother to get up," Dr. Levy said in a husky yet feminine voice. She thrust a hand at Sean.

Sean shook Dr. Levy's hand while balancing his coffee in the other. She gripped his fingers with unexpected strength and gave Sean's arm a shake that rattled his cup in its saucer. Her gaze bore into him with intensity.

"I've been instructed to say welcome," she said, sitting across from him. "But I think we should be honest about this. I'm not entirely convinced your visit is a good idea. I run a tight ship here in the lab. You'll either pitch in and work or you'll be out of here and on the next plane back to Boston. I don't want you to think . . ."

"I drove down," Sean interrupted. He knew he was already being provocative, but he couldn't help himself. He didn't expect such a brusque greeting from the head of research.

Dr. Levy stared at him for a moment before continuing. "The Forbes Cancer Center is no place for a holiday in the sun," she added. "Do I make myself clear?"

Sean cast a quick glance at Dr. Mason who was still smiling warmly.

"I didn't come here for a holiday. If Forbes had been in Bismarck, North Dakota, I would have wanted to come. You see, I've heard about the results you've been getting with medulloblastoma."

Dr. Mason coughed and moved forward in his seat, placing his coffee on the table. "I hope you didn't expect to work on the medulloblastoma protocol," he said.

Sean's gaze shifted between the two doctors. "Actually, I did," he said with some alarm.

"When I spoke with Dr. Walsh," Mason said, "he emphasized that you have had extensive and successful experience with the development of murine monoclonal antibodies."

"That was during my year at MIT," Sean explained. "But that's not my interest now. In fact, I feel it is already yesterday's technology."

"That's not our belief," Dr. Mason said. "We think it's still commercially viable and will be for some time. In fact, we've had a bit of luck isolating and producing a glycoprotein from patients with colonic cancer. What we need now is a monoclonal antibody in hopes it might be an aid to early diagnosis. But, as you know, glycoproteins can be tricky. We've been unable to get mice to respond antigenically, and we've failed to crystallize the substance. Dr. Walsh assured me you were an artist when it comes to this kind of protein chemistry."

"I was," Sean said. "I haven't been doing it for some time. My interest has changed to molecular biology, specifically oncogenes and oncoproteins."

"This is just what I feared," Dr. Levy said, turning to Dr. Mason. "I told you this was not a good idea. We are not set up for students. I'm much too busy to babysit a medical student extern. Now if you'll excuse me, I must get back to my work."

Dr. Levy got to her feet and looked down at Sean. "My rudeness is not meant to be personal. I'm very busy, and I'm under a lot of stress."

"I'm sorry," Sean said. "But it is difficult not to take it personally since your medulloblastoma results are the reason I took this elective and drove all the way the hell down here."

"Frankly, that's not my concern," she said, striding toward the door.

"Dr. Levy," Sean called out. "Why haven't you published any articles on the medulloblastoma results? With no publications, if you'd stayed in academia, you'd probably be out looking for a job."

Dr. Levy paused and cast a disapproving look at Sean. "Impertinence is not a wise policy for a student," she said, closing the door behind her.

Sean looked over at Dr. Mason and shrugged his shoulders. "She was the one who said we should be honest about all this. She hasn't published for years."

"Clifford warned me that you might not be the most diplomatic extern," Dr. Mason said.

"Did he now?" Sean questioned superciliously. He was already beginning to question his decision to come to Florida. Maybe everybody else had been right after all.

"But he also said you were extremely bright. And I think Dr. Levy came on a bit stronger than she meant. At any rate she has been under great strain. In fact we all have."

"But the results you've been getting with the medulloblastoma patients are fantastic," Sean said, hoping to plead his case. "There has to be something to be learned about cancer in general here. I want desperately to be involved in your protocol. Maybe by looking at it with fresh, objective eyes I'll see something that you people have missed."

"You certainly don't lack self-confidence," said Dr. Mason. "And perhaps someday we could use a fresh eye. But not now. Let me be honest and open with you and give you some confidential information. There are several reasons you won't be able to participate in our medulloblastoma study. First, it is already a clinical protocol and you are here for basic science research. That was made clear to your mentor. And second of all we cannot permit outsiders access to our current work because we have yet to apply for the appropriate patents on some of our unique biological processes. This policy is dictated by our source of funding. Like a lot of research institutions, we've had to seek alternate sources for operating capital since the government started squeezing research grants to everything but AIDS. We have turned to the Japanese."

"Like the Mass General in Boston?" Sean questioned.

"Something like that," Dr. Mason said. "We struck a

forty-million-dollar deal with Sushita Industries, which has been expanding into biotechnology. The agreement was that Sushita would advance us the money over a period of years in return for which they would control any patents that result. That's one of the reasons we need the monoclonal antibody to the colonic antigen. We have to produce some commercially viable products if we hope to continue to receive Sushita's yearly payments. So far we haven't been doing too well in that regard. And if we don't maintain our funding we'll have to shut our doors which, of course, would hurt the public which looks to us for care."

"A sorry state of affairs," Sean said.

"Indeed," Dr. Mason agreed. "But it's the reality of the new research environment."

"But your short-term fix will lead to future Japanese dominance."

"The same can be said about most industries," Dr. Mason said. "It's not limited to health-related biotechnology."

"Why not use the return from patents to fund additional research?"

"There's no place to get the initial capital," Dr. Mason said. "Well, that's not entirely true in our case. Over the last two years we've had considerable success with old-fashioned philanthropy. A number of businessmen have given us hefty donations. In fact, we are hosting a black-tie charity dinner tonight. I would very much like to extend an invitation to you. It's at my home on Star Island."

"I don't have the proper clothes," Sean said, surprised at being invited after the scene with Dr. Levy.

"We thought of that," Dr. Mason said. "We've made arrangements with a tux rental service. All you have to do is call in your sizes, and they will deliver to your apartment."

"That's very thoughtful," Sean said. He was finding it difficult to deal with this on-again, off-again hospitality.

Suddenly the door to Dr. Mason's office burst open and a formidable woman in a white nurse's uniform rushed in, planting herself in front of Dr. Mason. She was visibly distressed.

"There's been another one, Randolph," she blurted out. "This is the fifth breast cancer patient to die of respiratory failure. I told you that . . ."

Dr. Mason leapt to his feet. "Margaret, we have company."

Recoiling as if slapped, the nurse turned to Sean, seeing him for the first time. She was a woman of forty, with a round face, gray hair worn in a tight bun, and solid legs. "Excuse me!" she said, the color draining from her cheeks. "I'm terribly sorry." Turning back to Dr. Mason, she added, "I knew Dr. Levy had just come in here, but when I saw her return to her office, I thought you were alone."

"No matter," said Dr. Mason. He introduced Sean to Margaret Richmond, director of nursing, adding, "Mr. Murphy will be with us for two months."

Ms. Richmond shook hands perfunctorily with Sean, mumbling it was a pleasure to meet him. Then she took Dr. Mason by the elbow and steered him outside. The door closed, but the latch didn't catch, and it drifted open again.

Sean could not help but overhear, especially with Ms. Richmond's sharply penetrating voice. Apparently, another patient on standard chemotherapy for breast cancer had unexpectedly died. She'd been found in her bed totally cyanotic, just as blue as the others.

"This cannot go on!" Margaret snapped. "Someone must be doing this deliberately. There's no other explanation. It's always the same shift, and it's ruining our stats. We have to do something before the medical examiner gets suspicious. And if the media gets ahold of this, it will be a disaster."

"We'll meet with Harris," Dr. Mason said soothingly. "We'll tell him he has to let everything else slide. We'll tell him he has to stop it."

"It can't go on," Ms. Richmond repeated. "Harris has to do more than run background checks on the professional staff."

"I agree," Dr. Mason said. "We'll talk to Harris straight away. Just give me a moment to arrange for Mr. Murphy to tour the facility."

The voices drifted away. Sean moved forward on the couch hoping to hear more, but the outer office remained silent until once again the door burst open. Guiltily he sat back as someone else dashed into the room. This time it was an attractive woman in her twenties dressed in a checkered skirt and white blouse. She was tanned, bubbly, and had a great smile. Hospitality had refreshingly returned.

"Hi, my name's Claire Barington."

Sean quickly learned that Claire helped run the center's public relations department. She dangled keys in front of his face, saying: "These are to your palatial apartment at the Cow's Palace." She explained that the center's residence had gotten its nickname in commemoration of the size of some of its earlier residents.

"I'll take you over there," Claire said. "Just to make certain it's all in order and you're comfortable. But first Dr. Mason told me to give you a tour of our facility. What do you say?"

"Seems like a good idea to me," Sean said, pulling himself up from the couch. He'd only been at the Forbes Center for about an hour, and if that hour were any indication of what the two months would be like, it promised to be a curiously interesting sojourn. Provided, of course, he stayed. As he followed the shapely Claire Barington out of Dr. Mason's office, he began seriously considering calling Dr. Walsh and heading back to Boston. He'd certainly be able to accomplish more there than here if he was to be relegated to busywork involving monoclonal antibodies.

"This, of course, is our administrative area," Claire said as she launched into a practiced tour. "Henry Falworth's office is next to Dr. Mason's. Mr. Falworth is the personnel manager for all non-professional staff. Beyond his office is Dr. Levy's. Of course, she has another research office downstairs in the maximum containment lab."

Sean's ears perked up. "You have a maximum containment lab?" he asked with surprise.

"Absolutely," Claire said. "Dr. Levy demanded it when she came on board. Besides, the Forbes Cancer Center has all the most up-to-date equipment."

Sean shrugged. A maximum containment lab designed to safely handle infectious microorganisms seemed a bit excessive.

Pointing in the opposite direction, Claire indicated the clinical office shared by Dr. Stan Wilson, chief of the hospital's clinical staff, Margaret Richmond, director of nursing, and Dan Selenburg, hospital administrator. "Of course, these people all have private offices on the top floor of the hospital building."

"This doesn't interest me," Sean said. "Let's see the research areas."

"Hey, you get the twenty-five-dollar tour or none at all," she said sternly. Then she laughed. "Humor me! I need the practice."

Sean smiled. Claire was the most genuine person he'd met so far at the Center. "Fair enough. Lead on!"

Claire took him over to an adjacent room with eight desks manned by busy people. A huge collating copy machine stood off to the side busily functioning. A large computer with multiple modems was behind a glass enclosure like some kind of trophy. A small glass-fronted elevator that was more like a dumbwaiter occupied another wall. It was filled with what appeared to be hospital charts.

"This is the important room!" Claire said with a smile. "It's where all the bills are sent for hospital and outpatient services. These are the people who deal with the insurance companies. It's also where my paychecks come from."

After seeing more of administration than Sean would have liked, Claire finally took him downstairs to see the laboratory facilities which occupied the middle five stories of the structure.

"The first floor of the building has auditoriums, library, and security," Claire droned as they entered the sixth floor. Sean followed Claire down a long central corridor with labs off either side. "This is the main research floor. Most of the major equipment is housed here."

Sean poked his head into various labs. He was soon disappointed. He'd been expecting a futuristic lab, superbly designed and filled with state-of-the-art technology. Instead he saw basic rooms with the usual equipment. Claire introduced him to the four people they came upon in one of the labs: David Lowenstein, Arnold Harper, Nancy Sprague, and Hiroshi Gyuhama. Of these people only Hiroshi expressed any more than a passing interest in Sean. Hiroshi bowed deeply when introduced. He seemed genuinely impressed when Claire mentioned that Sean was from Harvard.

"Harvard is a very good school," Hiroshi said in heavily accented English.

As they continued down the corridor, Sean began to notice that most of the rooms were empty.

"Where is everybody?" he asked.

"You've met pretty much the whole research staff," Claire said. "We have a tech named Mark Halpern, but I don't see him at the moment. We don't have many personnel presently, although word has it that we are about to start expanding. Like all businesses, we've been through some lean times."

Sean nodded, but the explanation did little to allay his disappointment. With the impressive results of the medulloblastoma work, he'd envisioned a large group of researchers working at a dynamic pace. Instead, the place seemed relatively deserted, which reminded Sean of Ramirez's unsettling remark.

"Down in security they told me some of the researchers had disappeared. Do you know anything about that?"

"Not a lot," Claire admitted. "It was last year and it caused a flap."

"What happened?"

"They disappeared all right," Claire said. "They left everything: their apartments, their cars, even their girlfriends."

"And they were never found?" Sean asked.

"They turned up," Claire said. "The administration doesn't like to talk about it, but apparently they are working for some company in Japan."

"Sushita Industries?" Sean asked.

"That I don't know," Claire said.

Sean had heard about companies luring away personnel, but never so secretly. And never to Japan. He realized it was probably just another indication that times were changing in the arena of biotechnology.

Claire brought them to a thick opaque glass door barring

further progress down the corridor. In block letters were the words: No Entry. Sean glanced at Claire for an explanation.

"The maximum containment facility is in there," she said.

"Can we see it?" Sean asked. He cupped his hands and peered through the door. All he could see were doors leading off the main corridor.

Claire shook her head. "Off limits," she said. "Dr. Levy does most of her work in there. At least when she's in Miami. She splits her time between here and our Basic Diagnostic lab in Key West."

"What's that?" Sean asked.

Claire winked and covered her mouth as if she were telling a secret. "It's a minor entrepreneurial spin-off for Forbes," she said. "It does basic diagnostic work for our hospital as well as for several hospitals in the Keys. It's a way of generating some additional income. The trouble is the Florida legislature is giving us some trouble about self-referral."

"How come we can't go in there?" Sean asked, pointing through the glass door.

"Dr. Levy says there is some kind of risk, but I don't know what it is. Frankly, I'm happy to stay out. But ask her. She'll probably take you in."

Sean wasn't sure Dr. Levy would do him any favors after their initial meeting. He reached out and pulled the door open a crack. There was a slight hiss as the seal was broken.

Claire grabbed his arm. "What are you doing?" She was aghast.

"Just curious to see if it was locked," Sean said. He let the door swing shut.

"You are a trip," she said.

They retraced their route and descended another floor.

The fifth floor was dominated by a large lab on one side of the corridor and small offices on the other. Claire took Sean into the large lab.

"I was told that you would have this lab for your use," Claire said. She switched on the overhead lights. It was an enormous room by the standards of the labs Sean was accustomed to work in at both Harvard and MIT where fights for space among researchers were legendary for their acrimony. In the center was a glass-enclosed office with a desk, a telephone, and a computer terminal.

Sean walked around, fingering the equipment. It was basic but serviceable. The most impressive items were a luminescence-spectrophotometer and a binocular microscope to detect fluorescence. Sean thought he could have some fun with those instruments under the right circumstances, but he didn't know if the Forbes provided the right environment. For one thing, Sean realized that he'd probably be working in this large room alone.

"Where are all the reagents and things?" he asked.

Claire motioned for Sean to follow, and they descended another floor where Claire showed him the supply room. As far as Sean was concerned, this was the most impressive area he'd seen so far. The supply room was filled with everything a molecular biological lab would need. There was even a generous selection of various cell lines from the NIH.

After cursorily touring through the rest of the lab space, Claire led Sean down to the basement. Scrunching up her nose, she took him into the animal room. Dogs barked, monkeys glared, and mice and rats skittered about their cages. The air was moist and pungent. Claire introduced Sean to Roger Calvet, the animal keeper. He was a small man with a severe hunchback.

They only stayed a minute and as the doors closed behind them, Claire made a gesture of relief. "My least favorite part of the whole tour," she confided. "I'm not sure where I stand on the animal-rights issue."

"It's tough," Sean admitted. "But we definitely need them. For some reason mice and rats don't bother me as much as dogs or monkeys."

"I'm supposed to show you the hospital too," Claire said. "Are you game?"

"Why not?" Sean said. He was enjoying Claire.

They took the elevator back to the second floor and crossed to the clinic by way of the pedestrian bridge. The towers were some fifty feet apart.

The second floor of the hospital housed the diagnostic and treatment areas as well as the ICU and the surgical suites. The chemistry lab and radiology were also there along with medical records. Claire took Sean in to meet her mother, who was one of the medical librarians.

"If I can be of any assistance," Mrs. Barington said, "just give me a call."

Sean thanked her and moved to leave, but Mrs. Barington insisted she show him around the department. Sean tried to be interested as he was shown the Center's computer capabilities, the laser printers, the hoist they used to bring charts up from the basement storage vault, and the view they had over the sleepy Miami River.

When Claire and Sean got back to the corridor, she apologized.

"She's never done that," she added. "She must have liked you."

"That's just my luck," Sean said. "The older set and the prepubescent are taken by me. It's the women in between I have trouble with."

"I'm sure you expect me to believe that," Claire said sarcastically.

Sean was next treated to a rapid walk through the modern eighty-bed hospital. It was clean, well designed, and apparently well staffed. With its tropical colors and fresh flowers, it was even cheerful despite the gravity of many of the patients' illnesses. On this leg of the tour, Sean learned that the Forbes Cancer Center had teamed up with the NIH to treat advanced melanoma. With the powerful sunshine, there was a lot of melanoma in Florida.

With the tour completed, Claire told Sean it was time for her to lead him over to the Cow Palace and see that he got settled. He tried to suggest he'd be fine, but she wouldn't hear of it. With strict orders to stay close, he followed her car out of the Forbes Cancer Center and headed south on Twelfth Avenue. He drove carefully, having heard that most people in Miami carry pistols in their glove compartments. Miami has one of the world's highest mortality rates from fender-bender accidents.

At Calle Ocho they turned left, and Sean glimpsed the rich Cuban culture that has placed such an indelible mark on modern Miami. At Brickell they turned right and the city changed again. Now he drove past gleaming bank buildings, each an open testament to the financial power of the illicit drug trade.

The Cow Palace was not imposing to say the least. Like so many buildings in the area, it was two stories of concrete block with aluminum sliding doors and windows. It stretched for almost a block with asphalt parking in both the front and the back. The only attractive thing about the place was the tropical plantings, many of which were in bloom.

Sean pulled up next to Claire's Honda.

After checking the apartment number on the keys, Claire led the way upstairs. Sean's unit was halfway down the hall at the back. As Claire struggled to get the key into the lock, the door directly opposite opened.

"Just moving in?" a blond man of about thirty asked. He was stripped to the waist.

"Seems that way," Sean said.

"Name's Gary," the man said. "Gary Engels from Philadelphia. I'm an X-ray tech. Working nights, looking for an apartment by day. How about you?"

"Med student," Sean said as Claire finally opened the door.

The apartment was a furnished one-bedroom with a full kitchen. Sliding glass doors led from both the living room and the bedroom to a balcony that ran the length of the building.

"What do you think?" Claire asked as she opened the living-room slider.

"Much more than I expected," Sean said.

"It's hard for the hospital to recruit certain personnel," Claire said. "Especially high-caliber nurses. They have to have a good temporary residence to compete with other local hospitals."

"Thank you for everything," Sean said.

"One last thing," Claire said. She handed him a piece of paper. "This is the number of the tux rental place that Dr. Mason mentioned. I assume you'll be coming tonight."

"I'd forgotten about that," Sean said.

"You really should come," Claire said. "These affairs are one of the perks for working at the Center."

"Are they frequent?" Sean asked.

"Relatively," Claire said. "They really are fun."

"So you'll be there?" Sean asked.

"Most definitely."

"Well then, maybe I'll come," he said. "I haven't worn a tux too many times. It should be entertaining."

"Wonderful," Claire said. "And since you might have

trouble finding Dr. Mason's home, I don't mind picking you up. I live in Coconut Grove just down the way. How about seven-thirty?"

"I'll be ready," Sean said.

HIROSHI GYUHAMA had been born in Yokosuka, south of Tokyo. His mother had worked in the U.S. Naval base, and from an early age Hiroshi had been interested in America and Western ways. His mother felt differently, refusing to let him take English in school. An obedient child, Hiroshi acquiesced to his mother's wishes without question. It wasn't until after her death when he was at the university studying biology that he was able to take English, but once he began he displayed an unusual proficiency.

After graduation Hiroshi was hired by Sushita Industries, a huge electronics corporation that had just begun expanding into biotechnology. When Hiroshi's supervisors discovered how fluent he was in English, they sent him to Florida to supervise their investment in Forbes.

Except for an initial difficulty involving two Forbes researchers who refused to cooperate, a dilemma which had been handled expeditiously by bringing them to Tokyo and then offering them enormous salaries, Hiroshi had faced no serious problems during his tenure at Forbes.

Sean Murphy's unexpected arrival was a different story. For Hiroshi and the Japanese in general any surprise was disturbing. Also, for them, Harvard was more of a metaphor than a specific institution. It stood for American excellence and American ingenuity. Accordingly Hiroshi worried that Sean could take some of Forbes's developments back to Harvard where the American university might beat them to possible patents. Since Hiroshi's future advancement at Sushita rested on his ability to protect the Forbes investment, he saw Sean as a potential threat.

His first response had been to send a fax via his private telephone line to his Japanese supervisor. From the outset the Japanese had insisted they be able to communicate with Hiroshi without going through the Center switchboard. That had been only one of their conditions.

Hiroshi had then called Dr. Mason's secretary to ask if it would be possible for him to see the director. He'd been given a two o'clock appointment. Now, as he ascended the stairs to the seventh floor, it was three minutes before the hour. Hiroshi was a punctilious man who left little to chance.

As he entered Mason's office, the doctor leapt to his feet. Hiroshi bowed deeply in apparent respect though in reality he did not think highly of the American physician, believing Dr. Mason lacked the iron will necessary in a good manager. In Hiroshi's estimation, Dr. Mason would be unpredictable under pressure.

"Dr. Gyuhama, nice of you to come up," Dr. Mason said, motioning toward the couch. "Can we get you anything? Coffee, tea, or juice?"

"Juice, please," Hiroshi replied with a polite smile. He did not want any refreshment but did not care to refuse and appear ungrateful.

Dr. Mason sat down across from Hiroshi. But he didn't sit normally. Hiroshi noticed that he sat on the very edge of his seat and rubbed his hands together. Hiroshi could tell he was nervous, which only served to lower further Hiroshi's estimation of the man as a manager. One should not communicate one's feelings so openly.

"What can I do for you?" Dr. Mason asked.

Hiroshi smiled again, noting that no Japanese would be so direct.

"I was introduced to a young university student today," Hiroshi said.

"Sean Murphy," Dr. Mason said. "He's a medical student at Harvard."

"Harvard is a very good school," Hiroshi said.

"One of the best," Dr. Mason said. "Particularly in medical research." Dr. Mason eyed Hiroshi cautiously. He knew Hiroshi avoided direct questions. Mason always had to try to figure out what the Japanese man was getting at. It was frustrating, but Mason knew that Hiroshi was Sushita's front man, so it was important to treat him with respect. Right now it was apparent that he had found Sean's presence disturbing.

Just then, the juice arrived and Hiroshi bowed and said thank you several times. He took a sip, then placed the glass on the coffee table.

"Perhaps it might be helpful if I explain why Mr. Murphy is here," Dr. Mason said.

"That would be very interesting," Hiroshi said.

"Mr. Murphy is a third-year medical student," Dr. Mason said. "During the course of the year third-year students have blocks of time which they can use to choose an elective and study something that particularly interests them. Mr. Murphy is interested in research. He'll be here for two months."

"That's very good for Mr. Murphy," Hiroshi said. "He comes to Florida during the winter."

"It is a good system," Dr. Mason agreed. "He'll get the experience of seeing a working lab in operation, and we'll get a worker."

"Perhaps he'll be interested in our medulloblastoma project," Hiroshi said.

"He is interested," Dr. Mason said. "But he will not be

allowed to participate. Instead he will be working with our colonic cancer glycoprotein, trying to crystallize the protein. I don't have to tell you how good it would be for both Forbes and Sushita if he were able to accomplish what we've so far failed to do."

"I was not informed of Mr. Murphy's arrival by my superiors," Hiroshi said. "It is strange for them to have forgotten."

All at once, Dr. Mason realized what this circuitous conversation was about. One of Sushita's conditions was that they review all prospective employees before they were hired. Usually it was a formality, and where a student was concerned, Dr. Mason had not given it a thought, particularly since Murphy's stay was so temporary.

"The decision to invite Mr. Murphy for his elective happened rather quickly. Perhaps I should have informed Sushita, but he is not an employee. He does not get paid. Besides, he's a student with limited experience."

"Yet he will be entrusted with samples of glycoprotein," Hiroshi said. "He will have access to the recombinant yeast that produces the protein."

"Obviously he will be given the protein," Dr. Mason said. "But there is no reason for him to be shown our recombinant technology for producing it."

"How much do you know about this man?" Hiroshi asked.

"He comes with a recommendation from a trusted colleague," Dr. Mason said.

"Perhaps my company would be interested in his resumé," Hiroshi said.

"We have no resumé," Dr. Mason said. "He's only a student. If there had been anything important to know about him, I'm confident my friend Dr. Walsh would have informed me. He did say that Mr. Murphy was an artist when it came to protein crystallization and making murine monoclonal antibodies. We need an artist if we are going to come up with a patentable product. Besides, the Harvard cachet is valuable to the clinic. The idea we have been training a Harvard graduate student will not do us any harm."

Hiroshi got to his feet and, with his continued smile, bowed, but not as deeply nor for as long a period as when he'd first come into the office. "Thank you for your time," he said. Then he left the room.

AFTER THE door clicked behind Hiroshi, Dr. Mason closed his eyes and rubbed them with his fingertips. His hands were shaking. He was much too anxious, and if he wasn't careful, he'd aggravate his peptic ulcer. With the possibility of some psychopath killing metastatic breast cancer patients, the last thing he needed was trouble with Sushita. He now regretted doing Clifford Walsh the favor of inviting his graduate student. It was a complication he didn't need.

On the other hand, Dr. Mason knew he needed something to offer the Japanese or they might not renew their grant, irrespective of other concerns. If Sean could help solve the problem associated with developing an antibody to their glycoprotein, then his arrival could turn into a godsend.

Dr. Mason ran a nervous hand through his hair. The problem was, as Hiroshi made him realize, he knew very little about Sean Murphy. Yet Sean would have access to their labs. He could talk to other workers; he could access the computers. And Sean struck Dr. Mason as definitely the curious type.

Snatching up the phone, Dr. Mason asked his secretary to get Clifford Walsh from Boston on the line. While he waited, he ambled over to his desk. He wondered why he hadn't thought of calling Clifford earlier.

Within a few minutes, Dr. Walsh was available on the phone. Dr. Mason sat while he talked. Since they'd spoken just the previous week, their small talk was minimal.

"Did Sean get down there okay?" Dr. Walsh asked.

"He arrived this morning."

"I hope he hasn't gotten into trouble already," Dr. Walsh said.

Dr. Mason felt his ulcer begin to burn. "That's a strange statement," he said. "Especially after your excellent recommendations."

"Everything I said about him is true," Dr. Walsh said. "The kid is just short of a genius when it comes to molecular biology. But he's a city kid and his social skills are nowhere near his intellectual abilities. He can be headstrong. And he's physically stronger than an ox. He could have played professional hockey. He's the type of guy you want on your side if there's going to be a brawl."

"We don't brawl down here much," Dr. Mason said with a short laugh. "So we won't be taking advantage of his skills in that regard. But tell me something else. Has Sean ever been associated with the biotechnology industry in any way, like worked summers at a company? Anything like that?"

"He sure has," Dr. Walsh said. "He not only worked at one, he owned one. He and a group of friends started a company called Immunotherapy to develop murine monoclonal antibodies. The company did well as far as I know. But then I don't keep up with the industrial side of our field."

The pain in Mason's gut intensified. This was not what he wanted to hear.

Mason thanked Dr. Walsh, hung up the phone, and immediately swallowed two antacid tablets. Now he had to worry about Sushita learning of Sean's association with this Immunotherapy company. If they did, it might be enough to cause them to break the agreement.

Dr. Mason paced his office. Intuition told him he had to act. Perhaps he should send Sean back to Boston as Dr. Levy had suggested. But that would mean losing Sean's potential contribution to the glycoprotein project.

Suddenly Dr. Mason had an idea. He could at least find out all there was to know about Sean's company. He picked up the phone again. This number he didn't have his secretary dial. He dialed it himself. He called Sterling Rombauer.

TRUE TO her word, Claire showed up at Sean's apartment at seven-thirty on the dot. She was wearing a black dress with spaghetti straps and long dangly earrings. Her brunette hair was pulled back at the sides with rhinestone-studded barrettes. Sean thought she looked terrific.

He wasn't at all sure of his own outfit. The rented tux definitely needed the suspenders; the pants showed up two sizes too large and there hadn't been time to change them. The shoes were also a half size too large. But the shirt and the jacket fit reasonably well, and he tamed his hair back on the sides with some hair gel he borrowed from his friendly neighbor, Gary Engels. He even shaved.

They took Sean's 4×4 since it was roomier than Claire's tiny Honda. With Claire giving directions, they skirted the downtown high rises and drove up Biscayne Boulevard. People of all races and nationalities crowded the street. They passed a Rolls Royce dealership, and Claire said that she'd heard most of the sales were for cash; people walked in with briefcases full of twenty-dollar bills.

"If the drug traffic stopped tomorrow, it would probably affect this city," Sean suggested.

"The city would collapse," Claire said.

They turned right on the MacArthur Causeway and headed toward the southern tip of Miami Beach. On their right they passed several large cruise ships moored at the Dodge Island seaport. Just before they got to Miami Beach, they turned left and crossed a small bridge where they were stopped by an armed guard at a gatehouse.

"This must be a ritzy place," Sean commented as they were waved through.

"Very," Claire answered.

"Mason does okay for himself," Sean said. The palatial homes they were passing seemed inappropriate for a director of a research center.

"I think she's the one with the money," Claire said. "Her maiden name was Forbes, Sarah Forbes."

"No kidding." Sean cast a glance at Claire to be sure she wasn't teasing him.

"It was her father who started the Forbes Cancer Center."

"How convenient," Sean said. "Nice of the old man to give his son-in-law a job."

"It's not what you think," Claire said. "It's quite a soap opera. The old man started the clinic, but when he passed away he made Sarah's older brother, Harold, executor of the estate. Then Harold went and lost most of the foundation's money in some central Florida land development scheme. Dr. Mason was a latecomer to the Center and only arrived when it was about to go under. He and Dr. Levy have turned the place around."

They pulled into a sweeping drive in front of a huge white house with a portico supported by fluted Corinthian columns. A parking attendant quickly took charge of the car.

The inside of the house was equally impressive. Everything was white: white marble floors, white furniture, white carpet, and white walls.

"I hope they didn't pay a decorator a lot of money for picking the colors," Sean said.

They were motioned through the house to a terrace overlooking Biscayne Bay. The bay was dotted with lights from other islands as well as hundreds of boats. Beyond the bay was the city of Miami shimmering in the moonlight.

Nestled in the center of the terrace was a large kidney-shaped pool illuminated from beneath the water. To its left was a pink and white striped tent where long tables were laden with food and drink. A calypso steel band played next to the house and filled the velvety night air with melodious percussion. At the water's edge beyond the terrace was a gigantic white cruiser moored to a pier. Hanging from davits off the yacht's stern was yet another boat.

"Here come the host and hostess," Claire warned Sean, who'd been momentarily mesmerized by the scene.

Sean turned in time to see Dr. Mason guide a buxom bleached blonde toward them. He was elegant in a tuxedo that obviously was not rented and patent leather slippers complete with black bows. She was squeezed into a strapless peach gown so tight that Sean feared the slightest movement might bare her impressive breasts. Her hair was slightly disheveled and her makeup more suitable to a girl half her age. She was also clearly drunk.

"Welcome, Sean," Dr. Mason said. "I hope Claire has been taking good care of you."

"The best," Sean said.

Dr. Mason introduced Sean to his wife, who fluttered heavily mascaraed lashes. Sean dutifully squeezed her hand, drawing the line at her expected kiss on the cheek.

Dr. Mason turned and motioned for another couple to

join them. He introduced Sean as a Harvard medical student who would be studying at the Center. Sean had the uncomfortable feeling he was on display.

The man's name was Howard Pace, and from Dr. Mason's introduction, Sean learned that he was the CEO of an aircraft manufacturing company in St. Louis, and it was he who was about to make the donation to the Center.

"You know, son," Mr. Pace said, putting his arm around Sean's shoulder. "My gift is to help train young men and women like yourself. They are doing wonderful things at Forbes. You will learn a lot. Study hard!" He gave Sean a final man-to-man thump on the shoulder.

Mason began introducing Pace to some other couples and Sean suddenly found himself standing alone. He was about to snag a drink when a wavering voice stopped him. "Hello, handsome."

Sean turned to face the bleary eyes of Sarah Mason.

"I want to show you something," she said, grabbing Sean's sleeve.

Sean cast a desperate glance around for Claire, but she was nowhere in sight. With resignation rare for him, he allowed himself to be led down the patio steps and out onto the dock. Every few steps he had to steady Sarah as her heels slipped through the cracks between the planking. At the base of the gangplank leading to the yacht, Sean was confronted by a sizable Doberman with a studded collar and white teeth.

"This is my boat," Sarah said. "It's called Lady Luck. Would you like a tour?"

"I don't think that beast on deck wants company," Sean said.

"Batman?" Sarah questioned. "Don't worry about him. As long as you're with me he'll be a lamb."

"Maybe we could come back later," Sean said. "To tell the truth, I'm starved."

"There's food in the fridge," Sarah persisted.

"Yeah, but I had my heart set on those oysters I saw under the tent."

"Oysters, huh?" Sarah said. "Sounds good to me. We can see the boat later."

As soon as he got Sarah back on land, Sean ducked away, leaving her with an unsuspecting couple who'd ventured toward the yacht. Searching through the crowd for Claire, a strong hand gripped his arm. Sean turned and found himself gazing into the puffy face of Robert Harris, head of security. Even a tux didn't dramatically change his appearance, with his Marine-style crew cut. His collar must have been too tight since his eyes were bulging.

"I want to give you some advice, Murphy," Harris said with obvious disdain.

"Really?" Sean questioned. "This should be interesting, since we have so much in common."

"You're a wiseass," Harris hissed.

"Is that the advice?" Sean asked.

"Stay away from Sarah Forbes," Harris said. "I'm only telling you once."

"Damn," Sean said. "I'll have to cancel our picnic tomorrow."

"Don't push me!" Harris warned. With a final glare, he stalked off.

Sean finally found Claire at the table featuring oysters, shrimp, and stone crab. Filling his plate, he scolded her for allowing him to fall into the clutches of Sarah Mason.

"I suppose I should have warned you," Claire said. "When she drinks she's notorious for chasing anything in pants."

"And here I thought I was irresistible."

They were still busy with the seafood when Dr. Mason stepped to the podium and tapped the microphone. As soon as the crowd was silent, he introduced Howard Pace, thanking him profusely for his generous gift. After a resounding round of applause, Dr. Mason turned the microphone over to the guest of honor.

"This is a bit syrupy for my taste," Sean whispered.

"Be nice," Claire chided him.

Howard Pace began his talk with the usual platitudes, but then his voice cracked with emotion. "Even this check for ten million dollars cannot adequately express my feelings. The Forbes Cancer Center has given me a second chance at life. Before I came here all my doctors believed my brain tumor was terminal. I almost gave up. Thank God I didn't. And thank God for the dedicated doctors at the Forbes Cancer Center."

Unable to speak further, Pace waved his check in the air as tears streamed down his face. Dr. Mason immediately appeared at his side and rescued the check lest it waft out into the wine-dark Biscayne Bay.

After another round of applause, the formal events of the evening were over. The guests surged forward, all overcome with the emotion Howard Pace had expressed. They had not expected such intimacy from such a powerful person.

Sean turned to Claire. "I hate to be a drag," he said. "But I've been up since five. I'm fading fast."

Claire put down her drink.

"I've had enough as well. Besides, I've got to be at work early."

They found Dr. Mason and thanked him, but he was distracted and barely realized they were leaving. Sean was thankful Mrs. Mason had conveniently disappeared.

As they drove back over the causeway Sean was the first to speak. "That speech was actually quite touching," he said.

"It's what makes it all worthwhile," Claire agreed.

Sean pulled up and parked next to Claire's Honda. There was a moment of awkwardness. "I did get some beer this afternoon," he said after a pause. "Would you like to come up for a few minutes?"

"Fine," Claire said enthusiastically.

As Sean climbed the stairs behind her he wondered if he'd overestimated his endurance. He was almost asleep on his feet.

At the door to his apartment, he awkwardly fumbled with the keys, trying to get the right one in the lock. When he finally turned the bolt, he opened the door and groped for the light. Just as his fingers touched the switch, there was a violent cry. When he saw who was waiting for him, his blood ran cold.

"EASY NOW!" Dr. Mason said to the two ambulance attendants. They were using a special stretcher to lift Helen Cabot from the Lear jet that had brought her to Miami. "Watch the steps!"

Dr. Mason was still dressed in his tuxedo. Margaret Richmond had called just as the party was ending to say that Helen Cabot was about to land. Without a second's hesitation, Dr. Mason had jumped into his Jaguar.

As gently as possible the paramedics eased Helen into the ambulance. Dr. Mason climbed in after the gravely ill woman.

"Are you comfortable?" he asked.

Helen nodded. The trip had been a strain. The heavy medication had not completely controlled her seizures. On top of that they'd hit bad turbulence over Washington, D.C.

"I'm glad to be here," she said, smiling weakly. Dr. Mason gripped her arm reassuringly, then got out of the ambulance and faced her parents, who had followed the stretcher from the jet. Together they decided that Mrs. Cabot would ride in the ambulance while John Cabot would ride with Dr. Mason.

Dr. Mason followed the ambulance from the airport.

"I'm touched that you came to meet us," Cabot said. "From the look of your clothes I'm afraid we have interrupted your evening."

"It was actually very good timing," Mason said. "Do you know Howard Pace?"

"The aircraft magnate?" John Cabot asked.

"None other," Dr. Mason said. "Mr. Pace has made a generous donation to the Forbes Center, and we were having a small celebration. But the affair was winding down when you called."

"Still, your concern is reassuring," John Cabot said. "So many doctors are distracted by their own agendas. They are more interested in themselves than the patients. My daughter's illness has been an eye-opening experience."

"Unfortunately your complaints are all too common," Dr. Mason said. "But at Forbes it's the patient who counts. We would do even more if we weren't so strapped for funds. Since government began limiting grants, we've had to struggle."

"If you can help my daughter I'll be happy to contribute to your capital needs."

"We will do everything in our power to help her."

"Tell me," Cabot said. "What do you think her chances are? I'd like to know the truth."

"The possibility of a full recovery is excellent," Dr. Mason said. "We've had remarkable luck with Helen's type of tumor, but we must start treatment immediately. I tried to expedite her transfer, but your doctors in Boston seemed reluctant to release her."

"You know the doctors in Boston. If there's another test available, they want to do it. Then, of course, they want to repeat it."

"We tried to talk them out of biopsying the tumor," Dr. Mason said. "We can now make the diagnosis of medulloblastoma with an enhanced MRI. But they wouldn't listen. You see we have to biopsy it regardless of whether they did or not. We have to grow some of her tumor cells in tissue culture. It's an integral part of the treatment."

"When can it be done?" John Cabot asked.

"The sooner the better," Dr. Mason said.

"BUT YOU didn't have to scream," Sean said. He was still shaking from the fright he'd experienced when he'd flipped on the light switch.

"I didn't scream," Janet said. "I yelled 'surprise.' Needless to say, I'm not sure who was more surprised, me, you, or that woman."

"That woman works for the Forbes Cancer Center," Sean said. "I've told you a dozen times. She's in their public relations department. She was assigned to deal with me."

"And dealing with you means coming back to your apartment after ten at night?" Janet asked with scorn. "Don't patronize me. I can't believe this. You haven't even been here twenty-four hours and you have a woman coming to your apartment."

"I didn't want to invite her in," Sean said. "But it was awkward. She'd brought me here this afternoon, then took me to a Forbes function tonight. When we pulled up outside for her to get her car, I thought I'd try to be hospitable. I offered her a beer. I'd already told her I was exhausted. Hell, you're usually complaining about my lack of social graces."

"It seems strangely convenient for you to gain some manners just in time to bestow them on a young, attractive female," Janet fumed. "I don't think my being skeptical is unreasonable."

"Well, you're making more of this than it deserves," Sean said. "How did you get in here, anyway?"

"They gave me the apartment two doors down," Janet said. "And you left your sliding door open."

"Why are they letting you stay here?"

"Because I've been hired by the Forbes Cancer Center," Janet said. "That's part of the surprise. I'm going to work here."

For the second time that evening, Janet had Sean stunned. "Work here?" he repeated as if he hadn't heard correctly. "What are you talking about?"

"I called the Forbes hospital," Janet said. "They have an active nurses' recruitment program. They hired me on the spot. They, in turn, called the Florida Board of Nursing and arranged for a temporary 120-day endorsement so I can practice while the paperwork is being completed for my Florida nursing license."

"What about your job at Boston Memorial?" Sean asked.

"No problem," Janet said. "They gave me an immediate leave of absence. One of the benefits of being in nursing these days is that we are in demand. We get to call the shots about our terms of employment more than most employees."

"Well, this is all very interesting," Sean said. For the moment that was all he could think of to say.

"So we'll still be working at the same institution."

"Did you ever think that maybe you should have discussed this idea with me?" Sean asked.

"I couldn't," Janet said. "You were on the road."

"What about before I left?" Sean asked. "Or you could have waited until I'd arrived. I think we should have talked about this."

"Well, that's the whole point," Janet said.

"What do you mean?"

"I came here so we can talk," Janet said. "I think this is a perfect opportunity for us to talk about us. In Boston you're so involved with school and your research. Here your schedule will undoubtedly be lighter. We'll have the time we never had in Boston."

Sean pushed off the couch and walked over to the open slider. He was at a loss for words. This whole episode of coming to Florida was working out terribly. "How'd you get here?" he asked.

"I flew down and rented a car," Janet said.

"So nothing's irreversible?" Sean said.

"If you think you can just send me home, think again," Janet said, an edge returning to her voice. "This is probably the first time in my life I've gone out on a limb for something I think is important." She still sounded angry, but Sean sensed she could also be on the verge of tears. "Maybe we're not important in your scheme of things . . ."

Sean interrupted her. "It isn't that at all. The problem is, I don't know whether I'm staying."

Janet's mouth dropped open. "What are you talking about?" she asked.

Sean came back to the couch and sat down. He looked into Janet's hazel eyes as he told her about his disturbing reception at the Center with half the people being hospitable, the other half rude. Most importantly, he told her that

Dr. Mason and Dr. Levy were balking at allowing him to work on the medulloblastoma protocol.

"What do they want you to do?" she asked.

"Busywork as far as I'm concerned," Sean said. "They want me to try to make a monoclonal antibody to a specific protein. Failing that, I'm to crystallize it so that its three-dimensional molecular shape can be determined. It will be a waste of my time. I'm not going to be learning anything. I'd be better off going back to Boston and working on my oncogene project for my dissertation."

"Maybe you could do both," Janet suggested. "Help them with their protein and in return get to work on the medulloblastoma project."

Sean shook his head. "They were very emphatic. They are not about to change their minds. They said the medulloblastoma study had moved into clinical trials, and I'm here for basic research. Between you and me, I think their reluctance has something to do with the Japanese."

"The Japanese?" Janet questioned.

Sean told Janet about the huge grant Forbes had accepted in return for any patentable biotechnology products. "Somehow I think the medulloblastoma protocol is tied up in their deal. It's the only way I can explain why the Japanese would offer Forbes so much money. Obviously they expect and intend to get a return on their investment someday—and probably sooner rather than later."

"This is awful," Janet said, but her response was personal. It had nothing to do with Sean's research career. She'd been so consumed by the effort of coming to Florida that she'd not prepared herself for this kind of reversal.

"And there's another problem," Sean said. "The person who gave me the chilliest reception happens to be the director of research. She's the person I directly report to."

Janet sighed. She was already trying to figure how to undo everything she had done to get her down to the Forbes Center in the first place. She'd probably have to go back on nights at Boston Memorial, at least for a while. Janet pushed herself out of the deep armchair where she'd been sitting and wandered over to the sliding door. Coming to Florida had seemed like such a good idea to her when she'd been in Boston. Now it seemed like the dumbest thing she'd ever thought of.

Suddenly Janet spun around. "Wait a minute!" she said. "Maybe I have an idea."

"Well?" Sean questioned when Janet remained silent.

"I'm thinking," she said, motioning for him to be quiet for a moment.

Sean studied her face. A few moments ago she'd looked depressed. Now her eyes sparkled.

"Okay, here's what I think," she said. "Let's stay here and look into this medulloblastoma business together. We'll work as a team."

"What do you mean?" Sean sounded skeptical.

"It's simple," Janet said. "You mentioned that the project had moved into clinical trials. Well, no problem. I'll be on the wards. I'll be able to determine the treatment regiments: the timing, the dosages, the works. You'll be in the lab and you can do your thing there. That monoclonal stuff shouldn't take all your time."

Sean bit his lower lip as he gave Janet's suggestion some thought. He had actually considered looking into the medulloblastoma issue on the sly. His biggest obstacle had been exactly what Janet would be in a position to provide, namely clinical information.

"You'd have to get me charts," Sean said. He couldn't help but be dubious. Janet had always been a stickler for hospital procedures and rules, in fact for any rules.

"As long as I can find a copy machine, that should be no problem," she said.

"I'd need samples of any medication," Sean said.

"I'll probably be dispensing the medicine myself," she said.

He sighed. "I don't know. It all sounds pretty tenuous."

"Oh, come on," Janet said. "What is this, role reversal? You're the one who's always telling me I've lived too sheltered a life, that I never take chances. Suddenly I'm the one taking the chances and you turn cautious. Where's that rebel spirit you've always been so proud of?"

Sean found himself smiling. "Who is this woman I'm talking to?" he said rhetorically. He laughed. "Okay, you're right. I'm acting defeated before trying. Let's give it a go."

Janet threw her arms around Sean. He hugged her back. After a long moment, they looked into each other's eyes, then kissed.

"Now that our conspiracy has been forged, let's go to bed," Sean said.

"Hold on," Janet said. "We're not sleeping together if that's what you mean. That's not going to happen until we have some serious talk about our relationship."

"Oh, come on, Janet," Sean whined.

"You have your apartment and I have mine," Janet said as she tweaked his nose. "I'm serious about this talk business."

"I'm too tired to argue," Sean said.

"Good," Janet said. "Arguing is not what it's going to take."

AT ELEVEN-THIRTY that night, Hiroshi Gyuhama was the only person in the Forbes research building except for the security man whom Hiroshi suspected was sleeping at his post at the front entrance. Hiroshi had been alone in the building since nine when David Lowenstein had departed. Hiroshi wasn't staying late because of his research; he was waiting for a message. At that moment he knew it was one-thirty in the afternoon the following day in Tokyo. It was usually after lunch that his supervisor would get the word from the directors regarding anything Hiroshi had passed on.

As if on cue, the receiving light on the fax machine blinked on, and the LCD flashed the message: *receiving.* Eagerly Hiroshi's fingers grasped the sheet as soon as it slid through. With some trepidation he sat back and read the directive.

The first part was as he'd expected. The management at Sushita was disturbed by the unexpected arrival of the student from Harvard. They felt that it violated the spirit of the agreement with the Forbes. The directive went on to emphasize the company's belief that the diagnosis and treatment of cancer would be the biggest biotechnology/pharmaceutical prize of the twenty-first century. They felt that it would surpass in economic importance the antibiotic bonanza of the twentieth century.

It was the second part of the message that dismayed Hiroshi. It mentioned that the management did not want to take any risks, and that Hiroshi was to call Tanaka Yamaguchi. He was to tell Tanaka to investigate Sean Murphy and act accordingly. If Murphy was considered a threat, he was to be brought to Tokyo immediately.

Folding the fax paper several times lengthwise, Hiroshi held it over the sink and burned it. He washed the ashes down the drain. As he did, he noticed his hands were trembling.

Hiroshi had hoped the directive from Tokyo would have given him peace of mind. But it only left him even more agitated. The fact that Hiroshi's superiors felt that Hiroshi could not handle the situation was not a good sign. They hadn't said it directly, but the instruction to call Tanaka said as much. What that suggested to Hiroshi was he was not trusted in matters of crucial importance, and if he wasn't trusted, then his upward mobility in the Sushita hierarchy automatically was in question. From Hiroshi's perspective he'd lost face.

Unswervingly obedient despite his growing anxiety, Hiroshi got out the list of emergency numbers he'd been given before coming to Forbes over a year ago. He found the number for Tanaka and dialed. As the phone rang, Hiroshi felt his anger and resentment for the Harvard medical student rise. If the young doctor-to-be had never come to Forbes, Hiroshi's stature vis-à-vis his superiors would never have been tested this way.

A mechanical beep followed a message in rapid Japanese urging the caller to leave his name and number. Hiroshi did as he was told, but added he would wait for the call back. Hanging up the phone, Hiroshi thought about Tanaka. He didn't know much about the man, but what he did know was disquieting. Tanaka was a man frequently used by various Japanese companies for industrial espionage of any sort. What bothered Hiroshi was the rumor that Tanaka was connected to the Yakusa, the ruthless Japanese mafia.

When the phone rang a few minutes later, its raucous jangle sounded unnaturally loud in the silence of the deserted lab. Startled by it, Hiroshi had the receiver off the hook before the first ring had completed.

"Moshimoshi," Hiroshi said much too quickly, betraying his nervousness.

The voice that answered was sharp and piercing like a stiletto. It was Tanaka.

4

March 3
Wednesday, 8:30 A.M.

When Sean's eyes blinked open at eight-thirty, he was instantly awake. He snatched up his watch to check the time, and immediately became annoyed with himself. He'd intended to get to the lab early that day. If he was going to give this plan of Janet's a shot, he'd have to put in more of an effort.

After making himself reasonably decent by pulling on his boxer shorts, he padded down the balcony and gently knocked on Janet's slider. Her curtains were still closed. After he knocked again harder, her sleepy face appeared behind the glass.

"Miss me?" Sean teased when Janet slid the door open.

"What time is it?" Janet asked. She blinked in the bright light.

"Going to nine," Sean said. "I'll be leaving in fifteen or twenty minutes. Want to go together or what?"

"I'd better drive myself," Janet said. "I've got to find an apartment. I only get to stay here a few nights."

"See you this afternoon," Sean said. He started to leave.

"Sean!" Janet called.

Sean turned.

"Good luck!" Janet said.

"You too," Sean said.

As soon as he was dressed, Sean drove over to the Forbes Center and parked in front of the research building. It was just after nine-thirty when he walked in the door. As he did, Robert Harris straightened up from the desk. He'd been explaining something to the guard on desk duty. His expression was somewhere between angry and morose. Apparently the man was never in a good mood.

"Banker's hours?" Harris asked provocatively.

"My favorite Marine," Sean said. "Were you able to keep Mrs. Mason out of trouble, or was she desperate enough to take you on a tour of Lady Luck?"

Robert Harris glared at Sean as Sean leaned against the bar of the turnstile to show his ID to the guard at the desk. But Harris couldn't think of an appropriate retort fast enough. The guard at the desk released the bar and Sean pushed through.

Unsure how to approach the day, Sean first took the elevator to the seventh floor and went to Claire's office. He was not looking forward to meeting her since they'd parted on such uncomfortable terms. But he wanted to clear the air.

Claire and her superior shared an office with their desks facing each other. But when Sean found her, Claire was alone.

"Morning!" Sean said cheerfully.

Claire looked up from her work. "I trust you slept well," she said sarcastically.

"I'm sorry about last night," Sean offered. "I know it was unpleasant and awkward for everyone. I apologize that the evening had to end that way, but I assure you Janet's arrival was totally unexpected."

"I'll take your word for it," Claire said coolly.

"Please," Sean asked. "Don't you turn unfriendly. You're one of the few people here who has been nice to me. I'm apologizing. What more can I do?"

"You're right," Claire said, finally softening. "Consider it history. What can I do for you today?"

"I suppose I have to talk with Dr. Levy," Sean said. "How do you suggest I find her?"

"Page her," Claire said. "All of the professional staff carry beepers. You should get one yourself." She picked up the phone, checked with the operator that Dr. Levy was in, then had her paged.

Claire only had time to tell Sean where to go to get a beeper when her phone rang. It was one of the administrative secretaries calling to say that Dr. Levy was in her office only a few doors down from Claire's.

Two minutes later Sean was knocking on Dr. Levy's door, wondering what kind of reception he'd get. When he heard Dr. Levy call out to come in, he tried to talk himself into being civil even if Dr. Levy wasn't.

Dr. Levy's office was the first place that appeared like the academic scientific environment Sean was accustomed to. There was the usual clutter of journals and books, a binocular microscope, and odd assortments of microscopic slides, photomicrographs, scattered color slides, erlenmeyer flasks, culture dishes, tissue culture tubes, and lab notebooks.

"Beautiful morning," Sean said, hoping to start off on a better note than the day before.

"I asked Mark Halpern to come up when I heard you were on the floor," Dr. Levy said, ignoring Sean's pleasantry. "He is our chief and currently our only lab tech. He will get you started. He can also order any supplies and reagents you might need and we don't have, although we have a good stock. But I have to approve any orders." She pushed a small vial across her desk toward Sean. "Here is the glycoprotein. I'm sure you'll understand when I tell you that it does not leave this building. I meant what I said yesterday: stick to your assignment at hand. You should have more than enough to keep you busy. Good luck, and I hope you are as good as Dr. Mason seems to believe you are."

"Wouldn't it be more comfortable if we were a bit more friendly about all this?" Sean asked. He reached over and picked up the vial.

Dr. Levy pushed a few wayward strands of her glistening black hair away from her forehead. "I appreciate your forthrightness," she said after a brief pause. "Our relationship will depend on your performance. If you work hard, we'll get along just fine."

Just then, Mark Halpern entered Dr. Levy's office. As they were introduced, Sean studied the man and guessed he was around thirty. He was a few inches taller than Sean and was meticulously dressed. Sporting a spotless white apron over his suit, he looked more like men Sean had seen around cosmetic counters in department stores than a tech in a scientific lab.

Over the next half hour, Mark set Sean up for work in the large empty fifth floor that Claire had shown him the day before. By the time Mark left, Sean was satisfied with the physical aspects of his work situation; he only wished he was working on something he was truly interested in.

Picking up the vial Dr. Levy had given him, Sean unscrewed the cap and looked in at the fine white powder. He sniffed it; it had no smell. Pulling his stool closer to the counter, he set to work. First he dissolved the powder in a variety of solvents to get an idea of its solubility. He also set up a gel electrophoresis to get some approximation of its molecular weight.

After about an hour of concentration, Sean was suddenly distracted by movement that he thought he'd seen out of the corner of his eye. When he looked in that direction, all he saw was empty lab space extending over to the door to the stairwell. Sean paused from what he was doing. The only detectable sound came from the hum of a refrigerator compressor and the whirring of a shaking platform Sean was using to help super-saturate a solution. He wondered if the unaccustomed solitude was making him hallucinate.

Sean was seated near the middle of the room. Putting down the utensils in his hands, he walked the length of the lab, glancing down each aisle. The more he looked the more uncertain he became that he'd seen something. Reaching the door to the stairwell, he yanked it open and took a step forward, intending to look up and down the stairs. He hadn't really expected to find anything, and he involuntarily caught his breath when his sudden move put him face to face with someone who'd been lurking just beyond the door.

Recognition dawned swiftly as Sean realized that it was Hiroshi Gyuhama who stood before him, equally as startled. Sean remembered meeting the man the day before when Claire had introduced them.

"Very sorry," Hiroshi said with a nervous smile. He bowed deeply.

"Quite all right," Sean said, feeling an irresistible urge to bow back. "It was my fault. I should have looked through the window before opening the door."

"No, no, my fault," Hiroshi insisted.

"It truly was my fault," Sean said. "But I suppose it is a silly argument."

"My fault," Hiroshi persisted.

"Were you coming in here?" Sean asked, pointing back into his lab.

"No, no," Hiroshi said. His smile broadened. "I'm going back to work." But he didn't move.

"What are you working on?" Sean asked, just to make conversation.

"Lung cancer," Hiroshi said. "Thank you very much."

"And thank you," Sean said by reflex. Then he wondered why he was thanking the man.

Hiroshi bowed several times before turning and climbing the stairs.

Sean shrugged and walked back to his lab bench. He wondered if the movement he'd seen originally had been Hiroshi, perhaps through the small window in the stairwell door. But that would mean Hiroshi had been there all along, which didn't make sense to Sean.

As long as his concentration had been broken, Sean took the time to descend to the basement to seek out Roger Calvet. Once he found him, Sean felt uncomfortable talking to the man whose back deformity prevented him from looking at Sean when he spoke. Nonetheless, Mr. Calvet managed to isolate a group of appropriate mice so that Sean could begin injecting them with the glycoprotein in hopes of eliciting an antibody response. Sean didn't expect success from this effort since others at the Forbes Center had undoubtedly tried it already, yet he knew he had to start from the beginning before he resorted to any of his "tricks."

Back in the elevator Sean was about to press the button for the fifth floor when he changed his mind and pressed six. He wouldn't have guessed it of himself, but he felt isolated and even a bit lonely. Working at Forbes was a distinctly uncomfortable experience, and not simply because of the bevy of unfriendly people. There weren't *enough* people. The place was too empty, too clean, too ordered. Sean had always taken the academic collegiality of his previous work environments for granted. Now he found himself needing some human interaction. So he headed for the sixth floor.

The first person Sean encountered was David Lowenstein. He was an intense, thin fellow bent over his lab bench examining tissue culture tubes. Sean came up to his left side and said hello.

"I beg your pardon?" David said, glancing up from his work.

"How's it going?" Sean asked. He reintroduced himself in case David had forgotten him from the day before.

"Things are going as well as can be expected," David said.

"What are you working on?" Sean asked.

"Melanoma," David answered.

"Oh," Sean said.

The conversation went downhill from that point, so Sean drifted on. He caught Hiroshi looking at him, but after the stairwell incident Sean avoided him. Instead he moved on to Arnold Harper who was busily working under a hood. Sean could tell he was doing some kind of recombinant work with yeast.

Attempts at conversation with Arnold were about as successful as those with David Lowenstein had been. The only thing Sean learned from Arnold was that he was working on colon cancer. Although he'd been the source of the glycoprotein Sean was working with, he didn't seem the least interested in discussing it.

Sean wandered on and came to the glass door to the maximum containment lab with its No Entry sign. Cupping his hands as he'd done the day before, he again tried to peer through. Just like the previous day, all he could see was a corridor with doors leading off it. After glancing over his shoulder to make sure no one was in sight, Sean pulled open the door and stepped inside. The door shut behind him and sealed. This portion of the lab had a negative pressure so that no air would move out when the door was opened.

For a moment Sean stood just inside the door and felt his pulse quicken with excitement. It was the same feeling he used to get as a teenager when he, Jimmy, and Brady would go north to one of the rich bedroom communities like Swampscott or Marblehead and hit a few houses. They never stole anything of real value, just TVs and stuff like that. They never had trouble fencing the goods in Boston. The money went to a guy who was supposed to send it over to the IRA, but Sean never knew how much of it ever got to Ireland.

When no one appeared to protest Sean's presence in the No Entry area, Sean pushed on. The place didn't have the look or feel of a maximum containment lab. In fact, the first room he looked into was empty except for bare lab benches. There was no equipment at all. Entering the room, Sean examined the surface of the counters. At one time they had been used, but not extensively. He could see some marks where the rubber feet of a countertop machine had sat, but that was the only telltale sign of use.

Bending down, Sean pulled open a cabinet and gazed inside. There were a few half-empty reagent bottles as well as assorted glassware, some of which was broken.

"Hold it right there!" a voice shouted, causing Sean to whirl around and rise to a standing position.

It was Robert Harris poised in the doorway, hands on his hips, feet spread apart. His meaty face was red. Dots of perspiration lined his forehead. "Can't you read, Mr. Harvard Boy?" Harris snarled.

"I don't think it's worth getting upset over an empty lab," Sean said.

"This area is off limits," Harris said.

"We're not in the army," Sean said.

Harris advanced menacingly. Between his height and weight advantage, he expected to intimidate Sean. But Sean didn't move. He merely tensed. With all his street experience as a teenager, he instinctively knew what he'd hit and hit hard if Harris threatened to touch him. But Sean was reasonably confident Harris wouldn't try.

"You are certainly one wiseass," Harris said. "I knew you'd be trouble the moment I laid eyes on you."

"Funny! I felt the same way about you," Sean said.

"I warned you not to mess with me, boy," Harris said. He moved within inches of Sean's face.

"You have a couple of blackheads on your nose," Sean said. "In case you didn't know."

Harris glared down at Sean and for a moment he didn't speak. His face got redder.

"I think you are getting entirely too worked up," Sean said.

"What the hell are you doing in here?" Harris demanded.

"Pure curiosity," Sean said. "I was told it was a maximum containment lab. I wanted to see it."

"I want you out of here in two seconds," Harris said. He stepped back and pointed toward the door.

Sean walked out into the hall. "There are a few more rooms I'd like to see," he said. "How about we take a tour together?"

"Out!" Harris shouted, pointing toward the glass door.

JANET HAD a late morning meeting with the director of nursing, Margaret Richmond. She used the time from Sean's wakeup call until the moment she had to leave to take a long shower, shave her legs, blow-dry her hair, and press her dress. Although she knew her job at the Forbes hospital was assured, meetings such as the one she was anticipating still made her nervous. And on top of that, she was still anxious about Sean's potential for heading back to Boston. All in all she had plenty of reason to be upset; she had no idea what the next few days would bring.

Margaret Richmond was not what Janet anticipated. Her voice on the telephone had conjured up an image of a delicate, slight woman. Instead, she was powerful and rather severe. Yet she was still cordial and businesslike, and conveyed to Janet a sincere appreciation for Janet's coming to the Forbes hospital. She even gave Janet her choice of shifts. Janet was pleased to opt for days. She had assumed she'd have to start on nights, a shift she disliked.

"You indicated a preference for floor duty," Ms. Richmond said as she consulted her notes.

"Correct," Janet said. "Floor duty gives me the type of patient contact that I find the most rewarding."

"We have an opening for days on the fourth floor," Ms. Richmond said.

"Sounds good," Janet said cheerfully.

"When would you like to start?" Ms. Richmond asked.

"Tomorrow," Janet said. She would have preferred a few days' delay to give herself a chance to find an apartment and get settled, but she felt an urgency about delving into the medulloblastoma protocol.

"I'd like to use today to try to find a nearby apartment," Janet added.

"I don't think you should stay around here," Ms. Richmond said. "If I were you I'd go out to the beach. They've done a nice job restoring the area. Either that or Coconut Grove."

"I'll take your advice," Janet said. Assuming the meeting was over, she stood.

"How about a quick tour of the hospital?" Ms. Richmond asked.

"I'd like that," Janet said.

Ms. Richmond first took Janet across the hall to meet Dan Selenburg, the hospital administrator. But he wasn't available. Instead, they went to the first floor to see the outpatient facilities, the hospital auditorium, and the cafeteria.

On the second floor Janet peered into the ICU, the surgical area, the chemistry lab, the radiology department, and medical records. Then they went up to the fourth floor.

Janet was impressed with the hospital. It was cheerful, modern, and appeared to be adequately staffed, which was particularly important from a nursing point of view. She'd had her misgivings about oncology and the fact that all the patients would be cancer patients, but given the otherwise pleasant environment and the variety in the patients she saw—some old, some gravely ill, others seemingly normal—she decided the Forbes hospital was definitely a place she could work. In many ways, it wasn't dissimilar to the Boston Memorial, just newer and more pleasantly decorated.

The fourth floor was arranged in the same configuration as other patient floors. It was a simple rectangle with private rooms on either side of a central corridor. The nurses' station was situated in the middle of the floor near the elevators and formed a large U-shaped counter. Behind it was a utility room and a small closet-like pharmacy with a dutch door. Across from the nurses' station was a patients' lounge. A housekeeping closet with a slop sink was across from the elevators. At either end of the long central hall were stairways.

Once their tour was completed, Ms. Richmond turned Janet over to Marjorie Singleton, the head nurse on days. Janet liked Marjorie immediately. She was a petite redhead with a smattering of freckles across the bridge of her nose. She seemed in a constant flurry of activity and never without a smile. Janet met other staffers as well, but the profusion of names overwhelmed her. Aside from Ms. Richmond and Marjorie, she didn't think she'd remember a single person to whom she'd been introduced except for Tim Katzenburg, the ward secretary. He was a blond-haired Adonis who looked more like a beach boy than a hospital ward secretary. He told Janet he was taking pre-med courses at night school since discovering the limited utility of a philosophy degree.

"We're really glad to have you," Marjorie said when she rejoined Janet after taking care of a minor emergency. "Boston's loss is our gain."

"I'm happy to be here," Janet said.

"We've been short-handed since the tragedy with Sheila Arnold," Marjorie said.

"What happened?"

"The poor woman was raped and shot in her apartment," Marjorie said. "And not too far from the hospital. Welcome to big city life."

"How terrible," Janet said. She wondered if that was the reason Ms. Richmond had warned her against the immediate neighborhood.

"Currently we happen to have a small contingent of patients from Boston," Marjorie said. "Would you like to meet them?"

"Sure," Janet said.

Marjorie bounded off. Janet practically had to run to

keep up with her. Together they entered a room on the west side of the hospital.

"Helen," Marjorie called softly once she stood beside the bed. "You have a visitor from Boston."

Bright green eyes opened. Their intense color contrasted dramatically with the patient's pale skin.

"We have a new nurse joining our staff," Marjorie said. She then introduced the two women.

The name Helen Cabot immediately registered in Janet's mind. Despite the mildly jealous feelings she'd had back in Boston, she was pleased to find Helen at the Forbes. Her presence would undoubtedly help keep Sean in Florida.

After Janet had spoken briefly with Helen, the two nurses left the room.

"Sad case," Marjorie said. "Such a sweet girl. She's scheduled for a biopsy today. I hope she responds to the treatment."

"But I've heard that you people have had a hundred percent remission with her particular type of tumor," Janet said. "Why wouldn't she respond?"

Marjorie stopped and stared at Janet. "I'm impressed," she said. "Not only are you aware of our medulloblastoma results, you made an instantaneous and correct diagnosis. Are you endowed with powers we should know about?"

"Hardly," Janet said with a laugh. "Helen Cabot was a patient at my hospital in Boston. I'd heard about her case."

"That makes me feel more comfortable," Marjorie said. "For a second there I thought I was witnessing the supernatural." She began walking again. "I'm concerned about Helen Cabot because her tumors are far advanced. Why did you people keep her for so long? She should have been started on treatment weeks ago."

"That's something I know nothing about," Janet admitted.

The next patient was Louis Martin. In contrast to Helen, Louis did not appear ill. In fact, he was sitting in a chair fully dressed. He'd only arrived that morning and was still in the process of being admitted. Although he didn't look sick, he did appear anxious.

Marjorie went through introductions again, adding that Louis had the same problem as Helen, but that thankfully he'd been sent to them much more swiftly.

Janet shook hands with the man, noting his palm was damp. She looked into the man's terrified eyes, wishing there was something she could say that would comfort him. She also felt a little guilty realizing that she was somewhat pleased to learn of Louis's plight. Having two patients on her floor under the medulloblastoma protocol would give her that much more opportunity to investigate the treatment. Sean would undoubtedly be pleased.

As Marjorie and Janet returned to the nurses' station, Janet asked if the medulloblastoma cases were all on the fourth floor.

"Heavens no," Marjorie said. "We don't group patients according to tumor type. Their assignment is purely random. It just so happens we'll currently have three. As we speak we're admitting another case: a young woman from Houston named Kathleen Sharenburg."

Janet hid her elation.

"There's one last patient from Boston," Marjorie said as she stopped outside of room 409. "And she's a doll with an incredibly upbeat attitude that's been a source of strength and support for all the other patients. I believe she said she's from a section of town called the North End."

Marjorie knocked on the closed door. A muffled "Come in" could be heard. Marjorie pushed open the door and stepped inside. Janet followed.

"Gloria," Marjorie called. "How's the chemo going?"

"Lovely," Gloria joked. "I've just started the IV portion today."

"I brought you somebody to meet," Marjorie said. "A new nurse. She's from Boston."

Janet looked at the woman in the bed. She appeared to be about Janet's own age. A few years earlier, Janet would have been shocked. Prior to working in a hospital she'd been under the delusion that cancer was an affliction of the elderly. Painfully, Janet had learned that just about anyone was fair game for the disease.

Gloria was olive-complected with dark eyes and what had been dark hair. Presently her scalp was covered with a dark fuzz. Although she'd been a buxom woman, one side of her chest was now flat beneath her lingerie.

"Mr. Widdicomb!" Marjorie said with surprised irritation. "What are you doing in here?"

Her attention focused on the patient, Janet had not realized there was another person in the room. She turned to see a man in a green uniform with a mildly distorted nose.

"Don't go giving Tom a bad time," Gloria said. "He's only trying to help."

"I told you I wanted room 417 cleaned," Marjorie said, ignoring Gloria. "Why are you in here?"

"I was about to do the bathroom," Tom said meekly. He avoided eye contact while fidgeting with the mop handle sticking out of his bucket.

Janet watched. She was fascinated. Tiny Marjorie had been transformed from an amiable pixie to a commanding powerhouse.

"What are we to do with the new patient if the room is not ready?" Marjorie demanded. "Get down there at once and get it done." She pointed out the door.

After the man had left, Marjorie shook her head. "Tom Widdicomb is the bane of my existence here at Forbes."

"He means well," Gloria said. "He's been an angel to me. He checks on me every day."

"He's not employed as part of the professional staff," Marjorie said. "He's got to do his own job first."

Janet smiled. She liked working on wards that were well run by someone capable of taking charge. Judging by what she'd just seen, Janet was confident she'd get along fine with Marjorie Singleton.

SOME OF the soapy water sloshed out of his bucket as Tom raced down the corridor and into room 417. He released the doorstop and let the door close. He leaned against it. His breaths came in hissing gasps, a legacy of the terror that had flashed through him when the knock had first sounded on Gloria's door. He'd been seconds away from giving her the succinylcholine. If Marjorie and that new nurse had happened by a few minutes later, he would have been caught.

"Everything is fine, Alice," Tom reassured his mother. "There's no problem whatsoever. You needn't be worried."

Having reined in his fear, Tom was now angry. He'd never liked Marjorie, not from the first day that he'd met her. That bubbly good nature was just a sham. She was a meddlesome bitch. Alice had warned him about her, but he hadn't listened. He should have done something about her like he'd done to that other busybody nurse, Sheila Arnold, who'd started asking questions about why he was hanging around an anesthesia cart. All he'd have to do was get Marjorie's address sometime when he was cleaning up in administration. Then he'd show her who was in charge, once and for all.

Having calmed himself with thoughts of taking care of Marjorie, Tom pushed off from the door and eyed the room. He didn't care for the actual cleaning part of his job, just the freedom it provided. He'd preferred the job with the ambulance except for having to deal with fellow EMTs. With housekeeping, he didn't have to deal with anyone except for rare run-ins with the likes of Marjorie. Also, with housekeeping he could go anyplace in the hospital almost anytime he wanted. The only catch was he occasionally had to clean. But most of the time he was able to get by just pushing things around, since nobody was watching him.

If Tom was honest with himself, he had to admit that the job he'd liked the best had been one he'd held way back when he'd first left high school. He'd gotten a job with a vet. Tom liked the animals. After he'd worked there for a while the vet had designated Tom as the person in charge of putting the animals to sleep. They were usually old, sick animals that were suffering, and the work gave Tom a lot of satisfaction. He could remember being disappointed when Alice didn't share his enthusiasm.

Opening the door, Tom peered up the corridor. He had to return to the housekeeping closet to retrieve his housekeeping cart, but he didn't want to run into Marjorie for fear she'd start in on him again. Tom was afraid he might not be able to control himself. On many occasions he'd felt like striking her because that's what she needed. Yet he knew he couldn't afford to do that, no way.

Tom knew he would have trouble helping Gloria now that he'd been seen in her room. He would have to be more careful than usual. He'd also have to wait a day or so. He'd just have to hope she'd still be on IVs by then. He didn't want to inject the succinylcholine intramuscularly because that might make it detectable if it occurred to the medical examiner to look for it.

Slipping out of the room, Tom headed up the hall. As he passed 409, he glanced inside. He didn't see Marjorie, which was good, but he did see that other nurse, the new one.

Tom slowed his steps as a new fear gripped him. What if the new nurse who'd been hired to replace Sheila was actually hired to find him? Maybe she was a spy. That would explain why she had suddenly appeared in Gloria's room with Marjorie!

The more Tom thought about it, the more sure he became, especially since the new nurse was still in Gloria's room. She was out to trap him and stop his crusade against breast cancer.

"Don't worry, Alice," he assured his mother. "I'll listen this time."

Anne Murphy felt better than she had in weeks. She'd been depressed for several days after she'd learned of Sean's plans to go to Miami. To her, the city was synonymous with drugs and sin. Somehow, the news hadn't surprised her. Sean had been a bad child from an early age and, like men in general, he certainly wasn't likely to change, despite his surprising academic performances late in high school and then in college. At first when he talked about going to medical school, she'd felt a ray of hope. But the hope had been shattered when he told her he did not plan to practice medicine. Like so many other junctures in her life, Anne recognized she just had to endure and stop praying for miracles.

Still the question of why Sean couldn't be more like Brian or Charles plagued her. What had she done wrong? It had to have been her fault. Maybe it was because she hadn't been able to breast-feed Sean as a baby. Or maybe it was because she'd been unable to stop her husband from beating the child during some of his drunken rages.

Leave it to her youngest son, Charles, to provide a bright spot in the days subsequent to Sean's departure. Charles had called from his seminary in New Jersey with the glorious news that he would be home for a visit the following evening. Wonderful Charles! His prayers would save them all.

In anticipation of Charles's arrival, Anne had gone out shopping that morning. She planned to spend the day baking and preparing dinner. Brian said he'd try to make it although he had an important meeting that night that might run late.

Opening the refrigerator, Anne began putting away the cold items while her mind reveled in anticipation of the pleasures she'd enjoy that evening. But then she caught herself. She knew such thoughts were dangerous. Life was such a weak thread. Happiness and pleasure were invitations for tragedy. For a moment she tortured herself about how she'd feel if Charles were killed on the way to Boston.

The doorbell interrupted Anne's worries. She pressed the intercom and asked who was calling.

"Tanaka Yamaguchi," a voice said.

"What do you want?" Anne asked. The doorbell did not ring often.

"I want to talk to you about your son Sean," Tanaka said.

The color drained from Anne's face. Instantly she scolded herself for having entertained pleasurable thoughts. Sean was in trouble again. Had she expected anything less?

Pressing the door-release button, Anne went to the door to her apartment and pulled it open in anticipation of her unexpected guest. Anne Murphy was surprised enough that someone was paying a house call; when she saw that he was an Oriental, she was shocked. The fact that the man's name was Oriental hadn't registered.

The stranger was about Anne's height but stocky and muscular with coal-black short hair and tanned skin. He was dressed in a dark, slightly shiny business suit with a white shirt and dark tie. Over his arm he carried a belted Burberry coat.

"I beg your pardon," Tanaka said. He had only a slight accent. He bowed and extended his business card. The card simply read: Tanaka Yamaguchi, Industrial Consultant.

With one hand pressed against her throat and the other clutching the business card, Anne was at a loss for words.

"I must speak to you about your son Sean," Tanaka said.

As if recovering from a blow, Anne found her voice: "What's happened? Is he in trouble again?"

"No," Tanaka said. "Has he been in trouble before?"

"As a teenager," Anne said. "He was a very headstrong boy. Very active."

"American children can be troublesome," Tanaka said. "In Japan the children are taught to respect their elders."

"But Sean's father could be difficult," Anne said, surprised at her admission. She felt flustered and wasn't sure if she should invite the man in or not.

"I'm interested in your son's business dealings," Tanaka said. "I know he is a fine student at Harvard, but is he involved with any companies that produce biological products?"

"He and a group of his friends started a company called Immunotherapy," Anne said, relieved that the conversation was turning to the more positive moments of her son's checkered past.

"Is he still involved with this Immunotherapy?" Tanaka asked.

"He doesn't talk to me about it too much," Anne said.

"Thank you very much," Tanaka said with another bow. "Have a nice day."

Anne watched as the man turned and disappeared down the stairs. She was almost as surprised at the sudden end to the conversation as she'd been at the man's visit. She stepped out into the hall just in time to hear the front door close two floors down. Returning to her apartment, she closed the door and bolted it behind her.

It took her a moment to pull herself together. It had been a strange episode. After glancing at Tanaka's card, she slipped it into her apron pocket. Then she went back to putting food into the refrigerator. She thought about calling Brian but decided she could tell him about the Japanese man's visit that evening. Provided, of course, that Brian came. She decided that if he didn't come, then she'd call.

An hour later Anne was absorbed in making a cake when the door buzzer startled her again. At first she worried that the Japanese man had returned with more questions. Maybe she should have called Brian. With some trepidation she pressed the intercom button and asked who was there.

"Sterling Rombauer," a deep masculine voice replied. "Is this Anne Murphy?"

"Yes . . ."

"I would very much like to speak to you about your son Sean Murphy," Sterling said.

Anne caught her breath. She couldn't believe yet another stranger was there to ask questions about her second born.

"What about him?" she asked.

"I'd rather talk to you in person," Sterling said.

"I'll come down," Anne said.

Rinsing her hands of flour, Anne started down the stairs. The man was standing in the foyer, a camel-hair coat thrown over his arm. Like the Japanese man, he was wearing a business suit and white shirt. His tie was a bright red foulard.

"I'm sorry to bother you," Sterling said through the glass.

"Why are you asking about my son?" Anne demanded.

"I've been sent by the Forbes Cancer Center in Miami," Sterling explained.

Recognizing the name of the institution where Sean was working, Anne opened the door and gazed up at the stranger. He was an attractive man with a broad face and straight nose. His hair was light brown and mildly curly. Anne thought he could have been Irish except for his name. He was over six feet tall with eyes as blue as those of her own sons.

"Has Sean done something I should know about?" she asked.

"Not that I'm aware of," Sterling said. "The management of the clinic routinely looks into the background of the people who work there. Security is an important issue with them. I merely wanted to ask you a few questions."

"Like what?" Anne asked.

"Has your son been involved with any biotechnology companies to your knowledge?"

"You are the second person to ask that question in the last hour," Anne said.

"Oh?" Sterling said. "Who may I ask made similar inquiries?"

Anne reached into her apron pocket and drew out Tanaka's business card. She handed it to Sterling. Anne could see the man's eyes narrow. He handed her the card back.

"And what did you tell Mr. Yamaguchi?" Sterling asked.

"I told him my son and a few friends had started their own biotechnology company," Anne said. "They called it Immunotherapy."

"Thank you, Mrs. Murphy," Sterling said. "I appreciate your talking with me."

Anne watched the elegant stranger descend the steps in

front of her house and climb into the back seat of a dark sedan. His driver was in uniform.

More baffled than ever, Anne went back upstairs. After some indecision she picked up the phone and called Brian. After apologizing for interrupting his busy day, she told him about her two, curious visitors.

"That's odd," Brian said when she was finished.

"Should we be worried about Sean?" Anne asked. "You know your brother."

"I'll call him," Brian said. "Meanwhile, if anyone else comes asking questions, don't tell them anything. Just refer them to me."

"I hope I didn't say anything wrong," Anne said.

"I'm sure you didn't," Brian assured her.

"Will we be seeing you later?"

"I'm still working on it," Brian said. "But if I'm not there by eight eat without me."

WITH THE Miami street map open on the seat next to her, Janet managed to find her way back to the Forbes residence. She was pleased when she saw Sean's Isuzu in the parking lot. She was hoping to find him home since she had what she thought was good news. She'd found an airy, pleasant furnished apartment on the southern tip of Miami Beach that even had a limited view of the ocean from the bathroom. When she'd first started looking for apartments she'd been discouraged since it was "in season." The place she found had been reserved a year in advance, but the people had unexpectedly canceled. Their cancellation had come in five minutes before Janet stepped into the real estate office.

Grabbing her purse and her copy of the rental agreement, Janet went up to her apartment. She took a few minutes to wash her face and change into shorts and a tank top. Then with lease in hand she walked down the balcony to Sean's slider. She found him glumly slouched on the couch.

"Good news!" Janet said cheerfully. She plopped down in the armchair across from him.

"I could use some of that," Sean said.

"I found an apartment," she announced. She brandished the lease. "It's not fabulous, but it's a block from the beach, and best of all it's a straight shot out the expressway to the Forbes."

"Janet, I don't know whether I can stay here," Sean said. He sounded depressed.

"What happened?" Janet asked, feeling a shiver of anxiety.

"The Forbes is nuts," Sean said. "The atmosphere sucks. For one thing, there's a Japanese weirdo who I swear is watching me. Every time I turn around, there he is."

"What else?" Janet asked. She wanted to hear all Sean's objections so she could figure a way to deal with them. Having just signed a lease for two months made her commitment to remaining in Miami that much more binding.

"There's something basically wrong with the place," Sean said. "People are either friendly or unfriendly. It's so black and white. It's not natural. Besides, I'm working by myself in this huge empty room. It's crazy."

"You've always complained about the lack of space," Janet said.

"Remind me never to complain again," Sean said. "I never realized it, but I need people around me. And another thing: they have this secret maximum containment lab which is supposed to be off limits. I ignored the sign and went in anyway. You know what I found? Nothing. The place was empty. Well, I didn't get to go in every room. In fact, I hadn't gotten far when this frustrated Marine who heads up the security department stormed in and threatened me."

"With what?" Janet asked with alarm.

"With his gut," Sean said. "He came up real close and gave me this nasty look. I was this far from giving him a shot in the nuts." Sean held up his thumb and index finger about a half inch apart.

"So what happened?" Janet asked.

"Nothing," Sean said. "He backed off and just told me to get out. But he was all worked up, ordering me out of an empty room as if I'd done something really wrong. It was insane."

"But you didn't see the other rooms," Janet said. "Maybe they're redoing the room you were in."

"It's possible," Sean admitted. "There's a lot of potential explanations. But it's still weird, and when you add all the weird stuff together, it makes the whole joint seem plain crazy."

"What about the work they want you to do?"

"That's okay," Sean said. "In fact, I don't know why they've had so much trouble. Dr. Mason, the director, came in during the afternoon, and I showed him what I was doing. I'd already gotten some minuscule crystals. I told him that I could probably get some decent crystals in a week or so. He seemed pleased, but after he left, I thought about it, and I'm not wild about helping to make money for some Japanese holding company, which is essentially what I'd be doing if I get crystals that they can defract."

"But that's not all you'll be doing," Janet said.

"How's that?"

"You'll also be investigating the medulloblastoma protocol," Janet said. "Tomorrow I'm starting on the fourth floor and guess who's there?"

"Helen Cabot?" Sean guessed. He pulled in his feet and sat up.

"You got it," Janet said. "Plus another patient from Boston. A Louis Martin."

"Does he have the same diagnosis?" Sean asked.

"Yup," Janet said. "Medulloblastoma."

"That's amazing!" Sean remarked. "And they certainly got him down here quickly!"

Janet nodded. "Forbes is a bit perturbed that Helen had been kept in Boston so long," Janet said. "The head nurse is worried about her."

"There'd been a lot of argument about whether or not to biopsy her and which of her tumors to go after," Sean explained.

"And there was another young woman being admitted while I was there," Janet said.

"Medulloblastoma too?" Sean asked.

"Yup," Janet said. "So there are three patients on my floor who are just beginning their treatments. I'd say that was pretty convenient."

"I'll need copies of their charts," Sean said. "I'll need drug samples as soon as they start actual treatment, unless of course the drugs are named. But that's not going to be the case. They won't be using chemo on these people; at least not chemo exclusively. The drugs will probably be coded. And I'll need each patient's regimen."

"I'll do what I can," Janet said. "It shouldn't be difficult with the patients on my floor. Maybe I'll even be able to arrange to care for at least one of them personally. I've also located a convenient copy machine. It's in medical records."

"Be careful there," Sean warned. "The mother of the woman in public relations is one of the medical librarians."

"I'll be careful," Janet said. She eyed Sean warily before going on. She was learning what a mistake it was to push him to any conclusions before he was ready to make them. But she just had to know. "So this means you're still game?" she asked. "You'll stay? Even if it means doing that bit of work with the protein, even if it is for the Japanese?"

Sean leaned forward with his head down, elbows on his knees, and rubbed the back of his head. "I don't know," he said. "This whole situation is absurd. What a way to do science!" He looked up at Janet. "I wonder if anybody in Washington had any idea what limiting research funding would do to our research establishments. It's all happening just when the country needs research more than ever."

"All the more reason for us to try to do something," Janet said.

"You're serious about this?" Sean asked.

"Absolutely," Janet said.

"You know we'll have to be resourceful," Sean said.

"I know."

"We'll have to break a few rules," he added. "Are you sure you can handle that?"

"I think so," Janet said.

"And once we start, there's no turning back," Sean said.

Janet started to answer but the ringing of the phone on the desk startled them both.

"Who the hell could that be?" Sean wondered. He let it ring.

"Aren't you going to answer it?" Janet asked.

"I'm thinking," Sean said. What he didn't say was that he was afraid it might be Sarah Mason. She'd called him that afternoon, and despite a temptation to aggravate Harris,

Sean did not want any association with the woman whatsoever.

"I think you should answer it," Janet said.

"You answer it," Sean suggested.

Janet jumped to her feet and snatched up the receiver. Sean watched her expression as she asked who was calling. She showed no strong reaction as she extended the phone to him.

"It's your brother," she said.

"What the hell?" Sean mumbled as he pulled himself out of the couch. It wasn't like his brother to call. They didn't have that type of relationship, and they had just seen each other Friday night.

Sean took the phone. "What's wrong?" he asked.

"I was about to ask you the same question," Brian said.

"You want an honest answer or platitudes?" Sean asked.

"I think you'd better tell me straight," Brian said.

"This place is bizarre," Sean said. "I'm not so sure I want to stay. It might be a complete waste of time." Sean glanced over at Janet, who rolled her eyes in exasperation.

"Something weird's going on up here too," Brian said. He told Sean about the two men who'd visited their mother, asking about Immunotherapy.

"Immunotherapy is history," Sean said. "What did Mom say?"

"Not much," Brian said. "At least according to her. But she got a bit flustered. All she said was that you and some friends started it."

"She didn't say we sold out?"

"Evidently not."

"What about Oncogen?"

"She said she didn't mention it because we'd told her not to discuss it with anyone."

"Good for her," Sean said.

"Why would these people be up here talking to Mom?" Brian asked. "The Rombauer guy told her he represented the Forbes Cancer Center. He said that they routinely look into their employees for security reasons. Have you done anything to suggest you're a security risk?"

"Hell, I've only been here for a little over twenty-four hours," Sean said.

"You and I know of your penchant to provoke discord. Your blarney would try the patience of Job."

"My blarney is nothing compared to your blather, brother," Sean teased. "Hell, you've made an institution of it by becoming a lawyer."

"Since I'm in a good mood, I'll let that slam slide," Brian said. "But seriously, what do you think is going on?"

"I haven't the slightest idea," Sean said. "Maybe it's like the man said: routine."

"But neither guy seemed to know about the other," Brian said. "That doesn't sound routine to me. And the first man left his card. I have it right here. It says: Tanaka Yamaguchi, Industrial Consultant."

"Industrial consultant could mean anything," Sean said. "I wonder if his involvement is somehow related to the fact that a Japanese electronics giant called Sushita Industries has invested heavily in Forbes. They're obviously looking for some lucrative patents."

"Why can't they stick to cameras, electronics, and cars?" Brian said. "They're already screwing up the world's economy."

"They're too smart for that," Sean said. "They are looking toward the long term. But why they would be interested in my association with piss-ant Immunotherapy, I haven't the foggiest."

"Well, I thought you should know," Brian said. "It's still a little hard for me to believe you're not stirring things up down there, knowing you."

"You'll hurt my feelings talking like that," Sean said.

"I'll be in touch as soon as the Franklin Bank comes through for Oncogen," Brian said. "Try to stay out of trouble."

"Who, me?" Sean asked innocently.

Sean dropped the receiver into the cradle as soon as Brian said goodbye.

"Have you changed your mind again?" Janet asked with obvious frustration.

"What are you talking about?" Sean questioned.

"You told your brother that you weren't sure you wanted to stay," Janet said. "I thought we'd decided to go for it."

"We had," Sean said. "But I didn't want to tell Brian about the plan. He'd worry himself sick. Besides, he'd probably tell my mother and who knows what would happen then."

"THAT WAS very nice indeed," Sterling told the masseuse. She was a handsome, healthy Scandinavian from Finland, dressed in what could have passed for a tennis outfit. He gave her an extra five-dollar tip; when he'd made the arrangements for the massage through the Ritz's concierge, he'd already included an adequate tip in the charge added to his account, but he'd noticed she'd gone over the allotted time.

While the masseuse folded her table and gathered her oils, Sterling pulled on a thick white terrycloth robe and slipped off the towel cinched around his waist. Dropping into the club chair near the window he lifted his feet onto the ottoman and poured a glass of the complimentary champagne. Sterling was a regular visitor at Boston's Ritz Carlton.

The masseuse called a goodbye from the door, and Sterling thanked her again. He decided he'd ask for her by name the next time. A regular massage was one of the expenses Sterling's clients had learned to expect. They'd complain on occasion, but Sterling would merely say that they could accept his terms or hire someone else. Invariably they'd agree because Sterling was extremely effective at the service he performed: industrial espionage.

There were other, more sanitized, descriptions for Sterling's work such as trade counsel or business consultant, but Sterling preferred the honesty of industrial espionage, although for propriety's sake, he left it off his business card. His card merely read: consultant. It didn't read "industrial consultant" as did the card he'd seen earlier that day. He felt the word "industrial" suggested a limitation to manufacturing. Sterling was interested in all business.

Sterling sipped his drink and gazed out the window at the superb view. As usual, his room was on a high floor overlooking the magical Boston Garden. As the sunlight waned, the park's lamps lining the serpentine walkways had blinked on, illuminating the swan boat pond with its miniature suspension bridge. Although it was early March, the recent cold snap had frozen the pond solid. Skaters dotted its mirrored surface, weaving in effortless, intersecting arcs.

Raising his eyes, Sterling could see the fading dazzle of the gold-domed Massachusetts State House. Ruefully he bemoaned the sad fact that the legislature had systematically destroyed its own tax base by enacting short-sighted, anti-business legislation. Unfortunately Sterling had lost a number of good clients who'd either been forced to flee to a more business-oriented state or forced to leave business altogether. Nevertheless, Sterling enjoyed his trips to Boston. It was such a civilized city.

Pulling the phone over to the edge of the table, Sterling wanted to finish work for the day before he indulged in dinner. Not that he found work a burden. Quite the contrary. Sterling loved his current employ, especially considering that he didn't have to work at all. He'd trained at Stanford in computer engineering, worked for Big Blue for several years, then founded his own successful computer chip company, all before he was thirty. By his middle thirties he was tired of an unfulfilling life, a bad marriage, and the stultifying routine of running a business. First he divorced, then he took his company public and made a fortune. Then he engineered a buyout and made another fortune. By age forty he could have bought a sizable portion of the State of California if he'd so desired.

For almost one year he indulged himself in the adolescence he felt he'd somehow missed. Eventually, he got extremely bored with such places as Aspen. That was when a business friend asked him if he would look into a private matter for him. From that moment on, Sterling had been launched on a new career which was stimulating, never routine, rarely dull, and which utilized his engineering background, his business acumen, his imagination, and his intuitive sense for human behavior.

Sterling called Randolph Mason at home. Dr. Mason took the call from his private line in his study.

"I'm not sure you will be happy about what I've learned," Sterling said.

"It's better I learn it sooner rather than later," Dr. Mason responded.

"This young Sean Murphy is an impressive young fellow," Sterling said. "He founded his own biotechnology company called Immunotherapy while a graduate student at MIT. The company turned a profit almost from day one marketing diagnostic kits."

"How's it doing now?"

"Wonderfully," Sterling said. "It's a winner. It's done so well that Genentech bought them out over a year ago."

"Indeed!" Dr. Mason said. A ray of sunshine entered the picture. "Where does that leave Sean Murphy?"

"He and his young friends realized a considerable profit," Sterling said. "Considering their initial investment, it was extremely lucrative indeed."

"So Sean's no longer involved?" Dr. Mason asked.

"He's completely out," Sterling said. "Is that helpful?"

"I'd say so," Dr. Mason said. "I could use the kid's experience with monoclonals, but not if he's got a production facility behind him. It would be too risky."

"He could still sell the information to someone else," Sterling said. "Or he could be in someone else's employ."

"Can you find that out?"

"Most likely," Sterling said. "Do you want me to continue on this?"

"Absolutely," Dr. Mason said. "I want to use the kid but not if he's some kind of industrial spy."

"I've learned something else," Sterling said as he poured himself more champagne. "Someone besides myself has been investigating Sean Murphy. His name is Tanaka Yamaguchi."

Dr. Mason felt the tortellini in his stomach turn upside down.

"Have you ever heard of this man?" Sterling asked.

"No," Dr. Mason said. He'd not heard of him, but with a name like that, the implications were obvious.

"My assumption would be he's working for Sushita," Sterling said. "And I know that he is aware of Sean Murphy's involvement with Immunotherapy. I know because Sean's mother told him."

"He'd been to see Sean's mother?" Dr. Mason asked with alarm.

"As have I," Sterling said.

"But then Sean will know he's being investigated," Dr. Mason sputtered.

"Nothing wrong in that," Sterling said. "If Sean is an industrial spy, it will give him pause. If he's not, it will only be a matter of curiosity or at worst a minor irritation. Sean's reaction should not be your concern. You should be worried about Tanaka Yamaguchi."

"What do you mean?"

"I've never met Tanaka," Sterling said. "But I have heard a lot about him since we're competitors of sorts. He came to the United States many years ago for college. He's the eldest son of a wealthy industrial family, heavy machinery I believe. The problem was he adapted to 'degenerate' American ways a bit too easily for the family's honor. He was swiftly Americanized and became too individualistic for Japanese tastes. The family decided they didn't want him home so they funded a lavish lifestyle. It's been a kind of exile, but he's been clever to augment his allowance by doing what I do, only for Japanese companies operating in the U.S. But he's like a double agent of sorts, frequently representing the Yakusa at the same time he's representing a legitimate firm. He's clever, he's ruthless, and he's effective. The fact that he's involved means your Sushita friends are serious."

"You think he was involved with our two researchers who disappeared and whom you found happily working for Sushita in Japan?"

"I wouldn't be surprised," Sterling said.

"I can't afford to have this Harvard student disappear," Dr. Mason said. "That would be the kind of media event that could destroy the Forbes."

"I don't think there is a worry for the moment," Sterling said. "My sources tell me Tanaka is still here in Boston. Since he has access to a lot of the same information as I, he must think Sean Murphy is involved in something else."

"Like what?" Dr. Mason asked.

"I'm not sure," Sterling said. "I haven't been able to locate all that money those kids made when they sold Immunotherapy. Neither Sean nor his friends have any personal money to speak of, and none of them indulged themselves with expensive cars or other high-ticket items. I think they are up to something, and I believe Tanaka thinks so too."

"Good God!" Dr. Mason said. "I don't know what to do. Maybe I should send the kid home."

"If you think Sean can help you with that protein work you told me about," Sterling said, "then hold tight. I believe I have everything under control. I have made inquiries with numerous contacts, and because of the computer industry here, I'm well connected. All you have to do is tell me to remain on the case and continue paying the bills."

"Keep on it," Dr. Mason said. "And keep me informed."

5

March 4
Thursday, 6:30 A.M.

Janet was up, dressed in her white uniform, and out of the apartment early since her shift ran from seven to three. At that time of the morning there was very little traffic on I95, especially northbound. She and Sean had discussed driving together but in the end decided it would be better if each had their own wheels.

Janet felt a little queasy entering the Forbes Hospital that morning. Her anxiety went beyond the usual nervousness associated with starting a new job. The prospect of breaking rules was what had her on edge and tense. She already felt guilty to a degree; it was guilt by intent.

Janet made it to the fourth floor with time to spare. She poured herself a cup of coffee and proceeded to familiarize herself with the locations of the charts, the pharmacy locker, and the supply closet: areas she would need to be familiar with to carry out her job as a floor nurse. By the time she sat down for report with the night shift going off duty and the day shift coming on, she was significantly calmer than she had been when she first arrived. Marjorie's cheerful presence no doubt helped put her at ease.

Report was routine except for Helen Cabot's deteriorating condition. The poor woman had had several seizures during the night, and the doctors said that her intracranial pressure was rising.

"Do they think the problem is related to the CAT scan–driven biopsy yesterday?" Marjorie asked.

"No," Juanita Montgomery, the night shift supervisor, said. "Dr. Mason was in at three A.M. when she seized again, and he said the problem was probably related to the treatment."

"She's started treatment already?" Janet asked.

"Absolutely," Juanita said. "Her treatment started Tuesday, the night she got here."

"But she just had her biopsy yesterday," Janet said.

"That's for the cellular aspect of her treatment," Marjorie chimed in. "She'll be pheresed today to harvest T lymphocytes which will be grown and sensitized to her tumor. But the humoral aspect of her treatment was started immediately."

"They used mannitol to bring down her intracranial pressure," Juanita added. "It seemed to work. She hasn't seized again. They want to avoid steroids and a shunt if possible. At any rate, she's got to be monitored carefully, especially with the pheresis."

As soon as report was over and the bleary-eyed night shift had departed, the day's work began in earnest. Janet found herself extremely busy. There were a lot of sick patients on the floor, representing a wide range of cancers, and each was on an individual treatment protocol. The most heartrending for Janet was an angelic boy of nine who was on reverse precautions while they waited for a bone marrow transplant to repopulate his marrow with blood-forming cells. He'd been given a strong dose of chemotherapy and radiation to wipe out completely his own leukemic marrow. At the moment he was completely vulnerable to any microorganisms, even those normally not pathogenic for humans.

By mid-morning, Janet finally had a chance to catch her breath. Most of the nurses took their coffee breaks in the utility room off the nurses' station where they could put up their tired feet. Janet decided to take advantage of the time to have Tim Katzenburg show her how to access the Forbes computer. Every patient had a traditional chart and a computer file. Janet wasn't intimidated by computers, having minored in computer science in college. But it still helped to have someone familiar with the Forbes system get her started.

When Tim was distracted for a moment by a phone call from the lab, Janet called up Helen Cabot's file. Since Helen had been there less than forty-eight hours, the file was not extensive. There was a computer graphic showing which of her three tumors they had biopsied and the location of the trephination of the skull just above the right ear. The biopsy specimen was grossly described as firm, white, and of an adequate amount. It said that the specimen had been immediately packed in ice and sent to Basic Diagnostics. In the treatment section it said that she'd begun on MB-300C and MB-303C at a dosage of 100mg/Kg/day of body weight administered at 0.05 ml/Kg/minute.

Janet glanced over at Tim who was still busy on the phone. On a scrap of paper, she wrote down the treatment information. She also wrote down the alpha numeric designator, T-9872, that was listed as the diagnosis along with the descriptive term: medulloblastoma, multiple.

Using the diagnostic designator, Janet next called up the

names of the patients with medulloblastoma who were currently in the hospital. There were a total of five including the three on the fourth floor. The other two were Margaret Demars on the third floor, and Luke Kinsman, an eight-year-old, in the pediatric wings of the fifth floor. Janet wrote down the names.

"Having trouble?" Tim asked over Janet's shoulder.

"Not at all," Janet said. She quickly cleared the screen so that Tim wouldn't see what she'd been up to. She couldn't afford to arouse suspicion on her very first day.

"I've got to enter these lab values," Tim told her. "It will only take a sec."

While Tim was absorbed with the computer terminal, Janet scanned the chart rack for Cabot, Martin, or Sharenburg. To her chagrin, none of those charts was there.

Marjorie breezed into the station to get some narcotics from the pharmacy locker. "You're supposed to be on your coffee break," she called to Janet.

"I am," Janet said, holding up her Styrofoam cup. She mentally made a note to bring a mug into work. Everyone else had his or her own.

"I'm already impressed with you," Marjorie teased from inside the pharmacy. "You needn't work through your break. Kick back, girl, and take a load off your feet."

Janet smiled and said that she'd be taking that kind of break after she was fully acclimated to the ward's routine. When Tim was finished with the computer terminal, Janet asked him about the missing charts.

"They're all down on the second floor," Tim said. "Cabot's getting pheresed while Martin and Scharenburg are being biopsied. Naturally the charts are with them."

"Naturally," Janet repeated. It seemed tough luck that not one of those charts could have been there when she had the chance to look at them. She began to suspect that the clinical espionage she'd committed herself to might not be quite as easy as she'd thought when she suggested her plan to Sean.

Giving up on the charts for the moment, Janet waited for one of the other shift nurses, Dolores Hodges, to finish up in the pharmacy closet. Once Dolores had headed down the hall, Janet made sure no one was watching before slipping into the tiny room. Each patient had an assigned cubbyhole containing his or her prescribed medications. The drugs had come up from the central pharmacy on the first floor.

Finding Helen's cubbyhole, Janet quickly scanned the plethora of vials, bottles, and tubes that contained anti-seizure medication, general tranquilizers, anti-nausea pills, and non-narcotic pain pills. There were no containers designated MB300C or MB303C. On the chance that these medications were secured with the narcotics, Janet checked the narcotics locker, but she found only narcotics there.

Next Janet located Louis Martin's cubbyhole. His was a low one, close to the floor. Janet had to squat down to search through it, but first she had to close the lower half of the Dutch door to make room. As with Helen's cubby, Janet could find no drug containers with special MB code designations on the label.

"My goodness, you startled me," Dolores exclaimed. She had returned in haste and had practically tripped headlong over Janet crouched before Louis Martin's cubbyhole. "I'm so sorry," Dolores said. "I didn't think anyone was in here."

"My fault," Janet said, feeling herself blush. She was instantly afraid she was giving herself away and that Dolores would wonder what she'd been up to. Yet Dolores showed no signs of being suspicious. Instead, once Janet stepped back and out of the way, she came in to get what she needed. In a moment she was gone.

Janet left the pharmacy closet visibly trembling. This was

only her first day and though nothing terrible had happened, she wasn't sure she had the nerves for the furtive behavior espionage demanded.

When Janet reached Helen Cabot's room, she paused. The door was propped open by a rubber stopper. Stepping inside, Janet gazed around. She didn't expect to find any drugs there, but she wanted to check just the same. As she'd expected, there weren't any.

Having recovered her composure, Janet headed back toward the nurses' station, passing Gloria D'Amataglio's room on the way. Taking a moment, Janet stuck her head through the open door. Gloria was sitting up in her armchair with a stainless steel kidney dish clutched in her hand. Her IV was still running.

When they'd chatted the day before Janet had learned that Gloria had gone to Wellesley College just as she herself had. Janet had been in the class a year ahead. After thinking about it overnight, Janet had decided to ask Gloria if she'd known a friend of hers who'd been in Gloria's class. Getting Gloria's attention, she posed her question.

"You knew Laura Lowell!" Gloria said with forced enthusiasm. "Amazing! I was great friends with her. I loved her parents." It was painfully obvious to Janet that Gloria was making an effort to be sociable. Her chemotherapy was no doubt leaving her nauseous.

"I thought you might," Janet said. "Everybody knew Laura."

Janet was about to excuse herself and allow Gloria to rest when she heard a rattle behind her. She turned in time to see the housekeeping man appear at the door, then immediately disappear. Fearing her presence had interrupted his schedule, Janet told Gloria she'd stop by later and went out into the hall to tell the housekeeper the room was all his. But the man had disappeared. She looked up and down the corridor. She even checked a couple of the neighboring rooms. It was as if he'd simply vanished into thin air.

Janet headed back to the nurses' station. Noticing she still had a bit of break time left, she took the elevator down to the second floor in hopes of getting a glimpse at one or more of the missing charts. Helen Cabot was still undergoing pheresis and would be for some time. Her chart was unavailable. Kathleen Sharenburg was undergoing a biopsy at that moment, and her chart was in the radiology office. With Louis Martin, Janet lucked out. His biopsy was scheduled to follow Kathleen Sharenburg's. Janet discovered him on a gurney in the hallway. He was heavily tranquilized and soundly sleeping. His chart was tucked under the gurney pad.

After checking with a technician and learning that Louis would not be biopsied for at least an hour, Janet took a chance and pulled out his chart. Walking quickly as if leaving the scene of a crime with the evidence in hand, she carried the chart into medical records. It was all she could do not to break into a full sprint. Janet admitted to herself that she was probably the worst person in the world to be involved in this kind of thing. The anxiety she'd felt in the pharmacy locker came back in a flash.

"Of course you can use the copy machine," one of the medical record librarians told her when she asked. "That's what it's here for. Just indicate nursing on the log."

Janet wondered if this librarian was the mother of the woman in public relations who'd been in Sean's apartment on the night of her arrival. She'd have to be careful. As she walked over to the copy machine, she glanced over her shoulder. The woman had gone back to the task she'd been doing when Janet had entered, paying no attention to Janet whatsoever.

Janet quickly copied Louis's entire chart. There were more pages than she would have expected, particularly since he had only been hospitalized for one day. Glancing at some of them, Janet could tell that most of the chart consisted of referral material that had come from Boston Memorial.

Finished at last, Janet hurried the chart back to the gurney. She was relieved to see that Louis had not been moved. Janet slipped the chart under the pad, positioning it exactly as she'd found it. Louis didn't stir.

Returning to the fourth floor, Janet panicked. She hadn't given any thought to what she would do with the copy of the chart. It was too big to fit into her purse, and she couldn't leave it lying about. She had to find a temporary hiding place, somewhere the other nurses and nursing assistants would not be likely to go.

With no break time left, Janet had to think fast. The last thing she wanted to do on her first day of work was take more time off than she was due. Frantically, Janet tried to think. She considered the patient lounge, but it was currently occupied. She thought of one of the lower cabinets in the pharmacy closet, but dismissed that idea as too risky. Finally she thought of the housekeeping closet.

Janet looked up and down the corridor. There were plenty of people around, but they all seemed absorbed by what they were doing. She saw the housekeeper's cart parked outside a nearby patient room, suggesting the man was busy cleaning within. Taking a breath, Janet slipped into the closet. The door with its automatic closer shut behind her instantly, plunging her into darkness. She groped for the light switch and turned it on.

The tiny room was dominated by a generous slop sink. On the wall opposite was a countertop with undercounter cabinets, a bank of shallow overcounter wall cabinets, and a broom closet. She opened the broom closet. There were a few shelves above the compartment that held the brooms and mops, but they were too exposed. Then she looked at the overcounter cabinets and her eyes kept rising.

Placing a foot on the edge of the slop sink, she climbed up atop the counter. Reaching up, she groped the area above the wall cabinets. As she'd guessed, there was a narrow depressed space between the top of the cabinets and the ceiling. Confident she'd found what she'd been looking for, she slipped the chart copy over the front lip and let it drop down. A bit of dust rose up in a cloud.

Satisfied, Janet climbed down, rinsed her hands in the sink, then emerged into the hall. If anybody had wondered what she'd been up to, they didn't give any indication. One of the other nurses passed her and smiled cheerfully.

Returning to the nurses' station, Janet threw herself into her work. After five minutes she began to calm down. After ten minutes even her pulse had returned to normal. When Marjorie appeared a few minutes later, Janet was calm enough to inquire about Helen Cabot's coded medication.

"I've been going over each of the patients' treatments," Janet said. "I want to familiarize myself with their medications so I'll be prepared for whomever I'm assigned to for the day. I saw reference to MB300C and MB303C. What are they, and where would I find them?"

Marjorie straightened up from bending over the desk. She grasped a key strung around her neck on a silver-colored chain and pulled it out in front of her. "MB medicine you get from me," she said. "We keep it in a refrigerated lockup right here in the nursing station." She pulled open a cabinet to expose a small refrigerator. "It's up to the head nurse on each shift to dispense it. We control the MBs somewhat like narcotics only a bit stricter."

"Well that explains why I couldn't find it in the pharmacy," Janet said, forcing a smile. All at once she realized that getting samples of the medicine was going to be a hundred times more difficult than she'd envisioned. In fact, she wondered if it was possible at all.

TOM WIDDICOMB was trying to calm down. He'd never felt so wired in his life. Usually his mother was able to calm him down, but now she wouldn't even talk to him.

He'd made it a point to arrive extra early that morning. He'd kept an eye on that new nurse, Janet Reardon, from the moment she'd arrived. He'd trailed her carefully, watching her every move. After tracking her for an hour, he'd decided his concerns had been unjustified. She'd acted like any other nurse so Tom had felt relieved.

But then she'd ended up in Gloria's room again! Tom could not believe it. Just when he'd let his guard down, she'd reappeared. That the same woman would thwart his attempt to relieve Gloria's suffering not once but twice went past coincidence. "Two days in a row!" Tom had hissed in the solitude of his housekeeping closet. "She's gotta be a spy!"

His only consolation was that this time he'd walked in on her rather than vice versa. Actually, it was even better than that. He'd almost walked in on her. He didn't know whether she'd seen him or not, although she probably had.

From then on he'd followed her again. With her every step he became more and more convinced she was there to get him. She was not acting like a regular nurse, no way. Not with the sneaking around she was doing. The worst was when she'd sneaked into his housekeeping closet and started opening cabinets. He could hear her from the hall. He knew what she had been looking for, and he'd been sick with worry that she'd find his stuff. As soon as she'd left, he'd stepped inside. Climbing up on the counter, he'd blindly reached up on top of the wall cabinet at the very far end in the corner to feel for his succinylcholine and syringes. Thankfully they were there and hadn't been disturbed.

After climbing down from the cabinet, Tom struggled to calm himself. He kept telling himself he was safe since the succinylcholine was still there. At least he was safe for the moment. But there was no doubt that he would have to deal with Janet Reardon, just as he'd had to deal with Sheila Arnold. He couldn't let her stop his crusade. If he did, he might risk losing Alice.

"Don't worry, Mother," Tom said aloud. "Everything will be all right."

But Alice wouldn't listen. She was scared.

After fifteen minutes, Tom felt calm enough to face the world. Taking a fortifying breath, he pulled open the door and stepped into the hall. His housekeeping cart was to his right pushed against the wall. He grabbed it and started pushing.

He kept his eyes directed at the floor as he headed toward the elevators. As he passed the nurses' station he heard Marjorie yell to him about cleaning a room.

"I've been called to administration," Tom said without looking up. Every so often if there'd been an accident, like spilled coffee, he'd be called up there to clean it up. Regular cleaning of the administration floor was handled by the night crew.

"Well, get back here on the double," Marjorie yelled.

Tom swore under his breath.

When he got to the administration floor, Tom pushed his cleaning cart directly into the main secretarial area. It was always busy there, no one ever looking at him twice. He parked his cart directly in front of the wall chart of the floor plan of the Forbes residence in southeast Miami.

There were ten apartments on each floor, and each had a little slot for a name. Tom quickly found Janet Reardon's name in the slot marked 207. Even more handy was a key box attached to the wall just below the chart. Inside were multiple sets of keys, all carefully labeled. The box was supposed to be locked, but the key to open it was always in the lock. Since the box was obscured by his cart, Tom calmly helped himself to a set for apartment 207.

To justify his presence Tom emptied a few wastebaskets before pushing his cart back to the elevators.

As he waited for an elevator to arrive he felt a wave of relief. Even Alice was willing to talk to him now. She told him how proud of him she was now that he would be able to take care of things. She told him that she'd been worried about this new nurse, Janet Reardon.

"I told you that you didn't have to worry," Tom said. "Nobody will ever bother us."

STERLING ROMBAUER had always liked the adage that his schoolteacher mother had espoused: *Chance favors the prepared mind.* Figuring there were only a limited number of hotels in Boston that Tanaka Yamaguchi would find acceptable, Sterling had decided to try calling some of the hotel employee contacts he'd cultivated over the years. His efforts had been rewarded with immediate success. Sterling smiled when he learned that not only did he and Tanaka share the same profession, they shared the same taste in hotels.

This was a felicitous turn of events. Thanks to his frequent stays at Boston's Ritz Carlton, Sterling's contacts in the hotel were simply sterling. A few discreet inquiries revealed some helpful information. First, Tanaka had hired the same livery company Sterling himself used, which wasn't surprising since it was by far the best. Second, he was scheduled to remain in the hotel at least another night. Finally, he'd made a lunch reservation in the Ritz Café for two people.

Sterling went right to work. A call to the maître d' in the café, a rather crowded, intimate environment, produced a promise that Mr. Yamaguchi's party would be seated at the far banquette. The neighboring corner table, literally inches away, would be reserved for Mr. Sterling Rombauer. A call to the owner of the livery company resulted in a promise of the name of Mr. Yamaguchi's driver as well as a transcript of his stops.

"This Jap is well connected," the owner of the livery company said when Sterling phoned him. "We picked him up from general aviation. He came in on a private jet, and it wasn't one of those dinky ones either."

A call to the airport confirmed the presence of the Sushita Gulfstream III and gave Sterling its call number. Phoning his contact at the FAA in Washington and providing the call numbers, Sterling obtained a promise to keep him informed of the jet's movements.

With so much accomplished without even leaving his hotel room and a bit of time to spare before the luncheon rendezvous, Sterling walked across Newbury Street to Burberry's to treat himself to several new shirts.

WITH HIS legs crossed and stretched out in front of him, Sean sat in one of the molded plastic chairs in the hospital cafeteria. His left elbow was resting on the table, cradling his chin; his right arm dangled over the back of the chair.

Mood-wise, he was in approximately the same state of mind as he'd been the night before when Janet had come through his living-room slider. The morning had been an aggravating rerun of the previous day, confirming his belief that the Forbes was a bizarre and largely unfriendly place to work. Hiroshi was still trailing him like a bad detective. Practically every time Sean turned around when he was up on the sixth floor using some equipment not available on the fifth, he'd see the Japanese fellow. And the moment Sean looked at him, Hiroshi would quickly look away as if Sean were a moron and wouldn't know that Hiroshi had been watching him.

Sean checked his watch. The agreement had been that he'd meet Janet at twelve-thirty. It was already twelve-thirty-five, and although a steady stream of hospital personnel continued to pour by, Janet had yet to appear. Sean began to fantasize about going down to the parking lot, getting into his Isuzu, and hitting the road. But then Janet came through the door, and just seeing her lightened his mood.

Although Janet was still pale by Florida standards, her few days in Miami had already given a distinctively rosy cast to her skin. Sean thought she'd never looked better. As he admiringly watched her sensuous movements as she weaved through the tables, he hoped that he'd be able to talk her out of whatever it was that was keeping her in her own apartment and out of his.

She took the seat across from him, barely saying hello. Under her arm she clutched an unfolded Miami newspaper. He could tell she was nervous, the way she continually scanned the room like some wary, vulnerable bird.

"Janet, we're not in some spy movie," Sean said. "Calm down!"

"But I feel like I am," Janet said. "I've been sneaking

around, going behind people's backs, trying not to arouse suspicion. But I feel like everyone knows what I'm doing."

Sean rolled his eyes. "What an amateur I have for an accomplice," he joked. Then, more seriously, he added, "I don't know whether this is going to work if you're stressed out now, Janet. This is only the beginning. You haven't even done anything yet compared to what's coming. But, to tell you the truth, I'm jealous. At least you're doing something. I, on the other hand, have spent a good part of the morning in the bowels of the earth injecting mice with the Forbes protein plus Freund's adjuvant. There's been no intrigue and certainly no excitement. This place is still driving me nuts."

"What about your crystals?" Janet asked.

"I'm deliberately slowing down on that," Sean said. "I was doing too well. I won't let them know how far I've gotten. That way, when I need some time for some investigative work, I'll take it and still be able to have results to show as a cover. So how'd you do?"

"Not great," Janet admitted. "But I made a start. I copied one chart."

"Just one?" Sean questioned with obvious disappointment. "You're this nervous about one chart?"

"Don't give me a hard time," Janet warned. "This isn't easy for me."

"And I'd never say I told you so," Sean quipped. "Never. Not me. That's not my style."

"Oh, shut up," Janet said as she handed the newspaper to Sean under the table. "I'm doing the best I can."

Sean lifted the newspaper and placed it on top of the table. He spread it out and opened it, exposing the copied pages which he immediately removed. He pushed the newspaper aside.

"Sean!" Janet gasped, as she furtively scanned the crowded room. "Can't you be a little more subtle?"

"I'm tired of being subtle," he said. He started going through the chart.

"Even for my benefit?" Janet asked. "There might be some people from my floor here. They might have seen me give these copies to you."

"You give people too much credit," Sean said distractedly. "People aren't as observant as you might think." Then, referring to the copies Janet had brought, he said, "Louis Martin's chart is nothing but referral material from the Memorial. This history and physical is mine. That lazy ass on neurology just copied my workup."

"How can you tell?" Janet asked.

"The wording," Sean said. "Listen to this: the patient 'suffered through' a prostatectomy three months ago. I use expressions like 'suffered through' just to see who reads my workups and who doesn't. It's a little game I play with myself. No one else uses that kind of phraseology in a medical workup. You're supposed to just give facts, not judgments."

"Imitation is the highest form of flattery, so I guess you should be flattered," Janet said.

"The only thing of interest here is in the orders," Sean said. "He's being given two coded drugs: MB300M and MB305M."

"That code is comparable to the one I saw in Helen Cabot's computer file," Janet said. She handed him the paper on which she'd written the treatment information she'd gotten from the computer.

Sean glanced at the dosage and the administration rate.

"What do you think it is?" Janet asked.

"No idea," Sean said. "Did you get any of it?"

"Not yet," Janet admitted. "But I finally located the supply. It's kept in a special locker, and the shift supervisor has the only key."

"This is interesting," Sean said, still studying the chart. "From the date and time of the order they started treatment as soon as he got here."

"Same with Helen Cabot," Janet said. She told him what Marjorie had explained to her, namely that they started the humoral aspect of the treatment immediately whereas the cellular aspect didn't begin until after the biopsy and T-cell harvesting.

"Starting treatment so soon seems odd," Sean said. "Unless these drugs are merely lymphokines or some other general immunologic stimulant. It can't be some new drug, like a new type of chemo agent."

"Why not?" Janet asked.

"Because the FDA would have had to approve it," Sean said. "It has to be a drug that's already been approved. How come you only got Louis Martin's chart? What about Helen Cabot's?"

"I was lucky to get Martin's," Janet said. "Cabot is getting pheresed as we speak, and the other young woman, Kathleen Sharenburg, is being biopsied. Martin was a 'to follow' for his biopsy so his chart was available."

"So these people are on the second floor right now?" Sean asked. "Right above us?"

"I believe so," Janet said.

"Maybe I'll skip lunch and take a walk up there," Sean said. "With all the usual commotion in most diagnostic and treatment areas, the charts are usually just kicking around. I could probably get a look at them."

"Better you than me," Janet said. "I'm sure you're better at this than I."

"I'm not taking over your job," Sean said. "I'll still want copies of the other two charts as well as daily updates. Plus I want a list of all the patients they've treated to date who have had medulloblastoma. I'm particularly interested in their outcomes. Plus I want samples of the coded medicine. That should be your priority. I have to have that medicine; the sooner the better."

"I'll do my best," Janet said. Knowing how much trouble it had been merely to copy Martin's chart, she had misgivings about getting everything Sean wanted with the kind of speed he was implying. Not that she was about to voice those concerns to Sean. She was afraid he'd give up and leave for Boston.

Sean stood up. He gripped Janet's shoulder. "I know this isn't easy for you," he said. "But remember, it was your idea."

Janet put a hand on Sean's. "We can do it," she said.

"I'll see you at the Cow Palace," he said. "I suppose you'll be there around four. I'll try to get back about the same time."

"See you then," Janet said.

Sean left the cafeteria and used the stairs to get to the second floor. He emerged at the south end of the building. The second floor was a center of activity and as bustling as he'd expected. All the radiation therapy as well as diagnostic radiology was done there; so was all the surgery and any treatment that could not be done at the bedside.

With all the confusion Sean had to squeeze between gurneys carrying people to and from their procedures. A number of the gurneys with their human passengers were parked along the walls. Other patients sat on benches dressed in hospital robes.

Sean excused himself and pushed through the tumult,

bumping into hospital personnel as well as ambulatory patients. With a modicum of difficulty he proceeded down the central corridor, checking each door as he went. Radiology and chemistry were on the left, treatment rooms, ICU, and the surgical suites were on the right. Knowing that the pheresis was a long procedure and not labor-intensive, Sean decided to try to find Helen Cabot. Besides looking at her chart, he wanted to say hello.

Spotting a hematology technician sporting rubber tourniquets attached to her belt loops, Sean asked her where pheresis was done. The woman guided Sean through a side corridor and pointed toward two rooms. Sean thanked her and checked the first. A male patient was on the gurney. Sean closed the door and opened the other. Even from the threshold he recognized the patient: it was Helen Cabot.

She was the only one there. Outflow and inflow lines were attached to her left arm as her blood was being passed through a machine that separated the elements, isolating the lymphocytes and returning the rest of the blood to her body.

Helen turned her bandaged head in Sean's direction. She recognized him immediately and tried to smile. Instead, tears formed in her large green eyes.

From her color and general appearance Sean could see that her condition had dramatically worsened. The seizures she'd been suffering had been taking a heavy toll.

"It's good to see you," Sean said as he bent down to bring his face close to hers. He resisted an urge to hold and comfort her. "How are you doing?"

"It's been difficult," Helen managed to say. "I had another biopsy yesterday. It wasn't fun. They also warned me I might get worse when they started the treatment, and I have. They told me I was not to lose faith. But it's been hard. My headaches have been unbearable. It even hurts to talk."

"You have to hold on," Sean said. "Keep remembering that they have put every medulloblastoma patient into remission."

"That's what I keep reminding myself," Helen said.

"I'll try to come to see you every day," Sean said. "Meanwhile, where's your chart?"

"I think it's out in the waiting room," Helen said, pointing with her free hand toward a second door.

Sean gave her a warm smile. He squeezed her shoulder, then stepped into the small waiting room that connected to the corridor. On a counter was what he was searching for: Helen's chart.

Sean picked it up and flipped to the order sheets. Drugs similar to those he'd seen in Martin's chart were duly noted: MB300C and MB303C. He then turned to the beginning of the chart and saw a copy of his own workup which had been sent as part of the referral package.

Flipping the pages quickly, Sean came to the progress note section, and he read the entry for the biopsy that had been taken the day before, indicating they had gone in over the right ear. The note went on to say that the patient had tolerated the procedure well.

Sean had just begun to scan for the laboratory section to see if a frozen section had been done when he was interrupted. The door to the hallway crashed open and slammed against the wall with such force that the doorknob dented the plaster.

The sudden crash startled Sean. He dropped the chart onto the plastic laminate countertop. In front of him and filling the entire doorway was the formidable figure of Margaret Richmond. Sean recognized her immediately as the nursing director who'd burst into Dr. Mason's office. Apparently the woman made a habit of such dramatic entries.

"What are you doing in here?" she demanded. "And what are you doing with that chart?" Her broad, round face was distorted with outrage.

Sean toyed with the idea of giving her a flip answer, but he thought better of it.

"I'm looking in on a friend," Sean said. "Miss Cabot was a patient of mine in Boston."

"You have no right to her chart," Ms. Richmond blustered. "Patients' charts are confidential documents, available only to the patient and his doctors. We view our responsibility in this regard very seriously."

"I'm confident the patient would be willing to give me access," Sean said. "Perhaps we should step into the next room and ask her."

"You are not here as a clinical fellow," Ms. Richmond shouted, ignoring Sean's suggestion. "You are here in a research capacity only. Your arrogance in thinking that you have a right to invade this hospital is inexcusable."

Sean saw a familiar face appear over Ms. Richmond's intimidating shoulder. It was the puffy, smug countenance of the frustrated Marine, Robert Harris. Sean suddenly guessed what had happened. Undoubtedly he'd been picked up by one of the surveillance cameras, probably one in the second-floor corridor. Harris had called Richmond and then had come over to watch the slaughter.

Knowing that Robert Harris was involved, Sean could no longer resist the urge to lash back, particularly since Ms. Richmond wasn't responding to his attempts to be reasonable.

"Since you people aren't in the mood to discuss this like adults," Sean said, "I think I'll wander back to the research building."

"Your impertinence only makes matters worse," Ms.

Richmond sputtered. "You're trespassing, invading privacy, and showing no remorse. I'm surprised the governors of Harvard University would let someone like you into their institution."

"I'll let you in on a secret," Sean said. "They weren't all that impressed with my manners. They liked my facility with a puck. Now, I'd really like to stay and chat with you people, but I've got to get back to my murine friends who, by the way, have more pleasant personalities than most of the staff here at Forbes."

Sean watched as Ms. Richmond's face empurpled. This was just one more of a series of ridiculous episodes that had him fed up. Consequently he derived perverse pleasure out of goading and angering this woman who could easily have played linebacker for the Miami Dolphins.

"Get out of here before I call the police," Ms. Richmond yelled.

Sean thought that calling the police would be interesting. He could just imagine some poor uniformed rookie trying to figure out how to categorize Sean's offense. Sean could see it in the paper: Harvard extern actually looks into his patient's chart!

Sean stepped forward, literally eye to eye with Ms. Richmond. He smiled, pouring on his old charm. "I know you'll miss me," he said, "but I really must go."

Both Ms. Richmond and Harris followed him all the way to the pedestrian bridge that spanned the gulf between the hospital and the research building. The whole time they maintained a loud dialogue about the degeneracy of current-day youth. Sean had the feeling he was being run out of town.

As Sean walked across the bridge he recognized how much he would have to depend on Janet for clinical material pertaining to the medulloblastoma study, provided, of course, he stayed.

Returning to his fifth-floor lab, Sean tried to lose himself in his work to repress the anger and frustration he felt toward the ridiculous situation he found himself in. Like the empty room upstairs, Helen's chart didn't have anything in it to get upset about. But as he cooled down, Sean was able to acknowledge that Ms. Richmond did have a point. As much as he hated to admit it, the Forbes was a private hospital. It wasn't a teaching hospital like the Boston Memorial, where teaching and patient care went hand in hand. Here, Helen's chart was confidential. Yet even if it was, Ms. Richmond's fury was hardly appropriate for his infraction.

In spite of himself, within an hour Sean became engrossed in his crystal-growing attempts. Then, as he held a flask up against the overhead light, he caught a bit of movement out of the corner of his eye. It was a rerun of the incident on his first day. Once again the movement had come from the direction of the stairwell.

Without so much as looking in the direction of the stairwell, Sean calmly got off his stool and walked into the storeroom as if he needed some supplies. Since the storeroom was connected to the central corridor, Sean was able to dash the length of the building to the stairwell opposite the one where he'd seen the movement.

Racing down a flight, he ran the length of the fourth floor to enter the opposite stairwell. Moving as silently as possible, he climbed the stairs until the fifth-floor landing came into view. As he'd suspected, Hiroshi was there furtively looking through the glass of the door, obviously baffled as to why Sean had not returned from the storeroom.

Sean tiptoed up the remaining stairs until he was standing directly behind Hiroshi. Then he screamed as loud as he was able. Within the confines of the stairwell, Sean was impressed with the amount of noise he was capable of generating.

Having seen a few Chuck Norris martial arts movies, Sean had been a little concerned that Hiroshi might turn into a karate demon by reflex. But instead Hiroshi practically collapsed. Conveniently he'd had one hand on the door handle. It was that support which kept him standing.

When Hiroshi recovered enough to comprehend what had happened, he stepped away from the door and started to mumble an explanation. But he was backing up at the same time, and when his foot hit the riser of the first stair, he turned and fled up, disappearing from view.

Disgusted, Sean followed, not to pursue Hiroshi, but rather to seek out Deborah Levy. Sean had had enough of Hiroshi's spying. He thought Dr. Levy would be the best person to discuss the matter with since she ran the lab.

Going directly to the seventh floor, Sean walked down to Dr. Levy's office. The door was ajar. He looked in. The office was empty.

The pool secretaries did not have any idea of her whereabouts but suggested Sean have her paged. Instead, Sean went down to the sixth floor and sought out Mark Halpern, who was dressed as nattily as ever in his spotless white apron. Sean guessed he washed and ironed the apron every day.

"I'm looking for Dr. Levy," Sean said irritably.

"She's not here today," Mark said. "Is there something I can help you with?"

"Will she be here later?" Sean asked.

"Not today," Mark said. "She had to go to Atlanta. She travels a lot for work."

"When will she be back?"

"I'm not sure," Mark said. "Probably tomorrow late. She said something about going to our Key West facility on her way back."

"Does she spend much time there?" Sean asked.

"Fair amount," Mark said. "Several Ph.D.s who'd originally been here at Forbes were supposed to go to Key West, but they left instead. Their absence left Dr. Levy with a burden. She's had to pick up the slack. I think Forbes is having trouble replacing them."

"Tell her I'd like to talk to her when she comes back," Sean said. He wasn't interested in the Forbes's recruiting problems.

"Are you sure there's nothing I can do?" Mark said.

For a second Sean toyed with the idea of talking with Mark about Hiroshi's behavior, but decided against it. He had to speak to someone in authority. There wasn't anything Mark would be able to do.

Frustrated that he could get no satisfaction for his anger, Sean started back toward his lab. He was almost to the stairwell door when he thought of another question for Mark.

Returning to his tiny office, Sean asked the tech if the pathologists over in the hospital cooperated with the research staff.

"On occasion," Mark said. "Dr. Barton Friedburg has coauthored a number of research papers that require a pathologic interpretation."

"What kind of guy is he?" Sean asked. "Friendly or unfriendly? Seems to me that people fall into one camp or the other around here."

"Definitely friendly," Mark said. "Besides, I think you might be confusing unfriendly with being serious and preoccupied."

"You think I could call him up and ask him a few questions?" Sean asked. "Is he that friendly?"

"Absolutely," Mark said.

Sean went down to his lab, and using the phone in the glass-enclosed office so he could sit at a desk, he phoned Dr. Friedburg. He took it as an auspicious sign when the pathologist came on the line directly.

Sean explained who he was and that he was interested in the findings of a biopsy done the day before on Helen Cabot.

"Hold the line," Dr. Friedburg said. Sean could hear him talking with someone else in the lab. "We didn't get any biopsy from a Helen Cabot," he said, coming back.

"But I know she had it done yesterday," Sean said.

"It went south to Basic Diagnostics," Dr. Friedburg said. "You'll have to call there if you want any information on it. That sort of thing doesn't come through this lab at all."

"Who should I ask for?" Sean asked.

"Dr. Levy," Dr. Friedburg said. "Ever since Paul and Roger left, she's been running the show down there. I don't know who she has reading the specimens now, but it's not us."

Sean hung up the phone. Nothing about Forbes seemed to be easy. He certainly wasn't about to ask Dr. Levy about Helen Cabot. She'd know what he was up to in a flash, especially after she heard from Ms. Richmond about his looking at Helen's chart.

Sean sighed as he looked down at the work he was doing trying to grow crystals with the Forbes protein. He felt like throwing it all into the sink.

For Janet, the afternoon seemed to pass quickly. With patients coming and going for therapy and diagnostic tests, there was the constant tactical problem of organizing it all. In addition, there were complicated treatment protocols that required precise timing and dosage. But during this feverish activity Janet was able to observe the way patients were divided among the staff. Without much finagling she was able to arrange to be the nurse assigned to take care of Helen Cabot, Louis Martin, and Kathleen Sharenburg the following day.

Although she didn't handle them herself, she did get to see the containers the coded drugs came in when the nurses in charge of the medulloblastoma patients for the day got the vials from Marjorie. Once they'd received them, the nurses took them into the pharmacy closet to load the respective syringes. The MB300 drug was in a 10cc injectable bottle while the MB303 was in a smaller 5cc bottle. There was nothing special about these containers. They were the same containers many other injectable drugs were packaged in.

It was customary for everyone to have a mid-afternoon as well as a mid-morning break. Janet used hers to go back down to medical records. Once there she used the same ploy she'd used with Tim. She told one of the librarians, a young woman by the name of Melanie Brock, that she was new on the staff and that she was interested in learning the Forbes system. She said she was familiar with computers, but she could use some help. The librarian was impressed with Janet's interest and was more than happy to show her their filing format, using the medical records' access code.

Left on her own after Melanie's introduction, Janet called up all patients with the T-9872 designator which she'd used to pull up current medulloblastoma cases on the ward's work station. This time, Janet got a different list. Here there were thirty-eight cases on record over the last ten years. This list did not include the five cases currently in the hospital.

Sensing a recent increase, Janet asked the computer to graph the number of cases against the years. In a graph form, the results were rather striking.

LOOKING AT the graph, Janet noted that over the first eight years there had been five medulloblastoma cases, whereas during the last two years there had been thirty-three. She

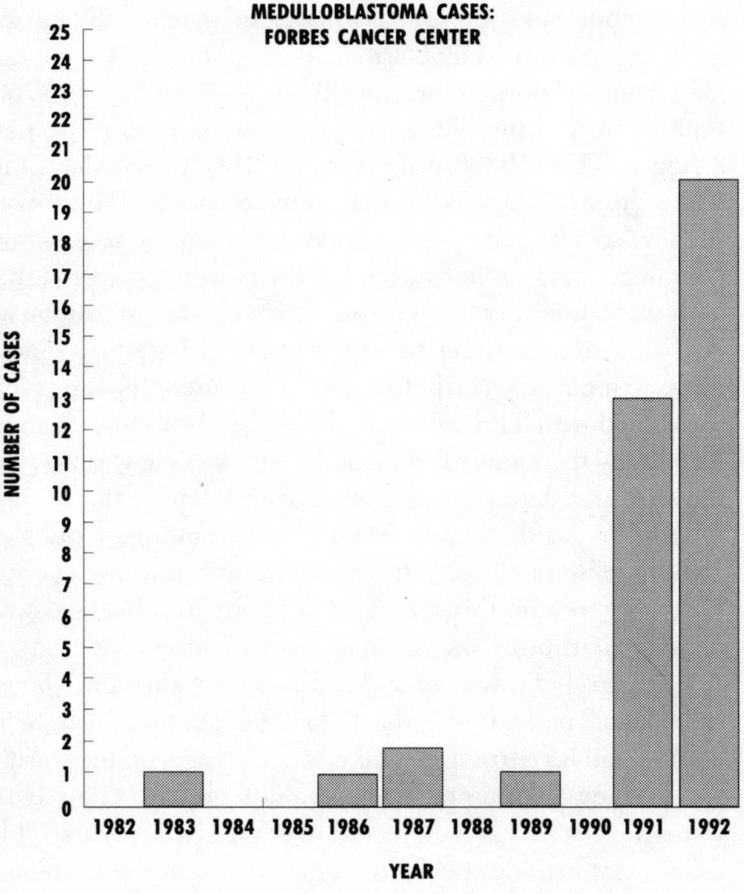

found the increase curious until she remembered that it had been in the last two years that the Forbes had had such success with its treatment. Success sparked referrals. Surely that accounted for the influx.

Curious about the demographics, Janet called up a breakdown by age and sex. Sex showed a preponderance of males in the last thirty-three cases: twenty-six males and seven females. In the earlier five cases there had been three females and two males.

When she looked at ages, Janet noted that in the first five cases there was one twenty-year-old. The other four were below the age of ten. Among the recent thirty-three cases Janet saw that seven cases were below the age of ten, two between the ages of ten and twenty, and the remaining twenty-four were over twenty years of age.

Concerning outcome, Janet noted that all of the original five had died within two years of diagnosis. Three had died within months. In the most recent thirty-three, the impact of the new therapy was dramatically apparent. All thirty-three patients were currently alive, although only three of them were nearing two years after diagnosis.

Hastily, Janet wrote all this information down to give to Sean.

Next Janet randomly picked out a name from the list. The name was Donald Maxwell. She called up his file. As she went through the information, she saw that it was rather abbreviated. She even found a notation that said: *Consult physical chart if further information is needed.*

Janet had become so absorbed in her investigative work, she was shocked when she glanced at her watch. She'd used up her coffee break and then some, just as she had that morning.

Quickly she had the computer print out a list of the

thirty-eight cases with their ages, sexes, and hospital numbers. Nervously, she went over to the laser printer as the sheet emerged. Turning from the printer, she half expected to find someone standing behind her, demanding an explanation. But no one seemed to have taken notice of her activities.

Before heading back to her floor, Janet sought out Melanie for one quick and final question. She found her at the copy machine.

"How do I go about getting the hospital chart of a discharged patient?" Janet asked.

"You ask one of us," Melanie said. "All you have to do is provide us with a copy of your authorization, which in your case would come from the nursing department. Then it takes about ten minutes. We keep the charts in the basement in a storage vault that runs beneath both buildings. It's an efficient system. We need access to them for patient care purposes, like when the patients come for outpatient care. Over in administration they need access to them for billing and actuarial purposes. The charts come up on dumbwaiters." Melanie pointed to the small glass-fronted elevator set into the wall.

Janet thanked Melanie, then hurried out to the elevator. She was disappointed about the authorization issue. She couldn't imagine how she would arrange that without completely giving herself away. She hoped Sean would have an idea.

As she pressed the elevator button impatiently, Janet wondered if she would have to apologize for again extending her break. She knew she couldn't keep doing it. It wasn't fair, and Marjorie was bound to complain.

STERLING WAS extremely pleased with the way the day was proceeding. He had to smile to himself as he rose up in the paneled elevator of the Franklin Bank's home office on Federal Street in Boston. It had been a sublime day with minimal effort and maximum gain. And the fact that he was being handsomely compensated for enjoying himself made it all that much more rewarding.

The luncheon at the Ritz had been heavenly, especially since the maître d' had been accommodating enough to bring a white Meursault down from the main dining room wine cellar. Sitting as close as he had to Tanaka and his guest, Sterling had been able to hear most of their conversation from behind his *Wall Street Journal.*

Tanaka's guest was a personnel executive from Immunotherapy. Since the buyout, Genentech had left the company largely intact. Sterling did not know how much money was in the plain white envelope that Tanaka had placed on the table, but he did notice that the personnel executive had slipped it into his jacket in the blink of an eye.

The information Sterling overheard was interesting. Sean and the other founding partners had sold Immunotherapy in order to raise capital for a totally new venture. Tanaka's informer wasn't one hundred percent certain, but it was his understanding that the new company would also be a biotechnology firm. He couldn't tell Tanaka its name or its proposed product line.

The gentleman knew there had been a holdup in forming the new company when Sean and his partners realized they would be undercapitalized. The reason he knew this was because he'd been approached to move to the new company and he'd agreed, only to be informed that there would be a delay until sufficient funds could be raised. From the sound of the gentleman's voice at this juncture, Sterling understood that the delay had engendered significant ill will between him and the new management.

The final bit of information that the gentleman had delivered was the name of the bank executive at the Franklin who was in charge of the negotiation of the loan for additional start-up capital. Sterling was acquainted with a number of people at the Franklin, but Herbert Devonshire was not one of them. But that was soon to change since it was Herbert whom Sterling was presently on his way to see.

The luncheon had also afforded Sterling an opportunity to observe Tanaka up close. Knowing a considerable amount about the Japanese character and culture, particularly in relation to business, Sterling was fascinated by Tanaka's performance. Flawlessly deferential and respectful, it would have been impossible for an uninitiated American to pick up the clues that suggested Tanaka clearly despised his lunch companion. But Sterling immediately discerned the subtle signs.

There'd been no way for Sterling to eavesdrop on Tanaka's meeting with Herbert Devonshire. Sterling had not even considered it. But he wanted to know its location so that he would be able to suggest he did know the content when he spoke to Mr. Devonshire. Accordingly, Sterling had the limousine company's president order Tanaka's driver to call it in to him. The president had then relayed the information to Sterling's driver.

After being tipped off, Sterling had entered City Side, a popular bar in the south building of Faneuil Hall Market. There'd been a chance Tanaka might recognize him from lunch, but Sterling had decided to risk it. He wouldn't be getting too close. He'd observed Tanaka and Devonshire from afar, noting their location in the bar and what they ordered. He also noted the time Tanaka had excused himself to make a call.

Armed with this information, Sterling had felt confident confronting Devonshire. He'd been able to get an appointment for that afternoon.

After a brief wait that he judged was designed to impress him with Mr. Devonshire's busy schedule, Sterling was shown into the banker's imposing office. The view was to the north and east, commanding a spectacular vista over the Boston Harbor as well as Logan International Airport in East Boston and the Mystic River Bridge arching over to Chelsea.

Mr. Devonshire was a small man with a shiny bald pate, wire-rimmed glasses, and conservative dress. He stood up behind his antique partner's desk to shake hands with Sterling. He couldn't have been over five feet five by Sterling's estimation.

Sterling handed the man one of his business cards. They both sat down. Mr. Devonshire positioned the card in the center of his blotter and aligned it perfectly parallel with the blotter's borders. Then he folded his hands.

"It's a pleasure to meet you, Mr. Rombauer," Herbert said, leveling his beady eyes at Sterling. "What can the Franklin do for you today?"

"It's not the Franklin I'm interested in," Sterling said. "It's you, Mr. Devonshire. I'd like to establish a business relationship with you."

"Our motto has always been personal service," Herbert said.

"I shall come directly to the point," Sterling said. "I'm willing to form a confidential partnership with you for our mutual benefit. There is information I need and information your superiors should not know."

Herbert Devonshire swallowed. Otherwise, he didn't move.

Sterling leaned forward to bring his eyes to bear on Herbert. "The facts are simple. You met with a Mr. Tanaka Yamaguchi this afternoon at the City Side Bar, not the usual business location, I'd venture to say. You ordered a vodka gimlet and then gave Mr. Yamaguchi some information, a service that while not illegal, is of questionable ethics. A short time later a sizable portion of the monies Sushita Industries keeps on deposit at the Bank of Boston was wire-transferred to the Franklin with you designated as the private banker involved."

Herbert's face blanched at Sterling's words.

"I have an extensive network of contacts throughout the business world," Sterling said. He settled back in his chair. "I'd very much like to add you to this intimate, very anonymous, but stellar network. I'm certain we can provide each other with useful information as time goes by. So the question is, would you care to join? The only obligation is that you never, ever, disclose the source of any information I pass on to you."

"And if I choose not to join?" Herbert asked, his voice raspy.

"I will pass on the information about you and Mr. Yamaguchi to people here at the Franklin who have some minor say in your future."

"This is blackmail," Herbert said.

"I call it free trade," Sterling said. "And as for your initiation fee, I would like to hear exactly what you told Mr. Yamaguchi about a mutual acquaintance, Sean Murphy."

"This is outrageous," Herbert said.

"Please," Sterling warned. "Let's not allow this conversation to dissolve into mere posturing. The fact is, your behavior was outrageous, Mr. Devonshire. What I am asking is a small price to pay for the benefits you will accrue from landing such a customer as Sushita Industries. And I can guarantee I will be useful to you in the future."

"I gave very little information," Herbert said. "Entirely inconsequential."

"If it makes you more comfortable to believe that, that's fine," Sterling said.

There was a pause. The two men stared at each other across the expanse of antique mahogany. Sterling was happy to wait.

"All I said was that Mr. Murphy and a few associates were borrowing money to start a new company," Herbert said. "I gave no figures whatsoever."

"The name of the new company?" Sterling asked.

"Oncogen," Herbert said.

"And the proposed product line?" Sterling asked.

"Cancer-related health products," Herbert said. "Both diagnostic and therapeutic."

"Time frame?"

"Imminent," Herbert said. "Within the next few months."

"Anything else?" Sterling asked. "I should add that I have ways of checking this information."

"No," Herbert said. His voice had developed an edge.

"If I learn you've deliberately prevaricated," Sterling warned, "the result will be as if you refused to cooperate."

"I have more appointments," Herbert said tersely.

Sterling stood up. "I know it is irritating to have your hand forced," he said. "But remember, I feel indebted and I always repay. Call me."

Sterling took the elevator down to the ground floor and hurried over to his sedan. The driver had locked the doors and had fallen asleep. Sterling had to thump on the window to get him to release the rear locks. Once inside, Sterling called his contact at the FAA. "I'm on a portable phone," he warned his friend.

"The bird's scheduled to leave in the morning," the man said.

"What destination?"

"Miami," the man said. Then he added: "I sure wish I was going."

"WELL, WHAT do you think?" Janet asked as Sean poked his head into the bedroom. Janet had brought Sean out to Miami Beach to see the apartment she'd rented.

"I think it's perfect," he said, looking back into the living room. "I'm not sure I could take these colors for long, but it does look like Florida." The walls were bright yellow, the rug was Kelly green. The furniture was white wicker with tropical floral print cushions.

"It's only for a couple of months," Janet said. "Come in the bathroom and look at the ocean."

"There it is!" Sean said as he peered through the slats of the jalousie window. "At least I can say I've seen it." A narrow wedge of ocean was visible between two buildings. Since it was after seven and the sun had already set, the water looked more gray than blue in the gathering darkness.

"The kitchen's not bad either," Janet said.

Sean followed her, then watched as she opened cabinets and showed him the dishes and glassware. She'd changed out of her nurse's uniform and had on her tank top and shorts. Sean found Janet incredibly sexy, particularly when she was so scantily clad. Sean felt himself at a distinct disadvantage with the way she was dressed, especially as she bent over showing him the pots and pans. It was difficult to think.

"I'll be able to cook," she said, straightening up.

"Wonderful," Sean said, but his mind was concerned with other basic appetites.

They moved back into the living room.

"Hey, I'm ready to move in tonight," Sean said. "I love it."

"Hold on," Janet said. "I hope I haven't given you the impression we're moving in together just like that. We've got some serious talking to do. That's the whole reason I came down here."

"Well, first we have to get going on this medulloblastoma thing," Sean said.

"I didn't think the two issues would be mutually exclusive," Janet said.

"I didn't mean to imply that they were," Sean said. "It's just that it's hard for me at the moment to think about much beyond my role here at Forbes and whether I should stay. The situation is kind of dominating my mind. I think it's pretty understandable."

Janet rolled her eyes.

"Besides, I'm starved," Sean said. He smiled. "You know I can never talk when I'm hungry."

"I'll be patient to a point," Janet conceded. "But I don't want you to forget I need some serious communicating. Now, as far as dinner is concerned, the real estate person told me there's a popular Cuban restaurant just up Collins Avenue."

"Cuban?" Sean questioned.

"I know you rarely venture from your meat and potatoes," Janet said. "But while we're in Miami we can be a bit more adventuresome."

"Groan," Sean murmured.

The restaurant was close enough to walk so they left Sean's 4×4 where they'd found a parking spot across from the apartment. Walking hand in hand, they wandered north up Collins Avenue beneath huge silver- and gold-tipped clouds that reflected the reddened sky over the distant Everglades. They couldn't see the ocean, but they could hear the waves hit against the beach on the other side of a block of recently renovated and refurbished Miami art deco buildings.

The entire beach neighborhood was alive with people strolling up and down the streets, sitting on steps or porches, roller blading, or cruising in their cars. Some of the car stereos had the bass pumped up to a point that Sean and Janet could feel the vibration in their chests as the cars thumped past.

"Those guys aren't going to have functional middle ears by the time they're thirty," Sean commented.

The restaurant gave the impression of frenzied disorganization with tables and people crammed everywhere. The waiters and waitresses were dressed in black pants or skirts and white shirts or blouses. Each had on a soiled apron. They ranged in age from twenty to sixty. Shouting back and forth, they communicated among themselves and to the steam table in expressive bursts of Spanish while they ran and weaved among the tables. Over the entire tumult hung a succulent aroma of roast pork, garlic, and dark roasted coffee.

Carried along by a current of people, Sean and Janet found themselves squeezed among other diners at a large table. Frosted bottles of Corona with lime wedges stuck in their mouths appeared as if by magic.

"There's nothing on here for me to eat," Sean complained after studying the menu for a few minutes. Janet was right; he rarely varied his diet.

"Nonsense," Janet said. She did the ordering.

Sean was pleasantly surprised when their food came. The marinated and heavily garlic-flavored roast pork was delicious, as was the yellow rice and the black beans covered with chopped onions. The only thing he didn't care for was the yucca.

"This stuff tastes like potato covered with mucoid exudate," Sean yelled.

"Gross!" Janet exclaimed. "Stop sounding so much like a medical student."

Conversation was almost impossible in the raucous restaurant, so after dinner they wandered over to Ocean Drive and ventured into Lummus Park where they could talk. They sat under a broad banyan tree and gazed out at the dark ocean dotted with the lights of merchant ships and pleasure boats.

"Hard to believe it's still winter in Boston," Sean said.

"It makes me wonder why we put up with slush and freezing rain," Janet said. "But enough small talk. If, as you said, you can't talk about us for the moment, then let's talk about the Forbes situation. Was your afternoon any better than your morning?"

Sean gave a short, mirthless laugh. "It was worse," he said. "I wasn't on the second floor for five minutes before the director of nursing burst into the room like a raging bull, yelling and screaming because I was looking at Helen's chart."

"Margaret Richmond was mad?" Janet asked.

Sean nodded. "All two hundred and fifty snarling pounds of her. She was out of control."

"She's always been civil with me," Janet said.

"I've only seen her twice," Sean said. "Neither time would I describe her as civil."

"How did she know you were there?" Janet asked.

"The Marine commando was with her," Sean said. "They must have picked me up on a surveillance camera."

"Oh, great!" Janet said. "Something else I have to worry about. I never thought of surveillance cameras."

"You don't have to worry," Sean said. "I'm the one who the head of security can't abide. Besides, the cameras are most likely only in the common areas, not patient floors."

"Did you get to talk with Helen Cabot?" Janet asked.

"For a moment," Sean said. "She doesn't look good at all."

"Her condition's been deteriorating," Janet said. "There's talk of doing a shunt. Did you learn anything from her chart?"

"No," Sean said. "I didn't have time. They literally chased me back over the bridge to the research building. Then, as if to cap off the afternoon, that Japanese guy appeared again, sneaking around, watching me in the lab from the stairwell. I don't know what his story is, but this time I got him. I scared the living willies out of him by sneaking up behind him and letting out this bloodcurdling yell. He nearly dropped his pants."

"The poor fellow," Janet said.

"Poor fellow nothing!" Sean said. "This guy's been watching me since I arrived."

"Well, I've had some luck," Janet said.

Sean brightened. "Really! Great! Did you get some of the miracle medicine?"

"No, no medicine," Janet said. She reached into her pocket and pulled out the computer printout and the sheet with her hastily scribbled notes. "But here's the list of all the medulloblastoma patients for the last ten years: thirty-eight in all; thirty-three in the past two years. I've summarized the data on the sheet."

Sean eagerly took the papers. But to read them he had to

hold it over his head to catch the light coming from the streetlights along Ocean Drive. As he looked it over, Janet explained what she'd learned about the sex and age distribution. She also told him that the computer files were abridged and that there had been a notation to consult the charts themselves for more information. Finally, she told him what Melanie had said about obtaining those charts in as little as ten minutes providing, of course, you had the proper authorization.

"I'll need the charts," Sean said. "Are they right there in medical records?"

"No." Janet explained what Melanie had said about the chart storage vaults extending beneath both buildings.

"No kidding," Sean said. "That might be rather handy."

"What do you mean?" Janet asked.

"It means that I might be able to get to them from the research building," Sean said. "After the episode today, it's pretty clear I'm persona non grata in the hospital. This way I can attempt to get at those charts without running afoul of Ms. Richmond and company."

"You're thinking of breaking into the storage vault?" Janet asked with alarm.

"I kinda doubt they'd leave the door open for me," Sean said.

"But that's going too far," Janet said. "If you did that, you'd be breaking the law, not just a hospital rule."

"I warned you about this," Sean said.

"You said we'd have to break rules, not the law," Janet reminded him.

"Let's not get into semantics," Sean said with exasperation.

"But there's a big difference," Janet said.

"Laws are codified rules," Sean said. "I knew we'd get

around to breaking the law in some form or fashion, and I thought you did too. But, be that as it may, don't you think we're justified? These Forbes people have obviously developed a very effective treatment for medulloblastoma. Unfortunately, they have chosen to be secretive about it, obviously so they can patent their treatment before anyone else catches on. You know, this is what bugs me about the private funding of medical research. The goal becomes a return on investment instead of the public interest. The public weal is in second place if it is considered at all. This treatment for medulloblastoma undoubtedly has implications for all cancers, but the public is being denied that information. Never mind that most of the basic science these private labs base their work on was obtained through public funds at academic institutions. These private places just take. They don't give. The public gets cheated in the process."

"Ends never justify means," Janet said.

"Go ahead and be self-righteous," Sean said. "Meanwhile, you're forgetting this whole thing was your idea. Well, maybe we should give up, and maybe I should go back to Boston and get something done on my dissertation."

"All right!" Janet said with frustration. "All right, we'll do what we have to do."

"We need the charts and we need the miracle medicine," Sean said. He stood up and stretched. "So let's go."

"Now?" Janet questioned with alarm. "It's nearly nine at night."

"First rule of breaking and entering," Sean said. "You do it when no one is at home. This is a perfect time. Besides, I have a legitimate cover: I should inject more of my mice with the primary dose of the glycoprotein."

"Heaven help me," Janet said as she allowed Sean to pull her up from the bench.

TOM WIDDICOMB guided his car into the slot at the extreme end of the parking area for the Forbes residence. He inched forward until the wheels touched the curb restraint. He had pulled up under the protective branches of a large gumbo-limbo tree. Alice had told him to park there just in case someone noticed the car. It was Alice's car, a lime green 1969 Cadillac convertible.

Tom opened the car door and stepped out after making certain no one was in sight. He pulled on a pair of latex surgical gloves. Then he reached under the front seat and grasped the chef's knife he'd brought from home. Light glinted off its polished surface. At first he'd planned on bringing the gun. But then thinking about noise and the thinness of the residence walls, he'd settled on the knife instead. Its only drawback was that it could be messy.

Being careful of the knife's cutting edge, Tom slipped the blade up inside the right sleeve of his shirt, cupping the handle in the palm of his hand. In his other hand he carried the keys to 207.

He made his way along the rear of the building, counting the sliders until he was below 207. There were no lights on in the apartment. Either that nurse was already in bed or she was out. Tom didn't care. Either way had its benefits and disadvantages.

Walking around to the front of the building, Tom had to pause while one of the tenants came out and headed for his car. After the man had driven away, Tom used one of the keys to enter the building. Once inside, he moved quickly. He preferred not to be seen. Arriving outside of 207, he inserted the key, opened the door, stepped inside, and closed the door behind him in one swift, fluid motion.

For several minutes he stood by the door without moving, listening for the slightest sound. He could hear several distant TVs, but they were from other apartments. Pocketing the keys, he allowed the long-bladed chef's knife to slide out from his sleeve. He clutched its handle as if it were a dagger.

Slowly he inched forward. By the light coming from the parking area he could see the outline of the furniture and the doorway into the bedroom. The bedroom door was open.

Looking into the gloom of the bedroom, which was darker than the living room due to the closed drapes, Tom could not tell if the bed was occupied or empty. Again he listened. Aside from the muffled sound of the distant TVs plus the hum of the refrigerator which had just kicked on, he heard nothing. There was no steady breathing of someone asleep.

Advancing into the room a half step at a time, Tom bumped gently against the edge of the bed. Reaching out with his free hand, he groped for a body. Only then did he know for sure: the bed was empty.

Not realizing he'd been holding his breath, Tom straightened up and breathed out. He felt relief of tension on the one hand, yet profound disappointment on the other. The anticipation of violence had aroused him and satisfaction would be delayed.

Moving more by feel than by sight, he managed to find his way to the bathroom. Reaching in, he ran his free hand up and down the wall until he found the light switch. Turning it on, he had to squint in the brightness, but he liked what he saw. Hanging over the tub were a pair of lacy pastel panties and a bra.

Tom placed the chef's knife down on the edge of the sink and picked up the panties. They were nothing like the ones Alice wore. He had no idea why such objects fascinated him, but they did. Sitting on the edge of the tub, he fingered the silky material. For the moment he was content, knowing that he'd be entertained while he waited, keeping the light switch and the knife close at hand.

"WHAT IF we get caught?" Janet asked nervously as they headed toward the Forbes Center. They'd just come from the Home Depot hardware store where Sean had bought tools that he said should work almost as well as a locksmith's tension bar and double ball pick.

"We're not going to get caught," Sean said. "That's why we're going there now when no one will be there. Well, we don't know that for sure, but we'll check."

"There will be plenty of people on the hospital side," Janet warned.

"And that's the reason why we stay away from the hospital," Sean said.

"What about security?" Janet asked. "Have you thought about that?"

"Piece of cake," Sean said. "Except for the frustrated Marine, I haven't been impressed. They're certainly lax at the front door."

"I'm not good at this," Janet admitted.

"Tell me something I didn't know!" Sean said.

"And how are you so acquainted with locks and picks and alarms?" Janet asked.

"When I grew up in Charlestown, it was a pure-blooded working-class neighborhood," Sean said. "The gentrification hadn't started. Each of our fathers was in a different trade. My father was a plumber. Timothy O'Brien's father was a locksmith. Old man O'Brien taught his son some of the tricks of the trade, and Timmy showed us. At first it was a game; kind of a competition. We liked to believe there weren't any locks in the neighborhood we couldn't open. And Charlie Sullivan's father was a master electrician. He put in fancy alarm systems in Boston, mostly on Beacon Hill. He often made Charlie come along. So Charlie started telling us about alarms."

"That's dangerous information for kids to have," Janet said. Her own childhood couldn't have been further from Sean's among the private schools, music lessons, and summers on the Cape.

"You bet," Sean agreed. "But we never stole anything from our own neighborhood. We'd just open up locks and then leave them open as a practical joke. But then it changed. We started going out to the 'burbs like Swampscott or Marblehead with one of the older kids who could drive. We'd watch a house for a while, then break in and help ourselves to the liquor and some of the electronics. You know, stereos, TVs."

"You stole?" Janet questioned with shock.

Sean glanced at her for a second before looking back at the road. "Of course we stole," he said. "It was thrilling at the time and we used to think all the people who lived on the North Shore were millionaires." Sean went on to tell how he and his buddies would sell the goods in Boston, pay off the driver, buy beer, and give the rest to a fellow raising money for the Irish Republican Army. "We even deluded ourselves into thinking we were youthful political activists even though we didn't have the faintest idea of what was going on in Northern Ireland."

"My God! I had no idea," Janet said. She'd known about Sean's adolescent fights and even about the joy rides, but this burglary was something else entirely.

"Let's not get carried away with value judgments," Sean said. "My youth and yours were completely different."

"I'm just a little concerned you learned to justify any type of behavior," Janet said. "I would imagine it could become a habit."

"The last time I did any of that stuff was when I was fifteen," Sean said. "There's been a lot of water over the dam since then."

They pulled into the Forbes parking lot and drove to the research building. Sean cut the engine and turned out the lights. For a moment neither moved.

"You want to go ahead with this or not?" Sean asked, finally breaking the silence. "I don't mean to pressure you, but I can't waste two months down here screwing around with busywork. Either I get to look into the medulloblastoma protocol or I go back to Boston. Unfortunately, I can't do it by myself; that was made apparent by the run-in with hefty Margaret Richmond. Either you help, or we cancel. But let me say this: we're going in here to get information, not to steal TV sets. And it's for a damn good cause."

Janet stared ahead for a moment. She didn't have the luxury of indecision, yet her mind was a jumble of confusing thoughts. She looked at Sean. She thought she loved him.

"Okay!" Janet said finally. "Let's do it."

They got out of the car and walked to the entrance. Sean carried the tools he'd gotten at the Home Depot in a paper bag.

"Evening," Sean said to the security guard who blinked repeatedly as he stared at Sean's ID card. He was a swarthy Hispanic with a pencil-line mustache. He seemed to appreciate Janet's shorts.

"Got to inject my rats," Sean said.

The security guard motioned for them to enter. He didn't speak, nor did he take his eyes off Janet's lower half. As Sean and Janet passed through the turnstile they could see he had a miniature portable TV wedged on top of the bank of security monitors. It was tuned to a soccer match.

"See what I mean about the guards?" Sean said as they used the stairs to descend to the basement. "He was more interested in your legs than my ID card. I could have had Charlie Manson's photo on it and he wouldn't have noticed."

"How come you said rats instead of mice?" Janet asked.

"People hate rats," Sean said. "I didn't want him deciding to come down and watch."

"You do think of everything," Janet said.

The basement was a warren of corridors and locked doors, but at least it was adequately lighted. Sean had made many trips to the animal room and was generally familiar with that area, but he hadn't gone beyond it. As they walked, the sound of their heels echoed off the bare concrete.

"Do you have any idea where we're going?" Janet asked.

"Vaguely," Sean said.

They walked down the central corridor taking several twists and turns before coming to a T intersection.

"This must be the way to the hospital," Sean said.

"How can you tell?"

Sean pointed to the tangle of pipes lining the ceiling. "The power plant is in the hospital," he said. "These lines are coming over to feed the research building. Now we have to figure out which side has the chart vault."

They proceeded down the corridor toward the hospital. Fifty feet down there was a door on either side of the narrow hall. Sean tried each. Both were locked.

"Let's give these a try," he said. He set down his bag and removed some tools, including a slender jeweler-like allen wrench and several short pieces of heavy wire. Holding the allen wrench in one hand and one of the pieces of heavy wire in the other, he inserted both into the lock.

"This is the tricky part," he said. "It's called raking the pins."

Sean closed his eyes and proceeded by feel.

"What do you think?" Janet asked as she looked up and down the corridor, expecting someone to appear at any moment.

"Piece of cake," Sean said. There was a click and the door opened. Finding a light, Sean turned it on. They had broken into an electrical room with huge wall-sized electrical buses facing each other.

Sean turned out the light and closed the door. Next he went to work on the door across the corridor. He had it open in less time than the first.

"These tools make a decent tension bar and pick," he said. "Nothing like the real thing, but not bad."

Switching on a light, he and Janet found themselves in a long, narrow room filled with metal shelving. Arranged on the shelves were hospital charts. There was a lot of empty space.

"This is it," Sean said.

"A lot of room to expand," Janet commented.

"Don't move for a couple of minutes," Sean said. "Let me make sure there are no alarms."

"Good grief!" Janet said. "Why don't you tell me these things in advance."

Sean took a quick turn around the room looking for infrared sensors or motion detectors. He found nothing. Rejoining Janet and taking out the computer printout sheet he said: "Let's divide these charts up between us. I only want the ones from the last two years. They'll reflect the successful treatment."

Janet took the top half of the list and Sean took the lower. In ten minutes they had a stack of thirty-three charts.

"It's easy to tell this isn't a teaching hospital," Sean said. "In a teaching hospital you'd be lucky to find one chart, much less all thirty-three."

"What do you want to do with them?" Janet asked.

"Copy them," Sean said. "There's a copy machine in the library. The question is, is the library open? I don't want the guard seeing me pick that lock. There's probably a camera there."

"Let's check," Janet said. She wanted to get this over with.

"Wait," Sean said. "I think I have a better idea." He started toward the research building end of the chart vault. Janet struggled to keep up. Rounding the last bank of metal shelves, they came to the end wall. In the center of the wall was a glass door. To the right of the door was a panel with two buttons. When Sean pushed the lower of the two, a deep whirring noise broke the silence.

"Maybe we're in luck," he said.

Within several minutes the dumbwaiter appeared. Sean opened the door and began removing the shelves.

"What are you doing?" she asked.

"A little experiment," Sean said. When he had enough of the racks removed, he climbed inside. He had to double up with his knees near his chin.

"Close the door and push the button," he said.

"Are you sure?" Janet asked.

"Come on!" Sean said. "But after the motor stops, wait for a couple of beats, then be sure to push the 'down' button to get me back."

Janet did as she was told. Sean ascended with a wave and disappeared from view.

With Sean gone, Janet's anxiety grew. The gravity of their actions hadn't sunk in when Sean had been with her.

But in the eerie silence the reality of where she was and what she was doing hit her: she was burglarizing the Forbes Cancer Center.

When the whirring stopped, Janet counted to ten, then pressed the down button. Thankfully, Sean quickly reappeared. She opened the door.

"Works like a charm," Sean said. "It goes right up to finance in administration. Best of all, they've got one of the world's best copy machines."

It took them only a few minutes to carry the charts over to the electric dumbwaiter.

"You first," Sean said.

"I don't know whether I want to do this," Janet said.

"Fine," Sean said. "Then you wait here while I copy the charts. It'll probably take about a half hour." He started to climb back in the dumbwaiter.

Janet grabbed his arm. "I changed my mind. I don't want to wait here by myself, either."

Sean rolled his eyes and got out of the dumbwaiter. Janet climbed into the hoist. Sean handed her most of the charts, closed the door, and pushed the button. When the motor stopped, he pressed again and the dumbwaiter reappeared. With the remaining charts in hand, he piled into the dumbwaiter a second time and waited a few uncomfortable minutes until Janet pushed the button upstairs in administration.

When Janet opened the door for him, he could tell she was becoming frantic.

"What's the matter now?" he asked as he struggled out of the dumbwaiter.

"All the lights are on up here," she said nervously. "Did you turn them on?"

"Nope," Sean said, gathering up an armload of the

charts. "They were on when I came up. Probably the cleaning service."

"I never thought of that," Janet said. "How can you be so calm through all this?" She sounded almost angry.

Sean shrugged. "Must have been all that practice I had as a kid."

They quickly fell into a system at the copy machine. By taking each chart apart, they could load it into the automatic feed. Using a stapler they found on a nearby desk, they kept the copies organized and reassembled the originals as soon as they'd been copied.

"Did you notice that computer in the glass enclosure?" Janet asked.

"I saw it on my tour on day one," Sean said.

"It's running some kind of program," Janet said. "When I was waiting for you to come up, I glanced in. It's connected to several modems and automatic dialers. It must be doing some kind of survey."

Sean looked at Janet with surprise. "I didn't know you knew so much about computers. That's rather odd for an English lit major."

"At Wellesley I majored in English literature but computers fascinated me," she explained. "I took a lot of computer courses. At one point I almost changed majors."

After loading more sets of charts into the copy machine, Sean and Janet walked over to the glass enclosure and looked in. The monitor screen was flashing digits. Sean tried the door. It was open. They went inside.

"Wonder why this is in a glass room?" he asked.

"To protect it," Janet said. "Big machines like this can be affected by cigarette smoke. There's probably a handful of smokers in the office."

They looked at the figures flashing on the screen. They were nine-digit numbers.

"What do you think it's doing?" Sean asked.

"No idea," Janet said. "They're not phone numbers. If they were, there'd be seven or ten digits, not nine. Besides, there's no way it can be calling phone numbers that rapidly."

The screen suddenly went blank, then a ten-digit number appeared. Instantly an automatic dialer went into motion, its tones audible above the hum of the air-conditioning fans.

"Now that's a phone number," Janet said. "I even recognize the area code. It's Connecticut."

The screen went blank again, then resumed flashing more nine-digit numbers. After a minute the list of numbers froze at a specific number and the computer printout device activated. Both Sean and Janet glanced over to the printer in time to see the nine-digit number print out followed by: *Peter Ziegler, age 55, Valley Hospital, Charlotte, North Carolina, Achilles tendon repair, March 11.*

Suddenly, an alarm sounded. As the computer reverted to flashing its nine-digit numbers, Sean and Janet looked at each other, Sean with confusion, Janet with panic.

"What's happening?" she demanded. The alarm kept ringing.

"I don't know," Sean admitted. "But it isn't a burglar alarm." He turned to look out into the office just in time to see the door to the hallway opening.

"Down!" he said to Janet, forcing her to her hands and knees. Sean figured that whoever was coming into the room was coming to check the computer. He frantically motioned to Janet to crawl behind the console. In utter terror, Janet did as she was told, fumbling over coiled computer cables. Sean was right behind her. Hardly had they gotten out of sight when the door to the glass enclosure was opened.

From where they were huddled, they could see a pair of legs enter the room. Whoever it was, it was a woman. The alarm that initiated the episode was turned off. The woman picked up a phone and dialed.

"We have another potential donor," she said. "North Carolina."

At that moment, the laser printer began printing yet again, and again the alarm sounded for a brief moment.

"Did you hear that?" the woman asked. "What a coincidence. We're getting another, as we speak." She paused, waiting for the printer. "Patricia Southerland, age forty-seven, San Jose General, San Jose, California, breast biopsy, March 14. Also sounds good. What do you think?"

There was a pause before she spoke again: "I know the team's out. But there's time. Trust me. This is my department."

The woman hung up. Sean and Janet heard her tear off the sheet that had just printed. Then the woman turned and left.

For a few minutes neither Sean nor Janet spoke.

"What the hell did she mean, a potential donor?" Sean whispered at last.

"I don't know and I don't care," Janet whispered back. "I want out of here."

"Donor?" Sean murmured. "That sounds creepy to me. What do we have here? A clearinghouse for body parts? Reminds me of a movie I saw once. I tell you, this place is nuts."

"Is she gone?" Janet asked.

"I'll check," Sean said. Slowly he backed out from their hiding place, then peeked over the countertop. The room was empty. "She seems to be gone," Sean said. "I wonder why she ignored the copy machine."

Janet backed out and gingerly raised her head. She scanned the room as well.

"Coming in, the computer alarm must have shielded the sound," Sean said. "But going out, she had to have heard it."

"Maybe she was too preoccupied," Janet offered.

Sean nodded. "I think you're probably right."

The computer screen that had been flashing the innumerable nine-digit numbers suddenly went blank.

"The program seems to be over," Sean said.

"Let's get away from here," Janet said, her voice quavering.

They ventured out into the room. The copy machine had finished the latest stack of charts and was silent.

"Now we know why she didn't hear it," Sean said, going up to the machine and checking it. He loaded the last of the charts.

"I want out of here!" Janet said.

"Not until I have my charts," Sean said. He pushed the copy button and the copier roared to life. Then he began removing the originals and the copies already done, stapling the copies and reassembling the charts.

At first, Janet watched, terrified that any moment the same woman would reappear. But after she recognized the faster they were finished, the sooner they would leave, she pitched in. With no further interruptions they had all the charts copied and stapled in short order.

Returning to the small elevator, Sean discovered that it was possible to push the button with the door ajar. Then, when the door was closed, the dumbwaiter operated. "Now I don't have to worry about you forgetting to bring me down," he said teasingly.

"I'm in no mood for humor," Janet remarked as she climbed into the hoist. She held out her arms to take as many charts and copies as possible.

Repeating the procedure that had brought them up to the

seventh floor, they returned the charts to the vault. To Janet's chagrin, Sean insisted they take the time to return the charts to their original locations. With that accomplished, they carried the chart copies to the animal room where Sean hid them beneath the cages of his mice.

"I should inject these guys," Sean said, "but to tell you the truth, I don't much feel like it."

Janet was pleased to leave but didn't start to relax until they were driving out of the parking lot.

"That has to have been one of the worst experiences of my life," she said as they traversed Little Havana. "I can't believe that you stayed so calm."

"My heart rate was up," Sean admitted. "But it went smoothly except for that little episode in the computer room. And now that it's over, wasn't it exciting? Just a little?"

"No!" Janet said emphatically.

They drove in silence until Sean spoke again: "I still can't figure out what that computer was doing. And I can't figure out what it has to do with organ donation. They certainly don't use organs from deceased cancer patients. It's too risky in relation to transplanting the cancer as well as the organ. Any ideas?"

"I can't think about anything at this point," Janet said.

They pulled into the Forbes residence.

"Geez, look at that old Caddy convertible," Sean said. "What a boat. Barry Dunhegan had one just like it when I was a kid, except his was pink. He was a bookmaker and all us kids thought he was cool."

Janet cast a cursory glance at the finned monster parked within the shadow of an exotic tree. She marveled how Sean could go through such a wrenching experience, then think about cars.

Sean pulled to a stop and yanked on the emergency

brake. They got out of the car and entered the building in silence. Sean was thinking about how nice it would be to spend the night with Janet. He couldn't blame the security guard for ogling her. As Sean climbed the stairs behind Janet, he was reminded how fabulous her legs were.

As they came abreast of his door he reached out and drew her to him, enveloping her in his arms. For a moment they merely hugged.

"What about staying together tonight?" Sean forced himself to ask. His voice was hesitant; he feared rejection. Janet didn't answer immediately, and the longer she delayed, the more optimistic he became. Finally he used his left hand to take out his keys.

"I don't think it's a good idea," she said.

"Come on," Sean urged. He could smell her fragrance from having held her close.

"No!" Janet said with finality after another pause. Although she'd been wavering, she'd made a decision. "I know it would be nice, and I could use the sense of security after this evening, but we have to talk first."

Sean rolled his eyes in frustration. She could be so impossibly stubborn. "Okay," he said petulantly, trying another tack. "Have it your way." He let go of her, opened his door, and stepped inside. Before shutting the door, he glanced at her face. What he wanted to see was sudden concern that he was miffed. Instead he saw irritation. Janet turned and walked away.

After closing his door, Sean felt guilty. He went to his slider, opened it, and stepped out on the balcony. A few doors down he saw Janet's light in her living room go on. Sean hesitated, not sure what to do.

"MEN," JANET said aloud with ire and exasperation. She hesitated inside her door, going over the conversation outside Sean's door. There was no reason for him to get angry with her. Hadn't she gone along with his risky plan? Didn't she generally defer to his wishes? Why couldn't he ever even try to understand hers?

Knowing that nothing would be solved that evening, Janet walked into the bedroom and turned on the light. Although she would later remember it, it didn't completely register that her bathroom door was closed. When Janet was by herself she never closed doors. It had been a habit developed as a child.

Pulling off her tank top and unhooking her bra, Janet tossed them on the armchair by the bed. She undid the clip on the top of her head and shook her hair free. She felt exhausted, irritable, and as one of her roommates at college used to say, fried. Picking up the hair dryer she'd tossed on her bed in haste that morning, Janet opened the bathroom and entered. The moment she turned on the light, she became aware of a hulking presence to her left. Reacting instinctively, Janet's hand shot out as if to fend off the intruder.

A scream started in Janet's throat but was stalled before it could get out by the hideousness of the image that confronted her. A man was in her bathroom dressed in baggy dark clothes. A knotted segment of nylon stocking had been drawn over his head so that his features were grotesquely compressed. At shoulder height he clutched a butcher's knife menacingly.

For an instant, neither of them moved. Janet quiveringly aimed the ineffectual hair dryer at the ghoulish face as if it were a magnum revolver. The intruder stared down the barrel in shocked surprise until he realized he was looking at heating coils, not the innards of a handgun.

He was the first to react, reaching out and snatching the hair dryer from Janet's hand. In a burst of rage he threw the apparatus aside; it smashed the mirror of the medicine cabinet. The shattering of the glass jolted Janet from her paralysis, and she bolted from the bathroom.

Tom reacted swiftly and managed to grab Janet's arm, but Janet's momentum pulled them stumbling into the bedroom. His original intent had been to stab her in the bathroom. The hair dryer had thrown him off guard. He hadn't planned on her getting out of the bathroom. And he didn't want her to scream, but she did.

Janet's first scream had been stifled by shock, but she more than made up for it with a second scream that reverberated in the confines of her small apartment and penetrated the cheaply built walls. It was probably heard in every apartment in the building, and it sent a shiver of fear down Tom's spine. As angry as he was, he knew that he was in trouble.

Still holding onto Janet's arm, Tom whipped her around so that she careened off the wall before falling crossways on the bed. Tom could have killed her there and then, but he didn't dare take the time. Instead he rushed to the slider. Fumbling with the curtains and then the lock, he yanked the door open and disappeared into the night.

SEAN HAD been loitering on the balcony outside Janet's open living room slider, trying to build up the courage to go in and apologize for trying to make Janet feel guilty. He was embarrassed at his behavior, but since apologies weren't his strong suit, he was having difficulty motivating himself.

Sean's hesitation dissolved in an instant at the sound of the shattering mirror. For a moment he struggled with the screen, trying to slide it open. When he heard Janet's bloodcurdling scream followed by a loud thud, he gave up opening the screen properly and threw himself through it. He ended up on the shag carpet, his legs still bound in the mesh. Struggling to his feet he launched himself through the doorway into the bedroom. He found Janet on the bed, wide-eyed with terror.

"What's the matter?" Sean demanded.

Janet sat up. Choking back tears, she said, "There was a man with a knife in my bathroom." Then she pointed to the open bedroom slider. "He went that way."

Sean flew to the sliding glass door and whipped back the curtain. Instead of one man, there were two. They came through the door in tandem, roughly shoving Sean back into the room prior to everyone recognizing each other. The newcomers were Gary Engels and another resident who'd responded to Janet's scream just as Sean had.

Frantically explaining that an intruder had just left, Sean led the two men back out onto the balcony. As they reached the handrail they heard the screech of tires coming from the parking lot behind the building. While Gary and his companion ran for the stairs, Sean returned to Janet.

Janet had recovered to a degree. She'd slipped on a sweatshirt. When Sean entered she was sitting on the edge of the bed finishing an emergency call to the police. Replacing the receiver, she looked up at Sean who was standing above her.

"You okay?" he asked gently.

"I think so," she said. She was visibly shaking. "God, what a day!"

"I told you you should have stayed with me." Sean sat next to her and put his arms around her.

In spite of herself, Janet gave a short laugh. Leave it to Sean to try to smooth over any situation with humor. It did feel wonderful to be in his arms.

"I'd heard Miami was a lively city," she said, taking his lead, "but this is too much."

"Any idea how the guy got in here?" Sean asked.

"I left the slider in the living room open," Janet admitted.

"This is learning the hard way," Sean said.

"In Boston the worst thing that ever happened to me was an obscene phone call," Janet said.

"Yeah, and I apologized," Sean said.

Janet smiled and threw her pillow at him.

It took the police twenty minutes to arrive. They pulled up in a squad car with lights flashing but no siren. Two uniformed officers from the Miami police department came up to the apartment. One was a huge bearded black man, the other was a slim Hispanic with a mustache. Their names were Peter Jefferson and Juan Torres. They were solicitous, respectful, and professional as they spent an unhurried half hour going over Janet's story. When she mentioned that the man was wearing latex rubber gloves, they canceled a crime scene technician who was scheduled to come over after finishing a homicide case.

"The fact that nobody got hurt puts this incident into a different category," Juan said. "Obviously homicides get more attention."

"But this could have been a homicide," Sean protested.

"Hey, we do the best we can with the manpower we got," Peter said.

While the policemen were still there gathering facts, someone else showed up: Robert Harris.

ROBERT HARRIS had carefully cultivated and nurtured a relationship with the Miami police department. Although he decried their lack of discipline and their poor physical shape, characteristics that set in approximately a year subsequent to their graduation from the police academy, Harris was enough of a pragmatist to understand that he needed to be on their good side. And this attack on a nurse at the Forbes residence was a case in point. Had he not developed the connections he had, he probably wouldn't have heard about the incident until the following morning. As far as Robert was concerned, such a situation would be unacceptable for the head of security.

The call had come from the duty commander while Harris was using his Soloflex machine in front of his TV at home. Unfortunately, there'd been a delay of nearly half an hour following the dispatch of the patrol car, but Harris was not in a position to complain. Arriving late was better than not arriving at all. Harris just didn't want the case to be cold by the time he got involved.

As Harris had driven to the residence, he thought back to the rape and murder of Sheila Arnold. He couldn't shake the suspicion—improbable though it might seem—that Arnold's death was somehow related to the deaths of the breast cancer patients. Harris wasn't a doctor so he had to go on what Dr. Mason had told him a few months ago, namely that it was his belief that the breast cancer patients were being murdered. The tip-off was the fact that these patients' faces were blue, a sign they were being somehow smothered.

Dr. Mason had made it clear that getting to the bottom of this situation should be Harris's primary task. If word leaked to the press, the damage to the Forbes might be irreparable. In fact, Dr. Mason had made it sound like Harris's tenure depended on a quick and unobtrusive resolution of this potentially embarrassing problem. The quicker that resolution came about, the better for everyone.

But Harris had not made any progress over the last few months. Dr. Mason's suggestion that the perpetrator was probably a doctor or a nurse had not panned out. Extensive background checks on the professional staff had failed to uncover any suspicious discrepancies or irregularities. Harris's attempts at keeping an unobtrusive eye on the Forbes breast cancer patients hadn't turned anything up. Not that he'd been able to keep watch over all of them.

Harris's suspicion that Miss Arnold's death was related to the breast cancer patient deaths had hit him the day after her murder while he'd been driving to work. It was then he'd remembered that the day before she was killed a breast cancer patient on her floor had died and turned blue.

What if Sheila Arnold had seen something, Harris wondered. What if she'd witnessed or overheard something whose significance she hadn't appreciated—something that made the perpetrator feel threatened nonetheless. The idea had seemed reasonable to Harris, although he did wonder if it were the product of a desperate mind.

In any case, Harris's suspicion hadn't left him with much to go on. He had learned from the police that a witness had seen a man leaving Miss Arnold's apartment the night of the murder, but the description had been hopelessly vague: a male of medium height and medium build with brown hair. The witness had not seen the man's face. In an institution the size of the Forbes Cancer Center, such a description had been of limited use.

So when Harris was told of yet another attack on a Forbes nurse, he again considered a possible connection to the breast cancer deaths. There had been another suspicious blue death on Tuesday.

Harris entered Janet's apartment eager to talk with her. He was extremely chagrined to find her in the company of the wiseass medical student, Sean Murphy.

Since the police were still questioning the nurse, Harris took a quick look around. He saw the shattered mirror in the bathroom along with the broken hair dryer. He also noticed the panties amid the debris on the floor. Wandering into the living room, he noted the large hole in the screen. It was obvious the screen had been a point of entry, not escape.

"Your witness," Peter Jefferson joked, coming into the living room. His partner followed in his shadow. Harris had met Peter on several occasions in the past.

"Anything you can tell me?" Harris asked.

"Not a whole lot," Peter said. "Perp was wearing a nylon stocking over his face. Medium build, medium height. Apparently didn't say a word. Girl's lucky. The guy had a knife."

"What are you going to do?" Harris asked.

Peter shrugged. "The usual," he said. "We'll file a report. We'll see what the sarge says. One way or another it'll get turned over to an investigative unit. Who knows what they'll do." Peter lowered his voice. "No injury, no robbery. It's not likely this will become a number-one priority. If she'd gotten whacked it'd be a different story."

Harris nodded. He thanked the officers and they left. Harris stepped into the bedroom. Janet was packing a bag; Sean was in the bathroom collecting her toiletries.

"On behalf of Forbes, I want to tell you I'm terribly sorry about this," he said.

"Thank you," Janet said.

"We've never felt the need for security here," Harris added.

"I understand," Janet said. "It could have happened anyplace. I did leave the door open."

"The police told me you had difficulty describing the guy," Harris said.

"He had a stocking over his head," Janet said. "And it all happened so fast."

"Is it possible that you might have seen him before?" Harris asked.

"I don't think so," Janet said. "But it really is impossible to say for sure."

"I want to ask you a question," Harris said. "But I want you to think for a minute before answering. Has anything unusual happened to you recently at Forbes?"

Janet's mouth went instantly dry.

Overhearing this exchange, Sean immediately guessed what was going through Janet's mind: she was thinking about their break-in into the chart room.

"Janet has had a rather difficult experience," Sean said, stepping into the room.

Harris turned. "I'm not talking to you, boy," he said menacingly.

"Listen, jughead," Sean said. "We didn't call the Marines. Janet has spoken to the police. You can get your information from them. She doesn't have to talk to you, and I think she's been through enough tonight. She doesn't need you pestering her."

The two men faced off, glaring at each other.

"Please!" Janet shouted. Fresh tears welled in her eyes. "I can't stand any tension just now," she told them.

Sean sat down on the bed, put his arm around her, and leaned his forehead against hers.

"I'm sorry, Miss Reardon," Harris said. "I understand. But it is important for me to ask you if you've seen anything unusual while you worked today. I know it was your first day."

Janet shook her head. Sean glanced up at Harris and with his eyes motioned for him to leave.

Harris fought hard to keep himself from slapping the kid around. He even fantasized about sitting on him and shaving his head. But instead he turned and left.

As THE night advanced toward dawn Tom Widdicomb's anxiety gradually increased. He was in the storeroom off the garage huddled in the corner beside the freezer. He had his arms around himself and his knees drawn up as if he were cold. He even intermittently shivered as his mind constantly tortured him by replaying over and over the disastrous events at the Forbes residence.

Now he was a total failure. Not only had he failed to put Gloria D'Amataglio to sleep, he'd failed to get rid of the nurse who'd prevented him from doing so. And despite the nylon stocking he'd worn, she'd seen him up close. Maybe she could recognize him. More than anything, Tom was mortified to have mistaken that stupid hair dryer for a gun.

Because of his idiocy, Alice wasn't speaking to him. He'd tried to talk with her, but she wouldn't even listen. He'd disappointed her. He wasn't "her little man" anymore. He deserved to be laughed at by the other children. Tom had tried to reason with her, promising that he would help Gloria that morning, and that as soon as he could he'd rid them of the meddlesome nurse. He promised and cried, but to no avail. Alice could be stubborn.

Getting stiffly to his feet, Tom stretched his cramped muscles. He'd been crouched in the corner without moving for hours, thinking his mother would eventually feel sorry for him. But it hadn't worked. She'd ignored him. So he thought he'd try talking to her directly.

Moving in front of the chest freezer he snapped open the lock and raised the lid. The frozen mist inside the freezer swirled as it mixed with a draft of moist, warm Miami air. Gradually the mist dissipated, and out of the fog emerged the desiccated face of Alice Widdicomb. Her dyed red hair was frozen into icy tangles. The skin of her face was sunken, blotchy, and blue. Crystals had formed along the edges of her open eyelids. Her eyeballs had contracted slightly, dimpling the surface of her corneas which were opaque with winter-like frost. Her yellow teeth were exposed by the retraction of her lips, forming a horrid grimace.

Since Tom and his mother had lived such isolated lives, Tom had little difficulty after he'd put her to sleep. His only mistake had been that he'd not thought of the freezer soon enough, and after a couple of days she'd started to smell. One of the few neighbors with whom they occasionally spoke had even mentioned it, throwing Tom into a panic. That was when he'd thought of the freezer.

Since then nothing had changed. Even Alice's social security checks continued to arrive on schedule. The only close call had been when the freezer compressor conked out one hot Friday night. Tom hadn't been able to get someone to come to fix it until Monday. He had been terrified the guy would need to open the freezer, but he didn't. The man did tell Tom that he thought he might have some bad meat in there.

Supporting the lid, Tom gazed at his mother. But she still refused to say a word. She was understandably scared.

"I'll do it today," Tom said pleadingly. "Gloria will still be on IVs. If not, I'll think of something. And the nurse. I'll get rid of her. There's not going to be any problem. No one is going to come to take you away. You're safe with me. Please!"

Alice Widdicomb said nothing.

Slowly Tom lowered the lid. He waited for a moment in case she changed her mind, but she didn't. Reluctantly he left her and went through to the kitchen into the bedroom they'd shared for so many years. Opening the bedside table he took out Alice's gun. It had been his father's originally, but after he'd died, Alice had taken it over, frequently showing it to Tom, saying that if anyone ever tried to come between them, she'd use it. Tom had learned to love the sight of the mother-of-pearl handle.

"Nobody's ever coming between us, Alice," Tom said. So far he'd only used the gun once, and that was when the Arnold girl tried to interfere by taking him aside to say she'd seen him take some medicine off the anesthesia cart. Now he'd have to use it again for this Janet Reardon before she caused more trouble than she already had.

"I'll prove to you that I'm your little man," Tom said. He slipped the cold gun into his pocket and went into the bathroom to shave.

6

March 5
Friday, 6:30 A.M.

As she drove along the General Douglas MacArthur Causeway heading for work, Janet tried to distract herself by admiring the impressive view over Biscayne Bay. She even tried to fantasize about taking a cruise with Sean on one of the dazzling white cruise ships lined up at the Dodge Island seaport. But nothing worked. Her mind kept returning to the previous night's events.

After confronting that man in her bathroom, Janet wasn't about to spend the night in 207. Not even Sean's apartment seemed a safe haven to her. Instead, she insisted on moving to the Miami Beach unit she'd rented. Not wanting to be alone, she'd invited Sean to come with her and was relieved when he accepted and even offered to sleep on the couch. But once they got there, even Janet's best resolutions fell to the wayside. They slept together in what Sean described as the "Platonic fashion." They didn't make love, but Janet had to admit, it felt good to be close to him.

Almost as much as the intruder's break-in, Janet was

troubled by her escapade with Sean. The episode in the administration office the previous night troubled her deeply. She couldn't stop thinking about what would have happened had they been caught. On top of that, she'd begun to wonder what kind of man Sean was. He was smart and witty, of that there was no doubt. But given this new revelation of his past experience of thievery, she questioned what his true morals were.

All in all Janet felt profoundly distraught, and to make matters worse she was facing a day in which she was expected to obtain deceitfully a sample of medicine that was highly controlled. If she failed, she faced the possibility of Sean packing his things and leaving Miami. As she neared the hospital Janet found herself thinking longingly about Sunday, the first day she was scheduled to have off. The fact that she was already thinking about vacation time at the start of her second day on the job gave an indication of her level of stress.

The bustling atmosphere of the floor turned out to be a godsend for Janet's troubled mind. Within minutes of her arrival, she was swept up in the tumult of the hospital. Nursing report gave the oncoming day shift a hint of the work ahead of them. Between diagnostic tests, treatments, and complicated medication protocols, all the nurses knew they would have little free time. The most disturbing news was that Helen Cabot had not improved overnight as the doctors had hoped. In fact, the night nurse taking care of her felt she'd actually lost ground, having had a small seizure around four A.M. Janet listened carefully to this part of the briefing since she'd arranged to be assigned to Helen Cabot for the day.

Regarding the controlled medicines, Janet had concocted a plan. Having seen the type of vials they came in, she'd made it a point to obtain similar vials that were empty. Now all she needed was some time alone with the medicine.

After report had concluded, Janet launched into work. The first order of business was to start an IV line for Gloria D'Amataglio. It was Gloria's last day of IV medication on her current chemotherapy cycle. Having shown an early facility with venipuncture, Janet was in demand for the procedure. During report she'd offered to start Gloria's IV since there had been some problems doing so in the past. The nurse scheduled to care for Gloria for the day had readily agreed.

Armed with all the necessary paraphernalia, Janet went into Gloria's room. Gloria was sitting on the bed, leaning against a bank of pillows, obviously feeling better than she had the day before. While they chatted nostalgically about the beauty of the pond on the Wellesley campus and how romantic it had been on party weekends, Janet got the IV going.

"I hardly felt that," Gloria said in admiration.

"Glad to help," Janet said.

Leaving Gloria's room, Janet felt her stomach tighten as she prepared herself for her next task: getting to the controlled medication. She had to dodge several gurneys, then did a kind of sidestep dance to get around the housekeeper and his bucket.

Reaching the nurses' station, Janet got out Helen Cabot's chart and turned to the order sheet. It indicated that Helen was to get her MB300C and MB303C starting at eight A.M. First Janet got the IV bottle and syringes; she then got the empty containers which she'd put aside. Finally she went to Marjorie and asked for Helen's medication.

"Just a sec," Marjorie said. She ran down the corridor to

the elevators to give a completed X-ray form to an orderly taking a patient down to X-ray.

"That guy never remembers the requisition," Tim commented with a shake of his head.

Marjorie returned to the nurses' station at a jog. As she rounded the counter, she was already removing the key from around her neck for the special medication locker.

"What a day!" she said to Janet. "And to think it's just starting!" She was obviously preoccupied with the welter of activity hospital wards faced at the beginning of each workday. Opening the small but stoutly built refrigerator, she reached in and brought out the two vials of Helen Cabot's medicine. Consulting a ledger that was also stored in the refrigerator, she told Janet she should take 2 ccs of the larger vial and a half cc of the smaller. She showed Janet where to initial after she administered the medication and where Marjorie would initial when Janet was finished.

"Marjorie, I have Dr. Larsen on the line," Tim said, interrupting them.

With the vials of clear fluid safely in hand, Janet retreated to the pharmacy closet. First she turned on the hot water in the small sink. After making sure no one was watching, she held the two MB vials under the hot water. When the gummed labels came loose, Janet pulled them off and placed them on the empty vials. She tucked the now unlabeled vials into the utility drawer back behind an assortment of plastic dosage cups, pencils, pads, and rubber bands.

After another precautionary glance into the busy nurses' station, Janet held the two empty vials over her head and let them fall to the tile floor. Both smashed into tiny shards. After pouring a small amount of water onto the glass pieces, Janet turned and left the pharmacy closet.

Marjorie was still on the phone, and Janet had to wait for

her to disconnect. As soon as she did, Janet put a hand on her arm.

"There's been an accident," Janet said. She tried to sound upset, which wasn't difficult considering her nervousness.

"What happened?" Marjorie asked. Her eyes widened.

"I dropped the two vials," Janet said. "They slipped out of my hand and broke on the floor."

"Okay, okay!" Marjorie said, reassuring herself as well as Janet. "Let's not get too excited. Accidents happen, especially when we're busy and rushing about. Just show me."

Janet led her back to the pharmacy closet and pointed at the remains of the two vials. Marjorie squatted down and, using her thumb and forefinger, gingerly pulled out the shards attached to the labels.

"I'm terribly sorry," Janet said.

"It's okay," Marjorie said. She stood up and shrugged. "As I said, accidents happen. Let's call Ms. Richmond."

Janet followed Marjorie back to the nurses' station where Marjorie placed a call to the director of nursing. After she explained what had happened, she had to get out the ledger from the medicine refrigerator. Janet could see the vials for the other two patients as she did so.

"There was 6cc in the larger and 4cc in the smaller," Marjorie said into the phone. She listened, agreed several times, then hung up.

"No problem," Marjorie said. She made an entry into the ledger, then handed the pen to Janet. "Just initial where I indicated what was lost," she said.

Janet wrote her initials.

"Now head over to Ms. Richmond's office in the research building, seventh floor," Marjorie said. "Bring these labels with you." She put the broken glass fragments with their attached labels in an envelope and handed them to Janet. "She'll give you several new vials, okay?"

Janet nodded and apologized again.

"It's all right," Marjorie assured her. "It could have happened to anyone." Then she asked Tim to page Tom Widdicomb to get him to mop up the pharmacy closet.

With her heart pounding and knowing her face was flushed, Janet walked toward the elevators as calmly as she could. Her ruse had worked, but she didn't feel good about it. She felt like she was taking advantage of Marjorie's trust and good nature. She was also concerned that someone might stumble across the unlabeled vials in the utility drawer. Janet would have liked to have removed them, but she felt she couldn't risk it until later when she could give them directly to Sean.

Despite her preoccupation with Helen's drugs, as Janet came abreast of Gloria's door she noticed it was closed. Having just started her IV, this disturbed her. Except for the one incident when Marjorie had introduced Janet to Gloria, Gloria's door was always ajar. Gloria had even commented that she liked to have it open so she could stay in touch with life on the ward.

Perplexed, Janet stopped and stared at the door, debating with herself what she should do. She was already behind with her work so she should get over to Ms. Richmond's office. Yet Gloria's door bothered her. Fearing Gloria might be feeling poorly, Janet stepped over to the door and knocked. When there was no response, she knocked again louder. When there was still no answer, Janet pushed the door open and peered inside. Gloria was flat on the bed. One of her legs was dangling over the side of the mattress. It seemed an unnatural position for a nap.

"Gloria?" Janet called.

Gloria didn't respond.

Propping the door open with its rubber foot, Janet approached the bed. Off to the side was a slop bucket with a mop, but Janet didn't see it because as she got closer she noted with alarm that Gloria's face was a deep cyanotic blue!

"Code, room 409!" Janet shouted at the operator after snatching the phone from its cradle. She tossed the envelope with the glass shards on the bedside table.

Pulling Gloria's head back and after making certain her mouth was clear, Janet started mouth-to-mouth resuscitation. With her right hand pinching Gloria's nostrils, Janet forcibly inflated Gloria's lungs several times. Noting the ease with which she was able to do this, she became confident there was no blockage. With her left hand she felt for a pulse. She found one, but it was weak.

Janet blew several more times as people began to arrive. Marjorie was there first, but soon others followed. By the time Janet was relieved from her resuscitative efforts by one of the other nurses, there were at least ten people in the room trying to help. Janet was impressed by the quick response: even the housekeeper was there.

Gloria's color responded quickly, to everyone's relief. Within three minutes several doctors including an anesthesiologist arrived from the second floor. By then a monitor had been set up showing a slow but otherwise normal heartbeat. The anesthesiologist deftly inserted an endotracheal tube and used an Ambu bag to inflate Gloria's lungs. This was more efficient than mouth-to-mouth, and Gloria's color improved even more.

But there were bad signs as well. When the anesthesiologist shone a penlight into Gloria's eyes her widely dilated pupils did not react. When another doctor tried to elicit reflexes, she was unable to do so.

After twenty minutes Gloria started to make efforts to breathe. Minutes later, she was breathing on her own. Reflexes also returned but in a fashion that did not bode well. Her arms and legs extended while her hands and feet flexed.

"Uh oh," the anesthesiologist said. "Looks like some signs of decerebrate rigidity. That's bad."

Janet did not want to hear this.

The anesthesiologist shook his head. "Too long without oxygen to the brain."

"I'm surprised," one of the other doctors said. She tilted the IV bottle to see what was running in. "I didn't think respiratory failure was a complication of this regimen."

"Chemo can do unexpected things," the anesthesiologist said. "It could have started with a cerebral vascular incident. I think Randolph better hear about this."

After rescuing her envelope, Janet stumbled out of the room. She knew scenes like this came with the territory, but knowing that hard fact didn't make them any easier to bear.

Marjorie came out of Gloria's room, saw Janet, and came over. She shook her head. "We're not having much luck with these advanced breast cancer patients," she said. "I think the powers that be better start questioning the treatment protocol."

Janet nodded but didn't speak.

"Being the first one on the scene is always tough," she said. "You did all you could."

Janet nodded again. "Thanks," she said.

"Now get that medicine for Helen Cabot before we have more trouble," Marjorie said. She gave Janet a sisterly pat on the shoulder.

Janet nodded. She took the stairs to get to the second floor, then crossed to the research building. She took an elevator to the seventh floor and, after asking for Ms. Richmond, was directed to her office.

The nursing director was expecting her and reached for the envelope. Opening it she poured the contents onto her desk blotter. With her index finger she pushed the shards around until she could read the labels.

Janet remained standing. Ms. Richmond's silence made her fear that somehow the woman knew exactly what Janet had done. Janet began to perspire.

"Did this cause a problem?" Ms. Richmond asked finally in her surprisingly soft voice.

"What do you mean?" Janet asked.

"When you broke these vials," Ms. Richmond said. "Did the glass cut you?"

"No," Janet said with relief. "I dropped them on the floor. I wasn't injured."

"Well, it's not the first time or the last," Ms. Richmond said. "I'm glad you didn't hurt yourself."

With surprising agility for her size, Ms. Richmond sprang up from behind her desk and went to a floor-to-ceiling cabinet that concealed a large, locked refrigerator. Unlocking and opening the refrigerator door, she took out two vials similar to the ones Janet had broken. The refrigerator was almost filled with such vials.

Ms. Richmond returned to her desk. Searching in a box in a side drawer, she took out printed labels identical to those on the shards on her desk. Licking the backs, she began applying the appropriate label to each vial. Before she was finished her phone rang.

Ms. Richmond answered and continued to work, holding the phone against her ear with a raised shoulder. But almost immediately the call took her full attention.

"What?" she cried. Her soft voice turned querulous. Her face reddened.

"Where?" Ms. Richmond demanded. "Fourth floor!" she said after a pause. "That's almost worse! Damnation!"

Ms. Richmond slammed the phone down and for a moment stared ahead without blinking. Then, noting Janet's presence with a start, she got up and handed over the vials. "I've got to go," she said urgently. "Be careful with that medicine."

Janet nodded and started to respond, but Ms. Richmond was already on her way out the door.

Janet paused at the threshold of Ms. Richmond's office and watched her walk rapidly away. Looking over her shoulder, she gazed at the cabinet which concealed the locked refrigerator. Something wasn't right about all this, but she wasn't sure what it was. Too much was happening.

RANDOLPH MASON marveled at Sterling Rombauer. He had some idea of Sterling's personal wealth as well as of his legendary business acumen, but he had no idea what motivated the man. Chasing around the country at other people's bidding would not be the life Mason would lead if he had command of the assets Sterling did. Nonetheless, Mason was grateful for Sterling's chosen occupation. Every time he hired the man, he got results.

"I don't think you have anything to worry about until the Sushita plane shows up here in Miami," Sterling was saying. "It had been waiting for Tanaka in Boston and was scheduled to go to Miami, but then it went to New York and on to Washington without him. Tanaka had to fly down here on a commercial flight."

"And you will know if and when the plane comes?" Dr. Mason asked.

Sterling nodded.

Dr. Mason's intercom crackled on. "Sorry to disturb you,

Dr. Mason," Patty, his secretary, said. "But you told me to warn you about Ms. Richmond. She's on her way in and she seems upset."

Dr. Mason swallowed hard. There was only one thing that could set Margaret off. He excused himself from Sterling and left his office to intercept his director of nursing. He caught her near Patty's desk and drew her aside.

"It's happened again," Ms. Richmond snapped. "Another breast cancer patient with a cyanotic respiratory arrest. Randolph, you have to do something!"

"Another death?" Dr. Mason asked.

"Not a death yet," Ms. Richmond said. "But almost worse, especially if the media gets involved. The patient is in a vegetative state with obvious brain damage."

"Good Lord," Dr. Mason exclaimed. "You're right; it could be worse if the family starts asking questions."

"Of course they will ask questions," Ms. Richmond said. "Once again, I must remind you that this could ruin everything we've worked for."

"You don't have to tell me," Dr. Mason said.

"Well, what are you going to do?"

"I don't know what else to do," Dr. Mason admitted. "Let's get Harris up here."

Dr. Mason had Patty call Robert Harris and told her to buzz him the moment Harris arrived. "I have Sterling Rombauer in my office," he told Ms. Richmond. "Maybe you should hear what he has to say about our medical student extern."

"That brat!" Ms. Richmond said. "When I caught him over in the hospital sneaking a look at Helen Cabot's chart I felt like throttling him."

"Calm down and come in and listen," Dr. Mason said.

Ms. Richmond reluctantly allowed Dr. Mason to lead her

into his office. Sterling got to his feet. Ms. Richmond told him he didn't have to stand on her account.

Dr. Mason had everybody sit, then asked Sterling to bring Ms. Richmond up to date.

"Sean Murphy is an interesting and complicated individual," Sterling said as he casually crossed his legs. "He's lived a rather double life, changing drastically when he got into Harvard undergraduate school, yet still clinging to his blue-collar Irish roots. And he's been successful. Currently he and a group of friends are about to start a company they intend to call Oncogen. Its goal will be to market diagnostic and therapeutic agents based on oncogene technology."

"Then it's clear what we should do," Ms. Richmond said. "Especially considering his being insufferably brash."

"Let Sterling finish," Dr. Mason said.

"He's extremely bright when it comes to biotechnology," Sterling said. "In fact I'd have to say he's gifted. His only real liability, as you've already guessed, is in the social realm. He has little respect for authority and manages to irritate a lot of people. That said, he's already been involved with the founding of a successful company that was bought out by Genentech. And he's had no significant difficulty finding funding for his second venture."

"He's sounding more and more like trouble," Ms. Richmond said.

"Not in the way you think," Sterling said. "The problem is that Sushita knows approximately as much as I do. It's my professional opinion that they will deem Sean Murphy a threat to their investment here at Forbes. Once they do, they'll be inspired to act. I'm not convinced a move to Tokyo and, essentially, a buyout, will work with Mr. Murphy. Yet if he stays here, I think they'll consider reneging on renewing your grant."

"I still don't understand why we don't send him back to Boston," Ms. Richmond said. "Then it's over. Why take the risk of jeopardizing our relationship with Sushita?"

Sterling looked at Dr. Mason.

Dr. Mason cleared his throat. "From my perspective," he said, "I don't want to be rash. The kid is good at what he does. This morning I went down to where he's working. He's got a whole generation of mice accepting the glycoprotein. On top of that, he showed me some promising crystals that he's been able to grow. He insists he'll have better in a week. No one else has been able to get this far. My problem is I'm caught between a rock and a hard place. A more dire threat to our Sushita funding is the fact that we have yet to provide them with a single patentable product. They expected something by now."

"In other words, you think we need this brat even with the risks," Ms. Richmond said.

"That's not the way I would phrase it," Dr. Mason said.

"Then why don't you call Sushita and explain it to them," Ms. Richmond said.

"That would not be advisable," Sterling said. "The Japanese prefer indirect communication so that confrontation can be avoided. They would not understand such a direct approach. Such a ploy would cause more anxiety than it would alleviate."

"Besides, I already alluded to all this with Hiroshi," Dr. Mason said. "And they still went ahead to investigate Mr. Murphy on their own."

"The Japanese businessman has a great problem with uncertainty," Sterling added.

"So what is your take on this kid?" Ms. Richmond asked. "Is he a spy? Is that why he's here?"

"No," Sterling said. "Not in any traditional sense. He's

obviously interested in your success with medulloblastoma, but it's from an academic point of view, not a commercial one."

"He was very open about his interests in the medulloblastoma work," Dr. Mason said. "The first time I met him he was clearly disappointed when I informed him he would not be permitted to work on the project. If he'd been some kind of spy, I think he'd keep a lower profile. Rocking the boat only draws further scrutiny."

"I agree," Sterling said. "As a young man he's still motivated by idealism and altruism. He has not yet been poisoned by the new commercialism of science in general and medical research in particular."

"Yet he's already started his own company," Ms. Richmond pointed out. "That sounds pretty commercial to me."

"But he and his partners were essentially selling their products at cost," Sterling said. "The profit motive did not play a role until the company was bought out."

"So what's the solution?" Ms. Richmond asked.

"Sterling will monitor the situation," Dr. Mason said. "He'll keep us informed on a daily basis. He'll protect Mr. Murphy from the Japanese as long as he is a help to us. If Sterling decides he is acting as a spy, he'll let us know. Then we'll send him back to Boston."

"An expensive babysitter," Ms. Richmond said.

Sterling smiled and nodded in agreement. "Miami in March is very agreeable," he said. "Particularly at the Grand Bay Hotel."

A short burst of static from Dr. Mason's intercom preceded Patty's voice: "Mr. Harris is here."

Dr. Mason thanked Sterling, indicating the meeting was over. As he accompanied Sterling out of the office, Dr. Mason couldn't help but agree with Ms. Richmond's assessment: Sterling was an expensive babysitter. But Dr. Mason was convinced the money was well spent and, thanks to Howard Pace, readily available.

Harris was standing next to Patty's desk, and for the sake of propriety, Dr. Mason introduced him to Sterling. As he did, he couldn't help but feel each man was the other's antithesis.

After sending Harris into his office, Dr. Mason thanked Sterling for all he'd done and implored him to keep them informed. Sterling assured him he would, and left. Dr. Mason then went back into his office to deal with the current crisis.

Dr. Mason closed the door behind him. He noticed Harris was standing stiffly in the center of the room; his patent leather visored hat with its gold trim was wedged under his left arm.

"Relax," Dr. Mason said as he went around behind his desk and sat down.

"Yes, sir," Harris said smartly. He didn't move.

"For crissake, sit down!" Dr. Mason said when he noticed Harris was still standing.

Harris took a seat, his hat remaining beneath his arm.

"I suppose you've heard another breast cancer patient has died," Dr. Mason said. "At least for all practical purposes."

"Yes, sir," Harris said crisply.

Dr. Mason eyed his head of security with mild irritation. On the one hand he appreciated the professionalism of Robert Harris; on the other hand the militaristic play-acting bothered him. It wasn't appropriate for a medical institution. But he'd never complained because until these breast cancer deaths, security had never been a problem.

"As we told you in the past," Dr. Mason said, "we believe

some misguided demented individual is doing this. It's becoming intolerable. It has to be stopped.

"I've asked you to make this your number-one priority. Have you been able to turn anything up?"

"I assure you, this problem has my undivided attention," Harris said. "Following your advice I've done extensive background checks on most all of the professional staff. I've checked references by calling hundreds of institutions. No discrepancies have turned up so far. I'll now be expanding the checks to other personnel who have access to patients. We tried to monitor some of the breast cancer patients, but there are too many to keep tabs on all the time. Perhaps we should consider putting security cameras in all the rooms." Harris did not mention his suspicion of the possible connection between these cases and the death of a nurse and the attempted assault of another. After all, it was only a hunch.

"Maybe cameras in every breast cancer patient's room is what we have to do," Ms. Richmond said.

"It would be expensive," Harris warned. "Not only the cost of the cameras and the installation, but also the additional personnel to watch the monitors."

"Expense might be an academic concern," Ms. Richmond said. "If this problem continues and the press gets hold of it, we might not have an institution."

"I'll look into it," Harris promised.

"If you need additional manpower, let us know," Dr. Mason said. "This has to be stopped."

"I understand, sir," Harris said. But he didn't want help. He wanted to do this on his own. At this point it had become a matter of honor. No screwball psychotic was going to get the best of him.

"And what about this attack last night at the residence?" Ms. Richmond asked. "I have a hard enough time recruiting nursing personnel. We can't have them attacked in the temporary housing we offer them."

"It is the first time security has been a problem at the residence," Harris said.

"Maybe we need security people there during the evening hours," Ms. Richmond suggested.

"I'd be happy to put together a cost analysis," Harris said.

"I think the patient issue is more important," Dr. Mason said. "Don't dilute your efforts at the present time."

"Yes, sir," Harris said.

Dr. Mason looked at Ms. Richmond. "Anything else?"

Ms. Richmond shook her head.

Dr. Mason glanced back at Harris. "We're counting on you," he said.

"Yes, sir," Harris said as he got to his feet. By reflex he started to salute, but he caught himself in time.

"VERY IMPRESSIVE!" Sean said aloud. He was sitting by himself in the glass-enclosed office in the middle of his expansive lab. He was at an empty metal desk, and he had the copies of the thirty-three charts spread out in front of him. He'd chosen the office in case someone suddenly appeared. If they did he'd have enough time to sweep the charts into one of the empty file drawers. Then he'd pull over the ledger featuring the protocol he'd developed to immunize the mice with the Forbes glycoprotein.

What Sean found so impressive were the statistics concerning the medulloblastoma cases. The Forbes Cancer Center had indeed achieved a one hundred percent remission rate over the last two years, which contrasted sharply with the one hundred percent fatality rate over the eight years prior to that. Through follow-up MRI studies, even large tumors were shown to have completely disappeared after successful treatment. As far as Sean was concerned, such consistent results were unheard of in the treatment of cancer except for the situation of cancer *in situ,* meaning extremely small, localized neoplasia that could be completely excised or otherwise eliminated.

For the first time since he'd arrived, Sean had had a reasonable morning. No one had bothered him; he hadn't seen Hiroshi or any of the other researchers. He'd started the day by injecting more of the mice which had given him a chance to get the copies of the charts up to his office. Then he'd toyed with the crystallization problem, growing a few crystals that he thought would keep Dr. Mason content for a week or so. He'd even had the director come down to see some of the crystals. Sean knew he'd been impressed. At that point, reasonably confident he wouldn't be disturbed, Sean had retired into the glass office to review the charts.

First he'd read through all the charts to gain an overall impression. Then he'd gone back, checking on epidemiological aspects. He'd noted that the patients represented a wide range of ages and races. They were also of varying sex. But the predominant group consisted of middle-aged white males, not the typical group seen with medulloblastoma. Sean guessed that the statistics were skewed due to economic considerations. The Forbes was not a cheap hospital. People needed adequate medical insurance or sizable savings accounts to be patients there. He also noted that the cases came from various major cities around the country in a truly national distribution.

But then, as if to show how dangerous generalizations were, he discovered a case from a small southwestern Florida town: Naples, Florida. Sean had seen the town on a map. It was the southern-most town on the west coast of Florida, just north of the Everglades. The patient's name was Malcolm Betencourt, and he was nearing two years since the commencement of his treatment. Sean noted the man's address and phone number. He thought he might want to talk with him.

As for the tumors themselves, Sean noted that most were multifocal rather than being a single lesion, which was more common. Since they were multifocal, the attending physicians in most cases had initially believed they were dealing with a metastatic tumor, one that had spread to the brain from some other organ like lung, kidney, or colon. In all these cases, the referring physicians had expressed surprise when the lesions turned out to be primary brain tumors arising from primitive neural elements. Sean also noted that the tumors were particularly aggressive and fast-growing. They would have undoubtedly led to rapid death had not therapy been instituted.

Concerning therapy, Sean noted that it did not vary. The dosage and rate of administration of the coded medication was the same for all patients although it was adjusted for weight. All patients had experienced about a week of hospitalization and after discharge were followed in the outpatient clinic at intervals of two weeks, four weeks, two months, six months, then annually. Thirteen of the thirty-three patients had reached the annual-visit stage. Sequelae from the illness were minimal and were associated with mild neurological deficits secondary to the expanding tumor masses prior to treatment rather than to the treatment itself.

Sean was also impressed with the charts themselves. He knew he was looking at a wealth of material that would probably take him a week to digest.

Concentrating as deeply as he was, Sean was startled when the phone on his desk began to ring. It was the first time it had ever rung. He picked it up, expecting a wrong number. To his surprise, it was Janet.

"I have the medicine," she said tersely.

"Great!" Sean said.

"Can you meet me in the cafeteria?" she asked.

"Absolutely," Sean said. He could tell something was wrong. Her voice sounded strained. "What's the matter?"

"Everything," Janet said. "I'll tell you when I see you. Can you leave now?"

"I'll be there in five minutes," Sean said.

After hiding all the charts, Sean descended in the elevator and crossed over the pedestrian bridge to the hospital. He guessed he was being observed by camera and felt like waving to indicate as much, but resisted the temptation.

When he arrived in the cafeteria Janet was already there, sitting at a table with a cup of coffee in front of her. She didn't look happy.

Sean slid into a chair across from her.

"What's wrong?" he asked.

"One of my patients is in a coma," Janet said. "I'd just started an IV on her. One minute she was fine, the next minute not breathing."

"I'm sorry to hear that," Sean said. He'd had some exposure to the emotional traumas of hospital life, so he could empathize to an extent.

"At least I got the medicine," she said.

"Was it difficult?" Sean asked.

"Emotionally more than anything else," Janet said.

"So where is it?"

"In my purse," she said. She glanced around to make sure no one was watching them. "I'll give the vials to you under the table."

"You don't have to make this so melodramatic," Sean

said. "Sneaking around draws more attention than just acting normal and handing them over."

"Humor me," Janet said. She fumbled with her purse.

Sean felt her hand hit his knee. He reached under the table and two vials dropped into his hand. Respecting Janet's sensitivity he slipped them into his pockets, one on each side. Then he scraped back his chair and stood up.

"Sean!" Janet complained.

"What?" he asked.

"Do you have to be so obvious? Can't you wait five minutes like we're having a conversation?"

He sat down. "People aren't watching us," he said. "When are you going to learn?"

"How can you be so sure?" she asked.

Sean started to say something, then thought better of it.

"Can we talk about something fun for a change?" Janet asked. "I'm completely stressed out."

"What do you want to talk about?"

"What we can do come Sunday," Janet said. "I need to get away from the hospital and all this tension. I want to do something relaxing and fun."

"Okay, it's a date," Sean promised. "Meanwhile, I'm eager to get back to the lab with this medicine. Would it be so obvious if I were to leave now?"

"Go!" Janet commanded. "You're impossible."

"See you back at the beach apartment," Sean said. He moved away quickly lest Janet say something about his not being invited. He looked back and waved as he left the cafeteria.

Hurrying over the bridge between the two buildings, he thrust his hands into his pockets and palmed the two vials. He couldn't wait to get started. Thanks to Janet, he felt some of the investigative excitement he'd expected when he'd made the decision to come to the Forbes Cancer Center.

ROBERT HARRIS carried the cardboard box of employee files into his small windowless office and set them on the floor next to his desk. Sitting down, he opened the top of the box and pulled out the first file.

After the conversation with Dr. Mason and Ms. Richmond, Harris had gone directly to personnel. With the help of Henry Falworth, the personnel manager, he'd compiled a list of non-professionals who had access to patients. The list included food service personnel who distributed menus and took orders and those who delivered meals and picked up the trays. The list also included the janitorial and maintenance staffs who were occasionally called to patient rooms for odd jobs. Finally, the list ran to housekeeping: those who cleaned the rooms, the halls, and the lounges of the hospital.

All in all, the number of people on the list was formidable. Unfortunately he had no other ideas to pursue save for the camera surveillance, and he knew such an operation would prove too costly. He would investigate prices and put together a proposal, but he knew Dr. Mason would find the price unacceptable.

Harris's plan was to go through the fifty or so files rather quickly to see if anything caught his attention, anything that might seem unlikely or strange. If he found something that was questionable, he'd put the file in a group to investigate first. Harris wasn't a psychologist any more than he was a doctor, but he thought that whoever was crazy enough to be killing patients would have to have something weird on his record.

The first file belonged to Ramon Concepcion, a food

service employee. Concepcion was a thirty-five-year-old man of Cuban extraction who'd worked a number of food service jobs in hotels and restaurants since he was sixteen. Harris read through his employment application and looked at the references. He even glanced at his health care utilization. Nothing jumped out at him. He tossed the file on the floor.

One by one, Harris worked through the box of files. Nothing caught his eye until he came to Gary Wanamaker, another food service employee. Under the heading experience Gary had listed five years' work in the kitchen at Rikers Island Prison in New York. In the employment photo the man had brown hair. Harris put that file on the corner of his desk.

It was only five files later that Harris came across another file that caught his eye. Tom Widdicomb worked in housekeeping. What got Harris's attention was the fact that the man had trained as an emergency medical technician. Even though he'd had a series of housekeeping jobs subsequent to his EMT training, including a stint at Miami General Hospital, the thought of a guy with emergency medical training working housekeeping seemed odd. Harris looked at the employment photo. The man had brown hair. Harris put Widdicomb's file on top of Wanamaker's.

A few files later, Harris came across another file that tweaked his curiosity. Ralph Seaver worked for the maintenance department. This man had served time for rape in Indiana. There it was right in the file! Included was even a phone number of the man's former probation officer in Indiana. Harris shook his head. He'd not expected to find such fertile material. The professional staff files had been boring in comparison. Except for a few substance abuse problems and one child molestation allegation, he'd not found anything. But with this group, he'd only gone through a quarter of the files and had already yanked three that he thought deserved a closer look.

INSTEAD OF sitting down and having coffee on her afternoon coffee break, Janet took the elevator to the second floor and visited the intensive care unit. She had a lot of respect for the nurses who worked there. She never understood how they could take the constant strain. Janet had tried the ICU after graduation. She found the work intellectually stimulating, but after a few weeks decided it wasn't for her. There was too much tension, and too little patient interaction. Most of the patients were in no position to relate on any level; many of them were unconscious.

Janet went over to Gloria's bed and looked down at her. She was still in a coma and had not improved although she was still breathing without mechanical assistance. Her widely dilated pupils had not constricted, nor did they react to light. Most disturbing of all, an EEG showed very little brain activity.

A visitor was gently stroking Gloria's forehead. She was about thirty years old with coloring and features similar to Gloria's. As Janet raised her head, their eyes met.

"Are you one of Gloria's nurses?" the visitor asked.

Janet nodded. She could tell the woman had been crying.

"I'm Marie," she said. "Gloria's older sister."

"I'm very sorry this happened," Janet said.

"Well," Marie said with a sigh, "maybe it's for the best. This way she won't have to suffer."

Janet agreed for Marie's benefit, although in her own heart she felt differently. Gloria had still had a shot at beating breast cancer, especially with her positive, upbeat attitude. Janet had seen people with even more advanced disease go into remission.

Fighting tears of her own, Janet returned to the fourth floor. Again, she threw herself into her work. It was the easiest way to avoid thoughts that would only leave her cursing the unfairness of it all. Unfortunately the ruse was only partly successful, and she kept seeing the image of Gloria's face as she thanked Janet for starting her IV. But then suddenly the ruse was no longer needed. A new tragedy intervened that matched Gloria's and overwhelmed Janet.

A little after two, Janet gave an intramuscular injection to a patient whose room was at the far end of the corridor. On her way back to the nurses' station, she decided to check in on Helen Cabot.

Earlier that morning and about an hour after Janet had added the coded medication to Helen's IV and adjusted the rate, Helen complained of a headache. Concerned about her condition, Janet had called Dr. Mason and informed him of this development. He'd recommended treating the headache minimally and asked to be called back if it got worse.

Although the headache had not gone away after the administration of an oral analgesic, it had not grown worse. Nevertheless, Janet had checked on Helen frequently at first, then every hour or so throughout the day. With the headache unchanged and her vital signs and level of consciousness remaining normal, Janet's concern had lessened.

Now, almost 2:15, as Janet came through the door, she was alarmed to discover that Helen's head had lolled to the side and off the pillow. Approaching the bed, she noticed something even more disturbing: the woman's breathing was irregular. It was waxing and waning in a pattern that suggested a serious neurological dysfunction. Janet phoned the nurses' station and told Tim she had to speak with Marjorie immediately.

"Helen Cabot is Cheyne-Stoking," Janet said when Marjorie came on the line, referring to Helen's breathing.

"Oh no!" Marjorie exclaimed. "I'll call the neurologist and Dr. Mason."

Janet took the pillow away and straightened Helen's head. Then she took a small flashlight she always carried and shined it in each of Helen's pupils. They weren't equal. One was dilated and unresponsive to the light. Janet shuddered. This was something she'd read about. She guessed that the pressure had built up inside Helen's head to the point that part of her brain was herniating from the upper compartment into the lower, a life-threatening development.

Reaching up, Janet slowed Helen's IV to a "keep open" rate. For the moment that was all she could do.

Soon other people started to arrive. First it was Marjorie and other nurses. Then the neurologist, Dr. Burt Atherton, and an anesthesiologist, Dr. Carl Seibert, rushed in. The doctors began barking orders in an attempt to lower the pressure inside Helen's head. Then Dr. Mason arrived, winded by his run from the research building.

Janet had never met Dr. Mason, although she'd spoken with him on the phone. He was titularly in charge of Helen's case, but in this neurological crisis he deferred to Dr. Atherton.

Unfortunately, none of the emergency measures worked, and Helen's condition deteriorated further. It was decided that emergency brain surgery was needed. To Janet's dismay, arrangements were made to transfer Helen to Miami General Hospital.

"Why is she being transferred?" Janet asked Marjorie when she had a moment.

"We're a specialty hospital," Marjorie explained. "We don't have a neurosurgical service."

Janet was shocked. The kind of emergency surgery Helen needed required speed. It did not require an entire neurosurgical service, just an operating room and someone who knew how to make a hole in the skull. Obviously with the biopsies they'd been doing, that expertise was available at the Forbes.

With frantic preparations, Helen was readied to leave. She was moved from her bed onto a gurney. Janet aided in the transfer, moving Helen's feet, then running alongside holding the IV bottle aloft as the gurney was rushed to the elevator.

In the elevator Helen took a turn for the worse. Her breathing, which had been irregular when Janet had entered her room, now stopped altogether. Helen's pale face quickly began to turn blue.

For the second time that day, Janet started mouth-to-mouth resuscitation while the anesthesiologist yelled for someone to get an endotracheal tube and an Ambu bag as soon as they got to the first floor.

When the elevator stopped and the doors opened, one of the fourth-floor nurses rushed out. Another kept the doors from closing. Janet continued her efforts until Dr. Seibert nudged her aside and deftly slipped in an endotracheal tube. After connecting the Ambu bag, he began to inflate Helen's lungs to near capacity. The blue cast to Helen's face transformed into a translucent alabaster.

"Okay, let's go," Dr. Seibert yelled.

The tightly packed group rushed Helen out to the ambulance receiving dock, collapsed the gurney, and pushed it inside the waiting vehicle. Dr. Seibert boarded with Helen, maintaining her respiration. The doors were slammed shut and secured.

With flashing light and piercing siren, the ambulance roared out of the parking bay and disappeared around the building.

Janet turned to look at Marjorie, who was standing next to Dr. Mason. She was consoling him with her hand on his shoulder.

"I can't believe it," Dr. Mason was saying with a halting voice. "I suppose I should have prepared myself. It was bound to happen. But we've been so lucky with our medulloblastoma treatments. With every success, I thought just maybe we could avoid this kind of tragedy."

"It's the people in Boston's fault," Ms. Richmond said. She'd appeared on the scene just before the ambulance had left. "They wouldn't listen to us. They kept her too long."

"We should have put her in the ICU," Dr. Mason said. "But she'd been so stable."

"Maybe they'll save her at Miami General," Marjorie said, trying to be optimistic.

"It would be a miracle," Dr. Atherton said. "It was pretty clear her uncus had herniated below the calyx and was compressing her medulla oblongata."

Janet repressed an urge to tell the man to keep his thoughts to himself. She hated the way some doctors hid behind their jargon.

All at once, as if on some unseen cue, the entire group turned and disappeared through the swinging doors of the Forbes ambulance dock. Janet was left outside. She was just as glad to be alone. It was suddenly so peaceful by the lawn. A huge banyan tree graced the grounds. Behind the banyan was a flowering tree Janet had never seen before. A warm, moist tropical breeze caressed her face. But the pleasant scene was still marred by the undulating siren of the receding ambulance. To Janet, it sounded like a death knell for Helen Cabot.

Tom Widdicomb wandered from room to room in his mother's ranch house, alternately crying and cursing. He was so anxious he couldn't sit still. One minute he was hot, the next freezing. He felt sick.

In fact, he'd felt so sick he'd gone to his supervisor and told him as much. The supervisor had sent him home, commenting that he was pale. He'd even noticed that Tom was shaking.

"You've got the whole weekend," the supervisor had said. "Go to bed, sleep it off. It's probably a touch of the 'snowbird flu.' "

So Tom had gone home, but he'd been unable to rest. The problem was Janet Reardon. He'd almost had a heart attack when she'd come knocking on Gloria's door minutes after he'd put Gloria to sleep. In an absolute panic he'd fled into the bathroom, sure that he'd been cornered. He'd gotten desperate enough to take his gun out.

But then the pandemonium in the room gave him the diversion he needed to get away. When he'd emerged from the bathroom, no one had even noticed. He'd been able to slip into the hall with his bucket.

The problem was that Gloria was still alive. Janet Reardon had saved her, and Gloria was still suffering, although now she was out of reach. She was in the ICU where Tom was not allowed to go.

Consequently, Alice still wouldn't talk to him. Tom had continued to plead, but without success. Alice knew Tom couldn't get to Gloria until she was transferred out of the ICU and put back into a private room.

That left Janet Reardon. To Tom, she seemed like a devil sent to destroy the life that he and his mother had created. He knew he had to get rid of her. Only now he didn't know where she lived. Her name had been removed from the residence chart in administration. She'd moved out.

Tom checked his watch. He knew her shift ended when his would have ended: three P.M. But he also knew nurses stayed longer because of their report. He'd have to be in the parking lot when she came out. Then he could follow her home and shoot her. If he was able to do that he was reasonably confident Alice would break this petulant silence and talk with him.

"HELEN CABOT died!" Janet repeated through sudden tears. As a professional it wasn't like her to cry over the death of a patient, but she was extra sensitive since there'd been two tragedies in the same day. Besides, Sean's response frustrated her. He was more interested in where Helen's body was than the fact that the woman was dead.

"I understand she died," Sean said soothingly. "I don't mean to sound callous. Part of the way I respond is to cover the pain I feel. She was a wonderful person. It's such a shame. And to think that her father runs one of the largest computer software companies in the world."

"What difference does that make?" Janet snapped. She wiped under her eyes with the knuckle of her index finger.

"Not much," Sean admitted. "It's just that death is such a leveler. Having all the money in the world makes no difference."

"So now you're a philosopher," Janet said wryly.

"All of us Irish are philosophers," Sean said. "It's how we deal with the tragedy of our lives."

They were sitting in the cafeteria where Sean had agreed to come when Janet called him. She'd called him after report, before she left for the apartment. She'd said she needed to talk.

"I don't mean to upset you," Sean continued. "But I'm truly interested in the location of Helen's body. Is it here?"

Janet rolled her eyes. "No, it's not here," she said. "I don't know where it is truthfully. But I suppose it's over at the Miami General."

"Why would it be there?" Sean asked. He leaned across the table.

Janet explained the whole episode, indicating her indignation that they couldn't do an emergency craniotomy at the Forbes.

"She was in extremities," Janet said. "They never should have transferred her. She never even made it to the OR. We heard she died in the Miami General emergency room."

"How about you and me driving over there?" Sean suggested. "I'd like to find her."

For a moment, Janet thought Sean was kidding. She rolled her eyes again, thinking Sean was about to make some sick joke.

"I'm serious," Sean said. "There's a chance they'll do an autopsy. I'd love to have a tumor sample. For that matter, I'd like to have some blood and even some cerebrospinal fluid."

Janet shuddered in revulsion.

"Come on," Sean said. "Remember, we're in this thing together. I'm really sorry she died—you know I am. But now that she's dead, we should concentrate on the science. With you in a nursing uniform and me in a white coat, we'll have the run of the place. In fact, let's bring some of our own syringes just in case."

"In case of what?" Janet asked.

"In case we need them," Sean said. He winked conspiratorially. "It's best to be prepared," he added.

Either Sean was the world's best salesman or she was so stressed out, she was incapable of resisting. Fifteen minutes later she found herself climbing into the passenger side of Sean's 4×4 to head over to a hospital she'd never visited, in hopes of obtaining the brain tissue of one of her patients who'd just expired.

"THAT'S HIM." Sterling pointed at Sean Murphy through the car's windshield for Wayne Edwards's benefit. Wayne was a formidable Afro-American whose services Sterling enlisted when he did business in south Florida. Wayne was an ex-Army sergeant, ex-policeman, and ex–small businessman who'd gone into the security business. He was an ex from as many things as Sterling was, and like Sterling, he now used his varied experience for a similar career. Wayne was a private investigator, and although he specialized in domestic squabbles, he was talented and effective in other areas as well. Sterling had met him a few years previously when both were representing a powerful Miami businessman.

"He looks like a tough kid," Wayne said. He prided himself on instantaneous assessments.

"I believe he is," Sterling said. "He was an all-star hockey player from Harvard who could have played professionally if he'd been inclined."

"Who's the chick?" Wayne asked.

"Obviously one of the nurses," Sterling said. "I don't know anything about his female liaisons."

"She's a looker," Wayne said. "What about Tanaka Yamaguchi? Have you seen him lately?"

"No, I haven't," Sterling said. "But I think I will. My contact at the FAA told me the Sushita jet has just refiled a flight plan to Miami."

"Sounds like action," Wayne said.

"In a way, I hope so," Sterling said. "It will give us a chance to resolve this problem."

Wayne started his dark green Mercedes 420SEL. The windows were heavily tinted. From the outside it was difficult to see within, especially in bright sunlight. He eased the car away from the curb and headed for the exit. Since a hospital shift had changed half an hour earlier, there was still considerable traffic leaving the parking area. Wayne allowed several cars to come between his car and Sean's. Once on Twelfth, they headed north over the Miami River.

"I got sandwiches and drinks in the cooler in the back seat," Wayne said while motioning over his shoulder.

"Good thinking," Sterling said. That was one of the things he liked about Wayne. He thought ahead.

"Well, well," Wayne said. "Short trip. They're turning already."

"Isn't this another hospital?" Sterling asked. He leaned forward to survey the building Sean was approaching.

"This area is hospital city, man," Wayne said. "You can't drive a mile without running into one. But they're heading to the mama hospital. That's Miami General."

"That's curious," Sterling said. "Maybe the nurse works there."

"Uh oh," Wayne said. "I do believe we have company."

"What do you mean?" Sterling asked.

"See that lime green Caddy behind us?" Wayne asked.

"It would be hard to miss it," Sterling said.

"I've been watching it since we crossed the Miami River," Wayne said. "I have the distinct impression it's following our Mr. Murphy. I wouldn't have noticed it except I used to have wheels just like it in my younger days. Mine was burgundy. Good car, but a devil to parallel park."

Sterling and Wayne watched as Sean and his companion

entered the hospital through the emergency entrance. Not far behind was the man who'd arrived in the lime green Cadillac.

"I think my initial impression was correct," Wayne said. "Looks to me like that dude is tighter on their tail than we are."

"I don't like this," Sterling said. He opened the passenger door, got out, and glanced back at the dumpy Cadillac. Then he bent down to talk to Wayne. "This is not Tanaka's style, but I can't risk it. I'm going in. If Murphy comes out, follow him. If the man in the Cadillac comes out first, follow him. I'll be in touch over the cellular phone."

Grabbing his portable phone, Sterling hurried after Tom Widdicomb, who was climbing the steps on the side of the ambulance dock outside the Miami General emergency room.

WITH THE assistance of a harried resident in the emergency room who'd given them directions, it did not take Sean and Janet long to find the pathology department. Once there, Sean sought out another resident. He told Janet that between the residents and the nurses you could find out anything you wanted to know about a hospital.

"I'm not doing autopsies this month," the resident said, trying to rush away.

Sean blocked his path. "How can I find out if a patient will be posted?" he asked.

"You have the chart number?" the resident asked.

"Just the name," Sean said. "She died in the ER."

"Then we probably won't be autopsying the case," the resident said. "ER deaths are usually assigned to the medical examiner."

"How can I be sure?" Sean persisted.

"What's the name?"

"Helen Cabot," Sean said.

The resident graciously went over to a nearby wall phone and made a call. It took him less than two minutes to ascertain that Helen Cabot was not scheduled.

"Where do bodies go?" Sean asked.

"To the morgue," the resident said. "It's in the basement. Take the main elevators to B1 and follow the red signs with the big letter M on them."

After the resident hurried on, Sean looked at Janet. "You game?" he asked. "If we find her then we'll know her disposition for sure. We might even be able to get a little body fluid."

"I've come this far," Janet said with resignation.

TOM WIDDICOMB felt calmer than he had all day. At first he'd been dismayed when Janet had appeared with a young guy in a white coat, but then things took a turn for the better when the two went directly to the Miami General. Having worked there, Tom knew the place from top to bottom. He also knew that Miami General would be crowded with people at that time of day since formal visiting hours had just started. And crowds meant chaos. Maybe he would get his chance at Janet and wouldn't even have to follow her home. If he had to shoot the fellow in the white coat, too bad!

Following the couple within the hospital had not been easy, especially once they went to pathology. Tom had thought he'd lost them and was about to return to the parking lot to keep an eye on the 4×4 when they suddenly reappeared. Janet came so close, he was sure she'd recognize him. He'd panicked, but luckily hadn't moved. Fearing

Janet would scream as she had in the Forbes residence, he'd gripped the pistol in his pocket. If she had screamed he would have had to shoot her on the spot.

But Janet glanced away without reacting. Obviously she'd failed to identify him. Feeling more secure, Tom followed the pair more closely. He even rode down in the same elevator with them, something he'd not been willing to do when they'd gone up to pathology.

Janet's friend pushed the button for B1, and Tom was ecstatic. Of all the locations in Miami General, Tom liked the basement the best. When he'd worked at this hospital, he snuck down there many times to visit the morgue or to read the newspaper. He knew the labyrinthine tunnels like the back of his hand.

Tom's anxiety about Janet recognizing him returned when everyone else but a doctor and a uniformed maintenance man got off on the first floor. But even with so slim a crowd to lose himself in, Janet failed to remember him.

As soon as the elevator reached the basement, the doctor and the maintenance man turned right and walked quickly away. Janet and Sean paused briefly, looking in both directions. Then they turned left.

Tom waited behind in the elevator until the doors began to shut. Bumping them open, he stepped out and followed the couple, keeping at a distance of about fifty feet. He slipped his hand in his pocket and gripped the gun. He even put his finger between the trigger and its guard.

The farther from the elevators the couple walked, the better Tom liked it. This was a perfect location for what he had to do. He couldn't believe his luck. They were entering an area of the basement few people visited. The only sounds were their footfalls and the slight hissing of steam pipes.

"THIS PLACE feels appropriately like Hades," Sean said. "I wonder if we're lost."

"There haven't been any turnoffs since the last M sign," Janet said. "I think we're okay."

"Why do they always put morgues in such isolated places?" Sean said. "Even the lighting is getting lousy."

"It's probably near a loading dock," Janet said. Then she pointed ahead. "There's another sign. We're on the right track."

"I think they want their mistakes as far away as possible," Sean quipped. "It wouldn't be good advertising to have the morgue near the front entrance."

"I forgot to ask how you made out with the medicine I got for you."

"I haven't gotten very far," Sean admitted. "What I did was start a gel electrophoresis."

"That tells me a lot," Janet said sarcastically.

"It's actually simple," Sean said. "I suspect the medicine is made up of proteins because they have to be using some sort of immunotherapy. Since proteins all have electric charges, they move in an electrical field. When you put them in a specific gel, which coats them with a uniform charge, they move only in relation to their size. I want to find out how many proteins I'm dealing with and what their approximate molecular weight is. It's a first step."

"Just make sure you learn enough to justify the effort for getting it," Janet said.

"I hope you don't think you're off the hook with this one sample," Sean said. "Next time I want you to get some of Louis Martin's."

"I don't think I can do it again," Janet said. "I can't break any more vials. If I do, they'll be suspicious for sure."

"Try a different method," Sean suggested. "Besides, I don't need so much."

"I thought by bringing the whole vial you'd have plenty," Janet said.

"I want to compare the medicines from different patients," Sean said. "I want to find out how they differ."

"I'm not sure they differ," Janet said. "When I went up to Ms. Richmond's office to get another vial, she took it from a large stock. I got the feeling they are all being treated by the same two drugs."

"I can't buy that," Sean said. "Every tumor is distinct antigenically, even the same kind of tumor. Oat cell cancer from one person will be different antigenically from the same type of cancer from another. In fact, if it arises as a new tumor even in the same person it will be antigenically distinct. And antigenically distinct tumors require different antibodies."

"Maybe they use the same drug until they biopsy the tumor," Janet suggested.

Sean looked at her with renewed respect. "That's an idea," he said.

Finally they rounded a corner and found themselves in front of a large insulated door. A metal sign at chest level read: *Morgue. Unauthorized Entry Forbidden.* Next to the door were several light switches.

"Uh oh," Sean said. "I guess they were expecting us. That's a rather formidable bolt action lock. And I didn't bring my tools."

Janet reached out and yanked on the door. It opened.

"I take that back," Sean said. "Guess they didn't expect us. At least not today."

A cool breeze issued from the room and swirled about their legs. Sean flipped on the lights. For a split second there was no response. Then raw fluorescent light blinked on.

"After you," Sean said gallantly.

"This was your idea," Janet said. "You first."

Sean stepped in with Janet immediately following. Several wide, concrete supporting piers blocked a view of the entire space, but it was obviously a large room. Old gurneys littered the room haphazardly. Each bore a shrouded body. The temperature, according to a gauge on the door, was forty-eight degrees.

Janet shivered. "I don't like this."

"This place is huge," Sean said. "Either the architects had a low opinion of the competence of the medical staff, or they planned for a national disaster."

"Let's get this over with," Janet said, hugging herself. The cold air was damp and penetrating. The smell was like a musty wet basement that had been closed for years.

Sean yanked back a sheet. "Oh, hello," he said. The bloodied face of a partially crushed construction worker stared up at him. He was still in his work clothes. Sean covered the man and went to the next.

Despite her revulsion, Janet did the same, going in the opposite direction.

"Too bad they're not in alphabetical order," Sean said. "There must be fifty bodies in here. This is one scene the Miami Chamber of Commerce wouldn't want to get up north."

"Sean!" Janet called, since they'd moved apart. "I think your humor is tasteless."

They worked around opposite ends of one of the concrete piers.

"Come on, Helen," Sean called in a childlike singsong. "Come out, come out wherever you are."

"That's especially crude," Janet said.

TOM WIDDICOMB was filled with excited anticipation. Even his mother had decided to break her long silence to tell him how clever he'd been to follow Janet and her friend into Miami General. Tom was well acquainted with the morgue. For what he intended to do, he couldn't have found a better place.

Approaching the insulated door, Tom pulled his gun from his pocket. Holding the pistol in his right hand, he pulled the thick door open and looked inside. Not seeing Janet or her friend, he stepped into the morgue and let the door ease closed. He couldn't see the couple but he could hear them. He distinctly heard Janet tell the man in the white coat to shut up.

Tom grasped the brass knob of the heavy lock on the door and slowly turned it. Silently the bolt slid into the striker plate. When Tom had worked at Miami General, the lock had never been used. He doubted if a key existed. Locking it ensured that he would not be disturbed.

"You're a smart man," Alice whispered.

"Thank you, Mom," Tom whispered back.

Holding the gun in both hands as he'd seen them do on TV, Tom moved forward, heading toward the nearest of the concrete piers. He could tell from Janet and her friend's voices that they were just on the opposite side of it.

"SOME OF these people have been in here for a while," Sean said. "It's like they've been forgotten."

"I was thinking the same thing," Janet said. "I don't think Helen Cabot's body is here. It would have been near the door. After all, she just died a few hours ago."

Sean was about to agree when the lights went out. With no windows and the door heavily girdled with insulating weather stripping, it wasn't just dark, it was absolutely black, like the vortex of a black hole.

The instant the lights went out there was an ear-piercing scream following by hysterical sobbing. At first Sean thought it was Janet, but having known where she was before the darkness enveloped him, he could tell that the crying was coming from behind the wall near the door to the hall.

So if it wasn't Janet, Sean thought, who was it?

The agony was infectious. Even the sudden darkness wouldn't have disturbed Sean ordinarily, but combined with the terrorized wailing, he found himself on the border of panic. What kept him from losing control was concern about Janet.

"I hate the dark," the voice cried out suddenly amid weeping. "Someone help me!"

Sean didn't know what to do. From the direction of the wailing came the sounds of frenzied commotion. Gurneys were bumping into each other, spilling their bodies onto the concrete floor.

"Help me!" the voice screamed.

Sean thought about calling out to try to calm the anguished individual, but he couldn't decide if that was a good idea or not. Unable to decide, he stayed quiet.

After the sound of more gurneys clanking against each other, there was a low-pitched thump as if someone had hit up against the insulated door. That was followed by a mechanical click.

For a moment a small amount of light fingered its way around the concrete pier. Sean caught sight of Janet with her hands pressed against her mouth. She was only about twenty feet from him. Then the darkness descended again like a heavy blanket. This time it was accompanied by silence.

"Janet?" Sean called softly. "You okay?"

"Yes," she answered. "What in God's name was that?"

"Move toward me," Sean said. "I'm coming toward you."

"All right," Janet said.

"This place is nuts," Sean said, wanting to keep talking as they groped toward each other. "I thought Forbes was weird, but this place takes the prize hands down. Remind me not to match here for my internship."

At last their groping hands met. Holding onto each other, they weaved their way through the gurneys in the direction of the door. Sean's foot nudged a body on the floor. He warned Janet she'd have to step over it.

"I'll have nightmares about this the rest of my life," Janet said.

"This is worse than Stephen King," Sean said.

Sean collided with the wall. Then, moving laterally, he felt the door. He pushed it open, and they both stumbled into the deserted corridor, blinking in the light.

Sean cupped Janet's face in his hands. "I'm sorry," he said.

"Life is never boring with you," Janet said. "But it wasn't your fault. Besides, we made it. Let's get out of here."

Sean kissed the end of her nose. "My feelings exactly."

Mild concern they would have trouble finding their way to the elevators proved unwarranted. In minutes the two were climbing into Sean's 4×4 and heading out of the parking lot.

"What a relief," Janet said. "Do you have any idea what happened in there?"

"I don't," Sean said. "It was so weird. It was like it was staged to scare us to death. Maybe there's some troll living in the basement who does that to everyone."

As they were about to exit the parking area, Sean put on

the brake suddenly, enough to make Janet reach out to support herself against the dash.

"What now?" she asked.

Sean pointed. "Look what we have here. How convenient," he said. "That brick building is the medical examiner's office. I had no idea it was so close. It must be fate telling us that Helen's body is over there. What do you say?"

"I'm not wild about the idea," Janet admitted. "But as long as we're here . . ."

"That's the ticket," Sean said.

Sean parked in visitor parking, and they entered the modern building. Inside they approached an information desk. A cordial black woman asked if she could be of assistance.

Sean told her that he was a medical student and Janet was a nurse. He asked to speak with one of the medical examiners.

"Which one?" the receptionist asked.

"How about the director?" Sean suggested.

"The chief is out of town," the receptionist said. "How about the deputy chief?"

"Perfect," Sean said.

After a short wait they were buzzed through an inner glass door and directed to a corner office. The deputy chief was Dr. John Stasin. He was about Sean's height but of slight build. He seemed genuinely pleased that Sean and Janet had stopped by.

"Teaching is one of our major functions," he said proudly. "We encourage the professional community to take an active interest in our work."

"We're interested in a specific patient," Sean said. "Her name is Helen Cabot. She died this afternoon in the Miami General emergency room."

"Name doesn't ring a bell," Dr. Stasin said. "Just a

minute. Let me call downstairs." He picked up the phone, mentioned Helen's name, nodded, and said "yeah" a few times, then hung up. It all happened extremely rapidly. It was apparent that grass did not grow under Dr. Stasin's feet.

"She arrived a few hours ago," Dr. Stasin said. "But we won't be posting her."

"Why not?" Sean asked.

"Two reasons," Dr. Stasin said. "First, she had documented brain cancer which her attending physician is willing to aver as the cause of death. Second, her family has expressed strong feelings against our posting her. In this kind of circumstance we feel it is better not to do it. Contrary to popular opinion, we're receptive to the family's wishes unless, of course, there is evidence of foul play or a strong suggestion that the public weal would be served by an autopsy."

"Is there a chance of getting any tissue samples?" Sean asked.

"Not if we don't do the autopsy," Dr. Stasin said. "If we did, the tissues removed would be available at our discretion. But since we're not posting the patient, property rights rest with the family. Besides, the body has already been picked up by the Emerson Funeral Home. It's on its way to Boston sometime tomorrow."

Sean thanked Dr. Stasin for his time.

"Not at all," he said. "We're here every day. Give a call if we can help."

Sean and Janet retraced the route to the car. The sun was setting; rush hour was in full swing.

"Surprisingly helpful individual," Janet said.

Sean only shrugged. He leaned his forehead against the steering wheel.

"This is depressing," he said. "Nothing seems to be going our way."

"If anyone should be melancholy it should be me," Janet reminded him, noting how glum he'd suddenly become.

"It's an Irish trait to be melancholy," Sean said. "So don't deny me. Maybe these difficulties we're having are trying to tell me something, like I should be heading back to Boston to do some real work. I never should have come down here."

"Let's go get something to eat," Janet said. She wanted to change the subject. "We could go back to that Cuban restaurant on the beach."

"I don't think I'm hungry," Sean said.

"A little *arroz con pollo* will make all the difference in the world," Janet said. "Trust me."

Tom Widdicomb had every light on in the house despite the fact that it wasn't even dark outside. But he knew it would be dark soon, and the idea terrified him. He did not like the dark. Even though it was hours after the terrible episode in the Miami General morgue he was still shaking. His mother had done something similar to him once when he was about six. He'd gotten irritated at her when she said he couldn't have any more ice cream, and he'd threatened to tell the teacher at school that they slept together unless she gave him more. Her response had been to shut him in a closet overnight. It had been Tom's worst experience. He'd been afraid of both the dark and closets ever since.

Tom had no idea how the lights had gone off in the morgue except that when he had finally found the door and pushed it open, he'd practically collided with a man dressed in a suit and tie. Since Tom had still had the gun in his hand, the man had backed away, giving Tom the opportunity to bolt down the corridor. The man had given chase, but Tom had lost him easily in the network of tunnels, corridors, and connecting rooms he knew so well. By the time Tom exited from an isolated basement door with outside steps leading to the parking area, the man was nowhere in sight.

Still panicked, Tom had run to his car, started it, and had headed toward the parking area exit. Fearing that whoever had chased him in the basement might have somehow gotten out faster than he, Tom had been watchful as he drove, and since the parking lot was not busy at that time, he'd seen the green Mercedes almost immediately.

Passing his intended exit, Tom had gone to another one that was seldom used. When the green Mercedes had followed suit, Tom was convinced he was being followed. Consequently, he concentrated on losing the car in the afternoon rush hour. Thanks to a traffic light and a few cars that had come between them, Tom had been able to speed away. He had driven aimlessly for half an hour just to make sure he was no longer being followed. Only then did he return home.

"You never should have gone into Miami General," Tom said, lambasting himself for his mother's benefit. "You should have stayed outside, waited, and followed her home."

Tom still had no idea where Janet lived.

"Alice, talk to me!" he shouted. But Alice wasn't saying a word.

All Tom could think to do was wait until Janet got off work on Saturday. Then he'd follow her. He'd be more careful. Then he'd shoot her.

"You'll see, Mom," Tom said to the freezer. "You'll see."

JANET HAD been right, although Sean wasn't about to admit it. What had especially perked him up were the tiny cups of Cuban coffee. He'd even tried what the people at the neighboring table had done. He'd drunk them like shots of alcohol, letting the mouthful of strong, thick, sweet fluid fall into his stomach in a bolus. The taste had been intense and the mild euphoria almost immediate.

The other thing that had helped Sean out of his dejected mood was Janet's positive attitude. Despite her difficult day and the episode at Miami General, she'd found the stamina to remain upbeat. She reminded Sean that they were doing rather well for only two days' effort. They had the thirty-three charts of the previous medulloblastoma patients and she'd managed to get two vials of the secret medicine. "I think that's pretty good progress," Janet said. "At this rate we're sure to get to the bottom of the Forbes success in treating these people. Come on, cheer up! We can do it!"

Janet's enthusiasm and the caffeine finally combined to win Sean over.

"Let's find out where this Emerson Funeral Home is located," he said.

"Why?" Janet asked, leery of such a suggestion.

"We can do a drive-by," Sean said. "Maybe they're working late. Maybe they give out samples."

The funeral home was on North Miami Avenue near the city cemetery and Biscayne Park. It was a well-cared-for two-story Victorian clapboard structure with dormers. It was painted white with a gray slate roof and was surrounded on three sides by a wide porch. It gave the impression that it had been a private home.

The rest of the neighborhood was not inviting. The immediately adjacent buildings were constructed of concrete block. There was a liquor store on one side and a plumbing supply store on the other. Sean parked directly in front in a loading zone.

"I don't think they're open," Janet said, gazing up at the building.

"Lots of lights," Sean said. All the ground-floor lights

were on except for the porch lights. The second floor was completely dark. "I think I'll give it a try."

Sean got out of the car, climbed the steps, and rang the bell. When no one answered, he looked into the windows. He even looked into some of the side windows before he came back to the car and got in. He started the engine.

"Where are we going now?" she asked.

"Back to the Home Depot," Sean said. "I need some more tools."

"I don't like the sound of this," Janet said.

"I can drop you off at the apartment," Sean suggested.

Janet was silent. Sean drove first to the apartment out on Miami Beach. He pulled over to the curb and stopped. They hadn't spoken en route.

"What exactly are you planning to do?" she asked at last.

"Continue my quest for Helen Cabot," Sean said. "I won't be long."

"Are you planning on breaking into that funeral home?" Janet asked.

"I'm going to 'ease in,' " Sean said. "That sounds better. I just want a few samples. If worst comes to worst, how bad is it? She's already dead."

Janet hesitated. At that point she had the door open and one foot out. As crazy as Sean's plan was, she felt responsible to a degree. As Sean had already pointed out several times, this whole venture had been her idea. Besides, she thought she'd go crazy sitting in the apartment waiting for him to return. Pulling her foot back into the car, Janet told Sean that she'd changed her mind and that she'd go along.

"I'm coming as a voice of rationality," she said.

"Okay by me," Sean said equably.

At Home Depot Sean bought a glass cutter, a suction device for lifting large pieces of glass, a sheet rock knife, a small hand-held jigsaw, and a cooler. After that he stopped at a 7-Eleven where he bought ice for the cooler and a few cold drinks. Then he drove back to the Emerson Funeral Home and parked again in the loading zone.

"I think I'll wait here," Janet said. "By the way, I think you're crazy."

"You're entitled to your opinion," Sean said. "I'd rather think of myself as determined."

"A cooler and cold drinks," Janet commented. "It's as if you think you're going on a picnic."

"I just like to be prepared," Sean said.

Sean hefted his pack of tools and the cooler and went up onto the funeral home porch.

Janet watched him check the windows. Several cars drove by in both directions. She was amazed at his sangfroid. It was as if he believed himself to be invisible. She watched as he went to a side window toward the back and put down his sack. Bending over, he took out some of the tools.

"Damn it all!" Janet said. With irritation she opened the door, climbed the funeral home's front steps, and walked around to where Sean was busily working. He'd attached the suction device to the window.

"A change of heart?" Sean asked without looking at Janet. He ran the glass cutter deftly around the perimeter of the window.

"Your lunacy floors me," Janet said. "I can't believe you're doing this."

"Brings back fond memories," Sean said. With a decisive tug, he pulled a large segment of the window glass out and laid it on the porch planking. After leaning inside, he told Janet that the alarm was a simple sash alarm which was what he'd guessed.

Sean reached in with his tools and the cooler and set them

on the floor. After stepping through the window himself, he leaned back out.

"If you're not coming in, it would be better if you waited in the car," he said. "A beautiful woman hanging around on a funeral home porch at this hour might attract some attention. This might take me a few minutes if I find Helen's body."

"Give me a hand!" Janet said impulsively as she tried to follow Sean's easy step through the window.

"Watch the edges!" Sean warned. "They're like razors."

Once Janet was inside, Sean hefted the tools and handed the cooler to Janet.

"Nice of them to leave the lights on for us," he said.

The two big rooms in the front were viewing rooms. The room they'd entered was a casket display room with eight caskets exhibited. Their lids were propped open. Across a narrow hall was an office. In the rear of the house, extending from one side to the other was the embalming room. The windows were covered with heavy drapes.

There were four stainless steel embalming tables. Two were occupied by shrouded corpses. The first was a heavyset woman who looked lifelike enough to be asleep except for the large Y-shaped, crudely sutured incision on the front of her torso. She'd been autopsied.

Moving to the second body, Sean lifted the sheet.

"Finally," Sean said. "Here she is."

Janet came over and mentally prepared herself before looking. The sight was less disturbing than she'd imagined. Like the other woman, Helen Cabot appeared in sleep-like repose. Her color was better than it had been in life. Over the last few days she'd become so pale.

"Too bad," Sean commented. "She's already been embalmed. I'll have to forego the blood sample."

"She appears so natural," Janet said.

"These embalmers must be good," Sean said. Then he pointed to a large glass-fronted metal cabinet. "See if you can find me some needles and a scalpel."

"What size?"

"I'm not choosy," Sean said. "The longer the needle the better."

Sean plugged in the jigsaw. When he tried it, it made a fearful noise.

Janet found a collection of syringes, needles, even suture material, and latex rubber gloves. But no scalpels. She brought what she'd found over to the table.

"Let's get the cerebrospinal fluid first," Sean said. He pulled on a pair of the gloves.

He had Janet help roll Helen onto her side so that he could insert a needle in the lumbar area between two vertebrae.

"This will only hurt for a second," Sean said as he patted Helen's upturned hip.

"Please," Janet said. "Don't joke around. You'll only upset me more than I already am."

To Sean's surprise he got cerebrospinal fluid on the first try. He'd only performed the maneuver on living patients a couple of times. He filled the syringe, capped it, and put it on the ice in the cooler. Janet let Helen roll back supine.

"Now for the hard part," he said, coming back to the embalming table. "I'm assuming you've seen an autopsy."

Janet nodded. She'd seen one but it had not been a pleasant experience. She braced herself as Sean prepared.

"No scalpels?" he asked.

She shook her head.

"Good thing I got this Sheetrock knife," Sean said. He picked up the knife and extended the blade. Then he ran it around the back of Helen's head from one ear to the other. Grasping the top edge of the incision, Sean yanked. With the kind of ripping sound of a weed being uprooted, Helen's scalp pulled away from her skull. Sean pulled it all the way down over Helen's face.

He palpated the craniotomy hole on the left side of Helen's skull that had been done at the Boston Memorial, then looked for the one on the right, the one done at Forbes two days previously.

"That's weird," he said. "Where the hell is the second craniotomy hole?"

"Let's not waste time," Janet said. Although she'd been nervous when they had entered, her anxiety was steadily increasing with each passing minute.

Sean continued to look for the second craniotomy hole, but finally gave up.

Picking up the jigsaw, he looked at Janet. "Stand back. Maybe you don't want to watch. This isn't going to be pretty."

"Just do it," Janet said.

Sean pushed the jigsaw blade into the craniotomy hole he'd found and turned the saw on. It bit into the bone and almost yanked itself out of his hands. The job would not be as easy as Sean had envisioned.

"You have to steady the head," Sean told Janet.

Grasping either side of Helen's face, Janet vainly tried to keep the head from jerking from side to side as Sean struggled to hold the bucking jigsaw. With great difficulty he managed to saw off a skull cap of bone. He had intended to keep the blade depth equal to the thickness of the skull, but it had been impossible. The saw blade had dug into the brain in several places, shredding the surface.

"This is disgusting," Janet said. She straightened up and brushed herself off.

"It's not a bone saw," Sean admitted. "We had to improvise."

The next part was almost as difficult. The Sheetrock knife was much larger than a scalpel, and Sean had difficulty inserting it below the brain to cut through the spinal cord and cranial nerves. He did the best he could. Then, inserting his hands on either side within the skull, he grasped the mutilated brain and yanked it out.

After taking the cold drinks out of the cooler, Sean dropped the brain onto the ice. Then he popped the top on one of the drinks and offered it to Janet. Sweat was beading his forehead.

Janet declined. She watched as he took a long drink, shaking her head in amazement. "Sometimes I don't believe you," she said.

Suddenly they both heard a siren. Janet panicked and started back for the display room, but Sean restrained her.

"We have to get out of here," Janet whispered urgently.

"No," Sean said. "They wouldn't come with a siren. It has to be something else."

The sound of the siren built. Janet felt her heart racing faster and faster. Just when the siren sounded as if it were coming into the house, its pitch abruptly changed.

"Doppler effect," Sean said. "A perfect demonstration."

"Please!" Janet pleaded. "Let's go. We got what you wanted."

"We have to clean up," Sean said, putting his drink down. "This is supposed to be a clandestine operation. See if you can find a broom or a mop. I'll put Helen back together so no one will know the difference."

Despite her agitation, Janet did as Sean asked. She worked feverishly. When she was done, Sean was still suturing the scalp back in place using subcutaneous stitches. When he was finished, he pulled her hair over the incision.

Janet was impressed. Helen Cabot's body appeared undisturbed.

They carried the tools and the cooler back to the casket display room.

"I'll go out first and you hand me the stuff," Sean said. He ducked and stepped through the window.

Janet handed out the things.

"You need help?" Sean asked. His arms were full.

"I don't think so," Janet said. Coming in had not been that difficult.

Sean started toward the car with his bundles.

Janet mistakenly grasped the edge of the glass before stepping through. In her haste she'd forgotten Sean's earlier warning. Feeling the razor-sharp edge cut into four of her fingers, she recoiled in pain. Glancing at her hand she saw an oozing line of blood. She clutched her hand and silently cursed.

Since she was on the inside now, she decided it would be far easier and less dangerous to get out by opening the window. There was no need to risk getting cut by the glass again. Without thinking, she undid the lock and pushed up the sash. Immediately the alarm sounded.

Struggling out the window, Janet ran after Sean. She got to the car just after he'd stashed the cooler on the floor of the back seat. In unison, they jumped into the front and Sean started the car.

"What happened?" he demanded as he pulled the car into the street.

"I forgot about the alarm," Janet admitted. "I opened the window. I'm sorry. I told you I wasn't good at this."

"Well, no problem," Sean said as he turned right at the first intersection and headed east. "We'll be long gone before anybody responds."

What Sean didn't see was the man who'd come out of the

liquor store. He'd responded to the alarm immediately, and he'd seen Janet and Sean getting into the 4×4. He also got a good look at the license plate. Returning inside his store he wrote down the numbers before he forgot them. Then he called the Miami police.

Sean drove back to Forbes so that Janet could get her car. By the time they pulled into the parking area, Janet had calmed down to some degree. Sean stopped next to her rental car. She opened the door and started to get out.

"Are you coming right back to the apartment?" she asked.

"I'm going to head up to my lab," Sean said. "You want to come?"

"I have to work tomorrow," Janet reminded him. "And it's been a tough day. I'm exhausted. But I'm afraid to let you out of my sight."

"I'm not going to be long," Sean said. "Come on! There are only a couple of things I want to do. Besides, tomorrow is Saturday and we'll go on that little vacation I promised you. We'll leave after you get off work."

"Sounds like you've already decided where we'll go," Janet said.

"I have," Sean said. "We'll drive across the Everglades to Naples. I hear it is quite a place."

"All right, it's a deal," Janet said, closing her door. "But tonight you have to get me home before midnight at the latest."

"No problem," Sean said as he drove around to the research building side of the parking lot.

"AT LEAST the Sushita jet hasn't left Washington," Sterling said. He was sitting in Dr. Mason's office. Wayne Edwards was there too, as were Dr. Mason and Margaret Richmond.

"I don't believe Tanaka will make a move until the jet is here and available," he added.

"But you said Sean had been followed," Dr. Mason said. "Who was following him?"

"I was hoping you could enlighten us," Sterling said. "Do you have any idea why someone would be following Mr. Murphy? Wayne noticed him when we crossed the Miami River."

Dr. Mason glanced at Ms. Richmond, who shrugged. Dr. Mason looked back at Sterling. "Could this mystery individual be in the employ of Tanaka?"

"I doubt it," Sterling said. "It's not Tanaka's style. If Tanaka makes a move, Sean will just disappear. There won't be any warning. It will be smooth and professional. The individual who was following Sean was disheveled. He was wearing a soiled open-necked brown shirt and trousers. And he certainly wasn't acting like the sort of professional Tanaka would enlist."

"Tell me exactly what happened," Dr. Mason demanded.

"We followed Sean and a young nurse out of the Forbes parking area around four," Sterling said.

"The nurse would be Janet Reardon," Ms. Richmond interjected. "The two are friends from Boston."

Sterling nodded. He motioned for Wayne to write the name down. "We'll need to investigate her as well. It's important to eliminate the possibility of them working as a team."

Sterling described following Sean to Miami General and his instructions to Wayne to follow the unknown man in brown if he came out first.

Dr. Mason was surprised to learn that Sean and his nurse friend had headed to the morgue. "What on earth were they doing there?"

"That was something else I was hoping you could tell us," Sterling said.

"I can't imagine," Dr. Mason said, shaking his head. He again looked at Ms. Richmond. She shook her head as well.

"When the mysterious man entered the morgue behind Sean Murphy and Miss Reardon," Sterling continued, "I only got a quick glimpse. But it was my impression he was holding a gun. That later proved to be correct. At any rate I was concerned for Mr. Murphy's safety, so I rushed to the morgue door only to find it locked."

"How dreadful," Ms. Richmond said.

"There was only one thing I could do," Sterling said. "I turned off the lights."

"That's a nice touch," Dr. Mason said. "Good thinking."

"I'd hoped the people within wouldn't hurt each other until I could conceive of a way to get the door open," Sterling said. "But there was no need. The man in brown apparently has a strong phobia of the dark. Within a short time he burst from the room significantly distraught. It was then that I saw the gun clearly. I gave chase, but unfortunately I was attired in leather-soled shoes, which put me at a distinct disadvantage to his running shoes. Besides, he seemed entirely familiar with the terrain. When it was clear that I'd lost him, I returned to the morgue. By then Sean and Miss Reardon had already departed as well."

"And Wayne followed the man in brown?" Dr. Mason asked.

"He tried," Sterling said.

"I lost him," Wayne admitted. "It was rush hour, and I was unlucky."

"So now we have no idea where Mr. Murphy is," Dr. Mason moaned. "And we have a new worry about an unknown assailant."

"We have a colleague of Mr. Edwards watching the

Forbes residence for Sean's return," Sterling said. "It is important we find him."

The phone on Dr. Mason's desk rang. Dr. Mason answered it.

"Dr. Mason, this is Juan Suarez in security," the voice at the other end told him. "You asked me to call if Mr. Sean Murphy appeared. Well, he and a nurse just came in and went up to the fifth floor."

"Thank you, Juan," Dr. Mason said with relief. He hung up the phone. "Sean Murphy is safe," he reported. "He just came into the building, probably to inject more mice. What dedication! I tell you, I think the kid is a winner and worth all this trouble."

IT WAS after ten o'clock at night when Robert Harris left Ralph Seaver's apartment. The man had not been particularly cooperative. He'd resented Harris's bringing up his rape conviction in Indiana which he'd dubbed "ancient history." Harris didn't think much of Seaver's self-serving assessment, but he mentally took the man off his list of suspects the minute he laid eyes on him. The attacker had been described as being of medium height and medium build. Seaver was at least six-eight and probably weighed two hundred and fifty pounds.

Climbing into his dark blue Ford sedan, Harris picked up the last file in his priority category. Tom Widdicomb lived in Hialeah, not too far from where Harris was. Despite the hour, Harris decided to drive by the man's home. If the lights were on, he'd ring the bell. Otherwise he'd let it go until morning.

Harris had already made several background calls regarding Tom Widdicomb. He'd found out that the man had taken an EMT course and had passed the exam for his license. A call to an ambulance firm where Tom had worked didn't yield much information. The owner of the company refused to comment, explaining that the last time he talked about a former employee the tires of two of his ambulances were slashed.

A call to Miami General had been a bit more helpful but not by much. A personnel officer said that Mr. Widdicomb and the hospital had parted ways by mutual agreement. The officer admitted he'd not met Mr. Widdicomb; he was merely reading from the employment file.

Harris had also checked with Glen, the housekeeping supervisor at the Forbes Hospital. Glen said that Tom was dependable from his point of view, but that he frequently clashed with his colleagues. He said that Tom worked better on his own.

The last call Harris had made was to a veterinarian by the name of Maurice Springborn. That number, however, was no longer in service and information did not have another number. So all in all, Harris hadn't turned up anything incriminating concerning Tom Widdicomb. As he drove into Hialeah and searched for 18 Palmetto Lane, he was not optimistic.

"Well, at least the lights are on," Harris said as he pulled over to the curb in front of an ill-kept ranch-style house. In sharp contrast to the other modest homes in the neighborhood, Tom Widdicomb's was lit up like Times Square on New Year's Eve. Every light inside and outside the house was blazing brightly.

Getting out of the car, Harris stared at the house. It was amazing how much light emanated from it. Shrubbery three houses away cast sharp shadows. As he walked up the driveway, he noticed the name on the mailbox was

Alice Widdicomb. He wondered how she and Tom were related.

Mounting the front steps, Harris rang the bell. As he waited he eyed the house. It was decorated in a plain style with faded pastel colors. The trim was badly in need of paint.

When no one responded to the bell, Harris rang again and put his ear to the door to make sure the bell was functioning. He heard it clearly. It was hard to believe no one was home with all the lights on.

After a third ring, Harris gave up and returned to his car. Rather than leave immediately, he sat staring at the house, wondering what could motivate people to illuminate their house so brightly. He was just about to start his engine when he thought he saw some movement by the living room window. Then he saw it again. Someone in the house had definitely moved a drape. Whoever it was seemed to be trying to catch a peek at Harris.

Without a moment's hesitation, Harris climbed out of his car and went back to the stoop. He leaned on the doorbell, giving it one long blast. But still no one came.

Disgustedly, Harris returned to his car. He used his car phone to call Glen to see if Tom Widdicomb was scheduled to work the next day.

"No, sir," Glen said with his southern accent. "He's not scheduled to work until Monday. Good thing, too. He was under the weather today. He looked terrible. I sent him home early."

Harris thanked Glen before hanging up. If Widdicomb wasn't feeling well and was home in bed, why all the lights? Was he feeling so bad he couldn't even come to the door? And where was Alice, whoever she was?

As Harris drove away from Hialeah he pondered what he should do. There was something weird going on at the

Widdicombs'. He could always go back and stake out the house, but that seemed extreme. He could wait until Monday when Tom showed up for work, but what about in the meantime? Instead, he decided he'd go back the following morning to see if he could catch a glimpse of Tom Widdicomb. Glen had said he was of medium height and medium build with brown hair.

Harris sighed. Sitting in front of Tom Widdicomb's house was not his idea of a great Saturday, but he was desperate. He felt he'd better make some headway on the breast cancer deaths if he was interested in remaining employed at Forbes.

SEAN WAS whistling softly while he worked, the picture of contented concentration. Janet watched from a high stool similar to Sean's that she'd dragged over to the lab bench. In front of him was an array of glassware.

It was at quiet times like this that Janet found Sean so appealingly attractive. His dark hair had fallen forward to frame his downturned face with soft ringlets, which had an almost feminine look in stark contrast to his hard, masculine features. His nose was narrow at the top where it joined the confluence of his heavy eyebrows. It was a straight nose except for the very tip where it slanted inward before joining the curve of his lips. His dark blue eyes were fixated unblinkingly on a clear plastic tray in his strong but nimble fingers.

He glanced up to look directly at Janet. His eyes were bright and shining. She could tell he was excited. At that moment she felt inordinately in love, and even the recent episode at the funeral home receded into her mind for the moment. She wanted him to take her in his arms and tell her that he loved her and wanted to spend the rest of his life with her.

"These initial silver stain electrophoresis gels are fascinating," Sean said, shattering Janet's fantasy. "Come and look!"

Janet pushed off her stool. At the moment she wasn't interested in electrophoresis gels, but she felt she had little choice. She didn't dare risk lessening his enthusiasm. Still, she was disappointed he didn't sense her affectionate feelings.

"This is the sample from the larger vial," Sean explained. "It's a non-reducing gel so you can tell by the control that it has only one component, and its molecular weight is about 150,000 daltons."

Janet nodded.

Sean picked up the other gel and showed it to her. "Now, the medicine in the small vial is different. Here there are three separate bands, meaning there are three separate components. All three have much smaller molecular weights. My guess is that the large vial contains an immunoglobulin antibody while the small vial most likely contains cytokines."

"What's a cytokine?" Janet asked.

"It's a generic term," Sean said. He got off his own stool. "Follow me," he said. "I've got to get some reagents."

They used the stairs. As they walked, Sean continued to explain. "Cytokines are protein molecules produced by cells of the immune system. They're involved in cell-to-cell communication, signaling cues like when to grow, when to start doing their thing, when to get ready for an invasion of virus, bacteria, or even tumor cells. The NIH has been busy growing the lymphocytes of cancer patients in vitro with a cytokine called interleukin-2, then injecting the cells back into the patient. In some cases they've had some good results."

"But not as good as the Forbes with their medulloblastoma cases," Janet said.

"Definitely not as good," Sean said.

Sean loaded himself and Janet with reagents from the storeroom; then they started back to his lab.

"This is an exciting time in biological science," Sean said. "The nineteenth century was the century for chemistry; the twentieth century was the century for physics. But the twenty-first century will belong to molecular biology; it's when all three—chemistry, physics, and biology—are going to merge. The results will be astounding, like science fiction come true. In fact, we're already seeing it happen."

By the time they got back in the lab Janet found herself becoming genuinely interested despite the day's emotional traumas and her fatigue. Sean's enthusiasm was infectious.

"What's the next step with these medicines?" she asked.

"I'm not sure," Sean admitted. "I suppose we should see what kind of reaction we get between the unknown antibody in the large vial and Helen Cabot's tumor."

Sean asked Janet to get out some scissors and a scalpel from a drawer near where she was standing. Sean took the cooler over to the sink, and after putting on a pair of latex rubber gloves, he lifted out the brain and rinsed it off. From beneath the sink he pulled out a cutting board. He put the brain on the board.

"I hope I don't have trouble finding the tumor," he said. "I've never tried to do anything like this before. Judging by the MRI we did in Boston, her largest tumor is in the left temporal lobe. That was the one they biopsied up there. I suppose that's the one I should go after." Sean oriented the brain so that he could determine the front from the back. Then he made several slices into the temporal lobe.

"I have an almost irresistible urge to joke about what I'm doing here," he said.

"Please don't," Janet said. It was hard for her to deal with the fact that this was the brain of a person with whom she'd so recently related.

"Now this looks promising," Sean said. He spread the edges of his most recent incision. At the base was a comparatively dense and more yellow-appearing tissue bearing tiny but visible cavities. "I think those spots might be areas where the tumor outgrew its own blood supply."

Sean asked Janet to give him a hand, so she pulled on a pair of the rubber gloves and held the cut edges of the brain apart while Sean took a sample of the tumor with the scissors.

"Now we have to separate the cells," he said, putting the sample in tissue culture medium, then adding enzymes. He put the flask in the incubator to give the enzymes a chance to work.

"Next we have to characterize this immunoglobulin," he said, holding up the larger of the two vials of unknowns. "And to do this we have a test called ELISA where we use commercially made antibodies to identify specific types of immunoglobulins." He placed the large vial on the countertop and picked up a plastic plate that had ninety-six tiny circular wells. In each of the wells he put a different capture antibody and allowed it to bind. Then he blocked any remaining binding sites in the wells with bovine serum albumin. Next he put a small aliquot of the unknown in each of the wells.

"Now I have to figure out which antibody has reacted to the unknown," he said, washing each of the wells to rid them of any of the unknown immunoglobulin that hadn't reacted. "We do this by adding to each well the same antibody that was originally in the well, only this time tagged with a compound that's enzymatically capable of yielding a colored reaction." This last substance had the characteristic of turning a pale lavender.

The whole time Sean was doing this test, he kept up a running explanation for Janet. She'd heard of the test but had never seen it performed.

"Bingo!" Sean said when one of the many wells turned the appropriate color to match controls he'd set up in sixteen of the end wells. "The unknown is no longer an unknown. It's a human immunoglobulin called IgGl."

"How did Forbes make it?" Janet asked.

"That's a good question," Sean said. "I'd guess by monoclonal antibody technique. Although it is not out of the question to make it by recombinant DNA technology. The problem there is that it's a big molecule."

Janet had a vague idea of what Sean was talking about and had definitely become interested in the process of figuring out what these unknown medicines were, but suddenly her physical exhaustion could no longer be ignored. Glancing at her watch she could understand why. It was almost midnight.

Feeling ambivalent about interrupting Sean's enthusiasm which she'd been trying hard to bolster, she reached out and grasped his arm. He was holding a Pasteur pipette. He'd started ELISA plates for the second unknown.

"Do you have any idea of the time?" she asked.

Sean glanced at his watch. "My word, time does fly when you're having a good time."

"I've got to work tomorrow," she said. "I've got to get some sleep. I suppose I could go back to the apartment by myself."

"Not at this hour," Sean said. "Just let me finish what I'm doing here, then I want to run a quick immuno-fluorescence test to see the level of reaction between the IgGl and Helen's tumor cells. I'll use an automatic diluter. It will only take a few minutes."

Janet reluctantly agreed. But she couldn't sit on a stool

any longer. Instead she dragged out an armchair from the glass-enclosed office. Less than half an hour later, Sean's enthusiasm went up another notch. The ELISA test on the second unknown had identified three cytokines: interleukin-2, which as he explained to Janet was a T lymphocyte growth factor; tissue necrosis factor alpha, which was a stimulant for certain cells to kill foreign cells like cancer cells; and interferon gamma, which was a substance that seemed to help activate the entire immune system.

"Aren't the T cells the ones that disappear in AIDS?" Janet asked. She was having progressive difficulty staying awake.

"Right on," Sean said. He was now holding a number of slides on which he'd run fluorescence antibody tests at different dilutions of the unknown immunoglobulin. Slipping one of the very high dilution slides under the objective of the fluorescein scope, Sean put his eyes to the eyepiece.

"Wow!" he exclaimed. "The intensity of this reaction is unbelievable. Even at a one to ten thousand dilution this IgGl antibody reacts with the tumor four plus. Janet, come and take a look at this!"

When Janet didn't respond, Sean looked up from the eyepieces of the binocular scope. Janet was slouched in the chair. She'd fallen fast asleep.

Seeing Janet sleeping, Sean immediately felt guilty. He hadn't considered how exhausted she must be. Standing up and stretching his tired arms, he stepped over to Janet and looked down at her. She seemed particularly angelic in her repose. Her face was framed by her fine blond hair. Sean felt an urge to kiss her. Instead, he gently shook her shoulder.

"Come on," he whispered. "Let's get you to bed."

Janet was already buckled in Sean's car when her sleepy mind reminded her she'd brought her own car that morning. She mentioned it to Sean.

"Are you in any condition to drive?" Sean asked.

She nodded. "I want my car," she said, leaving no room for discussion.

Sean pulled around to the hospital and let her out. Once she had her car started, he let her lead the way. And as they pulled out into the street, Sean was too intent on Janet to notice the dark green Mercedes which slowly began to follow them both without the benefit of its headlights.

7

March 6
Saturday, 4:45 A.M.

As soon as Sean's eyes fluttered open, he was instantly awake. He couldn't wait to get to the lab to unravel more of the medulloblastoma mystery cure. The little work that he'd been able to do the night before had merely whetted his appetite. Despite the early hour, he slipped out of bed, showered, and dressed.

When Sean was ready to leave for the lab he tiptoed back into the dark bedroom and gently nudged Janet. He knew she'd want to sleep until the last possible moment but there was something he wanted to tell her.

Janet rolled over and groaned: "Is it time to get up already?"

"No," Sean whispered. "I'm off to the lab. You can go back to sleep for a few minutes. But I wanted to remind you to pack some things for our overnight trip to Naples. I want to leave this afternoon when you get off work."

"Why do I have the feeling you have some ulterior motive in this?" Janet asked, rubbing her eyes. "What's with Naples?"

"I'll tell you on our way there," Sean said. "If we leave from the Forbes we'll beat the traffic out of Miami. Don't pack a lot of stuff. All you'll need is something for dinner tonight, a bathing suit, and jeans. One other thing," Sean added, leaning over her.

Janet looked into his eyes.

"I want you to get some of Louis Martin's medicine this morning," he said.

Janet sat up. "Great!" she exclaimed sarcastically. "How do you expect me to do that? I told you how hard it was to get Helen's samples."

"Calm down," Sean said. "Just give it a try. It could be important. You said that you thought the medicine all came from a single batch. I want to prove it's impossible. I don't need a lot, and just some from the larger vial. Even a few cc's will do."

"They control the medicine more carefully than a narcotic," Janet complained.

"What about diluting it with saline?" Sean suggested. "You know, the old trick of putting water in your parents' liquor bottles. They're not going to know the concentration changed."

Janet thought about the suggestion. "You think it could hurt the patient?"

"I can't see how," Sean said. "More than likely it's designed with a wide safety margin."

"All right, I'll try," Janet said with reluctance. She hated being deceptive and devious with Marjorie.

"That's all I can ask," Sean said. He kissed her on the forehead.

"Now I can't get back to sleep," she complained as Sean headed for the door.

"We'll be sure to get lots of sleep over the weekend," he promised.

As Sean made his way out to his 4×4 there was only a slight hint of dawn in the eastern sky. To the west the stars twinkled as if it were still the middle of the night.

Pulling away from the curb, he was already preoccupied with the work ahead in the lab and oblivious to his surroundings. Once again he failed to notice the dark green Mercedes as it too pulled out into the light traffic several cars behind.

Inside the Mercedes Wayne Edwards was dialing his car phone, calling Sterling Rombauer at the Grand Bay Hotel in Coconut Grove.

A sleepy Sterling picked up on the third ring.

"He's left the lair and is heading west," Wayne said. "Presumably to Forbes."

"Okay," Sterling said. "Stay with him. I'll join you. I was just informed a half an hour ago that the Sushita jet is winging south at this very moment."

"Sounds like game time," Wayne said.

"That's my assumption," Sterling said.

ANNE MURPHY was depressed again. Charles had come home, but he'd only stayed one night. And now that he was gone, the apartment seemed so lonely. He was such a pleasure to be with, so calm and so close to God. She was still in bed, wondering if she should get up, when the front door buzzer sounded.

Anne reached for her plaid robe and headed for the kitchen. She wasn't expecting anyone, but then she hadn't been expecting the two callers inquiring about Sean, either. She remembered her promise not to talk to any strangers about Sean or Oncogen.

"Who is it?" Anne asked, pressing the talk button of her intercom.

"Boston police," a voice replied.

A shiver went down Anne's spine as she buzzed the door open. She was sure this visit meant Sean had reverted to his old ways. After quickly brushing out her hair, she went to the door. A man and a woman were standing there, dressed in Boston police uniforms. Anne had never seen either of them before.

"Sorry to bother you, ma'am," the female officer said. She held up her identification. "I'm Officer Hallihan and this is Officer Mercer."

Anne was clutching the lapels of her robe, holding it closed. The police had come to the door a number of times when Sean had been a teenager. This visit brought back bad memories.

"What's the problem?" Anne asked.

"Are you Anne Murphy, mother of Sean Murphy?" Officer Hallihan asked.

Anne nodded.

"We're here at the request of the Miami police," Officer Mercer said. "Do you know where your son Sean Murphy is currently?"

"He's at the Forbes Cancer Center in Miami," Anne said. "What's happened?"

"We don't know that," Officer Hallihan said.

"Is he in trouble?" Anne asked, afraid to hear the answer.

"We really have no information," Officer Hallihan said. "Do you have an address for him there?"

Anne went to the telephone table in the hall, copied down the address of the Forbes residence, and gave it to the police.

"Thank you, ma'am," Hallihan said. "We appreciate your cooperation."

Anne closed the door and leaned against it. In her heart, she knew that what she'd feared had happened: Miami had been the bad influence she'd suspected; Sean was in trouble again.

As soon as she thought she was composed enough, Anne called Brian at home.

"Sean's in trouble again," she blurted when Brian answered. Tears came as soon as she got the words out.

"Mom, try to control yourself," Brian said.

"You have to do something," Anne said between sobs.

Brian got his mother to calm down enough to tell him what had happened and what the police had said.

"It's probably some traffic violation," Brian said. "He probably drove over someone's lawn, something like that."

"I think it's worse," Anne sniffled. "I know it is. I can feel it. That boy will be the death of me."

"How about if I come over?" Brian said. "I'll make some calls in the meantime and check it out. I bet it's something minor."

"I hope so," Anne said as she blew her nose.

While Anne waited for Brian to drive over from Marlborough Street, she dressed and began putting her hair up. Brian lived across the Charles River in Back Bay, and since it was Saturday with no traffic, he was there in half an hour. When he buzzed to let her know he was on his way up, Anne was putting in the last of her hairpins.

"Before I left my apartment I put in a call to a lawyer colleague in Miami by the name of Kevin Porter," Brian told his mother. "He works for a firm we do business with in the Miami area. I told him what had happened, and he said he had an in with the police and could find out what's going on."

"I know it's bad," Anne said.

"You don't know it's bad!" Brian said. "Now don't get yourself all worked up. Remember last time you ended up in the hospital."

The call from Kevin Porter came within minutes of Brian's arrival.

"I'm afraid I don't have great news for you," Kevin said. "A liquor store owner got your brother's tag leaving the scene of a burglary."

Brian sighed and looked at his mother. She was sitting on the very edge of a straight-backed chair with her hands clasped together in her lap. Brian was furious with Sean. Didn't he ever consider the effects of his escapades on their poor mother?

"It's a weird story," Kevin continued. "It seems that a dead body was mutilated and, you ready for this . . . ?"

"Let me have the whole story," Brian said.

"Somebody stole the brain out of the body," Kevin said. "And this body wasn't some derelict. The deceased was a young woman whose father is some business bigwig up there in Beantown."

"Here in Boston?"

"Yup, and there's a big ruckus down here because of his connections," Kevin said. "Pressure is being put on the police to do something. The state's attorney has drawn up a list of charges a mile long. The medical examiner who looked at the body guessed the skull had been opened with a jigsaw."

"And Sean's 4×4 was seen leaving the scene?" Brian asked. He was already trying to think of a defense.

"Afraid so," Kevin said. "Plus one of the medical examiners says your brother and a nurse were at the medical examiner's office only a few hours before asking about the same body. Seems they wanted samples. Looks like they got them. Obviously the police are looking for your brother and the nurse for questioning and probably arrest."

"Thanks, Kevin," Brian said. "Let me know where you'll be today. I might need you, especially if Sean is arrested."

"You can reach me all weekend," Kevin said. "I'll leave word at the station to call me if your brother is picked up."

Brian slowly replaced the receiver and looked at his mother. He knew she wasn't ready for this, especially since she thought Sean was alone in Sodom and Gomorrah.

"Do you have Sean's phone numbers handy?" he asked. He tried to keep the concern out of his voice.

Anne got them for him without speaking.

Brian called the residence first. He let it ring a dozen times before giving up. Then he tried calling the Forbes Cancer Center research building. Unfortunately all he got was a recording saying that the switchboard was open Monday through Friday, eight until five.

Picking the phone back up decisively, he called Delta Airlines and made a reservation on the noon flight to Miami. Something strange was going on, and he thought he'd better be there in the thick of things.

"I was right, wasn't I?" Anne said. "It's bad."

"I'm sure it's all some misunderstanding," Brian said. "That's why I think I should go down there and clear things up."

"I don't know what I did wrong," Anne said.

"Mother," Brian said. "It's not your fault."

HIROSHI GYUHAMA's stomach was bothering him. His nerves were on edge. Ever since Sean had frightened him in the stairwell, he'd been reluctant to spy on the man. But this morning he'd had no choice. He checked on Sean as soon as he saw the 4×4 in the parking lot so early in the day. When he saw that Sean was feverishly working in his lab, Hiroshi returned to his office.

Hiroshi was doubly upset now that Tanaka Yamaguchi

was in town. Hiroshi had met him at the airport two days earlier and had driven him to the Doral Country Club where he planned to stay and play golf until the final word came from Sushita.

The final word had come late Friday night. After reviewing Tanaka's memorandum, the Sushita board had decided that Sean Murphy was a risk to the Forbes investment. Sushita wanted him in Tokyo forthwith where they would "reason" with him.

Hiroshi was not at all comfortable around Tanaka. Knowing of the man's associations with the Yakusa made Hiroshi extremely wary. And Tanaka gave subtle hints that he did not respect Hiroshi. He'd bowed when they met, but he hadn't bowed very low, and not for very long. Their conversation on the way to the hotel had been inconsequential. Tanaka did not mention Sean Murphy. And once they arrived at the hotel, Tanaka had ignored Hiroshi. Worst of all he did not invite Hiroshi to play golf.

All these slights were painfully obvious to Hiroshi; the implications were clear.

Hiroshi dialed the Doral Country Club Hotel and asked to speak with Mr. Yamaguchi. He was transferred to the clubhouse since Mr. Yamaguchi had scheduled a tee time in twenty minutes.

Tanaka came on the line. He was particularly curt when he heard Hiroshi's voice. Speaking in rapid Japanese, Hiroshi got directly to the point.

"Mr. Sean Murphy is here at the research center," Hiroshi said.

"Thank you," Tanaka said. "The plane is on its way. All is in order. We will be at Forbes this afternoon."

SEAN HAD started the morning off in high spirits. After the initial ease of identifying the immunoglobulin and the three cytokines, Sean had expected just as rapid progress in determining exactly what kind of antigen the immunoglobulin reacted to. Since it reacted so strongly with the tumor cell suspension, he reasoned that the antigen had to be membrane-based. In other words, the antigen had to be on the surface of the cancer cells.

To assure himself of this assumption as well as confirm that the antigen was at least partially a peptide, Sean had treated intact cells from Helen's tumor with trypsin. When he tried to see if these digested cells reacted with the immunoglobulin, he quickly learned they did not.

But from that moment on, Sean had run into trouble. He could not characterize this membrane-based antigen. His idea was to try innumerable known antigens and see if they reacted with the antigen binding portion of the unknown immunoglobulin. None reacted. Using literally hundreds of cell lines grown in tissue culture, he spent hours filling the little wells, but he got no reaction. He was particularly interested in cell lines whose origins were from neural tissues. He tried normal cells and transformed or neoplastic cells. He tried digesting all the cells with detergents in increasing concentration, first to open the cell membranes and expose cytoplasmic antigens, then to open nuclear membranes to expose nuclear antigens. Still nothing reacted. There wasn't a single episode of immunofluorescence in any of hundreds of tiny wells.

Sean couldn't believe how difficult it was turning out to be to find an antigen to react with the mysterious immunoglobulin. So far he hadn't even gotten a partial reaction. Just when he was losing patience, the phone rang. He walked to a wall extension to answer it. It was Janet.

"How's it going, Einstein?" she asked brightly.

"Terrible," Sean said. "I'm not getting anywhere."

"I'm sorry to hear that," Janet said. "But I've got something that might brighten your day."

"What?" Sean asked. At the moment he couldn't imagine anything except the antigen he was seeking. But Janet certainly wouldn't be able to supply that.

"I got a sample of Louis Martin's large vial medicine," Janet said. "I used your idea."

"Great," Sean said without much enthusiasm.

"What's the matter?" Janet questioned. "I thought you'd be pleased."

"I am pleased," he said. "But I'm also frustrated with the stuff I have; I'm at a loss."

"Let's meet so I can give you this syringe," Janet said. "Maybe you need a break."

They met as usual in the cafeteria. Sean took advantage of the time to get something to eat. As before, Janet passed Sean the syringe under the table. He slipped it into his pocket.

"I brought my overnight bag, as requested," she said, hoping to lighten Sean's mood.

Sean merely nodded as he ate his sandwich.

"You seem a lot less excited about our trip than you did this morning," Janet commented.

"I'm just preoccupied," Sean said. "I never would have guessed I'd not find some antigen that would react with the mysterious immunoglobulin."

"My day hasn't been so great either," Janet said. "Gloria is no better. If anything, she's a little worse. Seeing her makes me depressed. I don't know about you, but I'm really looking forward to getting away. I think it will do us both some good. Maybe a little time away from the lab will give you some ideas."

"That would be nice," Sean said dully.

"I'll be off sometime around three-thirty," Janet said. "Where shall we meet?"

"Come over to the research building," Sean said. "I'll meet you downstairs in the foyer. If we leave from that side, we'll miss the shift-change crowd in the hospital."

"I'll be there with bells on," Janet said brightly.

STERLING REACHED over the seat and nudged Wayne. Wayne, who'd been sleeping in the back, sat up quickly.

"This looks promising," Sterling said. He pointed through the windshield at a black stretch Lincoln Town Car that was parking at the curb midway between the hospital building and the research building. Once the car stopped, a Japanese man got out of the rear and gazed up at the two buildings.

"That's Tanaka Yamaguchi," Sterling said. "Can you tell how many people are in the limousine with your glasses?"

"It's difficult to see through the tinted windows," Wayne said, using a small pair of binoculars. "There's a second man sitting in the back seat. Wait a sec. The front door is opening as well. I can see two more. That's four people total."

"That's what I'd expect," Sterling said. "I trust that they're all Japanese."

"You got it, man," Wayne said.

"I'm surprised they're here at Forbes," Sterling said. "Tanaka's preferred technique is to abduct people in an isolated location so there will be no witnesses."

"They'll probably follow him," Wayne suggested. "Then just wait for the right spot."

"I imagine you are right," Sterling said. He saw a second man get out of the limousine. He was tall compared to Tanaka. "Let me have a look with those binoculars," Sterling said. Wayne passed them over the seat. Sterling adjusted the focus of the glasses and studied the two Orientals. He didn't recognize the second one.

"Why don't we go over there and introduce ourselves?" Wayne suggested. "Let them know this is a risky operation. Maybe they'd give up the whole plan."

"That would only serve to alert them," Sterling said. "It's better this way. If we announce ourselves too soon they'll merely operate more clandestinely. We have to catch them in the act so we have something we can use to bargain with them."

"It seems like such a cat-and-mouse game," Wayne said.

"You are absolutely correct," Sterling said.

ROBERT HARRIS had been sitting in his car a few doors down from Tom Widdicomb's home on Palmetto Lane in Hialeah since early that morning. Although he'd been there for over four hours, Harris had seen no sign of life except that the lights had all gone out. Once he thought he saw the curtains move the way they had the night before, but he couldn't be certain. He thought maybe in his boredom his eyes were playing tricks on him.

Several times Harris had been on the verge of giving up. He was wasting too much valuable time on one individual who was suspicious only because of a career switch, the fact that he kept all his lights on, and because he wouldn't answer his doorbell. Yet the idea that the attack on the two nurses could be related to the cancer patient episodes gnawed at Harris. With no other current ideas or leads, he stayed where he was.

It was just after two P.M., and just when Harris was about to leave to deal with hunger and other bodily needs, that he first saw Tom Widdicomb. The garage door went up, and there he was, blinking in the bright sunlight.

Physically, Tom fit the bill. He was of medium height and medium build with brown hair. His clothes were mildly disheveled. His shirt and pants were unpressed. One sleeve of his shirt was rolled up to mid-forearm, the other was down but unbuttoned. On his feet were old, lightweight running shoes.

There were two cars in the garage: a huge, vintage lime green Cadillac convertible and a gray Ford Escort. Tom started the Ford with some difficulty. Once the engine caught, black smoke billowed out of the exhaust as if the car had not been started for some time. Tom backed it out of the garage, closed the garage door manually, then got back into the Escort. When he pulled out of the driveway, Harris let him build up a lead before following.

Harris did not have any preconceived plan. When he first saw Tom the moment the garage door opened, he considered getting out of the car and having a conversation with the man. But he'd held back, and now he was following him for no specific reason. But soon it became apparent where Tom was headed, and Harris got progressively interested. Tom was heading for the Forbes Cancer Center.

When Tom entered the parking lot, Harris followed but purposefully turned in the opposite direction to avoid Tom's noticing him. Harris stopped quickly, opened the door, and stood on the running board as he watched Tom cruise around the parking lot and finally stop near the entrance to the hospital.

Harris got back into his car and worked his way closer, finding a vacant spot about fifty feet from the Escort. What was going through his mind was the possibility that Tom Widdicomb might be stalking the second nurse to be attacked, Janet Reardon. If that were true, perhaps he'd been the one who had attacked her, and if he had, maybe he was the breast cancer patients' killer.

Harris shook his head. It was all so conjectural, with so many "ifs" and so contrary to the way he liked to think and act. He liked facts, not vague suppositions. Yet this was all he had for the moment, and Tom Widdicomb was acting strange: staying in a house with every light on; hiding out most of the day; now loitering in the hospital parking area on his day off, especially when he was supposed to be home sick. As ridiculous as it all might have sounded from a rational point of view it was enough to keep Harris sitting in his car wishing he'd had the foresight to bring sandwiches and Gatorade.

WHEN SEAN returned from his meeting with Janet, he changed the direction of his investigations. Instead of attempting to characterize the antigenic specificity of Helen Cabot's medicine, he decided to determine exactly how Louis Martin's medicine differed from hers. A rapid electrophoresis of the two showed them to be of approximately the same molecular weight, which he'd expected. An equally rapid ELISA test with the anti-human immunoglobulin IgGl confirmed it was the same class of immunoglobulins as Helen's. He'd also expected that.

But then he discovered the unexpected. He ran a fluorescence antibody test with Louis Martin's medicine with Helen's tumor and got just as strong a positive reaction as he'd gotten with Helen's medicine! Even though Janet believed that the medicines came from the same source, Sean did not believe they could be the same. From what he knew about the antigenic specificity of cancers and their antibodies, it was extremely improbable. Yet now he was faced with the fact that Louis's medicine reacted with Helen's tumor. He almost wished he could get his hands on Louis's biopsy just so he could run it against Helen's medicine to confirm this baffling finding.

Sitting at the lab bench, Sean tried to think what to do next. He could subject Louis Martin's medicine to the same battery of antigens he'd tried with Helen's medicine, but that would probably be futile. Instead, he decided to characterize the antigenic binding areas of the two immunoglobulins. Then he could compare their amino acid sequences directly.

The first step of this procedure was to digest each of the immunoglobulins with an enzyme called papain to split off the fragments that were associated with antigen binding. After the splitting, Sean separated these segments, then "unfolded" the molecules. Finally, he introduced these compounds into an automated peptide analyzer that would do the complicated work of sequencing the amino acids. The machine was on the sixth floor.

Sean went to the sixth floor and primed the automated instruments. There were a few other researchers working that Saturday morning, but Sean was too engrossed in his work to start any conversations.

Once the analyzer was prepared and set to run, Sean returned to his lab. Since he had more of Helen's medicine than he did of Louis's, he used hers to continue trying to find something that would react with its antigen binding area. He tried to think what kind of surface antigen could be on her tumor cells and reasoned that it was probably some kind of glycoprotein that formed a cellular binding site.

That was when he thought of the Forbes glycoprotein that he had been trying to crystallize.

As he had been doing with numerous other antigen candidates, he tested the reactivity of the Forbes glycoprotein with Helen's medicine using an immunofluorescence test. Just as he was scanning the plate for signs of reactivity, which he didn't see, he was startled by a husky female voice.

"Exactly what are you doing?"

Sean turned to see Dr. Deborah Levy standing directly behind him. Her eyes sparkled with a fierce intensity.

Sean was taken completely by surprise. He'd not even taken the precaution of coming up with a convincing cover story for all his immunological testing. He hadn't expected anyone to interrupt him on Saturday morning, particularly not Dr. Levy; he didn't even think she was in town.

"I asked a simple question," Dr. Levy said. "I expect an answer."

Sean looked away from Dr. Levy, his eyes sweeping over the mess of reagents on the lab bench, the profusion of cell culture tubes, and the general disarray. He stammered, trying to think up some reasonable explanation. Nothing came to mind except the crystal work he was supposed to be doing. Unfortunately that had nothing to do with immunology.

"I'm trying to grow crystals," Sean said.

"Where are they?" Dr. Levy asked evenly. Her tone indicated she would take some convincing.

Sean didn't answer right away.

"I'm waiting for an answer," Dr. Levy said.

"I don't know exactly," Sean said. He felt like a fool.

"I told you I run a tight ship here," Dr. Levy said. "I have a feeling you didn't take my word."

"I did," Sean hastened to say. "I mean, I do."

"Roger Calvet said you haven't been by to inject any more of your mice," Dr. Levy said.

"Yes, well . . ." Sean began.

"And Mr. Harris said he caught you in our maximum

containment area," Dr. Levy interrupted. "Claire Barington said she told you specifically that area was closed."

"I just thought . . ." Sean started to say.

"I let you know from the start that I did not approve of your coming here," Dr. Levy said. "Your behavior thus far has only confirmed my reservations. I want to know what you are doing with all this equipment and expensive reagents. One doesn't use immunologic materials to grow protein crystals."

"I'm just fooling around," Sean said lamely. The last thing he wanted to admit was that he was working on medulloblastoma, particularly after he'd been forbidden access.

"Fooling around!" Dr. Levy repeated contemptuously. "What do you think this place is, your personal playground?" Despite her dark complexion, color rose in her cheeks. "No one does any work around here without submitting a formal proposal to me. I'm in charge of research. You are to work on the colonic glycoprotein project and on that alone. Do I make myself clear? I want to see defractable crystals by next week."

"Okay," Sean said. He avoided looking at the woman.

Dr. Levy stayed for another minute, as if to make sure her words had sunk in. Sean felt like a child caught red-handed in a naughty act. He didn't have a thing to say for himself. His usual talent for witty retort had momentarily abandoned him.

At long last, Dr. Levy stalked out of the lab. Silence returned.

For a few minutes Sean merely stared at the mess in front of him without moving. He still had no idea where the crystal work was. It had to be there someplace, but he didn't make any move to find it. He simply shook his head. What a ridiculous situation. His sense of frustration came back in a rush. He'd really had it with this place. He never should have come—and never would have had he known the Forbes Center's terms. He should have left in protest as soon as he'd been informed. It was all he could do to restrain himself from using his hand to sweep the countertop of all the glassware, pipettes, and immunologic reagents and allow them to smash to the floor.

Sean looked at his watch. It was just after two in the afternoon. "The hell with it all," he thought. Gathering up the immunoglobulin unknowns, he stashed them in the back of the refrigerator along with Helen Cabot's brain and the sample of her cerebrospinal fluid.

Sean grabbed his jean jacket and headed for the elevators, leaving behind the mess he'd created.

Emerging into the bright, warm Miami sunshine, Sean felt a bit of relief. Tossing his jacket into the back seat of his 4×4, he climbed in behind the wheel. The engine roared to life. He made it a point to burn a little rubber as he exited the parking area and sped south toward the Forbes residence. He was so wrapped up in his thoughts, he didn't notice the stretch limo pull out after him, bumping its undercarriage on the dip as it struggled to keep Sean in sight, nor did he spot the dark green Mercedes tailing the limo.

Sean sped back to his apartment, slammed the car door with extra force, and kicked the front door of the residence shut. He was in a foul mood.

Going into his apartment, he heard the door across the hall open. It was Gary Engels dressed in his usual jeans without a shirt.

"Hey, man," Gary said casually, leaning against the door jamb. "You had some company earlier."

"What kind of company?" Sean asked.

"The Miami police," Gary said. "Two big burly cops

came in here nosing around, asking all sorts of questions about you and your car."

"When?" Sean asked.

"Just minutes ago," Gary said. "You could have passed them in the parking lot."

"Thanks," Sean said. He went into his apartment and closed the door, irritated anew with another problem. There was only one explanation for the police's visit: someone had noted his license plate after the funeral home alarm went off.

The last thing Sean wanted now was a hassle with the police. He grabbed a small suitcase and filled it with a dop kit, underwear, a bathing suit, and shoes. In his garment bag he packed a shirt, tie, slacks, and a jacket. In less than three minutes he was headed back down the stairs.

Before stepping out of the building he looked to see if there were any police cars, marked or otherwise. The only vehicle that looked out of place was a limousine. Confident the cops wouldn't be coming after him in a limo, Sean made a dash for his 4×4, then headed back to the Forbes Cancer Center. En route he stopped to use a pay phone.

The idea the police were looking for him bothered Sean immensely. It brought back bad memories of his unruly youth. Parts of his brief life of petty crime had been exhilarating, but his brushes with the judicial system had only been tedious and disheartening. He never wanted to get bogged down in that bureaucratic quagmire again.

The first person Sean thought to call after hearing about the police was his brother Brian. Before Sean spoke to any police, he wanted to speak to the best lawyer he knew. He hoped his brother would be home. He usually was on Saturday afternoon. But instead of Brian he got Brian's answering machine with its inane message complete with background elevator music. Sometimes Sean wondered how they could have grown up in the same house.

Sean left a message saying that it was important that they talk, but that he couldn't leave a number. He said he'd call later. Sean would try again once he got to Naples.

Returning to his car, Sean sped back toward the Forbes. He wanted to be sure to be at their appointed meeting place when Janet got off work.

8

March 6
Saturday, 3:20 P.M.

By three-twenty when the last details of report were being given, Janet fell asleep. She'd been exhausted when Sean had awakened her that morning, but after a shower and coffee, she'd felt reasonably good. She'd needed more coffee midway through the morning and then again in the middle of the afternoon. She'd done well until she'd sat down for report. As soon as she was stationary, her fatigue became overpowering, and she embarrassed herself by nodding off. Marjorie had to give her a nudge in the ribs.

"You look like you're burning the candle at both ends," Marjorie said.

Janet merely smiled. Even if she could tell Marjorie all she'd been up to the previous afternoon and evening, she doubted Marjorie would have believed her. In fact, she wasn't sure she believed it herself.

As soon as report was over, Janet got her things together and crossed over to the Forbes research building. Sean was sitting in the foyer reading a magazine. He smiled as soon as he saw her. She was glad to see his mood had improved since they'd met in the cafeteria.

"You ready for our little trip?" Sean asked, getting to his feet.

"Couldn't be more ready," Janet said. "Although I would like to get this uniform off and take a shower."

"The uniform we can handle," Sean said. "There's a ladies' room right here in the foyer where you can change. The shower will have to wait, but beating the traffic is worth the sacrifice. Our route will take us right by the airport, and I'm sure there's traffic there every afternoon."

"I was only kidding about the shower," Janet said. "But I will change."

"Be my guest," Sean said. He pointed to the ladies' room door.

TOM WIDDICOMB had his hand in his pants pocket clutching his pearl-handled "Saturday night special" revolver. He'd been standing off to the side of the hospital entrance watching for Janet Reardon to emerge. He thought that there might be a chance he could shoot her as she got into her car. In his mind's eye he saw himself walk up just as she got in behind the wheel. He'd shoot her in the back of the head and keep walking. With all the clutter and confusion of people and cars and the noise of car engines starting, the sound of the gun would be lost.

But there was one problem. Janet had not appeared. Tom had seen other familiar faces, including nurses from the fourth floor, so it was not as if report had held her up.

Tom looked at his watch. It was three-thirty-seven, and the mass exodus of the day shift had slowed to a trickle. Most people had now left, and Tom was confused and frantic; he had to find her. He'd made the effort to be sure she was working, but where was she?

Pushing off from where he'd been leaning against the building, Tom walked around the edge of the hospital and headed in the direction of the research building. He could see the walkway spanning the two structures. He wondered if she could have crossed and exited on the research side.

He was midway between the two buildings when the sight of a long black limousine gave him pause. Tom figured that some celebrity was being treated in the outpatient department. It had happened before.

Scanning the parking lot in a wide arc, Tom nervously tried to think what he should do. He wished he knew what kind of car Janet drove because then he'd know if she'd slipped away or not. If she had, there was a big problem. He knew she was scheduled to be off the next day, and unless he found out where she lived, she'd be inaccessible for the rest of the weekend. And that was trouble. Without some kind of definitive information, Tom hated the thought of going home to a silent house. Alice hadn't spoken to him all night.

Tom was still trying to figure out what to do when he saw the black 4×4 he'd followed the day before. He started moving toward it for a closer look when suddenly, there she was! She'd just exited the research building.

Tom was relieved to see her at last but chagrined that she was not alone. Accompanying her was the same man she'd been with the previous afternoon. Tom watched as they walked toward the 4×4. She was carrying an overnight bag. Tom was about to sprint back to his car when he saw that they weren't climbing into the Isuzu. Instead they merely got out an additional suitcase and a garment bag.

Tom knew that shooting Janet in the parking lot was out of the question now that the day shift had left. Besides, being with someone meant he'd have to shoot both if he didn't want to leave a witness.

Tom started back for his car, keeping an eye on the couple as he did. By the time he got to his Escort, Janet and Sean had arrived at a red Pontiac rent-a-car. Tom got into his car and started it while he watched Janet and Sean put their bags in the Pontiac's trunk.

ROBERT HARRIS had been watching every move Tom Widdicomb made. He'd seen Sean and Janet before Tom had, and when Tom initially didn't react, Harris had been disappointed, thinking that his whole "house of cards" theory was in error. But then Tom had spotted them and had scurried back to his Escort. In response Harris started his own car and drove out of the parking lot, thinking and hoping that Tom intended to follow Janet. At the corner of Twelfth Street he pulled over to the side of the road. If he were correct, Tom would soon be exiting, and Harris's suspicion would be significantly reinforced.

Presently Sean and Janet drove by and turned north to cross the Miami River. Then, just as Harris expected, Tom came and turned in the same direction. Only a black limo separated Tom from his apparent quarry.

"This is looking more and more interesting," Harris said to himself as he started to pull out. Behind him a horn blasted and Harris jammed on his brakes. A big green Mercedes missed him by inches.

"Damn!" Harris growled. He didn't want to lose Tom Widdicomb and had to tromp on the gas pedal to catch up. He was determined to follow the man to see if he made any overt threatening gestures toward Janet Reardon. If he did, then Harris would nail him.

Harris was content until Tom turned west instead of east on the 836 East-West Expressway. As he passed Miami International Airport, then merged with Florida's Turnpike heading south, Harris realized this was going to be a far longer trip than he'd anticipated.

"I DON'T like this," Sterling said as they exited Florida's Turnpike at Route 41. "Where are these people going? I wanted them to go home or stay in crowds."

"If they turn west up here at the next intersection, they're on their way into the Everglades," Wayne said. He was doing the driving. "Either that or they're heading across Florida. Route 41 cuts through the Everglades from Miami to the Gulf Coast."

"What's on the Gulf Coast?" Sterling asked.

"Not much, in my book," Wayne said. "Nice beaches and good weather, but it's subdued. Naples is the first real town. There are also a couple of islands like Marco and Sanibel. Mostly it's condo heaven with a lot of retirees. Pretty low-key, but high end. You can spend millions for a condo in Naples."

"Looks like they're turning west," Sterling said, his eyes on the limousine ahead of them. They were following Tanaka, not Sean, assuming Tanaka would keep Sean in sight.

"What's between here and Naples?" Sterling asked.

"Not a lot," Wayne said. "Just alligators, saw grass, and Cypress swamp."

"This is making me very nervous," Sterling said. "They're playing directly into Tanaka's hands. Let's hope they don't stop in some isolated pull-out."

Sterling glanced to the right and did a double-take. In the

blue sedan alongside them was a familiar face. It was Robert Harris, head of security at Forbes. Sterling had just been introduced to the man the previous day.

Sterling pointed Harris out to Wayne and explained who he was. "This is a disturbing complication," he said. "Why would Mr. Harris be following Sean Murphy? Chances are he'll only serve to make this situation significantly more difficult than it need be."

"Would he know about Tanaka?" Wayne asked.

"I cannot imagine he would," Sterling said. "Dr. Mason would not be so foolish."

"Maybe he's got a crush on the chick," Wayne offered. "Maybe he's following Reardon, not Murphy."

Sterling sighed. "It's disconcerting how quickly an operation can go awry. A minute ago I was confident we would be able to control the course of events since we had the informational edge. Unfortunately, I no longer believe that. I'm beginning to have that uncomfortable feeling that chance will become a major factor. Suddenly there are too many variables."

BRIAN HADN'T checked any luggage. He'd simply brought a carry-on and his briefcase. After getting off the plane he went directly to the Hertz counter. After a short ride on the Hertz shuttle bus he found his rental car in the lot: a cream-colored Lincoln Town Car.

Armed with a detailed street map of Miami, Brian first drove south to the Forbes residence. He'd tried calling Sean's number several times from the airport in Boston, but there hadn't been any answer. Concerned, he'd called Kevin from the plane, but Kevin had assured him that the police had not yet picked Sean up.

At the Forbes residence, Brian knocked on Sean's door, but there was no response. Hoping Sean would soon return, Brian left him a note saying that he was in town and would be staying at the Colonnade Hotel. Brian jotted down the hotel's phone number. Just as he was slipping the note under Sean's door, the door opposite opened.

"You looking for Sean Murphy?" a shirtless young man in jeans asked.

"Yes," Brian said. He then introduced himself as Sean's brother.

Gary Engels introduced himself. "Sean was here this afternoon around two-thirty," he said. "I told him the police had been here looking for him so he didn't stay long."

"Did he say where he was going?" Brian asked.

"Nope," Gary said. "But he took a suitcase and a garment bag with him when he left."

Brian thanked Gary, then returned to his rental car. The idea of Sean leaving with luggage did not sound promising. Brian only hoped his brother wasn't dumb enough to be trying to make a run for it. Unfortunately, with Sean, anything was possible.

Brian headed for the Forbes Cancer Center. Although the switchboard was closed, Brian thought that the building itself would be open, and it was. He went into the foyer.

"I'm looking for Sean Murphy," he told the guard. "My name is Brian Murphy. I'm Sean's brother from Boston."

"He's not here," the guard said with a heavy Spanish accent. He consulted a log in front of him. "He left at two-twenty. He came back at three-oh-five, but left again at three-fifty."

"Do you have any way to get in touch with him?" Brian asked.

The guard consulted another book. "He's staying at the Forbes residence. Would you like that address?"

Brian told the guard he already had that information and thanked him. He walked outside and got back into his car, wondering what he should do. He questioned the wisdom of his coming to Miami without having spoken to Sean first and wondered where his brother could be.

Deciding to check into his hotel, Brian started his car and made a U-turn to head out of the parking lot. In the process he spotted a black Isuzu that looked suspiciously like Sean's. Steering closer to it, he noticed that the plates were from Massachusetts. Putting his Lincoln in park, Brian hopped out to peer into the 4×4. It was Sean's, all right. The interior was filled with his fast-food wrappers and empty Styrofoam cups.

It seemed odd that Sean would leave it parked in the hospital lot. Going back into the building, Brian mentioned the car's presence to the guard and asked if he could account for it. The guard simply shrugged his shoulders.

"Is there any way to get in touch with the director of the Center before Monday?" Brian asked.

The guard shook his head.

"If I were to leave my name and hotel number," Brian said, "would you call your supervisor and ask if he could pass it on to the director of the Center?"

The guard nodded agreeably and even got out a pen and paper for Brian to write on. Brian wrote the note quickly, then handed it to the guard along with a five-dollar bill. The guard's face lit up with a big smile.

Brian returned to his car, drove to his hotel, and checked in. Once in his room, the first thing he did was call Kevin to give him the number. Kevin again assured him there'd been no arrest.

Brian then called Anne to reassure her that he'd gotten to Miami safely. He admitted he'd not yet spoken with Sean but expected to do so soon. He gave her his number at the hotel before hanging up.

After speaking with his mother, Brian kicked off his shoes and opened his briefcase. If he was stuck in a hotel room, at least he could get some work done.

"THIS IS more like the scenery I expected to see in South Florida," Sean said. They had finally left civilization behind. The four-lane highway lined with strip malls and condominiums had given way to a two-lane road slicing straight across the Everglades.

"It's breathtakingly beautiful," Janet said. "It looks almost prehistoric. I half expect to see a brontosaurus rise up from one of these ponds," she added with a laugh.

They were cruising past oceans of saw grass interspersed with hummocks of pine, palm, and cypress. Exotic birds were everywhere. Some were ghostly white, others iridescent blue. Huge cumulus clouds billowed in the distance, looking whiter than usual against the intense blue sky.

The drive had done much to help calm Janet. She was glad to be leaving Miami and her patients behind. With Sean driving, she had her shoes off and her bare feet planted on the dash. She was dressed in her most comfortable pair of jeans with a simple white cotton shirt. For work she'd had her hair tied back, but she'd taken it down as soon as they'd pulled out of the Forbes lot. With all the car windows rolled down, it was blowing free.

The only problem was the sun. Since they were heading due west, bright sunlight was streaming through the windshield with a vengeance. Both Sean and Janet were wearing their sunglasses, and they had tilted the sun visors in an attempt to keep their faces shaded from the harsh rays.

"I think I'm beginning to understand Florida's attraction," Janet said, the sun notwithstanding.

"It makes winter in Boston seem extra cruel," Sean said.

"How come you didn't want to take your Isuzu?" Janet asked.

"There's a little problem with my car," Sean said.

"What kind of problem?" Janet asked.

"The police are interested in talking to its owner."

Janet took her feet down from the dash. "I don't think I like what I'm hearing," she said. "What's with the police?"

"The police came to the Forbes residence," Sean said. "Gary Engels talked with them. I think someone got the tag number from my license plate after the alarm went off at the funeral home."

"Oh, no!" Janet exclaimed. "Then the police are looking for us."

"Correction," Sean said. "They're looking for me."

"Oh, God!" Janet said. "If someone saw the license plate then they saw both of us." She closed her eyes. This was the kind of nightmare she'd feared.

"All they have is a tag number," Sean said. "That's hardly evidence."

"But they can get our fingerprints," Janet said.

Sean shot her a look of mild disdain. "Be serious," he said. "They're not about to send a team of crime scene investigators out to dust the site over a broken window and a cadaver's missing brain."

"How do you know?" Janet shot back. "You're no law enforcement expert. I think we should turn ourselves in to the police and explain everything."

Sean gave a scornful laugh. "Please! We're not giving

ourselves up. Don't be ridiculous. Remember, they're looking for me. They want to talk with me. If worst comes to worst, I'll take the rap. But it's not going to come to that. I put in a call to Brian. He knows people in Miami. He'll fix it."

"Did you speak to Brian?" Janet asked.

"No, not yet," Sean admitted. "But I left a message on his answering machine. When we get to the hotel, I'll try again and leave the hotel number if he's still not in. By the way, did you bring your credit card?"

"Of course I brought my credit card," Janet said.

"Thank heaven for your trust fund," Sean said. He reached over and gave Janet's knee a playful slap. "I made a reservation at the Ritz Carlton. The Quality Inn was full."

Janet stared out the passenger-side window, wondering what she was doing with her life. It had nothing to do with the credit card issue. She didn't mind picking up the tab every now and again. Sean was generous with his money when he had it, and she had more than enough. What bothered her was the fact that they were wanted by the police. It was gallant of Sean to offer to take the rap alone, but Janet knew she couldn't let him do it even if it did fly, which it probably wouldn't. Whoever had seen that license plate had seen her too. Falling in love with Sean seemed to be bringing her nothing but grief, first emotionally and now potentially professionally. She wasn't sure how the Forbes Center would react to having a nurse on staff who was charged with God knows what in connection with a funeral home break-in. She couldn't think of too many employers who would view that kind of record as a plus.

Janet was on the verge of panic, yet there was Sean, as calm and cocky as ever. He really seemed to be enjoying himself. How he could be so cool and collected knowing the

Miami police were searching for him was beyond her. She wondered if she would ever truly understand him.

"What's the story with Naples, Florida?" Janet asked, deciding to change the subject. "You said you'd explain once we were on our way."

"Very simple," Sean said. "One of the patients from that group of thirty-three lives in Naples. His name is Malcolm Betencourt."

"One of the medulloblastoma patients in remission?" Janet asked.

"Yup," Sean said. "One of the first to be treated. He's been in remission for almost two years."

"What do you plan to do?"

"Call him up."

"And say what?"

"I don't know exactly," Sean said. "I'll have to improvise. I think it would be interesting to hear about the Forbes treatment from the patient's point of view. I'm especially curious as to what they told him. They had to have told him something just to get the informed consent forms signed."

"What makes you think he'll talk to you?" Janet asked.

"How could he resist my Irish charm?" Sean said.

"Seriously," Janet said. "People don't like to talk about their infirmities."

"Infirmities, perhaps," Sean admitted. "But recovery from an otherwise terminal illness is something else. You'd be surprised. People love to talk about that kind of thing and the world-famous doctor who made it happen. Have you ever noticed how people like to think their doctor is world famous, even if he practices someplace like Malden or Revere?"

"I think you have a lot of chutzpah," Janet said. She wasn't convinced that Malcolm Betencourt would be receptive to Sean's call, but she also knew she wouldn't be able to do anything to prevent Sean from trying. Besides, except for this new worry about the Miami police, the idea of a weekend away was still delicious, even if Sean had an ulterior aim in mind. She even thought that she and Sean might finally have a moment to talk about their future. After all, aside from Malcolm Betencourt, she'd have Sean to herself without interruption.

"How did you make out with the sample of Louis Martin's medicine?" Janet asked. She thought she'd keep the conversation light until they got to dinner. She could imagine a candlelight dinner on a terrace overlooking the sea. Then she'd talk about commitment and love.

Sean flashed Janet a look of frustration. "I was interrupted by the charming head of research," he said. "She read me the riot act and told me I had to go back to the Forbes glycoprotein baloney. She really caught me off guard; for once words failed me. I couldn't think of anything clever to say."

"I'm sorry," Janet said.

"Well, it was bound to happen sooner or later," Sean said. "But even before the harpy showed up I wasn't doing that great. I haven't been able to get Helen's medicine to react with any antigen, cellular, viral, or bacterial. But you must be right about the medicine all coming from a single batch. I ran a sample of Louis's medicine against Helen's tumor and it reacted just as strongly at the same dilutions as Helen's."

"So they use the same medicine," Janet said. "What's the big deal? When people are treated with an antibiotic, they all get the same drug. Labeling the drug for each patient is probably more a matter of control than anything else."

"But cancer immunotherapy is not comparable to antibiotics," Sean said. "Like I said before, cancers are antigenically distinct, even the same type of cancer."

"I thought one of the tenets of scientific reasoning involved the issue of an exception," Janet said. "If an exception is found to a hypothesis then one is forced to reconsider the original hypothesis."

"Yeah, but . . ." Sean said, but he hesitated. Janet was making good sense. The fact was that Forbes was getting one hundred percent remission, apparently with medication that was not individualized. Sean had seen that success documented in the thirty-three cases. Therefore, there had to be an error in his insistence on the immunological specificity of cancer cells.

"You have to admit I have a point," Janet persisted.

"Okay," Sean said, "but I still think there's something strange with all this. Something I'm missing."

"Obviously," Janet said. "You don't know what antigen the immunoglobulin reacts with. That's what's missing. Once you figure that out maybe everything else will fall into place. Let's see what a relaxing weekend will do for your creativity. Maybe by Monday you'll have an idea that will get you around this apparent roadblock."

After passing through the heart of the Everglades, Sean and Janet began to see signs of civilization. First there was an isolated resort or two, then the road expanded to four lanes. Quickly the saw grass gave way to strip malls, convenience gas station/food stores, and miniature golf courses equally as ugly as on the Miami side.

"I'd heard Naples was upscale," Janet said. "This hardly looks upscale."

"Let's hold our verdict until we get to the Gulf," Sean said.

The road suddenly turned north, and the unattractive

profusion of unrestricted signs and commercial development continued.

"How can so many strip malls survive?" Janet asked.

"It's one of the mysteries of American culture," Sean said.

With map in hand, Janet did the navigating. She gave Sean plenty of warning before they had to turn left toward the water.

"It's starting to look a bit more promising," Sean said.

After a mile or so of more scenic vistas, the Mediterranean-style Ritz Carlton loomed out of the mangroves to the left of the road. The profusion of lush tropical plants and exotic flowers was staggering.

"Ah, home!" Sean said as they pulled beneath the porte cochere.

A man in a blue morning coat and a black top hat opened their car doors. "Welcome to the Ritz Carlton," the liveried gentleman said.

They entered through oversized glass doors into a haze of polished pink marble, expansive Oriental carpets, and crystal chandeliers. High tea was being served on the dais beneath the huge arched windows. Off to the side was a grand piano complete with tuxedoed pianist.

Sean put his arm around Janet as they meandered over to the registration desk. "I think I'm going to like this place," he told her.

Tom Widdicomb had gone through a range of emotions during his two-hour pursuit. Initially when Janet and Sean had headed out of town toward the Everglades, he'd been disturbed. Then he'd decided it was a good thing. If they were on some mini-vacation, they'd be lax and unsuspecting. In the city, people were naturally more suspicious and careful. But as one hour turned into two, and Tom began to eye his gas gauge, he'd become angry. This woman had caused him so much trouble, he began to wish they'd just pull over to the side of the road. Then he could stop and shoot them both and put an end to it all.

As he pulled into the Ritz Carlton, he wondered if he had any gas at all. The gauge had registered empty for the last five miles.

Avoiding the front entrance, Tom drove around and parked in a large lot next to the tennis courts. Getting out of his car he ran up the drive, slowing when he saw the red rental car parked directly in front of the entrance. Clutching the handle of the pistol in his pocket, Tom walked around the car and fell in with a group of guests and entered the hotel. He was afraid someone might try to stop him, but no one did. Nervously, he scanned the lavish foyer. He spotted Janet and Sean standing at the registration desk.

With his anger giving him courage, Tom boldly walked to the registration desk and stood next to Sean. Janet was just on the other side of him. Being so close sent a shiver down Tom's spine.

"We're out of nonsmoking rooms with an ocean view," the desk person said to Sean. She was a petite woman with large eyes, golden hair, and the type of tan that made dermatologists cringe.

Sean looked at Janet and raised his eyebrows. "What do you think?" he asked.

"We can see how bad the smoking room is," she suggested.

Sean turned back to the receptionist. "What floor is your room with the ocean view?" he asked.

"Fifth floor," the receptionist said. "Room 501. It's a beautiful room."

"Okay," Sean said. "Let's give it a try."

Tom moved away from the registration desk, silently mouthing "Room 501" as he headed for the elevators. He saw a heavyset man in a business suit with a small earphone in his ear. Tom avoided him. The whole time he kept his hand in his pocket, clutching his pistol.

ROBERT HARRIS stood by the piano racked by indecision. Like Tom, he'd been exhilarated early in the chase. Tom's obvious pursuit of Janet seemed to confirm his fledgling theory. But as the procession left Miami, he'd become irritated, especially when he too thought he might run out of gas. On top of that, he was starved; his last meal had been early that morning. Now that they had made it all the way through the Everglades to the Ritz Carlton in Naples, he was having doubts as to what exactly the journey proved. It certainly was no crime to drive to Naples, and Tom could contend he hadn't been following anybody. Sadly, Harris had to admit that as of yet, he hadn't come up with anything conclusive. The link between Tom and the attack on Janet or the breast cancer patient deaths was tenuous at best, still made up only of hypothesis and conjecture.

Harris knew he'd have to wait for Tom to make an overtly aggressive move toward Janet, and he hoped he would. After all, Tom's apparent interest in the nurse could be chalked up to some crazy obsession. The woman wasn't bad. In fact she was reasonably attractive and sexy; Harris himself had appreciated that.

Feeling distinctly out of place dressed as he was in shorts and T-shirt, Harris skirted the piano as Tom Widdicomb disappeared from view down the hallway past reception. Walking quickly, Harris passed Janet and Sean, who were still busy checking in.

Up ahead, Harris could see Tom round a corner and disappear from sight. Harris was about to pick up his pace when he felt a hand grab his arm. Turning, he looked into the face of a heavyset man with an earphone stuck in his right ear. He was dressed in a dark suit, presumably to blend in with the guests. He wasn't a guest. He was hotel security.

"Excuse me," the security man said. "May I help you?"

Harris cast a quick glance in the direction Tom had gone, then looked back at the security man who still had hold of his arm. He knew he had to think of something quickly. . . .

"WHAT ARE we going to do?" Wayne asked. He was hunched over the steering wheel. The green Mercedes was parked at the curb near the main entrance to the Ritz Carlton. Ahead of them was the limousine parked on one side of the porte cochere. No one had gotten out of the limousine although the liveried doorman had spoken with the driver, and the driver had handed him a bill, presumably a large denomination.

"I truly don't know what to do," Sterling said. "My intuition tells me to stay with Tanaka, but I'm concerned about Mr. Harris's entering the hotel. I have no idea what he plans to do."

"Uh oh!" Wayne uttered. "More complications." Ahead they saw the front passenger-side door of the limousine open. An immaculately dressed, youthful Japanese man climbed out. He placed a portable phone on top of the car, adjusted his dark tie, and buttoned his jacket. Then he picked up the phone and went into the hotel.

"Do you think they might be considering killing Sean Murphy?" Wayne asked. "That dude looks like a professional to me."

"I would be terribly surprised," Sterling said. "It's not the Japanese way. On the other hand, Tanaka is not your typical Japanese, especially with his connections to the Yakusa. And biotechnology has become an extremely big prize. I'm afraid I'm losing confidence in my ability to predict his intentions. Perhaps you'd better follow the Japanese man inside. Whatever you do, make sure he does not harm Mr. Murphy."

Relieved to get out of the car, Wayne lost no time going into the hotel.

After Wayne slipped inside the hotel, Sterling's eyes drifted back to the limousine. He tried to imagine what Tanaka was thinking, what he was planning next. Absorbed by these thoughts, he suddenly remembered the Sushita jet.

Reaching for the car phone, Sterling called his contact at the FAA. The contact asked him to hold while he punched the query into his computer. After a brief pause, he came back on the line.

"Your bird has flown the coop," he said.

"When?" Sterling asked. This he didn't want to hear. If the plane was gone, Wayne might be correct. Tanaka certainly wasn't planning on bringing Sean to Japan if he no longer had the Sushita jet at his command.

"It left just a short time ago," the contact said.

"Is it going back up the east coast?" Sterling asked.

"Nope," the contact said. "It's going to Naples, Florida. Does that mean anything to you?"

"Indeed it does," Sterling said with relief.

"From there it's going to Mexico," the contact said. "That will take it out of our jurisdiction."

"You've been most helpful," Sterling said.

Sterling hung up the phone. He was glad he'd called. Now he was certain Sean Murphy was not about to be killed. Instead he was about to be offered a free trip across the Pacific.

"I CAN'T smell any cigarette smoke in here," Janet said as she sniffed around the spacious room. Then she opened the French doors and stepped out onto the terrace. "Sean, come out here!" she called. "This is gorgeous."

Sean was sitting on the edge of the bed reading the directions for making a long-distance call. He got up and joined Janet on the terrace.

The view was spectacular. A beach shaped like a scimitar swept to the north in a gigantic arc, ending in the distance at Sanibel Island. Directly below their terrace was the lush greenery of a mangrove swamp. To the south the beach ran a straight line, eventually disappearing behind a line of high-rise condominiums. To the west, the sun was slanting through a sheath of red clouds. The Gulf was calm and deep green. A few wind surfers dotted the surface, their sails offering bright splashes of color.

"Let's go to the beach for a swim," Janet suggested. Her eyes sparkled with enthusiasm.

"You're on," Sean said. "But first I want to call Brian and Mr. Betencourt."

"Good luck," Janet said over her shoulder. She was already on her way inside to change.

With Janet in the bathroom putting on her suit, Sean dialed Brian's number. It was after six, and Sean fully expected him to be home. It was disappointing to hear the damn answering machine kick on and have to sit through Brian's message yet again. After the beep Sean left the number of the Ritz and his room number and asked his brother to please call. As an afterthought he added that it was important.

Next, Sean dialed Malcolm Betencourt's number. Mr. Betencourt himself answered on the second ring.

Sean winged it. He explained that he was a medical student at Harvard who was taking an elective at the Forbes Cancer Center. He said he'd been reviewing charts of patients who'd been on the medulloblastoma protocol and who had been doing well. Having had an opportunity to review Mr. Betencourt's chart, he'd appreciate the chance to talk to Mr. Betencourt in person about his treatment, if that would be at all possible.

"Please call me Malcolm," Mr. Betencourt said. "Where are you calling from, Miami?"

"I'm in Naples," Sean said. "My girlfriend and I just drove over."

"Splendid. So you're already in the neighborhood. And you're a Harvard man. Just the med school or undergrad too?"

Sean explained that he was on leave from the M.D./Ph.D. program but that he'd been an undergrad at Harvard too.

"I went to Harvard myself," Malcolm said. "Class of '50. I'll bet that sounds like a century ago. You play any sports while you were there?"

Sean was somewhat surprised by the direction the conversation was taking, but he decided to go with it. He told Malcolm that he'd been on the ice hockey team.

"I was on the crew team, myself," Malcolm said. "But it's my time at the Forbes you're interested in, not my glory days of youth. How long will you be in Naples?"

"Just the weekend."

"Hang on a second, young fella," Malcolm said. In a minute, he came back on the line. "How about coming over for dinner?" he asked.

"That's awfully kind," Sean said. "Are you sure it's not an imposition?"

"Hell, I already checked with the boss," Malcolm said

cheerfully. "And Harriet will be tickled to have some youthful company. How's eight-thirty sound? Dress is casual."

"Perfect," Sean said. "How about some directions."

Malcolm told Sean that he lived on a street called Galleon Drive in Port Royal, an area just south of Naples's old town. He then gave specific directions which Sean wrote down.

No sooner had Sean hung up the phone than there was a knock on the door. Sean read over the directions as he walked to the door. Absentmindedly, he opened the door without asking who it was or looking through the security peephole. What he didn't realize was that Janet had hooked the security chain. When he pulled the door open, it abruptly stopped, leaving only a two-inch crack.

Through the crack Sean saw a momentary glint of metal in the hand of whoever was at the door. The significance of that glint failed to register. Sean was too embarrassed to have bungled opening the door to focus on it. As soon as he reopened the door properly, he apologized to the man standing there.

The man, dressed in a hotel uniform, smiled and said there was no need for an apology. He said he should apologize for disturbing them, but the management was sending up fruit and a complimentary bottle of champagne because of the inconvenience of not having a nonsmoking ocean-view room.

Sean thanked the man and tipped him before seeing him out, then he called to Janet. He poured two glasses.

Janet appeared at the bathroom doorway in a black one-piece bathing suit cut high on her thighs and low in the back. Sean had to swallow hard.

"You look stunning," he said.

"You like it?" Janet asked as she pirouetted into the room. "I got it just before I left Boston."

"I love it," Sean said. Once again he appreciated Janet's

figure, remembering it had been her figure that had first attracted him to her when he'd seen her climbing down from that countertop.

Sean handed her a glass of champagne, explaining the management's gift.

"To our weekend escape," Janet said, extending her glass toward Sean.

"Hear, hear!" Sean said, touching her glass with his.

"And to our discussions this weekend," Janet added, thrusting her glass at him again.

Sean touched her glass for a second time, but his face assumed a quizzical expression. "What discussions?" he asked.

"Sometime in the next twenty-four hours I want to talk about our relationship," Janet said.

"You do?" Sean winced.

"Don't look so mournful," Janet said. "Drink up and get your suit on. The sun's going to set before we get out there."

Sean's nylon gym shorts had to double as a bathing suit. He'd not been able to find his real bathing suit when he'd packed in Boston. But it hadn't worried him. He hadn't planned on going to the beach much, and if he did, it would have been just to walk and look at the girls. He hadn't planned on going into the water.

After they'd each had a glass of champagne, they donned terrycloth robes provided by the hotel. As they rode down in the elevator, Sean told Janet about Malcolm Betencourt's invitation. Janet was surprised by this development, and a little disappointed. She'd been envisioning a romantic dinner for just the two of them.

On the way to the beach they walked by the hotel's pool, which was a free-form variation of a clover leaf. There were half a dozen people in the water, mostly children. After crossing a boardwalk spanning a narrow tongue of mangrove swamp, they arrived at the Gulf of Mexico.

Even at this hour, the beach was dazzling. The sand was white and mixed with the crushed, sun-bleached remains of billions of shellfish. Redwood beach furniture and blue canvas umbrellas dotted the beach directly in front of the hotel. Groups of dawdling sunbathers were scattered to the north, but to the south, the sand was empty.

Opting for privacy, they turned to the south, angling across the sand to reach the apogee of the small waves as they washed up on the beach. Expecting the water to feel like Cape Cod in the summer, Sean was pleasantly surprised. It was still cool, but certainly not cold.

Holding hands, they walked on the damp, firm sand at the water's edge. The sun was dipping toward the horizon, casting a glistening path of golden light along the surface of the water. A flock of pelicans silently glided by overhead. From the depths of a vast mangrove swamp came the cry of a tropical bird.

As they walked past the beachfront condominiums just south of the Ritz Carlton, real estate development gave way to a line of Australian pine trees mixed with sea grapes and a few palms. The Gulf changed from green to silver as the sun sank below the horizon.

"Do you honestly care for me?" Janet asked suddenly. Since she wouldn't get a chance to talk seriously with Sean at dinner, she decided there was no time better than the present to at least get a discussion started. After all, what could be more romantic than a sunset walk on the beach?

"Of course I care for you," Sean said.

"Why don't you ever tell me?"

"I don't?" Sean asked, surprised.

"No, you don't."

"Well, I think it all the time," Sean said.

"Would you say you care for me a lot?"

"Yeah, I would," Sean said.

"Do you love me, Sean?" Janet asked.

They walked for a way in silence watching their feet press into the sand.

"Yeah, I do," Sean said.

"Do what?" Janet asked.

"What you said," Sean replied. He glanced off at the spot on the horizon where the sun had set. It was still marked by a fiery glow.

"Look at me, Sean," Janet said.

Reluctantly, Sean looked into her eyes.

"Why can't you tell me you love me?" she asked.

"I'm telling you," Sean said.

"You can't say the words," Janet said. "Why not?"

"I'm Irish," Sean said, trying to lighten the mood. "The Irish aren't good at talking about their feelings."

"Well, at least you admit it," Janet said. "But whether you truly care for me or not is an important issue. It's futile to have the kind of talk I want if the basic feelings aren't there."

"The feelings are there," Sean insisted.

"Okay, I'll let you off the hook for the moment," Janet said, pulling Sean to a halt. "But I have to say it's a mystery to me how you can be so expressive about everything else in life and so uncommunicative when it comes to us. But we can talk about that later. How about a swim?"

"You really want to go in the water?" he asked reluctantly. The water was so dark.

"What do you think going for a swim means?" Janet asked.

"I get the point," Sean said. "But this really isn't a bathing suit." He was afraid that once his shorts got wet it would be akin to wearing nothing.

Janet couldn't believe that after they'd come this far he was balking at going into the water because of his shorts.

"If there's a problem," she said, "why don't you just take them off?"

"Listen to this!" Sean said mockingly. "Miss Proper is suggesting I skinny-dip. Well, I'd be happy to as long as you'll do the same."

Sean glared at Janet in the half-light. Part of him relished making her feel uncomfortable. After all, hadn't she just made him squirm on this issue of expressing feelings? He wasn't quite sure she'd rise to his challenge, but then Janet had been surprising him a lot lately, starting with her following him to Florida.

"Who first?" she asked.

"We'll do it together," he said.

After a moment's hesitation they both peeled off their terrycloth robes, then their suits, and pranced naked into the light surf. As evening deepened toward night, they frolicked in the shallow water, letting the miniature waves cascade over their nude bodies. After the controlling grip of Boston winter it seemed like the epitome of abandon, especially for Janet. To her surprise, she was enjoying the sensation immensely.

Fifteen minutes later they drew themselves out of the water and rushed up the beach to gather their clothes, giggling like giddy adolescents. Janet immediately began to step into her suit, but Sean had different ideas. Grabbing her hand, he pulled her up into the shadows of the Australian pines. After spreading their robes on the sandy bed of pine needles at the edge of the beach, they lay down in tight, joyous embrace.

But it didn't last long.

Janet was the first to sense something was wrong. Lifting her head, she looked out at the luminous line of white sand beach.

"Did you hear that?" she asked.

"I don't think so," Sean replied without even listening.

"Seriously," Janet said. She sat up. "I heard something."

Before either could move a figure stepped out of the shadows enveloping the copse of pine trees. The stranger's face was lost in shadow. All they could see clearly was the pearl-handled gun pointed at Janet.

"If this is your property we'll just go," Sean said. He sat up.

"Shut up!" Tom hissed. He couldn't take his eyes off Janet's nakedness. He'd planned on stepping out of the darkness and immediately shooting them both, but now he found himself hesitating. Although he couldn't see much in the half-light, what he could see was mesmerizing. He was finding it difficult to think.

Sensing Tom's penetrating eyes, Janet snatched up her bathing suit and pressed it against her chest. But Tom was not to be denied. With his free hand he wrenched the suit away and let it drop to the sand.

"You never should have interfered," Tom snapped.

"What are you talking about?" Janet asked, unable to take her eyes off the gun.

"Alice told me girls like you would try to tempt me," Tom said.

"Who's Alice?" Sean asked. He got to his feet. He hoped to keep Tom talking.

"Shut up!" Tom barked, swinging the gun in Sean's direction. He decided it was time to get rid of this guy. He extended his arm, tightening his grip on the trigger until the gun fired.

But the bullet went wide. At the exact moment Tom pulled the trigger a second shadowy figure hurled out of the darkness, tackling Tom, knocking him sideways a number of yards.

The gun sprang from Tom's grip with the stranger's impact. It fell to the ground inches from Sean's foot. With the sound of the shot still ringing in his ears, Sean looked down at the weapon with shock. He couldn't believe it; someone had fired a gun at him!

"Get the gun!" Harris managed to grunt as he wrestled with Tom. They rolled against the trunk of one of the pine trees. Tom momentarily broke free. He started out onto the beach, but he only got fifty feet away before Harris tackled him again.

Both Sean and Janet got over their initial shock and began to react at the same moment. Janet snatched up their robes and suits. Sean picked up the gun. They could see Harris and Tom rolling around in the sand close to the water.

"Let's get out of here!" Sean said urgently.

"But who saved us?" Janet asked. "Shouldn't we help him?"

"No," Sean said. "I recognize him. He doesn't need any help. We're out of here."

Sean grabbed Janet's reluctant hand, and together they ran out from beneath the canopy of pine onto the beach and then north toward the hotel. Several times Janet tried to look over her shoulder, but each time Sean urged her on. As they neared the hotel they stopped long enough to slip into their robes.

"Who was that man who saved us?" Janet demanded between gasping breaths.

"Head of security at Forbes," Sean said, equally as winded. "His name is Robert Harris. He'll be okay. We should worry about that other fruitcake."

"Who was he?" Janet asked.

"I haven't the slightest idea," Sean said.

"What are we going to tell the police?" Janet asked.

"Nothing," Sean said. "We're not going to the police. I can't. They're looking for me. I can't go until I talk to Brian."

They ran past the pool and into the hotel.

"The man with the gun had to be associated with Forbes too," Janet said. "Otherwise, the head of security wouldn't have been here."

"You're probably right," Sean said. "Unless Robert Harris is after me just like the police are. He could be playing bounty hunter. I'm sure he'd like nothing better than to get rid of me."

"I don't like any of this," Janet admitted as they rode up in the elevator.

"Me neither," Sean said. "Something weird's happening, and we don't have a clue."

"What are we going to do?" Janet asked. "I still think we should go to the police."

"First thing we're going to do is change hotels," Sean said. "I don't like Harris knowing where we're staying. It's bad enough he knows we're in Naples."

Once in the room they quickly got their things together. Janet again tried to talk Sean into going to the police, but he adamantly refused.

"Now here's the plan," Sean said. "I'll take the bags and go down to the pool, then slip out by the tennis courts. You go down to the front door, get the car, then come and pick me up."

"What are you talking about?" Janet demanded. "Why all this sneaking around?"

"We were followed here at least by Harris," Sean said. "I want everybody to think we're still staying here."

Janet decided it was easier just to go along with Sean. She could tell he was in no mood to argue. Besides, he might be right to be this paranoid.

Sean left first with the bags.

WAYNE EDWARDS walked back to the Mercedes at a fast clip and climbed into the passenger seat. Sterling had moved behind the wheel.

Up ahead Sterling could see the youthful Japanese man climbing back into the limousine.

"What's happening?" Sterling asked.

"I'm not sure," Wayne said. "The Jap just sat in the foyer and read magazines. Then the girl appeared alone. She's under the porte cochere waiting for the car. No sign of Sean Murphy. I bet those guys in the limo are as confused as we are."

A parking valet drove by in the red Pontiac. He parked under the porte cochere.

The limousine started up, spewing a puff of black smoke from its tailpipe.

Sterling started the Mercedes. He told Wayne that the Sushita jet was on its way to Naples.

"Not much doubt something's going to happen," Wayne said.

"I'm sure it will be tonight," Sterling said. "We've got to be prepared."

Presently the red Pontiac went by with Janet Reardon at the wheel. Behind her came the limo. Sterling made a U-turn.

At the base of the drive the Pontiac turned right. The limo followed.

"I smell a fish," Wayne said. "Something's not right with

this picture. To get to the road you have to turn left. This right is a dead end."

Sterling turned right to follow the others. Wayne was correct; the road dead-ended. But just before the dead end they came to an entrance to a large parking lot that was partially obscured by foliage. Sterling pulled in.

"There's the limo," Wayne said, pointing off to the right.

"And there's the Pontiac," Sterling said, motioning toward the tennis courts. "And there is Mr. Murphy loading luggage in the trunk. This is a rather unorthodox departure."

"I suppose they think they're being clever," Wayne said, shaking his head.

"Maybe this move has something to do with Mr. Robert Harris," Sterling suggested.

They watched the red Pontiac drive by and out the exit. The limo followed. After waiting a bit, Sterling did the same.

"Watch for Harris's blue sedan," Sterling advised.

Wayne nodded. "I've been watching," he assured him.

They drove south for four or five miles, then cut west toward the Gulf. Eventually they ended up on Gulf Shore Boulevard.

"This area is a lot more built up," Wayne said. Either side of the road had condominium buildings with manicured lawns and pampered flower beds.

They drove for a short time before they saw the red Pontiac pull up a ramp to the first-floor entrance of the Edgewater Beach Hotel. The limo pulled off the road but remained on the ground level, turning in under the building. Sterling pulled off the road and parked in a diagonal spot to the right of the ramp. He turned off the ignition. At the top of the ramp they could see Sean directing the removal of their luggage from the Pontiac's trunk.

"A nice little hotel," Wayne said. "Less ostentatious."

"I believe you'll find the facade misleading," Sterling said. "Through some of my banking connections I've heard this place had been purchased by a charming Swiss fellow who added significant European elegance."

"You think Tanaka will try to make his move from here?" Wayne asked.

"I believe he's hoping Sean and his companion will go out so that he can corner them in some isolated location."

"If I were with that chick I think I'd bolt the door and order room service."

Sterling picked up the car phone. "Speaking of Mr. Murphy's companion, let's see what my contacts in Boston have learned about her."

9

March 6
Saturday, 7:50 P.M.

"This is a fabulous room," Janet said as she opened the large wooden tropical shutters.

Sean joined her. "It looks almost as if we're cantilevered out over the beach," he said. They were on the third floor. The beach was illuminated all the way down to the water's edge. A line of Hobie Cats were directly below them.

They were both making an attempt to put the disturbing beach experience behind them. At first Janet wanted to go back to Miami, but Sean talked her into staying. He'd said whatever the explanation for the episode was, at least it was now behind them. He'd said that since they'd driven all the way over to Naples, they should at least enjoy themselves.

"Let's get a move on," Sean said. "Malcolm Betencourt is expecting us in forty minutes."

While Janet showered, Sean sat down and tried Brian one more time. He was frustrated when he got the answering machine yet again. He left a third message instructing his brother to disregard the previous phone number. He gave the Edgewater Beach number and the room number, adding that he'd be out for dinner, but to call later, no matter the time. He said it was vitally important for them to talk.

Sean then called the Betencourt residence to say they might be a few minutes late. Mr. Betencourt assured him it wasn't a problem and thanked him for calling.

Sitting on the edge of the bed with Janet still in the shower, Sean took out the pistol he'd picked up on the beach. Snapping open the cylinder, he shook out some sand. It was an ancient .38 Smith and Wesson detective special. There were four remaining cartridges. Sean shook his head when he thought how close he'd come to being shot. He also thought about the irony of being saved by someone he'd disliked from the moment he'd first met him.

Snapping the cylinder of the revolver closed, Sean put the gun under his shirt. There had been a few too many inexplicable brushes with disaster in the last twenty-four hours for him to pass up this chance to arm himself. Sean sensed that something bizarre was happening, and like any good medical diagnostician, he was trying to relate all the symptoms to a single illness. Intuitively, he felt he should keep the gun just in case. Inwardly he was still shaking from the feeling of helplessness he'd had just before the gun had gone off.

After Janet got out of the shower, Sean got in. Janet was still complaining about not having reported the man with the gun, and said as much as she was applying her makeup. But Sean remained unwavering, adding that he believed Robert Harris was fully capable of handling the situation.

"Won't it look suspicious if we have to explain after the fact why we didn't go to the police?" Janet persisted.

"Probably," Sean agreed, "but it is just something else

Brian will have to handle. Let's stop talking about it for a while and try to enjoy ourselves a little."

"One more question," Janet said. "The man said something about my interfering. What do you think he meant?"

Sean threw up his hands in exasperation. "The guy was obviously crazy. He was probably in the middle of some acute paranoid psychotic episode. How am I supposed to know what he was talking about?"

"All right," Janet said. "Take it easy. Did you try Brian again?"

Sean nodded. "The bum is still not home," he said. "But I left this number. He'll probably call while we're at dinner."

When they were ready to leave, Sean phoned the parking valet to have the car brought up to the entrance. As they exited the room, Sean pocketed the Smith and Wesson, unbeknownst to Janet.

As they drove south on Gulf Shore Boulevard, Janet finally began to calm down. She even began to notice the surroundings again and to appreciate all the flowering trees. She noticed there was no debris or graffiti or any signs of homeless people. The problems of urban America seemed a long way from Naples, Florida.

While she was trying to get Sean to look at a particularly beautiful flowering tree, she noticed that he was spending an inordinate amount of time looking in the rearview mirror.

"What are you looking for?" she questioned.

"Robert Harris," Sean said.

Janet glanced behind them, then at Sean.

"Have you seen him?" she asked with alarm.

Sean shook his head. "No," he said. "I haven't seen Harris, but I think a car is following us."

"Oh great!" Janet said. The weekend was not turning out as she'd envisioned at all.

All of a sudden, Sean made a U-turn in the middle of the

road. Janet had to grab the dash to steady herself. In the blink of an eye they were traveling north, returning in the direction from which they'd come.

"It's the second car," Sean said. "See if you can tell what kind of car it is and if you can see the driver."

There were two cars bearing down on them from the opposite direction, their headlights cutting a swath in the darkness. The first car went by. Sean slowed, and then the second car passed them.

"It's a limousine," Janet said with surprise.

"Well, that shows how paranoid I'm getting," Sean said with a touch of chagrin. "That's certainly not the kind of car Robert Harris would be driving."

Sean made another sudden U-turn, and they were again heading south.

"Would you give me a little warning when you are about to do one of your maneuvers?" Janet complained. She resettled herself in her seat.

"Sorry," Sean said.

As they traveled south beyond the old section of town they noticed the homes got progressively larger and more impressive. Within Port Royal they were even more lavish, and when they pulled into Malcolm Betencourt's driveway lined with blazing torches, they were awed. They parked in an area designated "visitor parking" at least a hundred feet from the door.

"This looks more like a transplanted French château," Janet said. "It's huge. What does this man do?"

"He runs some enormous for-profit hospital corporation," Sean said. He got out of the car and came around to open the door for Janet.

"I didn't know there was so much money in for-profit medicine," Janet said.

The Betencourts were gracious hosts. They welcomed

Sean and Janet as if they were old friends. They even teased them for parking in an area reserved for the "trades."

Armed with glasses of the finest champagne flavored with a mere drop of cassis, Sean and Janet were treated to a grand tour of the twenty-thousand-square-foot home. They also had a walk around the grounds which included two pools, one cascading into the other, and a hundred-and-twenty-foot teak sailboat moored to a sizable pier.

"Some people might say that this house is a bit too big," Malcolm said when they were seated in the dining room. "But Harriet and I are accustomed to a lot of room. Our home up in Connecticut is actually a little larger."

"Plus we entertain regularly," Harriet said. She rang a little bell and a servant appeared with the first course. Another poured crisp white wine.

"So you are studying at Forbes?" Malcolm said to Sean. "You're a lucky man, Sean. It's a great place. You've met Dr. Mason, I presume?"

"Dr. Mason and Dr. Levy," Sean said.

"They're doing great things," Malcolm said. "Of course, I don't have to tell you that. As you know, I'm living proof."

"I'm certain you are grateful," Sean said. "But . . ."

"That's an understatement," Malcolm interrupted. "They've given me a second chance at life, so we're more than grateful."

"We've donated five million from our foundation," Harriet said. "We in the United States have to put our resources in those institutions that are successful instead of following those pork barrel policies of Congress."

"Harriet's sensitive about the research issue," Malcolm explained.

"She's got a good point," Sean admitted. "But Mr. Betencourt, as a medical student I'm interested in your experience as a patient, and I'd like to hear it in your own words. How did you understand the treatment you were given? Especially considering the business you are in, I'm sure you were interested."

"You mean the quality of the treatment or the treatment per se?"

"The treatment per se," Sean said.

"I'm a businessman, not a doctor," Malcolm said. "But I consider myself an informed layperson. When I got to Forbes they immediately started me on immunotherapy with an antibody. On the first day they took a biopsy of the tumor, and they took white blood cells from my body. They incubated the white blood cells with the tumor to sensitize them to become 'killer cells.' Finally, they injected my own sensitized cells back into my bloodstream. As I understand it, the antibody coated the cancer cells and then the killer cells came along and ate 'em up."

Malcolm shrugged and looked at Harriet to see if she wanted to add anything.

"That's what happened," she agreed. "Those little cells went in there and gave those tumors hell!"

"At first my symptoms got a little worse," Malcolm said. "But then they got progressively better. We followed the progression on MRI. The tumors just melted away. And today I feel great." To emphasize his point he gave his chest a thump with his fist.

"And now you are treated in the outpatient?" Sean asked.

"That's right," Malcolm said. "I'm scheduled at present to go back every six months. But Dr. Mason is convinced I'm cured, so I expect to extend it out to once a year. Each time I go I get a dose of antibody just to be sure."

"And no more symptoms?" Sean asked.

"Nothing," Malcolm said. "I'm fit as a fiddle."

The first-course dishes were removed. The main course arrived along with a mellow red wine. Sean felt relaxed despite the episode on the beach. He glanced at Janet, who was having a separate conversation with Harriet; it turned out they had family friends in common. Janet smiled back at Sean when he caught her eye. Clearly she, too, was enjoying herself.

Malcolm took an appreciative taste of his wine. "Not bad for an '86 Napa," he said. He put his glass down on the table and looked over at Sean. "Not only have I no symptoms from the brain tumor, but I feel great. Better than I have in years. Of course, I'm probably comparing it to the year before I got the immunotherapy which was pure hell. Not much else could have gone wrong. First I had knee surgery, which wasn't fun, then encephalitis, and then the brain tumor. This year I've been great. Haven't even had a cold."

"You had encephalitis?" Sean asked, his fork poised halfway to his mouth.

"Yes," Malcolm said. "I was a medical oddity. Somebody could have gone through medical school just studying me. I had a bout of headache, fever, and was generally feeling crappy, and . . ." Malcolm leaned over and spoke behind his hand. "There was some burning in my pecker when I peed." He glanced over to be sure the women hadn't overheard.

"How did you know it was encephalitis?" Sean asked. He put his full fork down on his plate.

"Well, the headache was the worst part," Malcolm said. "I went to my local internist who sent me down to Columbia Presbyterian. They're used to seeing strange stuff down there, all kinds of exotic, tropical diseases. They had these high-powered infectious-disease people see me. They were the ones who first suspected encephalitis and then proved it with some new method called polymerase something or other."

"Polymerase Chain Reaction," Sean said as if he were in a trance. "What kind of encephalitis was it?"

"They called it SLE," Malcolm said. "It stands for St. Louis encephalitis. They were all surprised, saying it was kinda out of season. But I had been on a couple of trips. Anyway, the encephalitis was mild, and after some bed rest I felt fine. Then of course, two months later, bam! I got a brain tumor. I thought I was done for. So did my doctors up north. First they thought it had spread from someplace else like my colon or my prostate. But when they all proved clean, they decided to biopsy. The rest, of course, is history."

Malcolm took another bite of his food, chewed and swallowed it. He took a taste of his wine, then glanced back at Sean. Sean hadn't moved. He appeared stunned. Malcolm leaned across the table to look him in the eye. "You okay, young fella?"

Sean blinked as if he were emerging from hypnosis. "I'm fine," he stammered. He quickly apologized for seeming distracted, saying that he was just astounded by Malcolm's story. He thanked Malcolm profusely for being willing to share it with him.

"My pleasure," Malcolm said. "If I can help train a few of you medical students, I'll feel like I'm repaying a little of the interest I owe on my debt to the medical profession. If it weren't for your mentor Dr. Mason and his colleague Dr. Levy, I wouldn't be here today."

Malcolm then turned his attention to the women, and while everyone but Sean ate his dinner, the conversation switched to Naples and why the Betencourts had decided to build their house there.

"How about we take our dessert out on the terrace above the pool," Harriet suggested after the dishes had been cleared.

"I'm sorry but we'll have to skip dessert," Sean said,

speaking up after a long silence. "Janet and I have been working tremendously hard. I'm afraid we'll have to get back to our hotel before we fall asleep on our feet. Right, Janet?"

Janet nodded and smiled self-consciously, but it was not a smile motivated by cheerful assent. It was an attempt to hide her mortification.

Five minutes later they were saying goodbye in the Betencourts' grand foyer with Malcolm insisting that if Sean had any more questions he should call him directly. He gave Sean his private direct-dial number.

When the door closed behind them, and they started out the massive driveway, Janet was incensed. "That was a rude way to end the evening," she said. "After they'd been so gracious with us, you practically walk out in the middle of the meal."

"That was the end of the meal," Sean reminded her. "Harriet was talking about dessert. Besides, I couldn't sit there another minute. Malcolm made me realize several extraordinary things. I don't know if you were listening when he described his illnesses."

"I was talking with Harriet," Janet said irritably.

"He told me he had an operation, encephalitis, and then his brain tumor all within a period of a few months."

"What did that tell you?" Janet asked.

"It made me realize that both Helen Cabot and Louis Martin had the same history," Sean said. "I know because I did their history and physicals."

"You think these illnesses are related somehow?" she asked. Some of the anger was gone from her voice.

"It seems to me I saw a similar sequence and timing in a number of the charts we copied," Sean said. "I'm not positive because I wasn't looking for it, but even with three, the possibility of it happening by chance is pretty small."

"What are you saying?" Janet asked.

"I don't know for sure," Sean said. "But it convinced me I want to go to Key West. Forbes has a spin-off diagnostic lab down there where they sent the biopsies. It's a favorite trick of hospitals to have quasi-independent labs to maximize the profits they can make out of diagnostic lab work, self-referral limitations be damned."

"I have next weekend off," Janet said. "Both Saturday and Sunday. I wouldn't mind visiting Key West."

"I don't want to wait," Sean said. "I want to go right away. I think we're on to something here." He was also thinking that between the police looking for him and not being able to reach Brian, he might not have the luxury of waiting a week.

Janet stopped dead in her tracks and glanced at her watch. It was after ten. "Are you talking about going there tonight?" she asked with disbelief.

"Let's find out how far it is," Sean said. "Then we can decide."

Janet started walking again, passing Sean who'd paused when she had. "Sean, you are getting more incomprehensible and crazier all the time," she said. "You call people up at the last minute, get them to graciously invite you to dinner, then you walk out in the middle because you suddenly have the idea of going to Key West. I give up. But I'll tell you something: this lady is not going to Key West tonight. This lady is . . ."

Janet didn't finish her angry monologue. Rounding the Pontiac, which was partially hidden by a large banyan tree, she'd practically collided with a figure in a dark suit, white shirt, and dark tie. His face and hair were obscured by shadows.

Janet gasped. She was still on edge from the episode on

the beach, and confronting yet another man coming out of the dark frightened her terribly. Sean started toward her but was stopped by a similarly shadowy figure on his side of the car.

Despite the darkness, Sean could tell the man before him was Asian. Before Sean knew it, a third man had stepped behind him. For a moment no one spoke. Sean glanced back at the house and estimated how long it would take him to cover the distance to the front door. He also thought about what he'd do once he got there. Unfortunately, a lot depended on how quickly Malcolm Betencourt responded.

"If you please," the man in front of Sean said in flawless English. "Mr. Yamaguchi would be most grateful if you and your companion would come and have a word with him."

Sean looked at each man in turn. All of them exuded an aura of total confidence and tranquility that Sean found unnerving. Sean could feel the weight of Tom's pistol in his jacket pocket, but he dared not pull it out. He had no experience with guns, and there was no way he could shoot these people. And he hesitated to think how these men might retaliate.

"It would be regretful if there is trouble," the same man said. "Please, Mr. Yamaguchi is waiting in a car parked on the street."

"Sean," Janet called over the top of the car in a wavering voice, "who are these people?"

"I don't know," Sean answered her. Then, to the man in front of him, he said: "Can you give me an idea who Mr. Yamaguchi is, and why he particularly wants to talk with us?"

"Please," the man repeated. "Mr. Yamaguchi will tell you himself. Please, the car is just a few steps away."

"Well, since you are being so nice about it," Sean said. "Sure, let's say hello to Mr. Yamaguchi."

Sean turned and started around the car. The man who was standing behind him stepped aside. Sean put an arm around Janet's shoulder and together they started toward the street. The taller Japanese man, the one who had been in front of Sean, led the way. The other two silently followed.

The limousine was parked beneath a line of trees and was so dark it was difficult to see it until they were only a few feet away. The taller man opened the rear door and motioned for Sean and Janet to climb inside.

"Can't Mr. Yamaguchi come out?" Sean asked. He wondered if this was the same limo that he thought had been following them on their way to the Betencourts'. He guessed it was.

"Please," the taller Japanese man said. "It will be far more comfortable inside."

Sean motioned for Janet to get in, and he climbed in after her. Almost immediately the other rear door opened, and one of the silent Japanese men crowded in next to Janet. Another man followed immediately behind Sean. The taller man got in the front behind the wheel and started the car.

"What's going on here, Sean?" Janet asked. Her initial shock was changing to alarm.

"Mr. Yamaguchi?" Sean asked. In front of him he could just make out the figure of a man sitting in one of the seats to the side of a console with a small built-in TV set.

"Thank you very much for joining me," Tanaka said with a slight bow. His accent was barely perceptible. "I apologize for the inconvenient seating, but we shall have only a short ride."

The car lurched forward. Janet grabbed Sean's hand.

"You people are very polite," Sean said. "And we appreciate that. But we would also appreciate some idea what this is all about and where we're going."

"You have been invited on a vacation," Tanaka said. His

white teeth flashed in the dark. When they passed a street lamp, Sean got his first glimpse of the man's face. It was calm but determined. There was no sign of emotion.

"Your trip is compliments of Sushita Industries," Tanaka continued. "I can assure you that you will be treated extremely well. Sushita would not go through this effort unless they had great respect for you. I am sorry it has to be done in this furtive, barbaric fashion, but I have my orders. I'm also sorry that your companion has been caught up in this affair, but your hosts will treat her with equal respect. Her presence at this point is helpful since I'm certain you would not want to see any harm befall her. So please, Mr. Murphy, do not attempt any heroics. My colleagues are professionals."

Janet began to complain, but Sean squeezed her hand to silence her.

"And where are we going?" Sean asked.

"To Tokyo," Tanaka said as if there had been no question.

They drove in strained silence as they worked their way in a northeasterly direction. Sean considered his options. There weren't many. The threat of violence toward Janet was sobering, and the pistol in his pocket was not reassuring.

Tanaka had been correct about the ride. In less than twenty minutes they pulled into the general aviation area of the Naples airport. As late as it was on a Saturday night, there were minimal signs of life, only a few lights in the main building. Sean tried to think of ways of alerting whomever he could, but the specter of harm to Janet kept him in check. Although he certainly did not want to be taken forcibly to Japan, he couldn't think of a plausible way to forestall it.

The limo drove through a gate in a chain link fence and out onto the tarmac. Skirting the rear of the general aviation building, they headed for a large private jet that was clearly prepared to take off at any moment. Its engines were running, its anti-collision and navigational lights were flashing, its door was open, and its retractable steps were extended.

The limousine stopped about fifty feet from the plane. Sean and Janet were politely asked to climb out of the car and walk the short distance to the steps. Cupping their hands over their ears to shield them from the whine of the jet engine, Sean and Janet reluctantly headed for the plane as commanded. Once again, Sean considered his options. Nothing seemed promising. He caught Janet's eye. She looked distraught. They paused at the base of the plane's steps.

"Please," Tanaka yelled over the sound of the engines as he motioned for Sean and Janet to move up the stairs.

Sean and Janet again exchanged glances. Sean nodded for her to board, then followed her up. They had to duck to enter, but once inside they could stand up. To their left was the cockpit with its door closed.

The interior of the plane was simple yet elegant, featuring darkly stained mahogany and tan leather. The carpeting was dark green. The seating included a banquette and a series of reclinable club chairs that could rotate to face any direction. Toward the rear of the plane was a galley and a door to a lavatory. On a counter in the galley was an open bottle of vodka and a sliced lime.

Sean and Janet paused near the door, unsure of where they were to go. One of the near club chairs was occupied by a Caucasian man dressed in a business suit. Like the Japanese, he exuded an aura of calm confidence. His features were angular and handsome; his hair was mildly curly. In his right hand he held a drink. Sean and Janet could hear the ice tinkle against the glass as he brought it to his lips.

Tanaka, who had boarded directly behind Sean and Janet, saw the Caucasian man seconds after Sean and Janet had. He seemed startled.

The taller of the Japanese men bumped into Tanaka since Tanaka had stopped so abruptly. The collision prompted a rapid outpouring of angry-sounding Japanese from Tanaka.

The taller Japanese began to respond, but he was interrupted by the Caucasian.

"I should warn you," he said in English. "I speak fluent Japanese. My name is Sterling Rombauer." He put his drink down in a depression in the arm of his chair made for that purpose, stood up, pulled out a business card, and handed it to Tanaka with a deferential bow.

Tanaka bowed in unison with Sterling as he accepted the card, and despite the surprise he obviously felt concerning Sterling's presence, he examined the card with care and bowed again. Then he spoke in rapid Japanese to his companion behind him.

"I believe I can best answer that," Sterling said casually as he reclaimed his seat and lifted his drink. "The pilot, copilot, and cabin crew are not in the cockpit. They are resting in the lavatory." Sterling gestured over his shoulder.

Tanaka spoke more angry Japanese to his cohort.

"Please excuse me for interrupting again," Sterling said. "But what you are asking your associate to do is unreasonable. I'm certain that if you carefully consider the situation, you'll agree that it would not serve my purposes to be here alone. And indeed, if you look out the starboard side you will see a vehicle occupied by an accomplice who is currently holding a portable phone programmed to speed dial the police. In this country, abduction is a crime, a felony to be more specific."

Tanaka looked again at Sterling's business card as if there was something he could have missed on his first examination. "What is it you want?" he asked in English.

"I believe we need to talk, Mr. Tanaka Yamaguchi," Sterling said. He rattled the ice cubes in his drink and took a last sip. "I am currently representing the interests of the Forbes Cancer Center," he continued. "Its director does not want to jeopardize the Center's relationship with Sushita Industries, but there are limits. He does not want to see Mr. Murphy spirited away to Japan."

Tanaka was silent.

"Mr. Murphy," Sterling called, ignoring Tanaka for the moment. "Would you mind allowing Mr. Yamaguchi and myself a few moments alone? I suggest you and your companion deplane and join my associate in the car. You can wait for me there; I will not be long."

Tanaka made no effort to countermand Sterling's suggestion. Not needing a second invitation, Sean grabbed Janet's hand, and together they pushed past Tanaka and his cohort, descended the short flight of stairs, and ran toward the darkened car parked perpendicular to the plane.

Reaching the Mercedes, Sean went to the passenger-side rear door and opened it. He allowed Janet to climb in. He followed. Before he closed the door Wayne Edwards greeted them with a warm, "Hi, folks." Although he'd briefly glanced at them as they got in, he quickly turned his attention back to the plane which could be seen clearly through his windshield. "I don't mean to sound inhospitable," he continued, "but maybe it would be better for you to wait in the terminal building."

"Mr. Rombauer told us to join you," Sean said.

"Hey, I know," Wayne said. "'Cause that was the plan. But I've been thinking ahead. If something goes awry, and that plane starts to move, I'm driving straight into its nose gear. There aren't any air bags in the back seat."

"I get the picture," Sean said. He got out and gave Janet a hand. Together they headed toward the general aviation building.

"This keeps getting more and more confusing," Janet complained. "Spending time with you is living on the edge, Sean Murphy. What is going on?"

"I wish I knew," Sean said. "Maybe they think I know more than I do."

"And what is that supposed to mean?"

Sean shrugged his shoulders. "One thing I do know is that we've just missed an unwanted trip to Japan," Sean said.

"But why Japan?" Janet asked.

"I don't know for sure," Sean said. "But that Hiroshi character at Forbes has been watching me ever since I showed up, and some Japanese man recently visited my mother asking about me. The only explanation I can think of is that they somehow see me as a risk to their investment in Forbes."

"This whole situation is insane," Janet said. "Who was that man in the plane who got us out of there?"

"I've never seen him before," Sean said. "It's just another part to the mystery. He did say he was working for Forbes."

They arrived at the general aviation building only to find the door locked.

"Now what?" Janet asked.

"Come on!" Sean said. "We're not staying here." He grabbed her hand, and together they skirted the two-story cement structure, exiting the airfield through the same gate the limo had entered through. In front of the building was a sizable parking lot. Sean began going from car to car, trying doors.

"Don't tell me, let me guess," Janet said. "Now you're going to steal a car just to round out the evening!"

"Borrow is a better term," Sean said. He found a Chevrolet Celebrity with its doors unlocked. After leaning in so he could feel under the dash, he got in behind the wheel. "Get in," he called to her. "This will be easy."

Janet hesitated, feeling more and more that she was being drawn into something she didn't want any part of. The idea of riding in a stolen car was not appealing, particularly given the trouble they were already in.

"Get in!" Sean called again.

Janet opened the door and did as she was told.

Sean got the car started instantly, much to Janet's dismay. "Still a pro," she commented scornfully.

"Practice makes perfect," Sean said.

Where the airport entrance met the county road, Sean took a right. They drove for a time in silence.

"Am I allowed to ask where we're going?" Janet asked.

"I'm not sure where," Sean said. "I'd like to find someplace where I can ask directions to Key West. Trouble is that this town is pretty quiet even though it's only eleven on a Saturday night."

"Why don't you take me back to the Betencourts'," Janet said. "I'll get my rental car and go back to the hotel. Then you can go to Key West if you're so inclined."

"I don't think that's a good idea," Sean said. "Those Japanese guys didn't show up at the Betencourts' by accident. They were in that limo that I thought was following us earlier. Obviously they followed us from the Edgewater Beach Hotel, which means they must have been following us from the Ritz Carlton. More likely, they've been following us all the way from Forbes."

"But the others had followed us, too," Janet said.

"We must have been a regular caravan coming across the

Everglades," Sean agreed. "But the point is we can't go back to the car or the hotel. Not unless we want to risk further pursuit."

"And I suppose we can't go to the police," Janet said.

"Of course not," Sean snapped.

"What about our belongings?" Janet asked.

"We'll call from Miami and have them sent," Sean said. "We'll call the Betencourts about the car. Hertz will have to get it. It's not that important. It's more important that we're no longer followed."

Janet sighed. She felt indecisive. She wanted to go to bed, yet Sean was making some sense in a situation that didn't make any sense whatsoever. The episode with the Japanese had frightened her, in some ways just as badly as the episode on the beach.

"Here are some people," Sean said. "I can ask them." Ahead, they could see a line of cars pulled up near a big sign heralding the Oasis, some sort of nightclub/disco. Sean pulled over to the side of the road. The line for valet parking snaked through a parking lot that was half-filled with trailered boats. The Oasis shared a parking lot with a landlocked marina.

Sean got out of the Celebrity and weaved his way among the parked cars toward the disco's entrance. Spine-jangling bass emanated from the open door. After waiting at the parking valet's podium, Sean cornered one of the men and asked directions to the city dock. The harried man quickly described the route to Sean with flamboyant hand gestures. A few minutes later Sean was back in the car. He repeated the directions to Janet so she could help.

"Why are we going to the city dock?" Janet asked. "Or is that a stupid question?"

"Hey, don't be mad at me," Sean complained.

"Who else can I be mad at?" Janet said. "This weekend so far is hardly what I had anticipated."

"Reserve your anger for that kook on the beach or those paranoid Japanese," Sean said.

"What about the city dock?" Janet asked again.

"Key West is due south of Naples," Sean said. "That much I remember from seeing it on a map. The Keys curve to the west. Going by boat could be easier and probably faster. We could even get some sleep. Plus, we wouldn't be using a 'borrowed' car."

Janet didn't even comment. The idea of a night-long boat ride would be a fitting end to such an insane day.

They found the city dock with ease at the base of a short cul de sac with a large flagpole at its entrance. But the docks were a disappointment as far as Sean was concerned. He'd expected it to be much busier, having heard that sports fishing was popular on the west coast of Florida. The only marina was shut tight. There were a few offers for fishing boat charters on a bulletin board, but not much else. After parking the car, they walked out on the pier. The larger, commercial boats were all dark.

Returning to the car, Janet leaned on the hood. "Any more bright ideas, Einstein?"

Sean was thinking. The idea of getting to Key West by boat still appealed to him. It was certainly too late to rent another car. Besides, they'd be exhausted when they arrived. Next to the city dock was a restaurant/bar appropriately called The Dock. Sean pointed.

"Let's go in there," he said. "I could use a beer, and we can see if the bartender knows any charter boat people."

The Dock was a rustic, casual affair constructed of planked, pressure-treated wood and furnished with epoxy-filled hatch-cover tables. There were no windows, just screened openings that could be closed with shutters. In lieu of drapes were a collection of fishnets, buoys and other nautical gear. Ceiling fans turned slowly overhead. A darkly burnished wood bar in the shape of a J stretched around one wall.

A small crowd was grouped around the bar watching a basketball game on a TV positioned high on the wall in a corner by the entrance. It wasn't like Old Scully's back in Charlestown, but Sean thought the place had a comfortable feel. In fact, it made him a little homesick.

Sean and Janet found room at the bar, their backs to the TV. There were two bartenders, one tall, serious, and mustached, the other stocky with a constant smirk on his face. Both were casually dressed in printed short-sleeved shirts and dark shorts. Short aprons were tied around their waists.

The taller bartender came over immediately and tossed circular cardboard coasters in front of Sean and Janet with a practiced flick of his wrist.

"What'll it be?" he asked.

"I see you have conch fritters," Sean said, eyeing a large menu attached to the wall.

"Sure do," the bartender said.

"We'll have an order," Sean said. "And I'll have a light draft." Sean looked at Janet.

"I'll have the same," she said.

Frosted mugs of beer were soon before them, and Sean and Janet had only a moment to comment on the relaxed character of the place before the conch fritters arrived.

"Wow!" Sean commented. "That was fast."

"Good food takes time," the bartender said.

In spite of all that had happened that evening, both Sean and Janet found themselves laughing. The bartender, like any good comedian, never cracked a smile.

Sean used the opportunity to ask about boats.

"What kind of boat you interested in?" the bartender asked.

Sean shrugged. "I don't know enough about boats to say," he admitted. "We want to go to Key West tonight. How long would it take?"

"Depends," the bartender said. "It's ninety miles as the crow flies. With a good-sized boat you can be down there in three or four hours."

"Any idea how we could find someone to take us?" Sean said.

"It'll cost you," the bartender said.

"How much?"

"Five, six hundred," the bartender said with a shrug.

"They take credit cards?" Sean asked.

Janet started to complain, but Sean gripped her leg under the edge of the bar. "I'll pay you back," he whispered.

The bartender stepped around the corner where he used a telephone.

STERLING DIALED Randolph Mason's home number with malicious pleasure. Well paid though he was, Sterling wasn't pleased to be working at two o'clock in the morning. He thought that Dr. Mason should be equally as inconvenienced.

Even though Dr. Mason's voice was groggy and full of sleep, he sounded pleased to hear from Sterling.

"I have resolved the Tanaka-Sushita conundrum," Sterling announced. "We even received fax confirmation from Tokyo. They will not abduct Mr. Murphy. He can stay at the Forbes Cancer Center provided you personally guarantee that he will not be exposed to patentable secrets."

"I cannot make that guarantee," Dr. Mason said. "It's too late."

Sterling was too surprised to speak.

"There's been a new development," Dr. Mason explained. "Sean Murphy's brother, Brian Murphy, has shown up here in Miami concerned about Sean. Unable to locate him, he got in touch with me. He has informed me that the Miami police are looking for Sean in connection with a break-in at a funeral home and the unauthorized theft of a cadaver's brain."

"Does this cadaver's brain involve the Forbes Cancer Center?" Sterling asked.

"Most definitely," Dr. Mason said. "The deceased was a patient at Forbes. She'd been one of our medulloblastoma patients, the only one to die in the last several years, I might add. The problem is, our treatment protocol has no patent protection yet."

"You mean to say that Sean Murphy could be in possession of patentable secrets by having this brain at his disposal?"

"Exactly," Dr. Mason said. "As usual, you are right on target. I've already instructed security at Forbes to deny Mr. Murphy access to our labs. What I want you to do is see that he is turned over to the police."

"That might be difficult," Sterling said. "Mr. Murphy and Miss Reardon have vanished. I'm calling from their hotel. They have left their belongings, but I do not think they are planning on returning. It's now after two in the morning. I'm afraid I underestimated their fortitude. I thought that after being rescued from the prospect of abduction, their relief would have rendered them passive. Quite the contrary. My guess is that they commandeered an automobile and drove away."

"I want you to find them," Dr. Mason said.

"I appreciate your confidence in my abilities," Sterling said. "But the character of this assignment is changing. I think you would do better to hire a regular private investigator whose fees are considerably less than mine."

"I want you to stay on the job," Dr. Mason said. There was a hint of desperation in his voice. "I want Sean Murphy turned over to the police as soon as possible. In fact, knowing what I now know, I wish you'd let the Japanese take him. I'll pay you time and a half. Just do it."

"That is very generous," Sterling said, "but, Randolph . . ."

"Double time," Dr. Mason said. "There'd be too much lag time attempting to get someone else involved at this point. I want Sean Murphy in police custody now!"

"All right," Sterling said reluctantly. "I will stay with the assignment. But I have to warn you that unless Miss Reardon uses her Visa card, I'll have no way of tracking him until he turns up in Miami again."

"Why her card?" Dr. Mason asked.

"That's how they paid for their hotel bills," Sterling said.

"You've never let me down," Dr. Mason said.

"I will do my best," Sterling promised.

After Sterling had disconnected, he indicated to Wayne that he had to make another call. They were in the lobby of the Edgewater Beach Hotel. Wayne was comfortably ensconced on a couch with a magazine in his lap.

Sterling dialed one of his many bank contacts in Boston. Once he was sure the man was awake enough to be coherent, Sterling gave him the details he'd learned about Janet Reardon, including the fact that she had used her Visa card at two hotels that evening. Sterling asked for him to call back on Sterling's portable line if the card was used again.

Rejoining Wayne, Sterling informed him that they were to remain on the assignment, but the goal had changed. He told him what Dr. Mason had said and that they were to see that Mr. Murphy was turned over to the police. Sterling also asked if Wayne had any suggestions.

"Just one," Wayne said. "Let's get a couple of rooms and get some shut-eye."

JANET FELT her stomach lurch. It was as if the steak with green peppercorn sauce she'd had for dinner at the Betencourts' had reversed its progress in her digestive tract. She was lying on a bunk in the bow of the forty-two-foot boat that was taking them to Key West. In the bunk across the narrow room, Sean was fast asleep. In the half-light he looked so peaceful. The fact that he could be so relaxed under the circumstances left Janet exasperated. It made her discomfort that much more trenchant.

Despite the Gulf's apparent calm during their sunset walk, it now felt as violent as a rough ocean. They were traveling due south and hitting oncoming swells at forty-five degrees. The boat alternately bounced dizzily up to the right only to crash down with a shudder to the left. Through it all was the constant, deep-throated roar of the diesel engines.

They had not been able to get under way until two-forty-five in the morning. At first they'd motored on calm waters with hundreds of dark mangrove-covered islands visible in the moonlight. As exhausted as she was, Janet had gone down to sleep only to be awakened by the sudden pounding of the boat against the waves and the sound of suddenly strong wind. She hadn't heard Sean come down, yet when she awoke, there he was, sleeping peacefully.

Throwing her feet over the side of the bunk, Janet braced

herself as the boat thumped into the trough of another wave. Holding on with both hands, she made her way aft and up into the main salon. She knew she would be sick if she didn't get air. Below deck the slight smell of diesel only compounded her nascent nausea.

Holding on for dear life, Janet managed to get to the stern of the careening boat where there were two swivel deep-sea fishing chairs mounted to the deck. Fearing these chairs were too exposed, Janet collapsed onto a series of cushions covering a seat along a port side. The starboard side was getting drenched with spray.

The wind and fresh air did wonders for Janet's stomach, but there was no opportunity for rest. She literally had to hold on. With the roar of the engines and the pounding magnified where she was in the stern, Janet could not fathom what people saw in power boating. Up ahead under a canopy sat Doug Gardner, the man who'd been willing to forgo a night's sleep to ferry them to Key West—for a price. He was silhouetted against an illuminated cluster of dials and gauges. He didn't have much to do since he'd put the boat on automatic pilot.

Janet looked up at the canopy of stars and recalled how she used to do the same thing on summer evenings when she was a teen. She'd lie there dreaming about her future. Now she was living it and one thing was for sure: it wasn't quite what she used to imagine.

Maybe her mother had been right, Janet thought reluctantly. Maybe it had been foolish for her to come to Florida to try to talk to Sean. She smiled a wry smile. The only talk they'd managed thus far was the little they'd done on the beach that evening, when Sean had merely echoed her own expression of love. It had been less than satisfying.

Janet had come to Florida in hopes of taking command

of her life, but the longer she was with Sean, the less in command she felt.

STERLING GOT even more satisfaction out of calling Dr. Mason at three-thirty A.M. than he had at two. It took four rings for the doctor to answer. Sterling himself had just been awakened by a call from his banking contact in Boston.

"I now know the destination of the infamous couple," Sterling said. "Fortunately, the young lady used her credit card again for a rather sizable sum. She paid five hundred and fifty dollars to be ferried from Naples to Key West."

"That's not good news," Dr. Mason said.

"I thought you'd be pleased to know we've learned where they're going," Sterling said. "I consider it a bit of good luck."

"The Forbes has a facility in Key West," Dr. Mason said. "It's called Basic Diagnostics. I imagine that's where Mr. Murphy is headed."

"Why do you believe he would go to Basic Diagnostics?" Sterling asked.

"We send a lot of our lab work there," Dr. Mason said. "With current third-party payment schemes, it's cost effective."

"Why do you care if Mr. Murphy visits the facility?"

"The medulloblastoma biopsies are sent there," Dr. Mason said. "I don't want Mr. Murphy exposed to our techniques of sensitizing patient T lymphocytes."

"And Mr. Murphy might be able to deduce these techniques by a mere visit?" Sterling asked.

"He's very savvy as far as biotechnology is concerned," Dr. Mason said. "I can't take the risk. Get yourself down there immediately and keep him out of that lab. See that he is turned over to the police."

"Dr. Mason, it is three-thirty in the morning," Sterling reminded him.

"Charter a plane," Dr. Mason said. "We're paying the expenses. The manager's name is Kurt Wanamaker. I'll give him a call right after I hang up and tell him to expect you."

After Sterling got Mr. Wanamaker's phone number, he hung up. Despite the money that he was being paid, he was not happy with the idea of rushing off to Key West in the middle of the night. He felt that Dr. Mason was overreacting. After all, it was Sunday and the lab very likely wasn't even open.

Yet Sterling got out of bed and walked into the bathroom.

10

March 7
Sunday, 5:30 A.M.

Sean's first glimpse of Key West in the pre-dawn light was of a line of low-rise clapboard buildings nestled in tropical greenery. A few taller brick structures poked out of the skyline here and there, but even they were no taller than five stories. The water's edge from the northwest was dotted with marinas and hotels all cheek to jowl.

"Where's the best place to drop us off?" Sean asked Doug.

"Probably the Pier House pier," Doug said as he cut back the engines. "It's right at the base of Duval Street which is Key West's main drag."

"You familiar with the area?" Sean asked.

"I've been here a dozen or so times," Doug said.

"Ever hear of an organization called Basic Diagnostics?"

"Can't say that I have," Doug said.

"What about hospitals?" Sean asked.

"There are two," Doug replied. "There's one right here in Key West, but it's small. There's a larger one on the next key called Stock Island. That's the main facility."

Sean went below and woke Janet up. She wasn't pleased about having to get up. She told Sean she'd only come down below fifteen or twenty minutes earlier.

"When I came down here hours ago you were sleeping like a baby," Sean said.

"Yeah, but as soon as we hit rough seas, I had to go back out on deck. I didn't get to sleep the whole trip like you did. Some restful weekend this has turned out to be."

The docking was uneventful since there was no other boating activity so early on a Sunday morning. Doug waved goodbye and motored away as soon as Sean and Janet jumped to the pier.

While Sean and Janet strolled off the pier and began to look around, they had the strange feeling they were the only living beings on the island. There was plenty of evidence of the previous night's partying; empty beer bottles and other debris were haphazardly strewn about in the gutters. But there were no people. There weren't even any animals. It was like the calm after the storm.

They walked up Duval Street with its compliment of T-shirt stores, jewelers, and souvenir shops all shuttered as if they expected a riot. The famous Conch Tour Train appeared abandoned by its bright yellow ticket kiosk. The place was as much of a honky-tonk as Sean expected, yet the net effect was surprisingly charming.

As they passed Sloppy Joe's Bar the sun peeked tentatively over the Atlantic Ocean and filled the deserted street with misty morning light. Half a block farther on they were enveloped by a delicious aroma.

"That smells suspiciously like . . ." Sean began.

"Croissants," Janet finished.

Following their noses they turned into a French bakery *cum* café. The delectable smell was coming from open windows off a terrace dotted with tables and umbrellas. The front door was locked so Sean had to yell through the open window. A woman with red frizzy hair came out wiping her hands on an apron.

"We're not open yet," she said with the hint of a French accent.

"How about a couple of those croissants?" Sean suggested.

The woman cocked her head while she gave the idea some thought. "I suppose," she said. "I could offer you some café au lait that I've made for myself. The espresso machine hasn't been turned on yet."

Sitting under one of the umbrellas on the deserted terrace, Sean and Janet savored the oven-fresh pastries. The coffee revived them.

"Now that we're here," Janet said, "what's the plan?"

Sean stroked his heavily whiskered chin. "I'll see if they have a phone book," he said. "That will give me the address of the lab."

"While you do that, I think I'll use the ladies' room," Janet said. "I feel like something the cat dragged in."

"A cat would be afraid to go near you," Sean said. He ducked when Janet threw her crumpled napkin at him.

By the time Janet returned, looking much fresher, Sean had not only gotten the address, he'd gotten directions from the red-haired woman.

"It's kinda far," he said. "We'll need a ride."

"And of course that will be easy," Janet said. "We can either hitchhike or just take one of the many cabs streaming by." They hadn't seen a single car since they'd arrived.

"I was thinking about something else," Sean said as he left a generous tip for their hostess. He stood up.

Janet looked at him questioningly for a moment before realizing what he had in mind. "Oh, no!" she said. "We're not stealing another car."

"Borrow," Sean corrected her. "I'd forgotten how easy it is."

Janet refused to have anything to do with "borrowing" a car, but Sean proceeded undeterred.

"I don't want to break anything," he said, going from car to car on a side street, trying all the doors. Every one was locked. "Must be a lot of suspicious people around here." Then he stopped, staring across the street. "I just changed my mind. I don't want a car."

Crossing over to a large motorcycle teetering on its kickstand, Sean got the engine going almost as quickly as he would have if he'd had the ignition key. Straddling the bike and kicking back the kickstand, he motioned for Janet to join him.

Janet studied Sean with his unshaven face and rumpled clothes as he revved the motorcycle's engine. How could she have fallen in love with a guy like this? she asked herself. Reluctantly, she threw a leg over the machine and threw her arms around Sean's waist. Sean hit the gas and they sped off, shattering the early morning silence.

They traveled back down Duval Street in the direction from which they'd come, then turned north at the Conch Train kiosk and followed the shoreline. Eventually they came to an old wharf. Basic Diagnostics occupied a two-story brick warehouse that had been nicely refurbished. Sean drove around to the back of the building and parked the bike behind a shed. Once the motorcycle engine was off the only sound they could hear was the cry of distant sea gulls. Not a soul was around.

"I think we're out of luck," Janet said. "It doesn't look open."

"Let's check it out," Sean said.

They mounted some back stairs and peered in the rear door. There were no lights on inside. A platform ran along the north side of the building. They tried the doors along the platform, including a large overhead door, but everything was locked tight. In the front of the building there was a sign on the double-door entry that announced that the lab was open from twelve noon to five P.M. on Sundays and holidays. There was a small metal drop door for leaving samples during off hours.

"Guess we'll have to come back," Janet said.

Sean didn't respond. He cupped his hands and peered through the front windows. Rounding the corner, he did the same at another window. Janet followed him as he went from window to window working his way back the way they'd come.

"I hope you're not getting any ideas," Janet said. "Let's find someplace where we can sleep for a few hours. Then we can return after noon."

Sean didn't answer. Instead he stepped away from the last window he'd been peering through. Without warning he gave the glass a sudden karate-like chop with the side of his hand. The window imploded, shattering on the floor within. Janet leapt back, then quickly looked over her shoulder to see if there were any witnesses. Then, looking back at Sean, she said: "Let's not do this. The police are already looking for us from the episode in Miami."

Sean was busy removing a few of the larger shards. "No shatter alarm," he said.

He quickly climbed through the window, then turned around to inspect it carefully. "No alarm at all," he said. Unlocking the sash, he pulled it up. Then he extended a hand toward Janet.

Janet held back. "I don't want to be part of this," she said.

"Come on," he insisted. "I wouldn't be breaking in here

unless I thought it was mighty important. Something bizarre is going on, and there might be some answers here. Trust me."

"What if someone comes?" Janet asked. She gave another nervous glance over her shoulder.

"No one is going to come," Sean said. "It's seven-thirty Sunday morning. Besides, I'm only going to look around. We'll be out of here in fifteen minutes, I promise. And if it makes you feel any better, we'll leave a ten-dollar bill for the window."

After everything they'd been through, Janet figured there wasn't much point in resisting now. She let Sean help her through the window.

They were standing in a men's lavatory. There was the scented smell of disinfectant coming from an oval pink cake in the base of the urinal attached to the wall.

"Fifteen minutes!" Janet said as they cautiously opened the door.

Outside the men's room was a hall running the length of the building. A cursory check of the floor revealed a large laboratory across from the men's room that also ran the length of the building. On the same side as the men's room were a ladies' room, a storeroom, an office, and a stairwell.

Sean opened each door and peered inside. Janet looked over his shoulder. Entering the laboratory proper he walked down the central aisle, glancing from side to side. The floor was a gray vinyl, the cabinets a lighter gray plastic laminant, and the countertops stark white.

"Looks like a normal, garden-variety clinical lab," he said. "All the usual equipment." He paused in the microbiological section and looked into an incubator filled with petri dishes.

"Are you surprised?" Janet asked.

"No, but I expected more," Sean said. "I don't see a pathology section where they'd process biopsies. I was told the biopsies are sent here."

Returning down the main hall, Sean went to the stairwell. He mounted the steps. At the top was a stout metal door. It was locked.

"Uh oh," Sean said. "This might take more than fifteen minutes."

"You promised," Janet said.

"So I lied," Sean said as he inspected the lock. "If I can find some appropriate tools it might be sixteen minutes."

"It's been fourteen already," Janet said.

"Come on," Sean said. "Let's see if we can find something to act as a tension bar and some heavy wire to use as picks." He retreated down the stairs. Janet followed.

STERLING'S CHARTERED Sea King touched down with a squeal of rubber at seven-forty-five in the morning at the Key West airport and taxied over to general aviation. At the commercial terminal right next door an American Eagle commuter plane was in the final boarding process.

By the time Sterling had gotten a call back from the charter company it had been close to five A.M. After some persuasion which included a promise of extra money, the plane was supposed to have departed around six, but because of refueling problems it wasn't ready to leave until six-forty-five.

Both Sterling and Wayne took advantage of the delay to catch some sleep, first at the Edgewater Beach Hotel, then in the waiting area at the airport. Then they had slept most of the flight.

Arriving at the general aviation building in Key West,

Sterling saw a short balding man in a floral print short-sleeved shirt gazing out the front window. He was holding a steaming Styrofoam cup.

As Sterling and Wayne deplaned, the balding man came out and introduced himself. He was Kurt Wanamaker. He was of stocky build with a broad, suntanned face. What hair he had was bleached by the sun.

"I went by the lab about seven-fifteen," Kurt said on the way to his Chrysler Cherokee. "Everything was quiet. So I think you've beaten them if they are planning on coming at all."

"Let's go directly to the lab," Sterling said. "I'd like to be there if and when Mr. Murphy breaks in. Then we could do more than merely deliver him to the police."

"THIS SHOULD work," Sean said. He had his eyes tightly closed while he fiddled with the two ballpoint pen refills. He'd bent the end of one to a right angle to serve as a tension bar.

"What exactly are you doing in there?" Janet asked.

"I told you back at Forbes," Sean said. "When we were trying to get in the chart vault. It's called raking the pins. There are five of the little guys in there keeping the cylinder from turning. Ah, there we go." The lock opened with a click. The door swung in.

Sean entered first. Since there were no windows, the interior was as dark as a moonless night, save for the light that spread up through the stairwell. Groping on the wall to the left of the door, Sean's hand hit against a panel of switches. He flipped them all on at once and the entire ceiling lit up in a wink.

"Well, look at this!" Sean said in utter amazement. Here

was the lab he'd expected to see at the Forbes Cancer Center research building. It was enormous, encompassing the entire floor. It was also very white, with its white floor tiles, white cabinets, and white walls.

Slowly Sean walked down the center aisle, appreciating the equipment. "Everything is brand new," he said admiringly. He put his hand on a desktop machine. "And strictly top notch. This is an automated southern blotting instrument. It runs at least twelve thousand dollars. And here is the latest chemiluminescence spectrophotometer. It's a cool twenty-three. And over there is a high phase liquid chromatography unit. That's around twenty grand. And here's an automatic cell sorter. That's at least one hundred and fifty thousand. And my God!"

Sean stopped in awe in front of a peculiar egg-shaped apparatus. "Don't let your credit card get near to this big guy," he said. "It's a nuclear magnetic resonator. You have any idea what this baby costs?"

Janet shook her head.

"Try half a million dollars," Sean said. "And if they have that, it means they have an X-ray defractor as well."

Walking on, Sean came to a glass-enclosed area. Inside he could see a Type III maximum containment hood as well as banks and banks of tissue culture incubators. Sean tried the glass door. It opened out, so he had to work against the suction holding it closed. In order to prevent the escape of any organisms, the pressure inside the viral lab was kept lower than the rest of the laboratory.

Stepping into the maximum containment area, Sean motioned for Janet to stay where she was. First he went to a floor freezer and opened its hood. The temperature on an internal gauge stood at minus seventy degrees Fahrenheit. Nestled inside the freezer were multiple racks containing small vials. Each vial contained a frozen viral culture.

Closing the freezer, Sean glanced in some of the tissue culture incubators. They were being kept at ninety-eight point six degrees Fahrenheit, mimicking the normal internal temperature of a human being.

Moving on to the desk, Sean picked up some electron photomicrographs of isometric viruses as well as accompanying engineering-style drawings of the viral capsids. The drawings were done to study the icosahedral symmetry of the viral shells and included actual measurement of the capsomeres. Sean noted that the viral particle had an overall diameter of 43 nanometers.

Leaving the maximum containment area, Sean proceeded into an area in which he felt very much at home. A whole section of the lab seemed dedicated to oncogene study, just what Sean was doing back in Boston. The difference, however, was that in this lab the equipment was all brand new. Sean longingly looked at shelf upon shelf of appropriate reagents for the isolation of oncogenes and their products, the oncoproteins.

"This place is state of the art in every regard," he said. In the oncogene section there were additional tissue culture incubators the size of thousand-bottle wine coolers. He opened the door of one and glanced at the cell lines. "This is a place I could work," he said, closing the incubator.

"Is this what you expected?" Janet asked. She'd followed behind like a puppy except when he went into the maximum containment area.

"More than I expected," Sean said. "This must be where Levy works. I'd guess that most of this equipment has come from the off-limits area of the sixth floor of the Forbes research building."

"What is all this telling you?" Janet asked.

"It's telling me I need a few hours in the lab back at Forbes," Sean said. "I believe . . ."

Sean didn't get to finish. The sounds of voices and footsteps were heard coming up the stairway. Janet put a hand over her mouth in panic. Sean grabbed her, his eyes desperately sweeping that area of the lab for a place to hide. There was no escape.

11

March 7
Sunday, 8:05 A.M.

"Here they are!" Wayne Edwards announced. He'd just pulled open a stout metal door to a small storage closet near the glass-enclosed maximum containment lab.

Sean and Janet blinked with the sudden intrusion of light.

Sterling stepped toward Wayne's discovery. Kurt was at his side.

"They may not look like fugitives or agents provocateurs," Sterling said. "Though of course we know the truth."

"Out of the closet!" Wayne commanded.

A subdued and remorseful Janet and a defiant Sean stepped out into the bright light.

"You people should not have left the airport last night," Sterling scolded. "And to think of the effort we'd expended on your behalf to thwart your abduction. Some gratitude. I'm curious to know if you're aware of how much trouble you've caused."

"How much trouble I *am* causing," Sean corrected.

"Ah, Dr. Mason mentioned you were brash," Sterling

said. "Well, we'll allow you to vent your impertinence on the Key West police. They can do battle with their Miami counterparts as to jurisdiction of your case now that you've committed a felony here as well."

Sterling picked up a phone in preparation to dial.

Sean pulled the long-dormant gun from his jacket pocket and pointed it at him. "Put the phone down," he commanded.

Janet sucked in her breath at the sight of the gun in Sean's hand.

"Sean!" she cried. "No!"

"Shut up," Sean snapped. The threesome surrounding him in a wide arc made him nervous. The last thing he wanted to do was let Janet give them an opportunity to overpower him.

As Sterling replaced the receiver, Sean motioned for the three men to group together.

"This is extremely foolish behavior," Sterling commented. "Breaking and entering in the possession of a deadly weapon is a far more serious crime than mere breaking and entering."

"Into the closet!" Sean commanded, motioning toward the space he and Janet had just vacated.

"Sean, this is going too far!" Janet said. She stepped up to Sean.

"Get out of my way!" Sean snarled. He shoved her roughly to the side.

Already dismayed at the appearance of the gun, Janet was doubly shocked at the sudden change in Sean's personality. The cruel and vicious sound of his voice and the expression on his face cowed her.

Sean succeeded in herding the three men into the narrow closet. He quickly closed and locked the door behind them.

Pocketing the gun, he moved some sizable furniture against the door, including a heavy five-drawer file cabinet.

Satisfied, he grabbed Janet's hand and started toward the exit. Janet tried to hold back. They got halfway to the stairway when she managed to pull free.

"I'm not going with you," she said.

"What are you talking about?" Sean whispered forcibly.

"The way you talked to me back there," she said. "I don't know you."

"Please!" Sean voiced through clenched teeth. "That was theatrics for the benefit of the others. If things don't go the way I imagine they will, you'll be able to contend that you were coerced into this whole affair. With the work I have to do back at the lab in Miami, there's a chance things might get worse before they get better."

"Be straight with me," Janet said. "Stop talking in riddles. What's going through your mind?"

"It's a bit much to explain at the moment," Sean said. "Right now we have to get out of here. I can't tell how long that storage closet will hold those three. Once they're out, the cat's out of the bag."

More confused than ever, Janet followed Sean down the stairs, through the first-floor lab, and out the front of the building. Kurt Wanamaker's Cherokee was angled in from the street. Sean motioned for Janet to get in.

"Convenient and thoughtful of them to have left the keys," Sean said.

"As if that would have made any difference to you," Janet said.

Sean started the car, but then immediately killed the engine.

"What now?" Janet asked.

"In the excitement I forgot that I need some of those

reagents from upstairs," Sean said. He got out of the car and leaned in the window. "This won't take but a minute. I'll be right back."

Janet tried to protest, but Sean was gone. Not that he'd cared much about her feelings about any of this mess so far. She got out of the car and began to pace the length of it nervously.

Thankfully, Sean returned in a few minutes carrying a large cardboard box which he shoved into the back seat. He got in behind the wheel and started the car. Janet got in next to him. They pulled out into the road and headed north.

"See if there's a map in the glove compartment," he said.

Janet searched and found one. She opened it up to the Florida Keys. Sean took the map and studied it while driving. "We can't count on getting all the way to Miami with this car," he said. "As soon as those three get out of the closet, they'll realize it's missing. The police will start looking for it and since there's only one road north, it won't be hard to find."

"I'm a fugitive," Janet marveled. "Just like the man said when they found us in the closet. I don't believe it. I don't know whether to laugh or cry."

"There's an airport at Marathon," Sean said, ignoring Janet's comment. "We'll leave the car there and either rent a car or fly depending on the flight schedule."

"I presume we're going back to Miami," Janet said.

"Absolutely," Sean said. "We'll go directly to Forbes."

"What's in the cardboard box?" Janet asked.

"A lot of reagents they don't have in Miami," Sean said.

"Like what?" Janet asked.

"Mostly DNA primer pairs and DNA probes for oncogenes," Sean said. "I also found some primers and probes for virus nucleic acid, particularly those used for St. Louis encephalitis."

"And you're not about to tell me what all this is all about?" Janet said.

"It will sound too preposterous," Sean admitted. "I want some proof first. I've got to prove it to myself before I tell anyone, even you."

"At least give me a general idea of what you use these primers and probes for," Janet said.

"DNA primers are used to find particular strands of DNA," Sean said. "They seek out a single strand from millions of others, then react with it. Then, by a process called the Polymerase Chain Reaction, the original DNA strand can be amplified billions of times. That way it can be easily detected by a labeled DNA probe."

"So using these primers and probes is like looking for the proverbial needle in the haystack with a powerful magnet," Janet said.

"Exactly," Sean said, impressed with how quickly she grasped the science. "A very, very powerful magnet. I mean, it can find one particular DNA strand out of a solution of millions of others. In that sense it's almost a magical magnet. I think the guy who developed the process should get the Nobel Prize."

"Molecular biology is making big strides," Janet said sleepily.

"It's unbelievable," Sean agreed. "Even those in the field have trouble keeping up."

Janet struggled against ponderously heavy eyelids made worse by the muffled drone of the engine and the gentle jostling. She wanted to press Sean for more of an explanation of what was going through his mind, and she thought the best way to do that was to get him to talk about molecular biology and what he was planning to do when he got back to the lab at Forbes. But she was too exhausted to go on.

Janet had always found driving calming. Between the little amount of sleep she'd gotten aboard the boat and all the running around they'd been doing, it wasn't long before she nodded off. She fell into a deep, much needed sleep and rested undisturbed until Sean pulled off Route 1 onto the grounds of the Marathon Airport.

"So far so good," Sean said when he noticed Janet was stirring. "No roadblocks and no police."

Janet sat up. For a moment she had no idea where she was, but then reality came back in a numbing flash. Now she felt worse than she had when she'd fallen asleep. Running her fingers through her hair made her think of a bird's nest. It was hard for her to imagine what she looked like. She decided not to try.

Sean parked the car in the most crowded part of the parking lot. He thought its presence would be less likely to be noticed that way and thereby give them more time. Hefting the cardboard box from the back seat, he carried it into the terminal. He sent Janet to check on commuter flights to Miami while he went to inquire about the availability of rental cars. He was still searching for a rental agent when Janet returned to tell him that a flight to Miami left in twenty minutes.

The airline agent helpfully taped Sean's box closed after plastering the outside with "fragile" stickers. The agent guaranteed the parcel would be treated with the utmost care. Later, as Sean was boarding the small turbo prop commuter plane, he saw someone casually tossing his box onto a luggage cart. But Sean wasn't worried. He'd found bubble wrap back at Basic Diagnostics when he packed the reagents. He was reasonably confident his primers and probes would survive the trip.

Once at the Miami airport, he and Janet rented a car.

They used Avis, avoiding Hertz in case the Hertz computer indicated that Janet Reardon was already in possession of a red Pontiac.

With the primers and probes in the back seat, they drove directly to Forbes. Sean parked next to his 4×4 near the entrance to the research building. He got out his Forbes ID card.

"You want to come in or what?" Sean asked. Exhaustion was catching up with him at this point too. "You can take this car back to the apartment if you want."

"I've come this far," Janet said. "I want you to explain what you're doing as you do it."

"Fair enough," Sean said.

They got out of the car and walked into the building. Sean did not expect any trouble, so he was surprised when the guard stood up. None of the guards had ever done that. This one's name was Alvarez. Sean had seen him before on several occasions.

"Mr. Murphy?" Alvarez questioned with a definite Spanish accent.

"That's me," Sean said. He'd bumped into the turnstile arm which Alvarez had failed to release. Sean had his ID in his hand visible for Alvarez to see. The cardboard box was under his other arm. Janet was behind him.

"You are not permitted in the building," Alvarez said.

Sean put down his cardboard box.

"I work here," Sean said. He leaned over to hold his ID closer to Alvarez's face in case the guard had missed it.

"Orders from Dr. Mason," Alvarez said. He leaned back from Sean's ID as if it were somehow repulsive. He picked up one of his telephones with one hand and flipped through a Rolodex with the other.

"Put the phone down," Sean said, struggling to control

his voice. Between everything he'd been through and his general fatigue, he was at the end of his patience.

The guard ignored Sean. He found Dr. Mason's phone number and started punching in the numbers.

"I asked you nicely," Sean said. "Put the phone down!" He spoke now with considerably more force.

The guard finished dialing, then calmly eyed Sean as he waited for the connection to go through.

With lightning speed, Sean reached across the Corian desk and grabbed the phone line where it disappeared into the woodwork. A sharp yank tore the cable free. Sean held the end of the cable up to the surprised guard's face. It was a tangled mass of tiny red, green, and yellow wires.

"Your phone is out of order," Sean said.

Alvarez's face turned red. Dropping the receiver, he snatched up a truncheon and started around the desk.

Instead of retreating, which the guard expected, Sean lunged ahead to meet Alvarez as if throwing a body check in a hockey game. Sean came up from below. The base of his forearm connected with the guard's lower jaw. Alvarez was lifted off his feet and smashed back against the wall before he could try anything with the truncheon. On impact Sean could hear a definite crack like a piece of dried kindling being snapped. Sean also heard the man grunt when he hit the wall as the breath was forced from his lungs. When Sean pulled away, Alvarez fell to the floor, his body limp.

"Oh, God!" Janet cried. "You've hurt him."

"Geez, what a jaw," Sean said as he rubbed the base of his forearm.

Janet stepped around Sean to get to Alvarez, who was bleeding from his mouth. Janet half feared that he was dead, but she quickly determined he was merely unconscious.

"When is this going to end?" she moaned. "Sean, I think you've broken this man's jaw, and he's bitten his tongue. You knocked him out."

"Let's walk him over to the hospital side," Sean suggested.

"They don't have trauma capability here," Janet said. "We'll have to take him over to Miami General."

Sean rolled his eyes and sighed. He eyed his cardboard box of primers and probes. He needed a few hours, maybe even as much as four, up in the lab. He looked at his watch. It was just after one in the afternoon.

"Sean!" Janet commanded. "Now! It's only three minutes away. We can come back once we've dropped him off. We can't just leave him this way."

Reluctantly, Sean pushed his cardboard box behind the guard's desk, then helped Janet carry Alvarez outside. Between the two of them, they got him out to the rental car and into the back seat.

Sean could see the wisdom in taking Alvarez to the emergency room at Miami General. It wasn't smart to leave a bleeding, unconscious man unattended. If Alvarez took a turn for the worse, Sean would be in serious trouble, the kind even his clever brother would have a hard time getting him out of. But Sean wasn't about to get caught now just because he'd agreed to this mission of mercy.

Even though it was midday Sunday, Sean counted on a busy ER. He wasn't disappointed. "This is a quick dropoff," he warned Janet. "A speedy in and out. Once we get him in the ER, we're out of there. The staff there will know what to do."

Janet wasn't in complete agreement, but she knew better than to disagree.

Sean left the engine idling, the gear in park, while he and

Janet struggled with Alvarez's still-limp body. "At least he's breathing," Sean said.

Just inside the door to the ER, Sean spotted an empty gurney. "Put him on this," he ordered Janet.

With Alvarez safely laid atop it, Sean gave the gurney a gentle shove. "Possible code," Sean shouted as the gurney rolled down the hall. Then he grabbed Janet by the arm. "Come on, let's go," he said.

As they raced back to the car, Janet said, "He wasn't a code."

"I know," Sean admitted. "But it was all I could think of to get some action. You know how emergency rooms are. Alvarez could have lain around for hours before anyone did something for him."

Janet only shrugged. Sean did have a point. And before they'd left she'd been relieved to see a male nurse already intercepting the gurney.

On the way back to Forbes, neither Sean nor Janet said another word. Both were exhausted. On top of that, Janet was unnerved by Sean's explosive violence; it was yet more behavior she had not anticipated from him.

Meanwhile, Sean was trying to figure out how he could ensure himself four hours of uninterrupted lab time. Between the unfortunate episode with Alvarez and the fact the Miami police were already looking for him, Sean knew he would have to come up with something creative to hold off the hordes. Suddenly he had an idea. It was radical, but it would definitely work. His plan brought a smile to his face despite his exhaustion. There was a kind of poetic justice involved that appealed to him.

Sean felt justified in using extreme measures at this point. The more he thought about his current theory of what was going on at the Forbes Cancer Center, the more convinced he was that he was correct. But he needed proof, and to get proof, he needed lab time. And to get the lab time, he needed something drastic. In fact the more drastic it was, the better it would work.

When they made the final turn into the parking lot at Forbes, Sean broke the silence: "The night you arrived in Florida I'd gone to an affair at Dr. Mason's," he said. "A medulloblastoma patient donated money to Forbes, big money. He headed up an airplane manufacturing firm in St. Louis."

Janet was silent.

"Louis Martin is the CEO of a computer hardware manufacturing firm north of Boston," Sean said. He glanced at Janet as he parked. She looked puzzled.

"Malcolm Betencourt runs a huge for-profit chain of hospitals," Sean continued.

"And Helen Cabot was a college student," Janet said at last.

Sean opened his door, but he didn't get out. "True, Helen was a college student. But it's also true that her father is founder and CEO of one of the world's top software companies."

"What are you trying to say?" Janet asked.

"I just want you to think about all this," Sean said as he finally got out of the car. "And when we get upstairs, I want you to look at the thirty-three charts we copied and think about the economic demographics. Just let me know what they say to you."

Sean was pleased that no new guard had come on duty. He retrieved his cardboard box from behind the front desk. Then both he and Janet ducked under the turnstile and took the elevator to the fifth floor.

Sean first checked the refrigerator to make certain that

Helen's brain and sample of cerebrospinal fluid had not been disturbed. Next he got the charts out from their hiding place and gave them to Janet. He eyed the mess at his lab bench but didn't touch it.

"While you're perusing the charts," Sean said casually, "I'll be heading out. But I'll be back shortly, maybe in an hour."

"Where are you going?" Janet asked. As usual, Sean was full of surprises. "I thought you needed lab time. That's why we rushed here."

"I do," Sean assured her. "But I'm afraid I'm going to be interrupted because of Alvarez and also because of that group I locked in the closet in Key West. They must be out and fit to be tied by now. I have to make some arrangements to keep the barbarians at bay."

"What do you mean by arrangements?" Janet asked warily.

"Maybe it's better if you don't know," Sean said. "I came up with a great idea that's guaranteed to work, but it's a bit drastic. I don't think you should be involved."

"I don't like the sound of this at all," Janet said.

"If anybody comes in here while I'm gone and asks for me," Sean said, ignoring Janet's concerns, "tell them that you have no idea where I am, which will be the truth."

"Who might come?" Janet asked.

"I hope no one," Sean said. "But if someone does come, it will probably be Robert Harris, the guy who saved the day on the beach. If Alvarez calls anyone, he'll call him."

"What if he asks what I'm doing here?"

"Tell him the truth," Sean said. "Tell him you're going over these charts to try to understand my behavior."

"Oh, please!" Janet said superciliously. "I'm not going to understand your behavior from these charts. That's ridiculous."

"Just read them and keep in mind what I just told you."

"You mean about the economic demographics?" Janet asked.

"Exactly," Sean said. "Now I've got to get out of here. But I need to borrow something. Can I have that container of Mace you always carry in your purse?"

"I don't like this at all," Janet repeated, but she got the container of Mace and handed it to Sean. "This is making me very nervous."

"Don't worry," Sean said. "I need the Mace in case I run into Batman."

"Give me a break," Janet said with exasperation.

SEAN KNEW his time was limited. Alvarez would be regaining consciousness soon if he hadn't already. Sean was quite confident the guard would eventually get the message to someone that he was no longer guarding the Forbes research building and that Sean Murphy was back in town.

Using the rental car, Sean drove to the City Yacht Basin near the municipal auditorium. He parked the car and went into one of the marinas where he rented a sixteen-foot Boston Whaler. Leaving the yacht basin, he drove the boat across Biscayne Bay and around the Dodge Island seaport. Since it was Sunday afternoon, a number of cruise ships were lined up at the dock with people boarding for Caribbean adventures. There was also a horde of pleasure craft, from jet skis to large oceangoing yachts.

Crossing the sea lane was treacherous because of the chop created by a combination of wind and other waterborne traffic, but Sean made it safely to the bridge connecting the MacArthur Causeway to Miami Beach. Passing under the bridge he saw his objective off to the left: Star Island.

It was easy to find the Masons' home since their huge

white yacht, *Lady Luck*, was moored to the pier in front. Sean angled his Boston Whaler in behind the yacht where a floating dock was connected to the pier by a ship's ladder. As Sean expected, by the time he secured his boat, Batman, the Masons' Doberman, was at the top of the ladder growling and baring his formidable teeth.

Sean climbed the ladder saying "good dog" over and over. Batman leaned out from the pier as far as he dared and responded to Sean's cajoling by curling his upper lip into a menacing snarl. The volume of his growling rose as he showed more teeth.

Coming within twelve inches of the canine's canines, Sean gave Batman a blast from Janet's Mace canister that sent the dog howling toward its lair on the side of the garage.

Confident that there was only one dog, Sean clambered up onto the pier and surveyed the grounds. What he had to do, he had to do quickly, before any phone calls could be made. The sliders opening out from the living room to the pool were cast open. The sound of opera issued forth.

From where he was standing, Sean couldn't see anyone. As nice a day as it was, he'd expected to see Sarah Mason sunning herself on one of the chaises by the pool. Sean did see a towel, some suntan lotion, and a portion of the Sunday paper, but no Sarah.

Moving quickly, Sean rounded the pool and approached the open sliders. Screen doors obscured his view inside. The closer he got to the house, the louder the music became.

Reaching the door, Sean tried the screen. It was unlocked. Silently he slid it open. Stepping into the room he tried to listen for sounds of people over the opera's sudden crescendo.

Advancing to the stereo, Sean searched among its dazzling array of dials and gauges. Finding the power button, he turned the system off, plunging the room into relative silence. He was hoping that cutting off the *Aida* aria in the middle would have a summoning effect. It did.

Almost immediately, Dr. Mason appeared at the door to his study, gazing at the stereo with a quizzical expression on his face. He took a few steps into the room before he saw Sean. He stopped, obviously flabbergasted.

"Good afternoon, Dr. Mason," Sean said with a voice that was more chipper than he felt. "Is Mrs. Mason around?"

"What in heaven's name is the meaning of this . . . ?" Dr. Mason blustered. He couldn't seem to find the right words.

"Intrusion?" Sean suggested.

Sarah Mason appeared, apparently equally baffled by the sudden silence. She was dressed, if that was the word, in a shiny black bikini. The skimpy suit barely covered her ample flesh. Over the bikini she wore a diaphanous jacket with rhinestone buttons, but the jacket was so transparent, it hardly made for a more modest appearance. Completing the outfit were black, backless high-heeled slippers decorated with a tuft of feathers over each instep.

"I've come to invite you two to the lab," Sean said matter-of-factly. "I suggest you bring some reading material. It may be a long afternoon."

Dr. and Mrs. Mason exchanged glances.

"Trouble is, I don't have a lot of time," Sean added. "Let's get a move on. We'll use your car since I came in a boat."

"I'm going to call the police," Dr. Mason announced. He started to turn back into his study.

"I don't think that is part of the game plan," Sean said. He pulled out Tom's gun and held it up in the air to be sure both of the Masons could see it clearly.

Mrs. Mason gasped. Dr. Mason stiffened.

"I was hoping a mere invitation would be sufficient," Sean said. "But I do have this gun if need be."

"I think you are making a big mistake, young man," Dr. Mason said.

"With all due respect," Sean said, "if my suspicions are correct, then you're the one who's made big mistakes."

"You won't get away with this," Dr. Mason warned.

"I don't intend to," Sean said.

"Do something!" Mrs. Mason commanded her husband. Tears had formed in the corners of her eyes, threatening her eyeliner.

"I want everybody to stay cool," Sean said. "No one will get hurt. Now if we can all just go to the car." Sean motioned with the gun.

"I'll have you know we're expecting company," Dr. Mason said. "In fact, we're expecting your . . ."

"That just means we have to get out of here faster," Sean interrupted. Then he yelled: "Move!" With gun in hand, he motioned to the hall.

Reluctantly, Dr. Mason put a protective arm around his wife and walked her to the front door. Sean opened it for them. Mrs. Mason was sobbing, saying that she couldn't go dressed as she was.

"Out!" Sean yelled, his impatience obvious.

They got halfway to Dr. Mason's parked car when another car pulled up to the curb.

Dismayed at this intrusion, Sean slipped the gun into his jacket pocket. He was thinking that he'd have to add this visitor to his pair of hostages. When he saw who it was, he had to blink several times: it was his own brother Brian.

"Sean!" Brian called the moment he recognized his brother. He ran up the lawn, his face reflecting both surprise and pleasure. "I've been looking for you for twenty-four hours! Where have you been?"

"I've been calling you," Sean said. "What in God's name are you doing in Miami?"

"It's a good thing you've arrived, Brian," Dr. Mason interjected. "Your brother was in the process of kidnapping us."

"He has a gun!" Mrs. Mason warned between sniffles.

Brian looked at his brother incredulously. "Gun?" he echoed in disbelief. "What gun?"

"It's in his pocket," Mrs. Mason snapped.

Brian stared at Sean. "Is this true?"

Sean shrugged. "It's been a crazy weekend."

"Let me have the gun," Brian said, extending his hand.

"No," Sean said.

"Let me have the gun," Brian repeated, this time more firmly.

"Brian, there's more involved here than meets the eye," Sean said. "Please don't interfere right now. Obviously I'm going to need your legal talents later, so don't go away. Just cool out for a few hours."

Brian took another step closer to Sean, bringing him within arm's reach. "Give me the gun," he repeated. "I'm not letting you commit this kind of crime. Abduction with a deadly weapon is a serious felony. It carries a compulsory prison term."

"I understand you have good intentions," Sean said. "I know you're older, and you are a lawyer. But I can't explain everything right now. Trust me!"

Brian reached out and jammed his hand into Sean's jacket pocket, groping toward the conspicuous bulge. His fingers wrapped around the gun. Sean grabbed Brian's wrist in an iron grip.

"You're older," Sean said, "but I'm stronger. We've been through this before."

"I'm not letting you do this," Brian said.

"Let go of the gun," Sean ordered.

"I'm not about to let you throw your life away," Brian said.

"Don't make me do this," Sean warned.

Brian tried to wrench his arm from Sean's grip while maintaining a hold on the gun.

Sean reacted by throwing a left uppercut into the pit of Brian's stomach. With lightning speed, he followed his punch with a sharp jab to the nose. Brian went down like a sack of potatoes, curling into a tight ball as he struggled to catch his breath. A bit of blood trickled out of his nose.

"I'm sorry," Sean said.

Dr. and Mrs. Mason, who'd been watching this exchange, bolted for the garage. Sean leapt after them, catching Mrs. Mason first. Dr. Mason, who had hold of Mrs. Mason's other arm, was pulled up short as well.

Having just struck his brother, Sean was in no mood for further argument. "In the car," he growled. "Dr. Mason, you drive."

Sheepishly, the Masons complied. Sean got in the back seat. "The lab, please," he said.

As they pulled out of the driveway, Sean caught a glimpse of Brian, who'd managed to push himself into a sitting position. Brian's face reflected a mixture of confusion, hurt, and anger.

"IT'S ABOUT time," Kurt Wanamaker snapped as he, Sterling, and Wayne stumbled out of the storage closet. They were dripping with perspiration. Despite the air-conditioning in the main lab, the temperature in the unventilated closet had soared.

"I just heard you," the technician explained.

"We've been shouting since noon," Kurt complained.

"It's hard to hear from downstairs," the technician said. "Especially with all the equipment running. Plus, we never come up here."

"I don't understand how you couldn't have heard," Kurt said.

Sterling went directly to a phone and dialed Dr. Mason's private number. When Dr. Mason didn't answer, Sterling cursed as he pictured Dr. Mason spending a relaxing Sunday afternoon at a country club.

Replacing the receiver, Sterling considered what he should do next. With decisive speed, he rejoined Kurt and Wayne and said that he'd like to go back to the airport.

As they descended the stairs, Wayne broke the strained silence. "I never would have picked Sean Murphy for somebody carrying a piece."

"It was a definite surprise," Sterling agreed. "I believe it is further evidence that Sean Murphy is a far more complex individual than we have surmised."

When they got to the front of the building, Kurt Wanamaker was thrown into a panic. "My car's gone!" he moaned.

"Undoubtedly compliments of Mr. Murphy," Sterling said. "He seems to be thumbing his nose at us."

"I wonder how Murphy and his girl got out here from the center of town," Wayne said.

"There's a motorcycle in the back that doesn't belong to anyone who works here," the technician said.

"I guess that answers it," Sterling said. "Call the police and give them the details about your missing automobile.

Since he took the car I think it's safe to presume he's left the island. Perhaps the police can pick him up."

"It's a new car," Kurt whined. "I've only had it three weeks. This is awful."

Sterling held his tongue. He felt nothing but contempt for this nervous, tiresome, balding man with whom he'd spent more than five uncomfortable hours crammed into a tiny closet. "Perhaps you could ask one of your technicians to give us a ride to the airport." He took solace in the hope that this would be the last thing he'd ever have to say to the man.

12

March 7
Sunday, 2:30 P.M.

As soon as Dr. Mason pulled into the Forbes parking lot, Sean tried to peer into the research building foyer to see if anything had changed since he'd left. With sunlight reflecting off the windows, it was impossible to see in. Sean couldn't tell if another guard had come on duty or not.

It was only after they'd parked, and Sean entered the building, keeping the Masons close ahead, that he saw another guard had indeed come on duty. The man's ID badge read "Sanchez."

"Tell him who you are and ask for his pass keys," Sean whispered as the trio neared the turnstile.

"He knows who I am," Dr. Mason snapped.

"Tell him you want no one else in the building until we come down," Sean said. He knew such a command would be ignored as the afternoon progressed, but he thought he might as well try.

Dr. Mason did as he was told. He passed the large key ring to Sean as soon as Sanchez had given it to him. The guard eyed them strangely as they went through the turnstile. Big-breasted blondes wearing black bikinis and feathered high heels weren't exactly regulars at the Forbes research building.

"Your brother was right," Dr. Mason said after Sean closed and locked the entrance doors beyond the turnstile. "This is a serious felony. You'll go to prison. You're not going to get away with this."

"I told you, I don't intend to get away with it," Sean said.

Sean locked the stairwell doors. On the second floor he closed and locked the fire doors leading to the bridge to the hospital. Once they got to the fifth floor he locked off the elevator, then summoned the second car. When it arrived, he locked that off as well.

Ushering the Masons into his lab, Sean waved to Janet. She was inside the glass-enclosed office reading the charts. She came out and looked quizzically at the Masons. Sean hastily introduced them, then sent the Masons into the glass-enclosed office, telling them to stay put. He closed the door behind them.

"What are they doing here?" Janet asked with concern. "And what's Mrs. Mason doing in a swimsuit? It looks like she's been crying."

"She's a bit hysterical," Sean explained. "There wasn't time for her to change. I brought them here to keep others from disturbing me. Besides, as soon as I do what I'm planning on doing, Dr. Mason is the first person I want to tell."

"Did you force them to come here?" Janet asked. Even after everything else Sean had resorted to, this had to be past the limit.

"They would have preferred to listen to the rest of *Aida,*" Sean admitted. He began clearing a work area on his bench, particularly under one of the exhaust hoods.

"Did you use that gun you're carrying?" Janet asked. She didn't want to hear the answer.

"I had to show it to them," Sean admitted.

"Heaven help us," Janet exclaimed, looking up toward the ceiling and shaking her head.

Sean got out some fresh glassware including a large Erlenmeyer flask. He pushed away some of the debris near the sink to make space.

Janet reached out and grasped Sean's arm. "This whole thing has gone too far," she said. "You've kidnapped the Masons! Do you understand that?"

"Of course," Sean said. "What do you think, I'm crazy?"

"Don't make me answer that," Janet said.

"Did anybody come by while I was gone?" Sean asked.

"Yes," Janet said. "Robert Harris came like you thought he might."

"And?" Sean asked, looking up from his work.

"I told him what you told me to say," Janet replied. "He wanted to know if you'd gone back to the residence. I said I didn't know. I think he went there to look for you."

"Perfect," Sean said. "He's the one I'm the most afraid of. He's too gung ho. Everything has to be in place by the time he returns." Sean went back to work.

Janet didn't know what to do. She watched Sean for a few minutes as he mixed reagents in the large Erlenmeyer flask, creating a colorless, oily liquid.

"What exactly are you doing?" she asked.

"I'm making a large batch of nitroglycerin," he said. "Plus an ice bath for it to sit in and cool."

"You're joking," Janet said with fresh concern. It was hard to keep up with Sean.

"You're right," Sean said, lowering his voice. "It's show time. This is really for the benefit of Dr. Mason and his beautiful bride. As a doctor, he knows just enough chemistry to make this believable."

"Sean, you're acting bizarre," Janet said.

"I am a bit manic," Sean agreed. "By the way, what did you think of those charts?"

"I guess you were right," Janet said. "Not all the charts had reference to economic status, but those that did indicated that the patients were CEOs or family members of CEOs."

"All part of the Fortune 500, I'd guess," Sean said. "What does that make you think?"

"I'm too exhausted to draw conclusions," Janet said. "But I suppose it's a strange coincidence."

Sean laughed. "What do you think the statistical probability would be of that happening by chance?"

"I don't know enough about statistics to answer that," Janet said.

Sean held up the flask and swirled the contained solution. "This looks good enough to pass," he said. "Let's hope old Doc Mason remembers enough of his inorganic chemistry to be impressed."

Janet watched Sean carry the flask into the glass enclosure. She wondered if he was losing touch with reality. Granted, he'd been driven to increasingly desperate acts, but abducting the Masons at gunpoint was a mind-numbing quantum leap. The legal consequences of such an act had to be severe. Janet didn't know much law, but she knew she was implicated to an extent. She doubted Sean's proposed coercion theory would spare her. She only wished she knew what to do.

Janet watched as Sean presented the fake nitroglycerin to the Masons as the real thing. Judging by the impression he made on Dr. Mason, she gathered that the Forbes director recalled enough of his inorganic chemistry to make the presentation plausible. Dr. Mason's eyes opened wide. Mrs. Mason brought a hand to her mouth. When Sean gave the flask a violent swirl both the Masons stepped back in fear. Then Sean jammed the flask into the ice bath he'd set up on the desk, collected the charts Janet had left in there, and came out into the lab. He dumped the charts on a nearby lab bench.

"What did the Masons say?" Janet asked.

"They were suitably impressed," Sean said. "Especially when I told them the freezing point is only fifty-five degrees Fahrenheit and that the stuff is extraordinarily unstable in a solid form. I told them to be careful in there because bumping the table would detonate it."

"I think we should call this whole thing off," Janet said. "You're going too far."

"I beg to differ," Sean said. "Besides, it's me that's doing this, not you."

"I'm involved," Janet said. "Just being here probably makes me an accessory."

"When all is said and done, Brian will work it out," Sean said. "Trust me."

Janet's attention was caught by the couple in the glass office. "You shouldn't have left the Masons alone," Janet said. "Dr. Mason is making a call."

"Good," Sean said. "I fully expected him to call someone. In fact, I hope he calls the police. You see, I want a circus around here."

Janet stared at Sean. For the first time, she thought he might be experiencing a psychotic break. "Sean," she said gently, "I have a feeling that you're decompensating. Maybe you've been under too much pressure."

"Seriously," Sean said. "I want a carnival atmosphere. It

will be much safer. The last thing I want is some frustrated commando like Robert Harris crawling around through the air ducts with a knife in his mouth trying to be a hero. That's when people would get hurt. I want the police and the fire department out there scratching their heads but keeping the would-be paladins at bay. I want them to think I'm crazy for four hours or so."

"I don't understand you," Janet said.

"You will," Sean assured her. "Meanwhile, I got some work for you to do. You told me you know something about computers. Head up to administration on the seventh floor." He handed her the ring of pass keys. "Go into that glass room that we saw when we copied the charts, the one where the computer was running that program, flashing those nine-digit numbers. I think those numbers are social security numbers. And the phone numbers! I think those were numbers for insurance companies that write health insurance. See if you can corroborate that. Then see if you can hack your way into the Forbes mainframe. I want you to look for travel files for the clinic, especially for Deborah Levy and Margaret Richmond."

"Can't you tell me why I'm doing this?" Janet asked.

"No," Sean said. "It's like a double blind study. I want you to be objective."

Sean's mania was oddly compelling—and persuasive. Janet took the keys and walked to the stairwell. Sean gave her a thumbs-up in parting. Whatever the resolution of this madcap, reckless escapade would be, she'd know within four or five hours.

Before he got down to work, Sean picked up a telephone and called Brian's number in Boston and left a long message. First he apologized for hitting him. Then he said that in case something happened to go horribly wrong, he wanted to tell him what he believed was happening at the Forbes Cancer Center. It took him about five minutes.

LIEUTENANT HECTOR Salazar of the Miami Police Department normally used Sunday afternoons as an opportunity to finish the reams of paperwork generated by Miami's typically busy Saturday nights. Sundays were generally quiet. Auto accidents, which the uniformed patrol and their sergeants could handle, comprised the biggest portion of the day's workload. Later on Sundays, after the football games were over, domestic violence often flared. Sometimes that could involve the watch commander, so Hector wanted to get as much done as he could before the phone started to ring.

Knowing that the Miami Dolphins game was still in progress, Hector answered the phone at three-fifteen with little concern. The call was patched through the complaint room to a land line.

"Sergeant Anderson here," the voice said. "I'm at the Forbes Cancer Center hospital building. We got a problem."

"What is it?" Hector asked. His chair squeaked as he leaned back.

"We got a guy holed up in the research building next door with two, maybe three hostages," Anderson said. "He's armed. There's also a bomb of some kind involved."

"Christ!" Hector said as his chair tipped forward with a thump. From experience, he knew the paperwork this kind of scene could generate. "Anyone else in the building?"

"We don't think so," Anderson said. "At least not according to the guard. To make matters worse, the hostages are VIPs. It's the director of the center, Dr. Randolph Mason, and his wife, Sarah Mason."

"You have the area secured?" Hector asked. His mind was already jumping ahead. This operation would be a hot potato. Dr. Randolph Mason was well known in the Miami area.

"We're doing it now," Anderson said. "We're running yellow crime scene tape around the whole building."

"Any media yet?" Hector asked. Sometimes the media got to a scene faster than backup police personnel. The media often monitored the police radio bands.

"Not yet," Anderson said. "That's why I'm using this land line. But we expect a blizzard any minute. The hostage taker's name is Sean Murphy. He's a medical student working at the clinic. He's with a nurse named Janet Reardon. We don't know if she's an accomplice or a hostage."

"What do you mean by 'some kind of bomb'?" Hector asked.

"He mixed up a big flask of nitroglycerin," Anderson said. "It's standing in ice on a desk in the room with the hostages. Once it freezes, slamming the door can set it off. At least, that's what Dr. Mason said."

"You've talked with the hostages?" Hector asked.

"Oh, yeah," Anderson said. "Dr. Mason told me he and his wife are in a glass office along with the nitro. They're terrified, but so far they're unharmed and they have a phone. He says he can see the perp. But the girl is gone. He doesn't know where she went."

"What's Murphy doing?" Hector asked. "Has he made any demands yet?"

"No demands yet," Anderson said. "Apparently he's real busy doing some kind of experiment."

"What do you mean experiment?" Hector asked.

"No clue," Anderson said. "I'm just repeating what Dr. Mason said. Apparently Murphy had been disgruntled because he'd been denied permission to work on a particular project. Maybe he's working on that. At any rate, he's armed. Dr. Mason said he waved the gun in front of them when he broke into their home."

"What kind of gun?"

"Sounds like a .38 detective special, from Dr. Mason's description," Anderson said.

"Make sure the building is secure," Hector said. "I want no one going in or out. Got it?"

"Got it," Anderson said.

After telling Anderson that he'd be out on site in a few minutes, Hector made three calls. First he called the hostage negotiating team and spoke with the supervisor, Ronald Hunt. Next he called the shift SWAT team commander, George Loring. Finally he called Phil Darell, the bomb squad supervisor. Hector told all three to assemble their respective teams and to rendezvous at the Forbes Cancer Center ASAP.

Hector heaved his two-hundred-and-twenty-pound frame out of the desk chair. He was a stocky man who'd been all muscle during his twenties. During his early thirties, a lot of that muscle had turned to fat. Using his stubby, shovel-like hands, he attached to his belt the police paraphernalia he'd removed to sit at his desk. He was in the process of slipping into his Kevlar vest when the phone rang again. It was the chief, Mark Witman.

"I understand there's a hostage situation," Chief Witman said.

"Yes, sir," Hector stammered. "I was just called. We're mobilizing the necessary personnel."

"You feel comfortable handling this?" Chief Witman said.

"Yes, sir," Hector answered.

"You sure you don't want a captain running the show?" Chief Witman asked.

"I believe there'll be no problem, sir," Hector said.

"Okay," Chief Witman said. "But I must tell you I have already had a call from the mayor. This is a politically sensitive situation."

"I'll keep that in mind, sir," Hector said.

"I want this handled by the book," Chief Witman said.

"Yes, sir," Hector said.

SEAN ATTACKED his work with determination. Knowing that his time was limited, he tried to work efficiently, planning each step in advance. The first thing he did was slip up to the sixth floor to check on the automatic peptide analyzer that he'd set up on Saturday to sequence the amino acids. He thought there was a good chance his run had been disturbed since Deborah Levy had appeared to read him the riot act just after he'd started it. But the machine hadn't been touched, and his sample was still inside. He tore off the readout from the printer.

The next thing Sean did was carry two thermal cyclers down from the sixth floor to the fifth. They were going to be his workhorses for the afternoon. It was in the thermal cyclers that the polymerase chain reactions were carried out.

After a quick check on the Masons, who seemed to be spending most of their time arguing over whose fault it was that they'd been taken hostage, Sean got down to real work.

First he went over the readout from the peptide analyzer. The results were dramatic. The amino acid sequences of the antigen binding sites of Helen Cabot's medicine and Louis Martin's medicine were identical. The immunoglobulins were the same, meaning all the medulloblastoma patients were being treated, at least initially, with the same antibody. This information was consistent with Sean's theory, so it fanned his excitement.

Next, Sean got out Helen's brain and the syringe containing her cerebrospinal fluid from the refrigerator. He took another general sample of tumor from the brain, then returned the organ to the refrigerator. After cutting it into small pieces, Sean put the tumor sample in a flask with the appropriate enzymes to create a cell suspension of the cancer cells. He put the flask in the incubator.

While the enzymes worked on the tumor sample, Sean began loading some of the ninety-six wells of the first thermal cycler with aliquots of Helen's cerebrospinal fluid. To each well of cerebrospinal fluid he added an enzyme called a reverse transcriptase to change any viral RNA to DNA. Then he put the paired primers for St. Louis encephalitis virus into the same well. Finally, he added the reagents to sustain the polymerase chain reaction. These reagents included a heat stable enzyme called Taq.

Turning back to the cell suspension of Helen's cancer, Sean used a detergent designated NP-40 to open the cells and their nuclear membranes. Then, by painstaking separation techniques, he isolated the cellular nucleoproteins from the rest of the cellular debris. In a final step he separated the DNA from the RNA.

He loaded samples of the DNA into the remaining wells of the first thermal cycler. Into these same wells Sean carefully added the paired primers for oncogenes, a separate pair for each well. Finally he dosed each well with an appropriate amount of reagents for the polymerase chain reaction.

With the first thermal cycler fully loaded, Sean turned it on.

Turning to the second thermal cycler, Sean added samples of Helen's tumor cell RNA to each well. In the second run he was planning to look for messenger RNA made from oncogenes. To do this he had to add aliquots of reverse transcriptions to each well, the same enzyme that he'd added to the samples of cerebrospinal fluid. While he was in the tedious process of adding the oncogene primer pairs, a pair in each well, the phone rang.

At first Sean ignored the phone, assuming that Dr. Mason would answer it. When Mason failed to do so, the continuous ringing began to grate on Sean's nerves. Putting down the pipette he was using, Sean walked over to the glass-enclosed office. Mrs. Mason was sitting glumly in an office chair pushed into the corner. She'd apparently cried herself out and was just sniffling into a tissue. Dr. Mason was nervously watching the flask in the ice bath, concerned that the ringing phone might disturb it.

Sean pushed open the door. "Would you mind answering the phone?" Sean said irritably. "Whoever it is, be sure to tell them that the nitroglycerin is just on the verge of freezing."

Sean gave the door a shove. As it clunked into its jamb, Sean could see Dr. Mason wince, but the doctor obediently picked up the receiver. Sean turned back to his lab bench and his pipetting. He'd only loaded a single well when his concentration was again broken.

"It's a Lieutenant Hector Salazar from the Miami Police Department," Dr. Mason called. "He'd like to talk with you."

Sean looked over at the office. Dr. Mason had the door propped open with his foot. He was holding the phone in one hand, the receiver in the other. The cord snaked back into the office.

"Tell him that there will be no problems if they wait for a couple more hours," Sean said.

Dr. Mason spoke into the phone for a few moments, then called out: "He insists on talking with you."

Sean rolled his eyes. He put his pipette back down on the lab bench, stepped over to the wall extension, and pushed the blinking button.

"I'm very busy right now," he said without preamble.

"Take it easy," Hector said soothingly. "I know you're upset, but everything is going to work out fine. There's someone here who'd like to have a word with you. His name is Sergeant Hunt. We want to be reasonable about all this. I'm sure you do too."

Sean tried to protest that he didn't have time for conversation when Sergeant Hunt's gruff voice came over the line.

"Now I want you to stay calm," Sergeant Hunt said.

"That's a little difficult," Sean said. "I've got a lot to do in a short time."

"No one will get hurt," Sergeant Hunt said. "We'd like you to come down here so we can talk."

"Sorry," Sean said.

"I've heard that you've been angry about not being able to work on a particular project," Sergeant Hunt said. "Let's talk about it. I can understand how upsetting that might be. You may want to lash out at the people you think are responsible. But we should also talk about the fact that holding people against their will is a serious offense."

Sean smiled when he realized the police had surmised he'd taken the Masons hostage as a result of being kept off the medulloblastoma protocol. In a way, they weren't far off.

"I appreciate your concern and your presence," Sean said. "But I don't have a lot of time to talk. I've got to get back to work."

"Just tell us what you want," Sergeant Hunt said.

"Time," Sean said. "I only want a little time. Two or three, or perhaps four hours at most."

Sean hung up. Returning to his bench, he lifted his pipette and went back to work.

RONALD HUNT was a six-foot redheaded man. At thirty-seven, he'd been on the police force for fifteen years, ever since graduating from community college. His major had been law enforcement, but he'd minored in psychology. Attempting to combine psychology with police work, he'd jumped at the chance to join the Hostage Negotiating Team when a slot became available. Although he didn't get to use his skills as often as he would have liked, when he did he'd enjoyed the challenge. He'd even been inspired to take more psychology at night school at the University of Miami.

Sergeant Hunt had been successful in all his previous operations and had developed confidence in his abilities. After the successful resolution of the last episode which involved a discontented employee at a soft-drink bottling plant who'd taken three female colleagues hostage, Ronald had received a citation from the force for meritorious service. So when Sean Murphy hung up on him, it was a blow to his ego.

"The twerp hung up on me!" Ron said indignantly.

"What did he say he wanted?" Hector asked.

"Time," Ron said.

"What do you mean, time?" Hector asked. "Like the magazine? Does he want to be in *Time*?"

"No," Ron said. "Time like hours. He told me he has to get back to work. He must be working on that project he'd been forbidden to work on."

"What kind of project?" Hector asked.

"I don't know," Ron said. He then pushed the redial on the portable phone. "I can't negotiate unless we talk."

Lieutenant Hector Salazar and Sergeant Ronald Hunt

were standing behind three blue-and-white Miami police cars parked in the Forbes parking lot directly across from the entrance to the Forbes research building. The squad cars were parked in the form of a letter U facing away from the building. In the heart of this U they'd set up a mini-command center with a couple of phones and a radio on a folding card table.

The police presence at the site had swelled considerably. Initially there had only been four officers: the original two uniformed patrolmen who'd answered the call, plus their sergeant and his partner. Now there was a small crowd. Besides dozens of regular uniformed police, including Hector, there was the two-man negotiating team, a five-man bomb squad, and a ten-man SWAT team dressed in black assault uniforms. The SWAT team was off to the side warming up with some jumping jacks.

In addition to the police, Forbes was represented by Dr. Deborah Levy, Margaret Richmond, and Robert Harris. They had been allowed near the command post but had been asked to keep to the side. A small crowd, including local media, had gathered just beyond the yellow crime scene tape. Several TV vans were parked as close as possible with their antennae extended. Reporters with microphones in hand and camera crews at their heels were scouring the crowd to interview anyone who seemed to have any information about the drama transpiring within.

While the crowd of spectators swelled, the police tried to go about their business.

"Dr. Mason says that Murphy flat out refuses to get back on the phone," Ron said. He was clearly offended.

"You keep trying," Hector advised him. Turning to Sergeant Anderson, Hector said: "I trust that all entrances and exits are covered."

"All covered," Anderson assured him. "No one is going

in or coming out without our knowing it. Plus we have sharpshooters on the roof of the hospital."

"What about that pedestrian bridge connecting the two buildings?" Hector asked.

"We got a man on the bridge on the hospital side," Anderson said. "There aren't going to be any surprises in this operation."

Hector motioned to Phil Darell to come over. "What's the story on the bomb?" Hector asked.

"It's a little unorthodox," Phil acknowledged. "I spoke with the doctor. It's a flask of nitroglycerin. He estimates about two or three hundred cc's. It's sitting in an ice bath. Apparently Murphy comes in every so often and dumps ice into the bath. Every time he does it, it terrifies the doctor."

"Is it a problem?" Hector asked.

"Yeah, it's a problem," Phil said. "Especially once it solidifies."

"Would slamming a door detonate it?" Hector asked.

"Probably not," Phil replied. "But a shake might. A fall to the floor certainly would."

"But can you handle it?"

"Absolutely," Phil said.

Next Hector waved Deborah Levy over.

"I understand you run the research here."

Dr. Levy nodded.

"What do you think this kid is doing?" Hector asked. "He told our negotiator he wanted time to work."

"Work!" Dr. Levy said disparagingly. "He's probably up there sabotaging our research. He's been angry that we haven't allowed him to work on one of our protocols. He has no respect for anyone or anything. Frankly, I thought he was disturbed from the first moment I met him."

"Can he be working on that protocol now?" Hector asked.

"Absolutely not," Dr. Levy said. "That protocol has moved into clinical trials."

"So you think he's up there causing trouble," Hector said.

"I know that he is causing trouble!" Dr. Levy said. "I think you should go up there and drag him out."

"We have the safety of the hostages to consider," Hector said.

Hector was about to confer with George Loring and his SWAT team when one of the uniformed patrolmen got his attention.

"This man insists on talking with you, Lieutenant," the patrolman said. "He claims to be the brother of the guy who's holed up inside."

Brian introduced himself. He explained that he was a lawyer from Boston.

"Any insight into what's going on here?" Hector asked.

"No, I'm sorry," Brian said. "But I know my brother. Although he's always been headstrong, he would not do anything like this unless there was a damn good reason. I want to be sure that you people don't do anything rash."

"Taking hostages at gunpoint and threatening them with a bomb is more than headstrong," Hector said. "That kind of behavior puts him in an unstable, unpredictable, and dangerous category. We have to proceed on that basis."

"I admit what he's done here appears foolhardy," Brian said. "But Sean's ultimately rational. Maybe you should let me talk to him."

"You think he might listen to you?" Hector asked.

"I think so," Brian said, despite still feeling the effects of the episode at the Masons'.

Hector got the phone away from Ronald Hunt and let Brian try calling. Unfortunately no one answered, not even Dr. Mason.

"The doctor has been answering until a few minutes ago," Ron said.

"Let me go in and talk with him," Brian said.

Hector shook his head. "There are enough hostages in there as it is," he said.

"Lieutenant Salazar," a voice called. Hector turned to see a tall, slender Caucasian approaching, along with a bearded, powerfully built Afro-American. Sterling introduced himself and Wayne Edwards. "I'm acquainted with your chief, Mark Witman, quite well," Sterling said after the introductions. Then he added: "We heard about this situation involving Sean Murphy so we came to offer our services."

"This is a police matter," Hector said. He eyed the newcomers with suspicion. He never liked anyone who tried to bully him by saying he was bosom buddies with the chief. He wondered how they'd managed to cross the crime scene barrier.

"My colleague and I have been following Mr. Murphy for several days," Sterling explained. "We are in the temporary employ of the Forbes Cancer Center."

"You have some explanation of what's going on here?" Hector asked.

"We know that this dude's been getting progressively crazy," Wayne said.

"He's not crazy!" Brian said, interrupting. "Sean is brash and imprudent, but he's not crazy."

"If someone does a string of crazy things," Wayne said, "it's fair to say he's crazy."

At that moment everyone ducked reflexively as a helicopter swept over the building, then hovered over the parking lot. The thunderous thump of the rotor blades rattled everyone's ribcage. Every bit of dust and dirt smaller than medium-sized gravel became airborne. A few papers on the card table were swept away.

George Loring, commander of the SWAT team, came forward. "That's our chopper," he yelled into Hector's ear. The noise of the aircraft was deafening. "I called it over so we can get to the roof the moment you give the green light."

Hector was having trouble keeping his hat on. "For crissake, George," he screamed back. "Tell the goddamn chopper to move off until we call it."

"Yes, sir!" George yelled back. He pulled a small microphone clipped to one of his epaulets. Shielding it with his hands he spoke briefly to the pilot. To everyone's relief the chopper dipped, then swept away to land on a helipad next to the hospital.

"What's your take on this situation?" Hector asked George now that they could talk.

"I looked at the floor plans supplied by the head of security, who's been very cooperative," George said, pointing out Robert Harris for Hector. "I think we'd only need a six-man team on the roof: three down each stairwell. The suspect's in the fifth-floor lab. We'd only need one, but we'd probably go ahead and use two concussion grenades. It would be over in seconds. A piece of cake."

"What about the nitroglycerin in the office?" Hector asked.

"I didn't hear about any nitro," George said.

"It's in a glass-enclosed office," Hector said.

"It would be a risk," Phil interrupted, having overheard the conversation. "The concussive waves could detonate the nitroglycerin if it's in a solid state."

"Hell, then," George said. "Forget the grenades. We can just come out of both stairwells simultaneously. The terrorist wouldn't know what hit him."

"Sean's no terrorist!" Brian said, horrified at this talk.

"I'd like to volunteer to be with the assault team," Harris said, speaking up for the first time. "I know the terrain."

"This is not amateur hour," Hector said.

"I'm no amateur," Harris said indignantly. "I trained as a commando in the service and carried out a number of commando missions in Desert Storm."

"I think something should be done sooner rather than later," Dr. Levy said. "The longer that crazy kid is left up there, the more damage he can do to our ongoing experiments."

Everyone ducked again as another helicopter made a low pass over the parking area. This one had "Channel 4 TV" on its side.

Hector yelled for Anderson to call the complaint room to have them call Channel 4 to get their goddamn helicopter away from the scene or he'd let the SWAT team have a go at it with their automatic weapons.

Despite the noise and general pandemonium, Brian picked up one of the telephones and pressed the redial button. He prayed it would be answered, and it was. But it wasn't Sean. It was Dr. Mason.

SEAN HAD no idea how many cycles he should let the thermal cyclers run. All he was looking for was a positive reaction in any of the approximately one hundred and fifty wells he'd prepared. Impatient, he stopped the first machine after twenty-five cycles and removed the tray containing the wells.

First he added a biotinylated probe and the enzymatic reagents used to detect whether the probe had reacted in the series of wells containing Helen Cabot's cerebrospinal fluid. Then he introduced these samples into the chemiluminescence instrument and waited by the printout to see if there was any luminescence.

To Sean's surprise, the very first sample was positive. Although he fully expected it to be positive eventually, he hadn't expected a reaction so soon. What this established was that Helen Cabot—just like Malcolm Betencourt—had contracted St. Louis encephalitis in the middle of the winter, which was strange since the normal vector for the illness is a mosquito.

Sean then turned his attention to the other wells where he would be searching for the presence of oncogenes. But before he could start adding the appropriate probes, he was interrupted by Dr. Mason.

Although the phone had rung intermittently after he'd spoken with Sergeant Hunt, Sean had ignored it. Apparently Dr. Mason had ignored it too, because on several occasions it rang for extended periods. Sean had finally turned the ringer off on his extension. But apparently it had rung again and apparently this time Dr. Mason had answered it because he'd gingerly opened the door to tell Sean that his brother was on the line.

Although Sean hated to interrupt what he was doing, he felt guilty enough about Brian to take his call. The first thing he did was apologize for striking him.

"I'm willing to forgive and forget," Brian said. "But you have to end this nonsense right now and come down here and give yourself up."

"I can't," Sean said. "I need another hour or so, maybe two at the most."

"What in God's name are you doing?" Brian asked.

"It'll take too long to explain," Sean said. "But it's big stuff."

"I'm afraid you have no idea of the hullabaloo you're

causing," Brian said. "They've got everyone here but the National Guard. You've gone too far this time. If you don't come out this minute and put a stop to this, I won't have anything to do with you."

"I only need a little more time," Sean said. "I'm not asking for the world."

"There's a bunch of gung ho nuts out here," Brian said. "They're talking about storming the building."

"Make sure they know about the purported nitroglycerin," Sean said. "That's supposed to dissuade them from heroics."

"What do you mean, 'purported nitroglycerin'?" Brian asked.

"It's mostly ethanol with just a little acetone," Sean said. "It looks like nitroglycerin. At least, it's close enough to fool Dr. Mason. You didn't think I'd make up a batch of the real thing, did you?"

"At this point," Brian said, "I wouldn't put anything past you."

"Just talk them out of any commando action," Sean said. "Get me at least one more hour."

Sean could hear Brian continue to protest, but Sean didn't listen. Instead he hung up the phone and turned back to the first thermal cycler tray.

Sean hadn't gotten far with the oncogene probes when Janet came through the stairwell door trailing computer printout sheets.

"No problem finding the Forbes travel file," she said. She thrust the computer paper at Sean. "For whatever it's worth, Dr. Deborah Levy does a lot of traveling, but it's mostly back and forth to Key West."

Sean glanced at the printout. "She does keep on the move," he agreed. "But notice all these other cities. That's what I expected. What about Margaret Richmond?"

"No travel to Key West," Janet said. "But moderate travel around the country. About once a month she's off to another city."

"What about that automated program we saw?" Sean asked.

"You were right about that," Janet said. "It was running when I got up there, so I copied two of the numbers we thought might have been phone numbers. When I tried to call direct I could tell it was a computer link, so I used the mainframe and its modem to connect. Both of them were insurance companies: one was Medi-First; the other was Healthnet."

"Bingo," Sean said. "It's all falling into place."

"How about letting me in on the revelation," Janet said.

"What I'd be willing to bet is that the computer searches for medical insurance companies' precertification files for specific social security numbers. It probably does it on a nightly basis during the week and on Sunday afternoons."

"You mean precertification for surgery?" Janet asked.

"That's exactly what I mean," Sean said. "In an attempt to cut down on unnecessary surgery, most if not all health plans require the doctor or the hospital to notify the insurance company of proposed surgery in advance. Usually it's merely a rubber-stamp exercise so it's pretty casual. I doubt there's any concern about confidentiality. That computer upstairs is printing out proposed elective surgery on a specific list of social security numbers."

"Those are the numbers that are flashing on the screen," Janet said.

"That's what it has to be," Sean said.

"So why?" Janet asked.

"I'll let you figure that out," Sean said. "While I continue processing these thermal cycler samples, you look at the referring histories on these thirty-three charts we copied. I think you'll find most will mention that the patient had elective surgery within a relatively short period before their diagnosis of medulloblastoma. I want you to compare the dates of those surgeries with Dr. Levy's travel schedule."

Janet stared at Sean without blinking. Despite her exhaustion, she was beginning to assimilate the facts as Sean understood them and therefore starting to comprehend the direction Sean's thoughts were headed. Without saying another word, she sat down with the charts and the computer printout she'd brought down from the seventh floor.

Turning back to his own work, Sean loaded a few more wells with the appropriate oncogene probes. He hadn't gotten far when Dr. Mason interrupted him.

"My wife is getting hungry," Dr. Mason announced.

With his general fatigue Sean's nerves were raw. After all that had happened he could not abide the Masons, particularly Mrs. Mason. The fact that they thought it appropriate to bother him with her being hungry threw him into a momentary rage. Putting down the pipette, he raced back toward the glass office.

Dr. Mason saw Sean coming and quickly guessed his state of mind. He let go of the door and backed into the office.

Sean threw open the office door so that it banged against the doorstop. He flew into the office, snatched the Erlenmeyer flask from the ice bath, and gave it a shake. Some of its contents had solidified and cakes of ice clunked against the sides of the container.

Dr. Mason's face blanched as he cringed in anticipation of an explosion. Mrs. Mason buried her face in her hands.

"If I hear one more sound from you people I'm going to come in here and shatter this flask on the floor," Sean yelled.

When no explosion occurred Dr. Mason opened his eyes. Mrs. Mason peeked out between her fingers.

"Do you people understand?" Sean snapped.

Dr. Mason swallowed hard, then nodded.

Disgusted with the Masons and his own temper tantrum, Sean went back to his lab bench. Guiltily he glanced over at Janet, but she'd not paid any attention. She was too engrossed in the charts.

Picking up the pipette, Sean went back to work. It was not easy, and he had to concentrate. He had to put the right probe in the right well, and he had the primer pairs and probes for over forty oncogenes, a rather extensive list.

A number of the first samples were negative. Sean didn't know if he'd taken them from the thermal cycler after an insufficient number of cycles or if they were truly negative. By the fifth sample he was beginning to become discouraged. For the first time since he'd put this drama into motion, he seriously questioned the conclusions which by then he'd come to view as rock solid. But then the sixth sample proved positive. He'd detected the presence of an oncogene known by the designation ERB-2, which referred to avian erythroblastosis virus, a virus whose normal host was chickens.

By the time Janet finished with the charts, Sean had found another oncogene, called v-myc, which stood for myelocytoma virus, another virus that grew in chickens.

"Only about three-quarters of the charts have the surgery dates," Janet said. "But of those, most of them match the dates and destinations of Dr. Levy's travel."

"Hallelujah!" Sean exclaimed. "It's all fitting into place like a jigsaw puzzle."

"What I don't understand," Janet said, "is what she did in those cities."

"Nearly everyone who's post-surgery is on an IV," Sean said. "It keeps people hydrated, plus if there's a problem the medical staff has a route for medication. My guess is that Deborah Levy gave them an injection into their IV."

"Of what?" Janet asked.

"An injection of St. Louis encephalitis virus," Sean said. He told Janet about the positive test for the SLE virus in Helen Cabot's cerebrospinal fluid. He also told her that Louis Martin had had transient neurological symptoms similar to Helen's several days after his elective surgery.

"And if you look back at the charts," Sean continued, "I think you'll find most of these people had similar fleeting symptoms."

"Why didn't they get full-blown encephalitis?" Janet asked. "Especially if it was injected through their IVs?"

"That's the truly clever part about all this," Sean said. "I believe the encephalitis viruses were altered and attenuated with the inclusion of viral oncogenes. I've already detected two such oncogenes in Helen's tumor. My guess is that I'll find another. One of the current theories on cancer is that it takes at least three isolated events in a cell to make it cancerous."

"How did all this occur to you?" Janet asked. It sounded too complicated, too involved, too complex, and most of all too hideous, to be true.

"Gradually," Sean said. "Unfortunately it took me a long time. I suppose initially my index of suspicion was so low; it's the last thing I expected. But when you told me they started immunotherapy with a specific agent from day one, I thought something was out of whack. That flew in the face of everything I knew about the specificity of immunotherapy. It takes time to develop an antibody and everybody's tumor is antigenically unique."

"But it was at the Betencourts' that you started acting strangely," Janet said.

"Malcolm Betencourt was the one who emphasized the sequence," Sean said. "Elective surgery, followed by neurological symptoms, and then brain tumor. Helen Cabot and

Louis Martin had the same progression. Until I heard Malcolm's story, I hadn't realized its significance. As one of my medicine professors said, if you are painstakingly careful in your history-taking, you should be able to make every diagnosis."

"So you believe the Forbes Cancer Center has been going around the country giving people cancer," Janet said, forcing herself to put into words her awful fear.

"A very special kind of cancer," Sean said. "One of the viral oncogenes I've detected makes a protein that sticks out through the cell membrane. Since it's homologous to the protein that forms the receptor for growth hormone, it acts like a switch in the 'on' position to encourage cell growth and cell division. But besides that, the portion that sticks through the cell is a peptide and probably antigenic. My guess is the immunoglobulin they give these people is an antibody for that extracellular part of the ERB-2 oncoprotein."

"You're losing me," Janet admitted.

"Let's give it a try," Sean said. "Maybe I can show you. It will only take a moment since I have some of the ERB-2 oncoprotein from the Key West lab. Let's see if Helen Cabot's medicine reacts with it. Remember that I wasn't able to get it to react with any natural cellular antigen. The only thing it would react with was her tumor."

As Sean quickly prepared the immunofluorescence test, Janet tried to absorb what Sean had said so far.

"In other words," Janet said after a pause, "what makes this medulloblastoma cancer so different is that not only is it manmade, it's curable."

Sean looked up from his work with obvious admiration. "Right on!" he said. "You got it. They created a cancer with a tumor-specific antigen for which they already had a monoclonal antibody. This antibody would react with the antigen and coat all the cancer cells. Then all they'd have to do was to stimulate the immune system both in vivo and in vitro to get as many 'killer' cells as possible. The only minor problem was that the treatment probably made the symptoms worse initially because of the inflammation it would undoubtedly cause."

"Which is why Helen Cabot died," Janet said.

"That's what I'd guess," Sean said. "Boston kept her too long during the diagnostic stage. They should have sent her right down to Miami. The trouble is that Boston can't believe someone else might be better for any medical problem."

"How could you be so sure of all this?" Janet asked. "By the time we got back here you hadn't any proof. Yet you were sure enough to force the Masons over here by gunpoint. Seems to me you were taking a huge risk."

"The clincher was some engineer-style drawings of viral capsids I saw in the lab in Key West," Sean explained. "As soon as I saw them, I knew it all had to be true. You see, Dr. Levy's particular area of expertise is virology. The drawings were of a spherical virus with icosahedral symmetry. That's the kind of capsule an SLE virus has. The scientifically elegant part of this vile plot is that Deborah Levy was able to package the oncogenes into the SLE viral capsule. There wouldn't be room for more than one oncogene in each virus because she'd have to leave much of the SLE virus genome intact so that it would still be infective. I don't know how she did it. She also must have included some retroviral genes as well as the oncogene in order to get the oncogene to insert into the infected cell's chromosomes. My guess is that she transformed a number of the viruses with the oncogenes and only those brain cells that were unlucky enough to get all the oncogenes simultaneously became cancerous."

"Why an encephalitis virus?" Janet asked.

"It has a natural predilection for neurons," Sean said. "If they wanted to cause a cancer they could treat, they needed a tumor which they could count on giving early symptoms. Brain cancer is one of them. Scientifically, it's all quite rational."

"Diabolical is a better term," Janet said.

Janet glanced over into the glass-enclosed office. Dr. Mason was pacing the room although carefully avoiding the desk and the flask in the ice bath. "Do you think he knows all this?" she asked.

"That I don't know," Sean said. "But if I had to guess, I'd say yes. It would be hard to run this elaborate operation without the director knowing. After all, it was a fund-raiser in the final analysis."

"That's why they targeted CEOs and their families," Janet said.

"That's my assumption," Sean said. "It's easy to find out which health insurance company a large firm uses. It's also not difficult to find out someone's social security number, especially for quasi-public figures. Once they had the subscriber's social security number, it would be an easy step to get their dependents'."

"So that evening when we were here copying the charts and heard the word donor, they were referring to money, not organs."

Sean nodded. "At that moment our imaginations were too active," he said. "We forgot that specialty hospitals and associated research centers have become increasingly desperate as NIH grants are getting harder and harder to come by. Creating a group of wealthy, grateful patients is a good way to make it through to the twenty-first century."

Meanwhile, the immunofluorescence test involving the

ERB-2 and Helen Cabot's medicine had registered strongly positive, even stronger than it had with the tumor cells. "There you go!" Sean said smugly. "There's the antigen-antibody reaction I've been searching for."

Next Sean turned back to his hundreds of samples in the two thermocyclers.

"Can I help?" Janet asked.

"Definitely," Sean said. He showed her how to handle a twelve-channel pipette, then gave her a series of oncogene probes to add to the thermocycler wells.

They worked together for almost three-quarters of an hour, concentrating on the meticulous work. They were both physically exhausted and emotionally overwrought from the magnitude of the conspiracy they suspected. After the final well was probed and analyzed for its luminescence, they'd uncovered two more oncogenes: Ha-ras, named after the Harvey sarcoma virus which normally infected rats, and SV40 Large T from a virus usually found in monkey kidneys. From the RNA studies in the second thermocycler, where Sean had run a quantitative polymerase chain reaction, it was determined that all the oncogenes were "mega" expressed.

"What an oncogene cocktail!" Sean said with awe as he stood and stretched his weary muscles. "Any nerve cell that got those four would undoubtedly become cancerous. Dr. Levy was leaving as little to chance as possible."

Janet put down the pipette she was holding and cradled her head in her hands. In a tired voice she spoke without looking up: "What now?"

"We give up, I guess," Sean said. As he tried to contemplate the next step, he glanced into the office at the Masons who were arguing again. Mercifully, the glass partition dampened the sound of their voices considerably.

"How are we going to manage the giving up?" Janet asked sleepily.

Sean sighed. "You know, I hadn't given it much thought. It could be tricky."

Janet looked up. "You must have had some idea when you came up with this plan."

"Nope," Sean admitted. "I didn't think that far ahead."

Janet pushed off her seat and went to the window. From there she could see down into the parking lot. "You got that circus you wanted," she said. "There are hundreds of people out there, including a group in black uniforms."

"They're the ones who make me nervous," Sean admitted. "I'd guess they're a SWAT team."

"Maybe the first thing we should do is send the Masons out to tell them that we're ready to come out."

"That's an idea," Sean said. "But you'll go with them."

"But then you'll be in here alone," Janet said. She came back and sat down. "I don't like that. Not with all those black-uniform guys itching to come charging in here."

"The biggest problem is Helen Cabot's brain," Sean said.

"Why?" Janet asked with a sigh of exasperation.

"It's our only evidence," Sean said. "We cannot allow the Forbes people to destroy the brain which I'm certain they'd do if given the chance. My guess is that I'll not be very popular with anybody when we end this. During the confusion there's a good chance the brain could get into the wrong hands. I doubt anyone is going to take the time to stop and hear me out."

"I'd have to agree," Janet said.

"Wait a second!" Sean said with sudden enthusiasm. "I've got an idea."

13

March 7
Sunday, 4:38 P.M.

It took Sean twenty minutes to convince Janet that the best thing for her to do was join the Masons in the office. It was Sean's hope that the idea she'd been coerced would be easier to put forth if she was considered a hostage. Janet was skeptical, but in the end she relented.

With that issue decided, Sean packed Helen Cabot's brain in ice and put it in the cooler he'd used to transport it to the lab. Then with some cord that he'd found in the supply closet, he made a large parcel out of the thirty-three chart copies plus the computer printout of the Forbes Cancer Center travel file. When all was ready, Sean picked up the pass keys and with the cooler in one hand and the charts in the other, he climbed up to the administration floor.

Using the pass key, Sean went into the finance section. After taking out the shelving from the dumbwaiter, he squeezed himself in along with his two parcels. He rode the dumbwaiter down the seven floors to the basement, trying hard to keep his elbows in so they wouldn't rub on the walls.

The chart vault was a problem. The light switch was at

the entrance, and Sean had to negotiate the entire length of the room in utter blackness. Remembering at least the general layout of the shelving, he was able to move with a modicum of confidence although several times he became disoriented. Eventually, he found the sister dumbwaiter. Within minutes he was riding up the two stories to medical records in the hospital building.

When he opened the dumbwaiter door he was thankful for the lights being on but disappointed to hear someone giving muffled dictation. Before stepping out of the cramped car, Sean determined that the voice was coming from a small cubicle that was out of sight. As quietly as possible he got himself out of the hoist; then he crept into the hall, clutching his two parcels, one under each arm.

Once in the hall, Sean could sense the electricity in the air. It was apparent that the clinical chemistry and radiology departments had been informed of the hostage situation in the neighboring building; the excitement provided an almost holiday atmosphere for the weekend skeleton staff. Most of them were in the hall at the floor-to-ceiling windows opposite the elevators that faced the research building. None of them paid any attention to Sean.

Shunning the elevators, Sean took the stairs down to the first floor. When he came out into the main lobby, he felt immediately at ease. Conveniently, it was visiting hours so there was quite a mob of people clustered around the lobby entrance. Despite his bulky parcels, two-day growth of whiskers, and rumpled clothes, Sean was able to blend in.

Sean walked out of the hospital unimpeded. Crossing the parking lot to the research side he began to appreciate the number of people who'd showed up for his hostage show. They were milling about the handful of cars parked there, including his own 4×4.

Passing near his Isuzu, Sean contemplated dropping the

brain and the charts off. But he decided it would be better to give them directly to Brian. Sean was confident his brother was still there despite his threats to abandon him.

The police had stretched the yellow vinyl crime scene tape from vehicle to vehicle all the way around the front of the research building. Behind the building they used trees to seal off the area completely. All along the tape at regular intervals uniformed police officers stood guard.

Sean noticed that the police had set up a command central at a card table positioned behind a group of squad cars. A crowd of several dozen police officials were gathered in the vicinity in the central spot. Off to the left was the black-suited SWAT team, some of whom were doing calisthenics, others checking an assortment of impressive weaponry.

Sean paused at the tape and scanned the crowd. He was able to pick Brian out instantly. He was the only man dressed in a white shirt and paisley suspenders. Brian was off to the side locked in an animated conversation with a black-suited SWAT team member with black face paint smeared under each eye.

Stepping over to one of the uniformed police officers manning the crime scene tape, Sean waved to get his attention. He was busy clipping his nails.

"Sorry to be a bother," Sean said. "I'm related to the individual who took the hostages and that's my brother over there talking with a member of the SWAT team." Sean pointed toward Brian. "I think I can help resolve the dilemma."

The policeman raised the tape without saying a word. He merely gestured for Sean to enter. Then he went back to his nails.

Sean kept clear of Deborah Levy and Robert Harris, who he spotted near one of the squad cars. Fortunately they weren't looking in his direction. He also steered away from one of the men he'd locked in the closet in Key West, the same man who'd been waiting on the Sushita jet in Naples, whom he saw near the card table.

Sean went directly to his brother, coming up behind him. He caught bits and pieces of the argument which dealt with the issue of storming the building. It was obvious they held contrary views.

Sean tapped Brian on the shoulder, but Brian shrugged the intrusion off with a disinterested shrug. He was busy making a point by pounding a fist into an open palm. He continued his emotional monologue until Sean drifted around into the corner of his vision. Brian stopped in mid-sentence, his mouth agape.

George Loring followed the line of Brian's gaze, sized Sean up as a homeless person, then looked back at Brian. "You know this guy?" he asked.

"We're brothers," Sean said as he nudged the shocked Brian aside.

"What the hell . . . ?" Brian exclaimed.

"Don't make a scene!" Sean warned, pulling his brother further away. "If you're still mad about me tagging you, I'm sorry. I didn't want to hit you, but you left me with little choice. It was an inconvenient moment for you to pop up."

Brian threw a quick but concerned glance toward the command post a mere forty feet away. Redirecting his attention to Sean, he said: "What are you doing here?"

"I want you to take this cooler," Sean said, handing it over. "Plus these chart copies. But it's the cooler that's most important."

Brian adjusted his posture to deal with the weight of the charts. "How on earth did you get out of there? They assured me the place had been sealed off: that no one could go in or out."

"I'll tell you in a few minutes," Sean said. "But first about this cooler: it's got a brain in it. Not a very pretty brain, but an important one."

"Is this the brain you stole?" Brian asked. "If it is, it's stolen property."

"Hold your legal blarney," Sean said.

"Whose brain is it?"

"A patient's," Sean said. "And we'll need it to indict a number of people here at Forbes Cancer Center."

"You mean it's evidence?" Brian asked.

"It's going to blow a lot of people's minds," Sean promised.

"But there's no appropriate chain of custody," Brian complained.

"The DNA will solve that," Sean said. "Just don't let anybody have it. And the chart copies are important too."

"But they're no good as evidence," Brian said. "They're not authenticated copies."

"For crissake, Brian!" Sean snapped. "I know it was thoughtless of me not to have had the foresight to have a notary with me when I copied them, but we can use them for the grand jury. Besides, the copies will show us what we need to subpoena, and we can use them to be sure they don't change any of the originals." Sean lowered his voice. "Now, what do we do to end this carnival with no loss of life, particularly mine? These idle SWAT team guys give me the willies."

Brian glanced around again. "I don't know," he said. "Let me think. You're always throwing me off balance. Being your brother is a full-time job for several lawyers. I wish I could trade you in for a nice sister."

"That's not how you felt when we sold the stock in Immunotherapy," Sean reminded him.

"I suppose we could just walk away from here," Brian said.

"Whatever is best," Sean said agreeably.

"But then they could charge me as an accessory after the fact," Brian mused.

"Whatever you say," Sean said. "But I should tell you that Janet is upstairs."

"Is she that rich girl you've been dating in Boston?" Brian asked.

"That's the one," Sean said. "She surprised me and showed up down here the same day I arrived."

"Maybe it's best if you just give yourself up right here," Brian reasoned. "It will probably sit well with the judge. The more I think about it, the more I like it. Come on, I'll introduce you to Lieutenant Hector Salazar. He's running the show, and he seems like a decent guy."

"Fine by me," Sean said. "Let's do it before one of these black-suited SWAT team members doing calisthenics pulls a groin muscle and I get sued for loss of consortium."

"You'd better have one hell of an explanation for all of this," Brian warned.

"It'll blow your socks off," Sean said. "Guaranteed."

"Let me do the talking," Brian said. They started toward the card table.

"I wouldn't think of interfering," Sean said. "It's the one thing you do well."

As they approached the card table Sean eyed Sterling Rombauer and Robert Harris, who were arguing off to the side. Sean tried to turn away from them and walk sideways lest they recognize him and cause some kind of panic. But he needn't have been concerned. They were too engrossed in their conversation to notice him.

Coming up behind Hector Salazar's bulk, Brian cleared

his throat to get the policeman's attention, but to no avail. Hector had taken over where Brian had left off with George Loring. George was eager to get the nod for action. Hector was advocating patience.

"Lieutenant!" Brian called.

"Goddamn it," Hector bellowed. "Anderson, did you call complaints about that TV chopper? Here it comes again."

All conversation had to halt as the Channel 4 helicopter flew low overhead and banked around the parking area. Hector flipped the cameraman a finger which he'd later regret when he had to watch it replay again and again on TV.

Once the helicopter disappeared, Brian got Hector's attention.

"Lieutenant," Brian said buoyantly. "I'd like you to meet my brother Sean Murphy."

"Another brother!" Hector said, not making the proper connection. "What is this, a family reunion?" Then to Sean he said: "Do you think you might have some influence on that nutty brother of yours up in the lab? We have to get him to start talking to our negotiating team."

"This is Sean!" Brian said. "He's the one who was up there. But he's out now, and he wants to apologize for all this trouble."

Hector looked back and forth between the two brothers as his mind tried to make sense of this sudden, mind-boggling turn of events.

Sean stuck his hand out. Hector took it automatically, still too stunned to speak. The two men shook hands as if they'd just been introduced at a cocktail party.

"Hi!" Sean said, giving Hector one of his best smiles. "I want to personally thank you for all your effort. It really saved the day."

14

March 8
Monday, 11:15 A.M.

Sean preceded Brian through the swinging doors of the Dade County Courthouse and let the sun and cool fresh air wash over him while he waited for Brian to emerge. Sean had been in the lockup overnight after having been arrested and booked the previous evening.

"That was worse than medical school," Sean said, referring to the night in jail, as he and Brian descended the broad, sun-drenched steps.

"You're eyeball to eyeball with a long prison sentence if this case doesn't go perfectly smoothly," Brian said.

Sean stopped. "You're not serious, are you?" he asked with alarm. "Not after what I've told you these Forbes people have been up to."

"It's now in the hands of the judicial system," Brian said with a shrug. "Once it goes to a jury, it's a crap shoot. And you heard that judge in there at your arraignment. He was none too happy with you despite your giving yourself up and despite the nitroglycerin's not being nitroglycerin. As long as your captives thought it was nitroglycerin, it makes no difference what it was. You'd better thank me that I took the time and trouble to get your juvenile record sealed. If I hadn't you probably wouldn't have gotten out on bail."

"You could have made sure Kevin Porter told the judge there were extenuating circumstances," Sean complained.

"An arraignment is not a trial," Brian explained. "I told you that already. It's only a time for you to hear the formal charges against you and for you to enter your plea. Besides, Kevin alluded to extenuating circumstances during the bail portion."

"That's another thing," Sean said. "Five hundred thousand dollars bail! My God! Couldn't he have done better than that? Now we've tied up part of our seed capital of Oncogen."

"You're lucky to be out on bail, period," Brian said. "Let's go over your charges again: conspiracy, grand larceny, burglary, burglary with a deadly weapon, assault, assault with a deadly weapon, false imprisonment, kidnapping, mayhem, and mutilation of a dead body. My God, Sean, why'd you leave out rape and murder!"

"What about the Dade County District Attorney?" Sean asked.

"They call him State's Attorney down here," Brian said. "I met with him and with the U.S. District Attorney last night. While you were comfortably sleeping in jail, I was working my butt off."

"What did they say?"

"They were both interested, obviously," Brian said. "But without any evidence to present to them other than some circumstantial travel records and copies of hospital charts, they wisely withheld comment."

"What about Helen Cabot's brain?" Sean asked. "That's the evidence."

“It’s not evidence yet,” Brian said. “The tests you say you ran haven’t been reproduced.”

“Where is the brain itself?” Sean asked.

“It’s been impounded by the police,” Brian said. “But it is in the physical custody of the Dade County Medical Examiner. Remember, it’s stolen property. So that’s an added problem about its status as evidence.”

“I hate lawyers,” Sean said.

“And I have a feeling you’ll be liking them even less by the time this is over,” Brian said. “I heard this morning that in light of your irresponsible and slanderous statements that Forbes has retained one of the country’s most successful and flamboyant lawyers as well as the backup of Miami’s largest firm. A number of powerful people from all over the country are incensed by your allegations and are flooding Forbes with money for legal representation. In addition to the criminal charges, you’ll be facing a blizzard of civil suits.”

“I’m not surprised that important business people are standing behind Forbes,” Sean said. “But these same people will have a change of heart when they learn that the fantastic cure Forbes provided them was for a brain cancer that Forbes caused.”

“You’d better be right about that,” Brian said.

“I’m right,” Sean said. “The tumor I checked had four viral oncogenes. Even finding one in a natural tumor would have been astounding.”

“But that’s only one tumor out of thirty-eight cases,” Brian said.

“Don’t worry,” Sean said. “I’m right about this.”

“But the other evidence has already been thrown into question,” Brian said. “Through its lawyers, Forbes is saying that the fact that Dr. Deborah Levy happened to be in relevant cities the same day subsequent Forbes patients underwent elective surgery was purely coincidental.”

"Oh, sure," Sean said sarcastically.

"They do have a point," Brian said. "First of all, her travel did not match all the cases."

"So they sent someone else," Sean said. "Like Margaret Richmond. You'll have to subpoena all their travel records."

"There's more to it," Brian said. "Forbes contends that Dr. Levy is an on-site inspector for the College of American Pathology. I already checked it out. It's true. She often travels around the country making clinical lab inspections necessary for hospitals to maintain accreditation. I've also already checked some of the hospitals. It seems Dr. Levy did make inspections on those specific days."

"What about the program running at night with the social security numbers?" Sean asked. "That's pretty incriminating."

"Forbes has already categorically denied it," Brian said. "They say that they access insurance companies on a regular basis but purely to process claims. They say they never access precertification files for elective surgery. And what's more, the insurance companies claim that all their files are secure."

"Of course the companies would say that," Sean said. "I'm sure they're all quaking in their boots that they might be drawn in on the civil side of this. But in regard to the program at Forbes, Janet and I saw it running."

"It will be tough to prove," Brian said. "We'd need the program itself, and they certainly aren't going to give it to us."

"Well, damn!" Sean said.

"It's all going to come down to the science and whether we can get a jury to believe it or even understand it," Brian said. "I'm not sure I do. It's pretty esoteric stuff."

"Where's Janet?" Sean asked. They started walking again.

"She's in my car," Brian said. "Her arraignment was much earlier and a bit easier, but she wanted to get out of the courthouse. I can't blame her. This whole experience has unnerved her. She's not accustomed to being in trouble the way you are."

"Very funny," Sean said. "Is she being charged?"

"Of course she's being charged," Brian said. "What do you think, these people down here are morons? She was an accomplice for everything except assault with a deadly weapon and the kidnapping. Fortunately, the judge seemed to believe her biggest crime is associating with you. He didn't set bail. She was released on her own recognizance."

As they neared Brian's rental car, Sean could see Janet sitting in the front seat. She had her head leaning back on the headrest and she appeared to be asleep. But as Sean came alongside the car, her eyes popped open. Seeing Sean, she scrambled out of the car and hugged him.

Sean hugged her back, feeling self-conscious with his brother standing next to them.

"Are you all right?" Janet asked, pulling her head away but keeping her arms around Sean's neck.

"Fine, and you?"

"Being in jail was an eye-opener," she admitted. "I guess I got a little hysterical at first. But my parents flew down with a family attorney who speeded up my arraignment."

"Where are your parents now?" Sean asked.

"Back at a hotel," Janet said. "They're mad I wanted to wait for you."

"I can imagine," Sean said.

Brian consulted his watch. "Listen, you two," he said. "Dr. Mason has scheduled a news conference at noon at Forbes. I think we should go. I was worried we'd still be tied up here at the courthouse, but there's time. What do you say?"

"Why should we go?" Sean asked.

"I'm concerned about this case, as you can tell," Brian said. "I'm worried about getting a fair trial here in Miami. I'd prefer that this news conference not turn into the public relations bonanza I believe Forbes expects it to be. Your being there will tone down their rhetoric. It will also help establish you as a responsible individual who is serious about his allegations."

Sean shrugged. "Okay by me," he said. "Besides, I'm curious what Dr. Mason will say."

"Okay by me," Janet said.

Because of traffic, it took more time than Brian expected to drive from the Dade County Courthouse, but they were still on time for the news conference when they finally pulled into the Forbes parking area. The conference was scheduled to be held in the hospital auditorium, and all the parking spaces near the hospital were occupied. Several TV vans were parked in the fire lane near the hospital's front door. Brian had to drive around by the research building to find a space.

As they walked around to the hospital, Brian commented on how much media attention the affair was getting. "Let me warn you, this is hot. It's just the kind of case that gets played out in the media as much as it gets played out in the courts. What's more, it's being played on the Forbes's turf. Don't be surprised if your reception is less than cool."

A throng of people was milling about in front of the hospital. Many were reporters, and unfortunately several recognized Sean. They mobbed him, fighting with each other to thrust microphones into his face, everyone asking hostile questions at the same time. Flashbulbs flashed; TV camera lights flooded the scene. By the time Sean, Brian, and Janet reached the front door, Sean was angry. Brian had to restrain him from taking a swing at a few of the photographers.

Inside wasn't much better. News of Sean's arrival sent ripples through the surprisingly large crowd. As the three entered the auditorium, Sean heard a chorus of boos rise from the members of the Forbes medical staff who were attending.

"I see what you mean about chilly receptions," Sean said as they found seats. "Hardly neutral territory."

"It's a lynch mob mentality," Brian said. "But this gives you an idea of what you're up against."

The booing and hissing directed at Sean ceased abruptly and was replaced by respectful applause when Dr. Randolph Mason appeared from the wings of the small stage. He walked resolutely to the podium, placing a sizable manila envelope on it. Grasping either side of the podium, he looked out over the audience with his head slightly tilted back. His bearing and appearance were commendably professional, his classically graying hair perfectly coiffed. He was dressed in a dark blue suit, white shirt, and subdued tie. The only splash of color was a lavender silk foulard handkerchief in his breast pocket.

"He looks like everyone's romantic image of a physician," Janet whispered. "The kind you'd see on TV."

Brian nodded. "He's the kind of man juries tend to believe. This is going to be an uphill battle."

Dr. Mason cleared his throat, then began speaking. His resonant voice easily filled the small auditorium. He thanked everyone for coming and for supporting the Forbes Cancer Center in the face of the recent accusations.

"Will you be suing Sean Murphy for slander?" one of the reporters yelled out from the second row. But Dr. Mason didn't have to answer. The entire auditorium erupted in a sustained hiss in response to the reporter's rudeness. The reporter got the message and meekly apologized.

Dr. Mason adjusted the position of the manila envelope as he collected his thoughts.

"These are difficult times for hospitals and research facilities, particularly specialty hospitals which have the dual objectives of patient care and research. Clinical reimbursement schemes based on diagnosis and standard therapy do not work in environments such as Forbes where treatment plans often follow experimental protocols. Treatment of this sort is intensive and therefore expensive.

"The question is, where is the money supposed to come from for this type of care? Some people suggest it should come from research grants since it is part of the research process. Yet our public funding for general research has gone down, forcing us to seek other sources for financial support, like industry, or even, in exceptional cases, foreign industry. But even this source has limits, especially when the global economy is floundering. Where else can we turn but to the oldest method: private philanthropy."

"I can't believe this guy," Sean whispered. "This is like a fund-raiser pep talk."

A few people turned to glare at Sean.

"I have devoted my life to the relief of suffering," Dr. Mason continued. "Medicine and the fight against cancer have been my life since the day I entered medical school. I have always kept the good of mankind as my motivating force and goal."

"Now he sounds like a politician," Sean whispered. "When is he going to address the issue?"

"Quiet!" a person behind Sean snapped.

"When I took the position as director of the Forbes Center," Dr. Mason continued, "I knew the institution was in financial difficulty. Restoring the institution to a solid financial basis was a goal consistent with my desire to work for the good of mankind. I've given this task my heart and my soul. If I've made some mistakes, it is not for lack of altruistic motives."

There was spotty applause when Dr. Mason paused and fumbled with his manila envelope, undoing the string that held it closed.

"This is a waste of time," Sean whispered.

"That was just his introduction," Brian whispered in return. "Pipe down. I'm sure he's about to get to the meat of the news conference now."

"At this time I would like to take leave of you," Dr. Mason said. "To those who have helped me in this difficult period, my heartfelt thanks."

"Is this whole rigmarole so he can resign?" Sean asked out loud. He was disgusted.

But no one answered Sean's question. Instead, gasps of horror rippled through the audience when Dr. Mason reached into the envelope and pulled out a nickel-plated .357 magnum revolver.

Murmurs crescendoed as a few people nearest the podium rose to their feet, unsure whether to flee or approach Dr. Mason.

"I don't mean for people to become upset," Dr. Mason said. "But I felt . . ."

It was clear Dr. Mason had more to say, but two reporters in the front row made a move for him. Dr. Mason motioned them to keep away, but the two men edged closer. Dr. Mason took a step back from the podium. He looked panicked, like a cornered deer. All the color had drained from his face.

Then, to everyone's dismay, Dr. Mason put the barrel of

the revolver in his mouth and pulled the trigger. The bullet went through his hard palate, liquified part of his brain stem and cerebellum, and carried away a five-centimeter disk of skull before burying itself deeply into the wooden cornice molding. Dr. Mason fell backward while the gun was propelled forward. The revolver hit the floor and skidded beneath the first row of seats, sending the people still seated there scattering.

A few people screamed, a few cried, most felt momentarily ill. Sean, Janet, and Brian looked away at the moment the gun went off. When they looked again the room was in pandemonium. No one knew quite what to do. Even the doctors and nurses felt helpless; clearly Dr. Mason was beyond help.

All Sean, Janet, and Brian could see of Dr. Mason were his shoes pointing upward and a foreshortened body. The wall behind the podium was splattered as if someone had hurled a handful of ripe red berries against it.

Sean's mouth had gone dry. He found it difficult to swallow.

A few tears welled in Janet's eyes.

Brian murmured: "Holy Mary, mother of God!"

Everyone was stunned and emotionally drained. There was little conversation. A few hearty souls, including Sterling Rombauer, ventured up to view Dr. Mason's corpse. For the moment most people remained where they were—all except for one woman, who got up from her seat and struggled toward an exit. Sean saw her pushing dumbfounded people aside in her haste. He recognized her immediately.

"That's Dr. Levy," Sean said, getting to his feet. "Somebody should stop her. I'll bet she's planning on fleeing the country."

Brian grabbed Sean by the arm, preventing him from

giving chase. "This is not the time or place for you to play a paladin. Let her go."

Sean watched as Dr. Levy got to an exit and disappeared from view. He looked down at Brian. "The charade is beginning to unravel."

"Perhaps," Brian said evasively. His legal mind was concerned about the sympathy this shocking event was likely to evoke in the community.

Gradually, the crowd began to disperse. "Come on," Brian said. "Let's go."

Brian, Janet, and Sean shuffled out in silence and pushed through the subdued crowd gathered at the hospital entrance. They headed toward Brian's car. Each struggled to absorb the horrible tragedy they'd just had the misfortune of witnessing. Sean was the first to speak.

"I'd say that was a rather dramatic mea culpa," he said. "I suppose we have to give him credit for at least being a good shot."

"Sean, don't be crude," Brian said. "Black humor is not my cup of tea."

"Thank you," Janet said to Brian. Then to Sean she said: "A man is dead. How can you joke about it?"

"Helen Cabot is dead, too," Sean said. "Her death bothers me a lot more."

"Both deaths should bother you," Brian said. "After all, Dr. Mason's suicide could be attributed to all the bad publicity Forbes has received thanks to you. The man had reason to be depressed. His suicide wasn't necessarily an admission of guilt."

"Wait a second," Sean said, bringing the party to a halt. "Do you still have any doubts about what I've told you concerning this medulloblastoma issue after what we just witnessed?"

"I'm a lawyer," Brian said. "I'm trained to think in a specific fashion. I try to anticipate the defense."

"Forget being a lawyer for two seconds," Sean said. "What do you feel as a human being?"

"Okay," Brian relented. "I'll have to admit, it was an extremely incriminating act."

EPILOGUE

May 21
Friday, 1:50 P.M.

The big Delta jet banked, then entered its final approach into Logan Airport. It was landing to the northwest, and Sean, sitting in a window seat, had a good view of Boston out the left side of the plane. Brian was sitting next to him but had his nose buried in a law journal. Below they passed over the Kennedy Library on Columbus Point and then the tip of South Boston with its shorefront of clapboard three-decker houses.

Next Sean was treated to a superb view of the downtown Boston skyline with the Boston inner harbor in the foreground. Just before they touched down, he caught a quick glimpse of Charlestown with the Bunker Hill obelisk jutting up into the afternoon sky.

Sean breathed a sigh of relief. He was home.

Neither of them had checked luggage, so after deplaning they went directly to a cab stand and got a taxi. First they went to Brian's office in Old City Hall on School Street. Sean told the cabbie to wait and got out with Brian. They hadn't spoken much since they'd left Miami that morning, mainly because they'd been under such tension and had spoken so much during the prior three days. They had gone to Miami so Sean could testify before a Florida grand jury concerning the case *The State of Florida v. The Forbes Cancer Center.*

Sean eyed his brother. Despite their differences and their frequent arguments, he felt a rush of love for Brian. He stuck out his hand. Brian grasped it firmly and they shook. But it wasn't enough. Sean let go of Brian's hand and embraced him in a strong, sustained hug. When they parted both felt a moment of awkwardness. Rarely did they convey their affection physically. Generally they didn't touch save for jabs to the shoulder and pats on the back.

"Thanks for all you've done," Sean said.

"It pales in comparison to what you've done for a lot of potential Forbes victims," Brian said.

"But without your legal follow-through," Sean said, "Forbes would still be in business today."

"It's not over yet," Brian cautioned. "This was merely the first step."

"Well, whatever," Sean said. "Let's get back to putting our efforts into Oncogen. The Forbes matter is in the hands of the Florida State's Attorney and the U.S. District Attorney. Who do you think will prosecute the case?"

"Maybe they'll cooperate," Brian said. "With all the media attention, both obviously see the case as having great political potential."

Sean nodded. "Well, I'll be in touch," he said as he climbed back into the cab.

Brian grabbed the door before Sean had a chance to pull it closed. "I hate to sound captious," Brian said, "but as your older brother, I feel I should offer some advice. You'd make things so much easier for yourself if you'd only tone down that brazen side of your personality. I'm not talking about a big change, either. If you could just shed some of that townie abrasiveness. You're holding on to your past way too much."

"Aw, come on," Sean said with a wry smile. "Lighten up, Brian."

"I'm serious," Brian said. "You make enemies of those people less intelligent than yourself, which unfortunately is most of us."

"That's the most backhanded compliment I've ever received," Sean said.

"Well, it's not meant as a compliment," Brian said. "You're like some idiot savant. As smart as you are in some areas, you're retarded in others, like social skills. Either you're unaware of what other people are feeling, or you don't care. But either way, the results are the same."

"You're out of control!" Sean said with a laugh.

"Give it some thought, brother," Brian said. He gave Sean's shoulder a friendly poke.

Sean told the cabdriver to take him to the Boston Memorial Hospital. It was getting on toward three, and Sean was eager to catch Janet before her shift was over. Sitting back, Sean thought about what Brian had said. He smiled. As likable as his brother was, he could be such a nerd at times.

At the hospital, Sean went straight to Janet's floor. At the nurses' station he learned she was down in 503 medicating Mrs. Mervin. Sean headed down the hall toward the patient's room. He couldn't wait to give Janet the good news. He found her injecting antibiotic into Mrs. Mervin's IV.

"Well hello, stranger," Janet said when she caught sight of Sean. She was pleased to see him although she was obviously preoccupied. She introduced Sean to Mrs. Mervin, telling her that he was one of the Harvard medical students.

"I just love all you boys," Mrs. Mervin said. She was an elderly white-haired woman with pink cheeks and sparkling eyes. "You can come visit me anytime," she said with a titter.

Janet winked at Sean. "Mrs. Mervin is on the mend."

"I can see that," Sean agreed.

Janet made a notation on a 3×5 card and stuck it into her pocket. After picking up her medication tray, she said good-bye to Mrs. Mervin, advising her to ring if she wanted anything.

In the hall, Sean had to scurry to keep up with Janet's pace.

"I'm anxious to talk with you," Sean said, coming alongside. "In case you couldn't guess."

"I'd love to chat," Janet said, "but I'm really busy. Report's coming up and I've got to finish these medications."

"The indictment against Forbes was handed down by the grand jury," Sean said.

Janet stopped and gave him a big, warm smile.

"That's great!" she said. "I'm pleased. And I'm proud of you. You must feel vindicated."

"As Brian says, it's an important first step," Sean said. "The indictment includes Dr. Levy, although she hasn't been seen or heard from since Mason's mea culpa news conference. No one knows where the heck she is. The indictment also includes two clinical staff doctors and the director of nursing, Margaret Richmond."

"It's still all so hard to believe," Janet said.

"It is until you realize how thankful the Forbes medulloblastoma patients have been," Sean said. "Up until we put an end to it all, they'd given over sixty million dollars in essentially unrestricted donations."

"What's happened to the hospital?" Janet asked, eyeing her watch.

"The hospital is in receivership," Sean said. "But the research institute is closed. And in case you're interested, the Japanese were fooled by the scam as well. They had no part in it. Since the lid blew off, they cut their losses and ran."

"I'm sorry about the hospital," Janet said. "I personally think it's a good hospital. I hope they make it."

"One other piece of news," Sean said. "You know that crazy guy that caught us on the beach and scared us half to death? His name is Tom Widdicomb, and he's crazier than the mad hatter. He'd kept his dead mother in a freezer at his house. Seems he thought she was telling him to put all advanced breast cancer patients to sleep with succinylcholine. The mother had had the same disease."

"My God," Janet said. "Then that's what happened to Gloria D'Amataglio."

"Apparently so," Sean said. "And a number of others."

"I even remember Tom Widdicomb," Janet said. "He was the housekeeper who bugged Marjorie so much."

"Well, apparently you bugged him," Sean said. "Somehow in his distorted thinking, he decided that you had been sent to stop him. That's why he was after you. They think he was the guy in your bathroom at the Forbes residence, and he definitely was the person who followed us into the Miami General morgue."

"Good Lord!" Janet exclaimed. The idea that a psychotic had been stalking her was terribly unnerving. It reminded her again of how different her trip to Florida had been from what she'd anticipated when she'd decided to go.

"Widdicomb will be tried," Sean continued. "Of course he's pleading insanity, and if they bring the mother in the freezer in to testify, he won't have a problem." Sean laughed. "Needless to say it's because of him that the hospital is in receivership. Every family that lost a breast cancer patient under suspicious circumstances is suing."

"None of the medulloblastoma cases are suing?" Janet asked.

"Not the hospital," Sean said. "There'd been two entities: the hospital and the research center. The medulloblastoma patients will have to sue the research center. After all, at the hospital, they got cured."

"All except for Helen Cabot," Janet said.

"That's true," Sean agreed.

Janet glanced at her watch again and shook her head. "Now I'm really behind," she said. "Sean, I've got to go. Can't we talk about all this tonight, maybe over dinner or something?"

"Not tonight," Sean said. "It's Friday."

"Oh, of course!" Janet said coolly. She thumped her head with the heel of her hand. "How stupid of me to forget. Well then, when you get a chance, give me a call." Janet started down the hall.

Sean took a few steps and grasped her arm, pulling her to a stop.

"Wait!" he said, surprised at her abrupt end to their conversation. "Aren't you going to ask me about the charges against you and me?"

"It's not that I'm not interested," Janet said. "But you've caught me at a bad time, and of course, you're busy tonight."

"It'll only take a second," he said with exasperation. "Brian and I spent most of last evening bargaining with the State's Attorney. We got his word that all charges against you will be dropped. As far as I'm concerned, in return for testifying, all I have to do is plead guilty to disturbing the peace and malicious mischief. What do you think?"

"I think that's great," Janet said. "Now if you'll excuse me." She tried to get her arm free, but Sean wouldn't let go.

"There's something else," Sean said. "I've been doing a lot of thinking now that this Forbes thing is out of the way." Sean averted his gaze and shifted his weight uneasily. "I don't know how to say this, but remember when you said you wanted to talk about our relationship when you came down to Florida, how you wanted to talk about commitment and all that? Well, I think I want to do that. That is, if you're still thinking about what I think you were."

Stunned, Janet looked Sean directly in his deep blue eyes. He tried to look away. Janet reached out and, grasping his chin, turned his head back to face her. "Is all this double-talk an attempt to talk about marriage?"

"Well, yeah, sorta," Sean equivocated. He pulled away from Janet's hold on his chin to gaze down the hall. It was difficult for him to look at her. He made some gestures with his hands as if he were about to say more, but no words came.

"I don't understand you," Janet said, color spreading across her cheeks. "To think of all the times I wanted to talk and you wouldn't, and now you bring this up here and now! Well, let me tell you something, Sean Murphy. I'm not sure I can deal with a relationship with you unless you're willing to make some big changes, and frankly I don't think you're capable. After that experience down in Florida, I'm not sure you are what I want. It doesn't mean I don't love you, because I do. It just means I don't think I could live with the kind of relationship you're capable of."

Sean was shocked. For a moment he was incapable of speech. Janet's response had been totally unexpected. "What do you mean by change?" he asked finally. "Change what?"

"If you don't know and if I have to tell you, then it's futile. Of course, we could talk about it more tonight, but you have to go out with the boys."

"Don't get on my case," Sean said. "I haven't seen the guys for weeks with all this legal malarkey going on."

"That's undeniably true," Janet said. "And you have fun." Again she started down the hall. After a few steps she turned to face him. "Something else unexpected came out of my Florida trip," she said. "I'm seriously thinking of going to medical school. Not that I don't love nursing, and God only knows what a challenge it is, but all that material you introduced me to concerning molecular biology and the medical revolution it's spawning has turned me on in a way no other academic subject has been able to do. I think I want to be a part of it.

"Well, don't be a stranger, Sean," Janet added as she continued down the hall. "And close your mouth."

Sean was too stunned to speak.

IT WAS a little after eight when Sean pushed into Old Scully's Bar. Not having been able to go for many weeks, he was filled with pleasant anticipation. The bar was jammed with friends and acquaintances and was brimming with good cheer. A number of people had been there since five and were feeling no pain. A Red Sox game was on the tube and at the moment Sean looked at it, Roger Clemens was giving the camera the evil eye while waiting for the sign from the catcher. There were a few cheers of encouragement from a knot of diehard fans grouped directly under the TV. The bases were loaded.

Standing just inside the door, Sean paused to take in the scene. He saw Jimmy O'Connor and Brady Flanagan at the dart board laughing to the point of tears. Someone's dart had missed the board. In fact, it had missed the wall and was embedded in one of the muntin bars of the window. Obviously, the two were smashed.

At the bar, Sean could see Molly and Pete tirelessly going about their business filling mugs of ale and stout, occasionally holding four or five of the frosted, brimming glasses in a single hand. Shots of Irish whiskey dotted the bar. The day's problems melted into oblivion much faster with these nips between the drafts of beer.

Sean eyed the guys at the bar. He recognized Patrick FitzGerald, or Fitzie, as they called him. He'd been the most popular guy in high school. Sean could remember as if it were yesterday how Fitzie had stolen his girl when they were in ninth grade. Sean had fallen head over heels for Mary O'Higgins only to have her disappear at a party he'd brought her to in order to make out with Fitzie in the back of Frank Kildare's pickup.

But since his high school triumph, Fitzie had put on considerable weight around his middle and his face had assumed a puffy, pasty look. He worked on the maintenance crew down at the old Navy Yard when he worked, and he was married to Anne Shaughnessy, who'd blown up to two hundred pounds after giving birth to twins.

Sean took a step toward the bar. He wanted to be drawn into his old world. He wanted people to slap him on the back, tease him about his brother becoming a priest. He wanted to remember those days when he thought his future was a limitless road to be traveled along with the whole gang. Fun and meaning were to be had in shared experiences that could be enjoyed over and over through reminiscences. In fact, the experiences became more enjoyable with the inevitable embellishment that accompanied each retelling.

But something held Sean back. With a disturbing, almost tragic sense, he felt apart. The feeling that his life had taken a different track from his old friends came back to him with crushing clarity. He felt more like an observer of his old life; he was no longer a participant. The events at the Forbes clinic were forcing him to look at broader issues beyond the confines of his old friends in Charlestown. He no longer had the insulation that innocence of the world provided. Seeing his former friends all half drunk or worse made him appreciate their limited opportunities. For a confusing combination of social and economic reasons, they were caught in a web of repeated mistakes. They were condemned to repeat the past.

Without having spoken a single word to anyone, Sean abruptly turned and stumbled out of Old Scully's Bar. He quickened his step when he felt a powerful voice coaxing him back to the warm familiarity of this haven of his youth. But Sean had made up his mind. He would not be like his father. He would look to the future, not to the past.

RESPONDING TO a knock on her apartment door, Janet heaved her feet off the ottoman and struggled out of her deep club chair. She'd been perusing a ponderous book she'd picked up in the medical school bookstore called *Molecular Biology of the Cell.* At the door she peered through the security port. She was shocked to see Sean making a stupid face at her.

Fumbling with the locks, Janet finally swung the door open wide.

"I hope I'm not disturbing you," Sean said.

"What happened?" Janet asked. "Did that favorite haunt of yours burn down?"

"Maybe figuratively," Sean said.

"None of your old friends show up?" Janet asked.

"They were all there," Sean said. "May I come in?"

"I'm sorry," Janet said. "Please." She stepped aside, then closed the door behind him. "I've forgotten my manners. I'm just so surprised to see you. Can I get you something? A beer? A glass of wine?"

Sean thanked her but said no. He sat awkwardly on the edge of the couch. "I went as usual to Old Scully's . . ." he began.

"Oh, now I know what happened," Janet interrupted. "They ran out of beer."

"I'm trying to tell you something," Sean said with exasperation.

"Okay, I'm sorry," Janet said. "I'm being sarcastic. What happened?"

"Everybody was there," Sean said. "Jimmy O'Connor, Brady Flanagan, even Patrick FitzGerald. But I didn't talk to anyone. I didn't get much past the door."

"Why not?"

"I realized by going there I was condemning myself to the past," Sean said. "All of a sudden I had an idea about what you and even Brian were talking about concerning change. And you know something? I want to change. I'm sure I'll have occasional relapses, but I certainly don't want to be a 'townie' all my life. And what I'd like to know is whether or not you'd be willing to help me a little."

Janet had to blink away a sudden rush of tears. She looked into Sean's blue eyes and said, "I'd love to help you."